LOCHRANZA

A Fantasy by

Mark Haviland

Paperback: 978-1-967820-56-6
eBook: 978-1-967820-57-3
Library of Congress Control Number: 2025910115

This is a work of fiction.

Ordering Information:

Prime Seven Media
518 Landmann St.
Tomah City, WI 54660

Printed in the United States of America

TABLE OF CONTENTS

ACKNOWLEDGEMENTS.

I am utterly indebted to my wife Judy for giving me the priceless gift of the freedom to pursue my writing. It means more to me than I can say.

My heartfelt thanks go to CC, my teacher, my mentor and my friend. He has been my guide on the druic path, which is the inspiration for this work. He has made available to me some rare and - shall we say? - esoteric books, and has contributed countless pearls of wisdom, without which my efforts would be infinitely the poorer.

Sandy Semple has similarly made available to me his superlative collection of books on mediaeval history, as well as teaching me so much about how to make things in wood and metal.

Dr. Denise Finlay's remarkable library of texts on Antarctica have proved invaluable for the writing of the polar section of the tale, and to her I am also profoundly grateful.

My thanks go to the lovely Marie Keyser, whose miniscule handwriting was an inspiration.

Thanks also to Maggie Stevens for giving me some insight into what it is that a seer sees.

Further, a big thank you goes to the Danelaw Mediaeval Fighting Society of Sydney for allowing me to "borrow" the name of Dunghaven.

A number of friends, past and present, have served as models for characters. Some have given their consent to being used in this way, others have not. I hope I have not taken too many liberties.

An asterisk (*) denotes an entry in the glossary at the
end of the book.

CHAPTER ONE.

Fate is a most peculiar thing. It rules and shapes our lives, it nudges and prods us, or else holds us back, so that we walk down that particular street or make a certain choice, but we are blissfully unaware of its workings until it is too late, and fate has done its job. All through life, we encounter crossroads, but we only ever recognise them for what they are by looking back over our shoulder at them, when our feet are irrevocably set on a certain path. Often, if that path proves to be stony or steep, we may find ourselves wondering about the paths left untravelled, and even if a voice within us tells us that we are *destined* for the steep and stony path, nevertheless, we cannot help but wonder. It is a futile pursuit, but sometimes it is irresistible all the same.

And so it was for Ben Troon on that crisp autumn morning when fate stepped into his path and sent his life skittering off in a new and utterly unforeseen direction.

Ben, in his late teens, although he could not be sure of his exact age, was beginning his first term as a student - a "wyffen", as they were called - at the celebrated Dundonald Academy of Magecraft. However, the academy had been his home for much longer, in fact, for as long as he could remember. He had been adopted as a baby by the caretaker, and his wife, . Who his real parents were, and where he had come from, remained a mystery.

Having become a student, he had elected to move out of the caretaker's cottage and into one of the student dwellings, which he shared with three new chums, .

The great rambling edifice that was Dundonald sat atop a large outcrop of rock that stood out by being an unusual ochre colour, very different from the surrounding grey granite. It was commonly believed to be the residual plug of an ancient volcano that had eroded away. Clinging to its sides was a village, with shops catering to the every need of Mages and students. They lined a steep path that wound up from the base to the Academy itself, a street that was essentially a continuous flight of steps. Leading off it were small side streets with houses belonging to the Mages and their support staff.

From the base of the mound, the students' houses fanned out in a semicircle lining a small bay. Students used small coracles to cross the bay to the village or to one another's homes.

The small bay itself opened off a much larger one. On a map, the entire body of water resembled nothing so much as a woman's breast in profile. As a consequence, those who studied at Dundonald were said to be "sucking at Wisdom's teat".

On that morning, Ben was awakened by the trilling of a blackbird outside his window, and looking up with a start he saw, from the position of the sun in the sky, that he was late. Yet again.

He had spent a goodly part of the evening in the tavern, carousing with his friends, and had then returned to his room to complete the written assignment which was due in that day. He had burned a considerable amount of midnight oil in so doing, before crawling into bed to snatch a few hours' sleep.

One glance out of the window told him that his companions had had a similar experience, and were now rowing furiously across the bay, having in their haste neglected to call him before racing out of the door.

Ben threw on his clothes and grabbed his satchel of books, clattering down the stairs into the little communal parlour. Snatching a hunk of bread from the table as he passed, he raced out onto the terrace. A small gate opened at the top of an iron ladder that led down the sea wall to the water, where his coracle was the last still tied up. In moments he had untied the painter and was paddling breathlessly across the water.

As he drew closer, the great bulk of the Academy seemed to loom accusingly above him. Along the edge of the water was a boardwalk, with jetties extending out from it, to which students tied up their craft. Beside the boardwalk was a large stone with a flat face into which was incised a spiral, an indication that this was indeed the place for tying up boats. Ben's boat was one of the last to arrive, and he had to step through several others before he reached dry land. His feet pounded the boardwalk as he ran. At the end was a great stone archway. Above it was the insignia of the Academy, a pair of scales over a pair of crossed Magestaffs. Beneath it was inscribed the Academy's motto: 'I Am No One'.

Panting heavily now, Ben passed through the arch and began the laborious climb. He passed a few stragglers, and felt relief that he was now, at any rate, not the absolute last, but he knew he was still in deep trouble.

At the top of the hill, he took the broad steps leading to the imposing Grand Entrance Hall, lined with portraits of famous past Mages. Everywhere, the stonework was richly carved to suggest twisting vines, foliage, reeds, grass, trees and flowers, the whole panoply of nature. Scattered amongst the branches could be seen birds and small animals so startlingly realistic that one almost expected them to flit or scurry into hiding as one passed. In many places, there were faces to be seen amidst this vegetative richness, smiling, grinning, even leering in a way that could be taken as perhaps a little sinister, some of them even with creepers issuing out of their mouths.

Ben began to ascend the stairs to his classroom. He was almost completely out of breath, but he knew he could not slow down. Up two flights of stairs, he just had one long gallery to go. It had classrooms on one side, where he could hear Mages already beginning their lessons, and windows on the other, looking down into an internal courtyard. At the end, another gallery intersected the first, and his classroom was just a short distance along it. Not far to go now.

He reached the intersection of the two galleries, and...

Wham!

He collided with another student, in just as much of a hurry as he was, and before he knew it, he was sitting on the floor. Winded, he stared at the other student, sitting facing him, looking similarly nonplussed.

And she was beautiful.

Light brown hair, simply parted in the middle, and falling to her shoulders, framed a perfect oval face. Dark brows arched above large eyes of a striking blue, soulful in the extreme, and expressive of some deep inner sadness. There was a somewhat prominent nose, and rosy cheeks over high, strongly sculpted cheekbones, and soft pink lips curved into a smile that was half of surprise and half of greeting.

She was dressed in a breacan*-patterned cloak in shades of soft green and violet, with a hint of stronger yellow running through it.

She, for her part, took in his appearance. He had grey, expressive eyes, a high forehead suggestive of great intelligence, and a mane of wavy fair hair that fell down onto his shoulders.

As the daughter of a weaver, she noted the cloth of his tunic and pants as being of the simple homespun material striped in three colours, known as tabby. The bands alternated between light and dark, and were of varying widths, with narrow lines marking their edges. Indigotin, she surmised, for the blue - her mother was the dyer of the family, crozophora tinctora for the light mauve, and iron mordant for the dark red. It bespoke modest means, and that was a source of great relief to her, for her own people were far from wealthy.

As they sat there for what seemed an eternity, diminutive Mage Adoy shuffled past. Leaning heavily on his Magestaff, he contemplated the pair of them for a moment. He smiled a smile that was not so much knowing as foreknowing, and nodded in satisfaction.

"Well, hurry along!" he said, a little sharply, but at the same time not unkindly. "Classes have begun."

And he moved slowly away.

Ben and the young woman looked around them. In the collision, their satchels had spilled their contents. Books were scattered everywhere in a jumble, and they hastily began gathering them up, until one book remained between them, a notebook bearing the initials B.T.

Both of them reached for it at the same time. Ben was fractionally slower, and his hand came down on the top of hers. As he touched her, it felt as if a bolt of lightning had run up his arm, thrilling and wonderful. The touch of another human being, even one so light and innocent as this, was an act of intimacy. A bonding, however momentary, gave comfort and reassurance, and was to be treasured.

He stared at her hand. It was elegant, with long, tapering fingers, and nails over which she appeared to have expended a good deal of care in the filing and shaping, so fine they might have been carved in marble, so different to the hands of the working women he had seen around the Academy, including his mother's, with their broken nails and swollen knuckles.

His gaze moved up, and he found himself looking again into those exquisite eyes. He slowly withdrew his hand.

She, for her part, felt an unaccountable shiver of fear run through her. She looked at her own hand as it lay atop the book, and felt the tingle of his touch. She could not be sure, but she felt that he had deliberately squeezed her hand, tenderly, lovingly, before withdrawing his own.

He struggled to speak. "B.T.," he said hesitantly. "Ben Troon. It's mine I believe."

She smiled again. "B.T. Bliss Tarrant. Mine, I believe."

They were the first words she had uttered, and they fell upon his ears like the singing of angels, some strange ethereal music that captivated him completely. Her voice was gentle, lilting, and utterly sweet.

Drawing his eyes from hers with considerable effort, he looked again at the notebook, and realised that he didn't even recognise the handwriting.

"The same initials!" he gasped. "Wow!"

She replaced the notebook in her satchel.

Ben got to his feet and helped Bliss to hers. It was, after all, an excuse to touch again, to feel the one magic that the Academy did not teach. Together they hurried the last little distance to the classroom.

Mage Waerferth was of course holding forth as they entered. He was a tall, angular man, with deep creases incised into both cheeks, and spiky silvery grey hair. "Ah, Mr. Troon," he said oleaginously. "And I presume Miss Tarrant?" Bliss nodded. "Welcome to Dundonald, Miss Tarrant. Please be seated, both of you."

As chance would have it, there were two vacant seats together. Ben and Bliss hastened to occupy them, and pulled the appropriate books from their bags.

Ben glanced around at his classmates as he did so. His best friend, Bubonax Angenwit, his dark hair parted in the middle, was staring at him goggle-eyed, bewildered by his appearance in the company of a female of the species, and a decidedly pretty one at that. The others, Godric Mappestone, Atilla Hegedus, Opabinia van Millingen, peering over her thick spectacles, Brilliana Harvey, that cunning fox Brancepeth-Raginhard Raby and all the rest, displayed a variety of expressions of surprise and curiosity.

"Now, as I was saying," Mage huffed, picking up the thread of his diatribe, "who can tell me what our purpose is, as Mages, in respect to evil?" There was a stony silence. "No one? Surely, Mr. Troon, you of all people should be able to answer that one."

Ben felt all the eyes in the room upon him, not least those of Bliss. "Well," he said after a pause, "surely we are meant to defeat it?"

Mage Waerferth sighed audibly. "Alas, that is the answer I feared you would give, and alas, it is not the right one. I dare say this morning you were in too much of a hurry to notice the insignia of the Academy as you passed beneath it, but there have surely been other occasions when you have not been in quite such a hurry, when you may have paused a little to ponder its significance."

Tubby Exomphalus Trillibub chuckled.

Mage Waerferth's gaze fell upon him. "I shall attend to you shortly, Mr. Trillibub."

Somewhere inside Ben's mind, illumination. "Sir, crossed Magestaves and scales."

"A balance, Mr. Troon. A balance. Because evil cannot and should not be eradicated, merely kept in balance with the good. Balance is what we are all about, Mr. Troon, balance. Good and evil cannot exist without one another. That is fundamental. Please write that in your notebooks."

There was a rustling of pages as the students opened their notebooks, and then the soft scratching of their pens as they noted down Mage Waerferth's pearls of wisdom.

He held up the silver pendant that he wore on a chain around his neck. It consisted of a six-pointed star comprised of two intersecting triangles, one pointing upward, the other downward. It was the Seal of Manred, a Mage's amulet of protection.

"Consider Manred," he said. "It represents the underlying structure of physical existence, in which every part of the cosmos is ensouled, with no blank spaces. It also speaks of the highest universal law, the balance of opposites, the balance between the macrocosm that is the Cosmos, and the microcosm that is humanity. The two interwoven triangles tell us, 'As it is above, so may it be below'. Strange as it may seem, evil profits from *either* extreme chaos *or* extreme order. Good profits from a balance between the two.”

Bliss glanced across at Ben as he wrote. Their eyes met again, and he gave her a shy smile, which she reciprocated.

Then she noticed the page he was writing on and gave a little inward start. Ben’s writing was the smallest she had ever seen. The pen he wrote with was tiny, with the finest nib imaginable, and the pages of his book were filled with miniscule, exquisitely neat script, with tiny, jewel-like sketches inserted into the margin.

She could not help herself. She leaned closer, which Ben was delighted to see. During the first days of the semester, the quirk of his tiny writing had excited some degree of curiosity, but the fuss had soon died down. Now it had attracted the attention of the heavenly creature sitting beside him, and his heart soared once more.

“So,” huffed Mage Waerferth, when he deemed that sufficient time had been allowed for the writing, “to continue...”

*****

The morning seemed to drag on interminably, but at last the lunch break came. Having appointed himself as Bliss's personal guide, Ben escorted her to a large cloistered quadrangle where students gathered to talk. He was aching to take her hand, but was careful not to: Mages were not supposed to form romantic attachments, although invariably many did, and on the whole an official blind eye was turned in such cases.

"Can I show you something?" he asked.

"Yes, of course," she replied. There was that intoxicating smile again.

"Follow me," he said. "But we must be discreet."

Bliss nodded.

Ben led her into the cloisters. In a dark corner, partially concealed behind a statue, was a small door. Ben opened it, ushered Bliss inside, and then closed it behind her.

Lamps illuminated a narrow staircase that clearly saw little use. Ben led the way up the worn stone steps that turned repeatedly, until Bliss began to wonder if they would *ever* reach the top.

"Ben, where are we going?" she asked.

"Not far now," was the reply that came down from above her.

A few minutes later they arrived on a small landing that was lit by a circular window over a door. Ben took the ring on the door in his hand and turned it. It was stiff, and when he pulled on the door, it opened only with considerable effort and groaning of hinges.

They emerged onto a high sloping roof, patterned with centuries of lichen in shades of pale grey and green against the dark blue-grey of the slates, with a parapet wall all around. In one direction was the rambling roofscape of the Academy, which had clearly had additional wings tacked on at different times in its long history, in a hotchpotch of architectural styles. Ben led Bliss around the edge of the roof to a point where a small stone bridge spanned the gap between two high walls. They crossed over, Bliss doing her level best not to look down, and on the further side, at a corner of the building, they entered a small open pavilion made of a clover leaf of small turrets, each with its own conical roof. It was clearly intended to serve as a sheltered lookout, perhaps in times past when Mages had been threatened by locals who feared their influence.

Looking in one direction, the whole edifice was laid out before their eyes, tall walls like cliffs, pocked here and there with what seemed random patterns of windows, like small caves amid the crags. Bliss clutched nervously at Ben's arm, which was what he had rather hoped might happen.

In another direction, the view was of the small bay in the foreground, with the students' lodgings all around it, then the strait connecting it with the Great Bay beyond. In the distance could be seen the two peninsulae which almost closed it off, leaving a narrow gap through which shipping could pass to the open sea. On the far horizon could be seen a string of islands that lay before the opening, seemingly barring the way, and which thus earned them the name of the Tollgate Islands.

"That's my home," said Bliss softly.

"The Tollgates?"

She nodded. "And that's sort of the reason why I'm only starting at the Academy today."

"Oh?"

She took a handful of his tunic and held his gaze with her own. "But you must promise not to tell anyone."

"I promise."

"I was all set to make the sea crossing to the Academy at the start of the semester, just a short trip. But the weather was terrible for days on end."

"Yes," said Ben. "I remember."

"Well, I started to think I would never get here, that I had missed something vitally important. I had worked so hard to be admitted here, and it seemed as if my life was over before it had even begun." She hesitated. "Well," she went on, "I got very down about it, and, well, I took a draught. I tried to kill myself."

She held Ben's gaze with her own. She wasn't sure quite why she was telling a complete stranger this most personal part of her life, but there was something about him that made her feel that she could trust him with anything.

"Clearly you didn't succeed," Ben said softly.

"No," she said, recalling how it had been. "My brother Ekkehard found me in time, and was able to bring an apothecary that we knew, who brought me back from the brink of death.

"I'm glad of it," said Ben in a voice scarcely above a whisper.

"What about you?" said Bliss. "Where are you from?"

"Well, here really," said Ben. "My foster-father, Hasupada, is the caretaker of the Academy, and Halldis, his wife, is my foster-mother. They gave me the name Ben, short for Bendigeidfran, the Blessed Raven."

"So you weren't born here?"

"I don't know where I was born, to be honest," said Ben with a sigh. He pointed out at the great bay. "You see the bay there?"

"Yes," said Bliss, wondering where this was leading.

"There is a powerful current that sweeps in through the gap between the two headlands at its mouth, and runs in a circle right the way around the bay. Every year the top twelve students of the Academy are strapped down in coracles and covered over, and set adrift on the current. It carries them around the bay and brings them back to the point of departure. It comes from the story of Taliesin in the *Magichronicon…*"

"'Nine months was I in the womb of the hag Ceridwen,'" Bliss recited. "Yes, I've read the books on the reading list."

"Ah, good," said Ben. "Well, eighteen years ago, twelve coracles were launched, and the next morning thirteen were recovered. I was in the thirteenth. I still use the coracle to this day."

"I see," said Bliss thoughtfully. "So your origins are a complete mystery?"

"That about sums it up," Ben agreed.

There was a silence between them. They were looking into each other's eyes with intensity. The breeze swept Bliss's hair this way and that with playful abandon, making her look wonderfully wild. The desire that swept Ben was the most powerful thing he could remember, but he didn't want to destroy this moment by making the wrong move. He leaned in closer, expecting every second that Bliss would back away, but she didn't. Instead she seemed to be leaning in also, closer and closer.

Their lips met, their arms closed tightly around each other, tongue locked against tongue in a moment of glorious fulfilment that neither wanted to end. End it did only when the requirement to breathe made it unavoidable to break.

Sucking air into their lungs, they engaged once more, each growing more hungry for the other as they did so.

They broke again, looking into each other's eyes once more, and each seeing there a wordless affirmation that they shared the same thought: that an event of cosmic significance had occurred, that two souls had found a soulmate in each other, and that whatever the future might throw at them, that fact could never be annulled. It was a moment of exquisite joy, and each grasped the hands of the other, simply staring, drinking in every feature of that beloved face. It made them want to throw up their hands and call a halt to the passage of time, to bid this most wonderful of moments, "Stay!"

But time was deaf to such urging, and dreary practical considerations, such as the growing chill and, perhaps, the need for physical sustenance, brought them down from the clouds. Grasping Bliss' hand in his own, Ben led the way back down off the roof.

CHAPTER TWO.

In the evening they went to the students' tavern, the *Brasseur de Bourbourg*, to sup on hearty bowls of partan bree*, soaked up with slabs of oaten bread. There were tankards of ale to accompany it. Some students were already launching into games of fidhchneall*, also known as the 'Game of the Wise'.

Surrounded by friends - Bubonax in particular was staring unashamedly at Ben, who was not known for keeping female company, shaking his shaggy locks in utter disbelief - there was little opportunity for intimate conversation between two newly minted lovers. However, there was one question that Bliss could not keep from asking.

"Why do you write so small?"

Ben smiled. "It's just something that I do. I think that ever since I learned to write, it has amused me to try and write as small as possible, while still keeping my writing legible. Hasupada and Halldis have no complaints as it saves on writing paper."

"I see," said Bliss, smiling in turn.

On this night, however, it was not possible to enjoy more than one tankard of ale, as there was another class to attend, Mage Cassegrain's astronomy class.

"Well," said Ben, stretching, as their classmates began making their way towards the door of the tavern, "I suppose it's time to pay a visit to old Brasenose."

"Old Brasenose?" asked Bliss.

"Mage Cassegrain," Ben explained, pushing back his chair. "He has a brass prosthesis for a nose. The story is that he lost his own nose when he was young, in a duel over a woman. It's hard to imagine Cassegrain being young, let alone fighting a duel over a woman! Still, who knows what some of these Mages got up to in times past?"

"Mmm," Bliss conceded, as they emerged into the cold and the dark.

"Oh, one thing," Ben added, gathering his cloak more tightly around himself, "if you want to stay on the right side of him. Try not to stare at the schnoz." He looked up. "Ah well, it's a clear night. Old Brase… Cassegrain will be happy about that, at any rate."

And so they made their way up a narrow spiral stair to the rooftop observatory.

Mage Cassegrain was waiting for them at the door, rubbing his hands, though whether from the cold or in imitation of a stage villain welcoming new victims into his lair was unclear. The beaky brass appendage glinted in the starlight, and Bliss made every effort to appear to be focussed on him without staring at it. He was clad in black academic robes, but not above average height, and certainly did not appear villainous. Indeed, with his balding dome of a head and thick spectacles which exaggerated the size of his glistening dark eyes, the overriding impression was more owlish than anything.

"Welcome," he beamed as the students emerged from the staircase turret onto the flat roof which formed a forecourt in front of the observatory. "Before we go inside, ladies and gentlemen, I would like to take a brief moment to consider the night sky in all its glory. Please, look up."

During their ascent of the dark stairway, the students' night vision had come into play, and now, as they stared upwards at the indigo bowl of the heavens, they were able to perceive the breathtaking spectacle of the night sky down to the least twinkling star. To the east, a cheeseparing of a moon was rising above the mountains, but that part of the moon that was nominally dark could nevertheless be seen quite distinctly against the darker backdrop of the sky.

However, Mage Cassegrain directed the students' attention to the opposite side of the sky. Clearly visible above the ocean horizon was a distinct point of red.

"That, ladies and gentlemen, is Pyrois, which we call the fiery one. Pyrois is of course not a star but a planet, which is to say, another solid body like our own Anoone, which circles the sun. There are seven visible planets, Phaenon, Phaeton, Enkidu, known as the Evening Star, which will be rising shortly, Aurvaudil, which will appear a little later, Pyrois, of course, Stilbon and Vesperugo. Beyond these, according to ancient stargazers such as Hevelius, Timocharis, Naburianna and Vesto Slipher, there are a further eight so-called invisible planets, which are of course not invisible at all but have such long cycles that many people go their whole lives without seeing more than a couple. Er... I won't trouble you with the names of these eight planets just at the moment, as the study of them is not a priority for you. Should you wish to specialise in astronomy later, all the relevant texts are naturally in the Academy library."

In the dark, Ben and Bliss clasped hands, pressing close together for warmth as much as passion.

"Of course," he went on, "it was Ponthaeus who determined that all the planets lie in a single plane, which he called the Malkuth. From earliest times, it was assumed that the planets moved in perfect circles, because it was thought inconceivable that the gods would create anything that was less than perfect. However, movement in perfect circles would not give the results that we observe. The assumption did not tally with the facts. It was Cornelius Gemma who finally determined that the planets in fact move in ellipses, which is of course what gives us our seasons. Before him, it was the writings of Osiander that were considered the last word on celestial mechanics. But Osiander put Anoone at the centre of all things, whereas now we know that the sun is at the centre. Of course, even now, we understand that the motions of the planets and the stars cannot be reduced to a simple formula, and astronomers still cannot agree on the number of deferents and epicycles needed to make the whole system work as we see that it does. But it is unquestionable that Osiander and the Alphonsine Tables fall short in representing what we see above us with our own eyes. In the end, we must follow nature, who, in her wisdom, not only takes pains not to create superfluity, but moreover often endows one thing with multiple effects."

It was quite a speech, and a lot to take in all at once. There was a shuffling of feet as the students tried to keep warm. Mage Cassegrain seemed oblivious.

"Now," he continued, "some constellations. Look a little to the right of Pyrois, and up the sky a bit. There's another bright star. Do you see it?" There were murmurs of assent. "That is Orwendil, popularly known as the Giant's Toe, because it forms the bottom end of the constellation of Vafthrudnir, the Giant." He raised his Magestaff and sent a thin beam of light up into the sky. With it he pointed to a succession of stars. "Do you see a rough human figure there?" There were louder murmurs this time, as the students saw the shape of the constellation pointed out to them.

"Here's another," Mage Cassegrain went on, clearly warming to his subject. "This one's easier." The shaft of light picked out a number of stars forming a rough U shape.

"Ah!" exclaimed Allegra Claremont. "That has to be the Cauldron of Ceridwen."

"Well done, Allegra," said Mage Cassegrain. "Now, this one is the easiest of them all…"

The light beam moved from one star to another, describing a large circle.

"Oh!" exclaimed the whole class in unison. "The Circle of Arianrod!"

"Excellent!" beamed Mage Cassegrain. "Now, shall we go inside, as it is getting rather chilly?"

The students followed him inside the observatory building. The interior was lit by just a few small lamps, but they gave enough light to see the enormous telescope, tilted up at a steep angle towards the sloping roof. Mage Cassegrain strode to the wall and unwound a rope from a cleat affixed there. He pulled on the rope, and a pair of large panels in the roof slid apart on rollers, revealing the night sky beyond.

The lesson seemed to last forever, but eventually, Mage Cassegrain came to the end of his diatribe. "For next week, please read chapter four of the *Picatrix**."

They made their way back down to the *Brasseur* for a final tankard of ale and a warming nightcap of kuass*.

By this time, the mutual attraction of Ben and Bliss was plain for all to see.

They left the tavern and descended the steps to the water's edge hand in hand. In the same way, they walked slowly along the boardwalk, speaking very little, just absorbed in the wonder of what they had found in one another.

They came to the spot where Ben's coracle was tied up. Having been one of the last to arrive in the morning, he was now among the last to leave at night.

"Where are you living?" he asked.

Bliss pointed along the boardwalk. "Just a little further that way," she replied softly.

"Can I walk you there?"

She nodded. "Mmm-hmm."

And so they walked on to the door of her cottage, where a friendly yellow lantern beamed a welcome. Ben drew her into his arms for one more lingering kiss, and then slowly, reluctantly, drew away.

"See you tomorrow," he murmured.

"Yes." Once more she gave him that heart-stopping smile. "Sleep well."

Sleep? he wondered, walking back to his boat. How in Anoone was he going to sleep after a day like today?

*****

They slipped into a comfortable routine as a couple, sitting side by side in classes, and spending their evenings either in the tavern or else in study, usually at Bliss' cottage rather than Ben's, as his flatmates could be rowdy at times, and not always considerate of the need of others to complete assignments. There was always time for some passionate kissing, but however much Ben might yearn for greater physical intimacy, Bliss would always put him off, telling him "When the time is right," and becoming occasionally quite annoyed at his insistence. It was not that she didn't want him as he wanted her, he knew - he could feel it when they lay together, and she would draw her leg across his belly and rub herself against his hip bone - but he could not fathom why she held back. Still, that was her rule, and however much it pained him, he had to comply.

On the first study-free day, Ben took Bliss to the caretaker's cottage, tucked away in a corner of the grounds, but conveniently located for getting to most parts of the Academy in a few minutes.

Hasupada was short, bald and tubby, and gave Bliss a welcoming hug on the doorstep. Halldis was much taller than him, lean, with iron grey hair and a look that bespoke many years of struggling to make ends meet. She was reserved, but not unfriendly.

"What's for lunch?" asked Ben as they sat down at the dining table.

"Lammsmäcka," said Halldis, laying the serving platter in the middle of the table. A grilled, parboiled half lamb skull, complete with eye, lay amid mountains of mashed neeps*.

"Lammsmäcka!" echoed Ben with delight. "We haven't had this in ages!"

"Well, no," said Hasupada, pouring the wine. "We generally only serve it when you bring a woman home."

Ben blushed, and Bliss glanced across to see Hasupada wearing an impish grin. He gave her a wink.

"Here," said Hasupada, spooning the eyeball onto Bliss's plate. "Always given to the guest of honour."

"Why thank you," she said, cutting into it. It was a little tough. She forked a piece into her mouth. It was salty, but tasted principally of the savoury sauce that accompanied it. "Mmm," she smiled. "It's very good."

Halldis smiled radiantly. Bliss was now officially one of the family.

After lunch, they sat and talked amicably about life at the Academy, and inquired about Bliss's family and the Tollgate Islands in general. Hasupada passed around the kuass flask.

In the late afternoon, Ben and Bliss walked away from the cottage hand in hand.

"Well done," said Ben.

"What?"

"Giving you the lamb's eye was a bit of a test. Some folk don't care for it. By showing appreciation, I think you won their hearts on the spot."

"We have lammsmäcka in the islands too," said Bliss with a smile. "And much the same tradition applies. So it didn't come as such a shock. Your foster parents are very sweet."

"They're good people," Ben agreed. "I'll miss them when we go out into the wider world."

"Yes," said Bliss. "And they'll miss you."

She didn't want to dwell on the subject of the "wider world". When their studies at Dundonald were complete, they would be told where they were to go afterwards, and there was absolutely no guarantee that the two of them would be sent to the same place. It was something they would have to deal with when the time came.

The Magyck year was marked by ceremonies every few weeks. The month of Zehnar* was the time for Dadanhudd, the ceremony of uncovering the hearth in autumn. And then at the month's end came Samhain, the end and beginning of the year.

In preparation for this event, particularly as it was their first at Dundonald, the wyffens were to receive special tuition from the Academy's Grand Mage himself, Styrmir the Learned. Styrmir himself did not normally teach, and was seen only occasionally, and generally at a distance, so it was with considerable anticipation that the young students looked forward to his classes.

They gathered in the Great Hall on a chilly and misty autumn morning, all wearing garlands in brown autumnal tones. There was the usual hubbub of low conversation as they hovered in small knots, much of their discussion revolving around what they might expect from this august teacher.

The sudden rapping of a staff on the flagstones brought all chatter to an abrupt halt, and all turned to look in the direction from which the sound had come.

Grand Mage Styrmir stood before them, in a patch of deep shadow, although none had marked his approach. In many respects, he was much as they might have expected him to be, tall and angular, with a slight stoop. His hair, long and grey, beneath a circlet of interwoven silver strands about his brows, swept down over his shoulders. He wore the beard that was customary for Mages in the winter months, and shot them a benign, avuncular smile. He was clad in a hooded robe of deep forest green, with a border of crimson velvet. Embroidered on the right shoulder were six acorns, indicating that he was a sixth generation Son of the Oak. The cloak was fastened at the throat with a large circular brooch of silver knotwork with a carnelian at the centre, and in his hand he clasped a Magestaff almost as tall as himself, bound with a complex, almost three dimensional pattern of criss-cross binding in colours that matched those of the students' garlands. Atop the staff was a large crystal of distinctly phallic shape, which glowed a soft pink in the dim light of the Hall.

All this was much as might be expected. What took the students by surprise was that draped over Grand Mage Styrmir's shoulders was a large snake, which coiled and uncoiled lengths of its body languorously the whole time. Then Ben recalled having read that Mages often had serpents as protective familiars. Not so surprising after all, he reflected.

Styrmir tutted loudly. "You really must work on your observation skills," he declared. "I have been standing here quite a few minutes, and not one of you noticed me." The avuncular smile evaporated momentarily. Then it returned. "Well," he said brightly, "let me welcome you all, somewhat belatedly, to Dundonald Academy. As you know, Samhain is nearly upon us, and it falls to me to give you some introduction to the conduct of ceremonies. Now, I don't know what your experience of ceremonies has been in the past, but certainly some Mages, rather too fond of the sound of their own voices, are apt to make their ceremonies terribly long-winded. My own view is that a ceremony is an observance of the season, which does not need to be wordy, and, above all, a celebration. Now, if you would care to follow me, we will make our way to the henge*"

He walked across the Hall to a door which the students had not noticed before, opened it, and led them through. Beyond it lay the walled kitchen garden, where assistant cooks were digging vegetables and herbs in readiness for the evening meal. Another door on the far side issued onto a cloister with ornate pillars of varying shapes, looking out on a small garden for quiet meditation. Styrmir took them round two sides of the cloister and through a vaulted passageway, emerging into the open on a lawn, still while with early frost. The students looked around with curiosity, having never seen this part of the Academy before.

The far side of the lawn was bordered by a wood. A path through the wood was defined by a series of flat round stones, which wound their way in a sinuous fashion somewhat recalling Styrmir's reptilian companion. Birds called cheerily from the branches. Shortly, the trees petered out and they found themselves standing on the edge of an open grassy space. Before them, large and clearly very old oak trees marched away to left and right, forming a circle. A grove, in fact. Styrmir beckoned, and led them between the trees into the centre.

They looked about them with wonder and awe. The boughs of the oaks spread above them, meeting in the middle and becoming densely interwoven, such as to exclude most of what little sunlight there was. And there was a sudden absence of calls, no bird made its presence felt amid this sombre foliage. It was not silent in the grove, however: the boughs whispered as they brushed against each other, even though no breath of wind could be felt. Olloudius, the god of the Great Tree, seemed not to belong here, nor the usual beneficent woodland spirits. This seemed to be the home of much darker things.

"Gather round," he urged. "I don't want to have to strain my voice more than necessary. Now, this is our oak grove. It has been here as long as the Academy, which is to say, quite a few centuries. Now, we need to clear a few things up about groves. You have probably all heard lurid tales of human sacrifice, the altars heaped with the dead, the trees spattered with the gore, the dripping bodies of horses, dogs and men hung from the limbs. Food for the tiecelin*, traditional messengers of Uxellimus*. Yes? Well, let me tell you here and now… it's all true."

A faint murmur went through Styrmir's audience.

"Our ancestors did conduct these practices, certainly. This grove has unquestionably witnessed such things." He could almost feel a shudder pass through the students. "But no more. We have long since put these things behind us. Now, onward, to the henge!"

It never ceased to impress. A large, sweeping circle of dressed stone slabs quarried far to the south at Finnbennach, or 'Whitehorn', in the Eternity Mountains. Styrmir bade them take off their shoes.

As they passed barefoot between the stones into the centre, they all sensed a powerful presence, as if the spirits of those who had conducted ceremonies here in centuries and millennia past still walked here, keeping guard, ensuring that only those who merited it were permitted to walk on this sacred soil.

The other thing that they noticed at once was a strong animal smell, and it was most certainly not the kasturi* which commonly passed this way. It suggested something very ancient and earthy.

Styrmir stood at the centre of the henge, his arms outstretched, gripping his staff, his head turned to the sky. His expression was one close to ecstasy. He was murmuring something in Vargulets*, the language of the cosmos. Slowly, he lowered his head again, and as he did so, the students gave a collective gasp. For the face he showed them was not that they were familiar with, but rather the face of something much, much older, dark and terrifying, with a greenish tint to its skin and eyes that betrayed untold depths. And then, as suddenly as it had appeared, it vanished, replaced by the familiar face of Styrmir.

"Now," he said, as if nothing at all untoward had happened, "as you are all no doubt aware, this henge is very old, dating back, indeed, to the Age of Unpolished Stone*. The distances between the stones have been measured very precisely with a measure which is no longer in use but which we may term the megalithic metre. It is slightly less than an ell*. The people who built it, our ancestors, were master architects and builders, and, moreover, gifted mathematicians and astronomers, and with this henge we are able to predict the rising and setting of the moon at eight critical junctures. Even after all this time, the positioning is only fractionally altered, and still holds good for practical purposes. Plantings, harvests, hunting times, all the major annual events, could be calculated with these stones."

*****

When Samhain arrived, there was no question in anyone's mind that winter was well and truly on its way. The festival actually ran over three nights (Mages reckoned in nights rather than days), the 'Three Nights of Samhain', during which time there was much festive eating, drinking, singing and general merrymaking, but it was the middle night, the last night of Zehnar, New Year's Eve, when the grand ceremony took place. It was foggy, such that it was hard to tell exactly when sunset was, but Grand Mage Styrmir had conducted the ceremony so many times that he knew instinctively when the correct time was. The full student body and all the Mages were gathered, in green robes (freshly minted for the wyffens, stained, ripped and generally in disrepair for the older Mages, for one kept a robe for life, and indeed wore it into the funeral pyre when this life was past) and bare feet. They gathered at the edge of the henge while Styrmir advanced into the middle.

There, an altar had been erected, covered with a cloth bearing a pentacle, and patterned in the colours of the order. On it were lighted candles, at the corners and in the centre, a phial of salt, some incense, and a large ornate golden goblet lavishly decorated with knotwork and inset with precious stones. To one side was an assemblage of late flowers and herbs, and a small loaf of bread.

Styrmir stood erect, impressive and impassive. The crystal at the head of his staff came to life, emitting a rosy glow. Taking the staff in both hands, he swept it in a circle around himself, uttering an ancient incantation in the Goidelic tongue which amounted to "I declare this circle open."

Mages went first, in order of seniority, then older students, and finally the wyffens, each doing a little jump across the invisible perimeter of the circle, then they walked around the circle, working inwards with each pass, until everyone was inside it.

"Ladies and gentlemen, Samhain is upon us once again!" Styrmir declared. "We begin, as always, with a prayer to the Cailleach.

Cailleach beloved ancestral mother
of prosperity and plenty
From whose starry womb the green earth springs
You who are the bearer of all life
We pray you bless and uphold this rite. Cailleach,
Earth Mother, accept our offering!

Ancient dark ones, we made this offering to you.
You who dwell in the outer dark
You who stood against the gods
You twisted and misshapen
You cold of heart and dim of mind
Take this offering and trouble not our working.
Likewise we acknowledge in ourselves
Weakness and perversity
Hatred and spite
Cowardice and ignorance

We contemplate these ills and enemies and for this sacred time, we set them aside! Accept our offering!"

He paused for breath.

"What follows is our statement of purpose and precedent. We gather here on the Feast of Samhain, the End and Beginning of the Sacred Year, the Time of Turning, of twilight, when the Dark Time begins. This is the Last Harvest. The fields lie empty, sinking into Winter's Sleep and our larders hold what gain we have reaped from our labours. As our forebears did, so do we now, and so may our descendants do in time. We are here to offer worship to the Lord of the House of the Dead and to the Queen of Phantoms; to the God of the Dead and the Sidhe, and reverence to our honoured dead here at this their Feast. We offer to Donn the Dark One, the Antlered God who offers hospitality and peace to those bound for the Ancestors' Country. We offer to Morrigan, the Great Queen of Battle and Sorcery, the Old Woman of Death and the Cauldron of Rebirth. In this Season of Change we honour the Holy Dead as the ancients did and seek the omen for the coming year while the veil between the Worlds is thin."

He poured a libation of wine from the goblet onto the grass.

"What follows is an offering to our ancestors. The children of the earth call out to the mighty dead. Hear us, our ancestors, our kindred. To all whose bones lie in this land, whose hearts are tied to it, whose memory holds it; ancient tribes of this place, we offer you welcome. To all of our grandmothers and grandfathers, our own beloved dead, blood-kin and heart-kin, ancient tribes of our blood, we offer you welcome. To all those elder wise ones who guide their people, poets and seers, judges and magicians, wise women and men of ancient days, we offer you welcome. So, o mighty ones, we call to you as our kin, in the love of the all-mother, to join in our magic. Come to our fire, spirits; meet us at the boundary. Guide and ward us as we walk the elder ways. Ancestors, accept our sacrifice!"

Styrmir then took the loaf from the altar. He walked slowly around the circle, breaking off small pieces and casting them on the ground to either side of him, until there was none left.

"We now similarly make an offering to the nature spirits of this place. The children of earth call out to the spirits of this land. Hear us, companions and teachers. To all our allies, kindreds of stone and stream, crystal and fertile soil, pools and mighty seas, kins of the earth, we offer you welcome. To all our allies, kindreds of the growing green, herb and flower, shrub and mighty trees, root and stem and fruit. Green kins, we offer you welcome. To all our allies, kindreds of fur and feather and scale, all who walk or fly or swim or crawl, we offer you welcome. So, o noble ones, we call to you as our allies, in the joy of life upon earth, to join in our magic. Come to our fire, spirits meet us at the boundary. Guide and ward us as we walk the elder ways. Land-spirits, accept our sacrifice!"

Gathering up the flowers and herbs, he once more perambulated the circle, scattering the sacrificial greenery at random, until that too was gone.

"The Great Wheel turns!" Styrmir announced, seeming to direct his words more towards the heavens than to his earthly audience. "And having turned, moves ever on. Ladies and gentlemen, that concludes our ceremony. The traditional Samhain feast awaits you in the Hall."

The order of entering the henge was reversed for the departure. The last of the wyffens to enter, little Haxor Kolchak, led the departure, with Styrmir bringing up the rear. They eagerly headed back to the entrance hall of the Academy, where their shoes were neatly ranked, and, being reshod, joyously made their way into the Great

Hall, where the candles, the wreaths of greenery, and the merry music being played in the gallery, gave the whole scene a delightfully festive air, and all swung their legs over the long benches in keen anticipation of the fine fare that was about to be set before them.

CHAPTER THREE.

Radnyr* brought biting winds and hard, sleety rain. It was a time of year when, as Bliss observed, it was most pleasurable to be indoors, particularly if there was a loved one with whom one could cuddle up on the pretext of maintaining bodily warmth, and look at the bleak weather outside from the side of a cheery flickering fire, whilst testing each other on the names of the major constellations for Mage Cassegrain's assignment.

As the term progressed, they became familiar with all the other Mages and their particular areas of erudition. Mage Grimbald taught them fios*, the esoteric knowledge of the workings of the universe, which was traditionally taught orally, passed down by word of mouth from one generation of Mages to the next. Mage Aud, called the Deep-Minded, her deep mind concealed beneath a frizzy bush of red-brown hair, gave them an introduction to metagnomy, or, in other words, awareness beyond intelligence, and how to access their megin, or inner power. Mage Zalmoxis took them for studies in astrology as well as study of the signs of the earth, the signs of the sun and the course of the moon. Mage Proinsias gave instruction on weather lore and the knowledge of the clouds, while Mage Plegmund taught enchantments and the resolving of enchantments, and Mage Semjaza taught root-cuttings and all matters botanical.

At around Atenoux*, the time of the division between the light and the dark halves of the month, Mage Grimbald had the wyffens in a workshop, building their first hengeforms. Each student would build a wooden board, then draw upon it a sequence of circles. The circles had to be divided into seven, eleven, thirteen, twenty-four and thirty-two equal segments. A nail was hammered into the circumference of the circle at each of the divisions, and then a long skein of wool, dyed in the red, green, blue and purple of the order, was tied at one end to one of the nails. The wool was then stretched to and wound around each nail in turn such that every nail was connected to every other nail. It was a relatively simple matter with the lower numbers, but by the time they came to the thirty-two point hengeform, the tension in the wool was such that it would often simply spring off the nails, and the workshop echoed with all manner of profanities as the students groaned in frustration and proceeded to rethread the wool. When it was completed, the wool formed a three-dimensional pattern as thick as the nails were high, with nothing at all of the board beneath visible.

The month of Midyar* came, and the students began eagerly to anticipate the Solstice celebrations. Ben's close chums, not least the stalwart Bubonax, had noticed that he was spending a good deal less time in the *Brasseur de Bourbourg,* and put this down to his infatuation - as they saw it - with Bliss. This was true, he was choosing to spend more of his free time in private as a twosome with her, but it was also true that he was deliberately spending less of his allowance on beer, in order to save for a Solstice present to give to his beloved.

And now he had enough, it was time to go shopping. The shops on the main street leading up from the waterside to the Academy buildings and the narrow side alleys leading off it provided for every possible need of the students and the teaching staff. On a wintry afternoon when there were few people about, Ben, his hood raised, paused in front of the premises of Greywacke Thangobrind, bespoke goldsmith and jeweller. He looked around to see if he was observed, but there was not a soul to be seen, and he pushed open the door of the shop.

A small bell tinged over his head as he entered. The shop was unoccupied. It was for the most part quite gloomy, with the main sources of light concentrated at the counter, which doubled as a workbench, with a tiny anvil, small hammers, tweezers, rasps and snippers, and rolls of gold, silver and bronze wire. To one side was a small brazier to provide heat for brazing articles of jewellery.

The sound of heavy, shuffling footsteps drew Ben's eyes to the doorway in the corner of the shop, leading to the back room. The heavy curtain covering the doorway was pushed aside, and the proprietor of the shop appeared. Greywacke Thangobrind was not above average height, and had a girth that bespoke an appreciation of fine food and the best sipping mead. Beneath a round cap of wine-coloured velvet sprouted a wild profusion of grey hair which, lower down, merged into an enormous grey beard that extended down across his chest. A small space amid this grey forest was occupied by a pair of twinkly blue eyes, rosy cheeks, and a well-proportioned nose that supported a pair of half-moon spectacles, essential for the fine detailed work that was the hallmark of his jewellery.

He moved slowly, and leaned heavily upon a sturdy staff of polished wood, almost as tall as himself, which ended in a bulbous knot, offering his hand an excellent grip. Although he would not speak of it himself, it was common knowledge throughout the Academy that he had fought in the wars against the Quaaman Empire.

In centuries past, Quaama, far to the south on the great continent of Laurentia, had grown from a collection of villages into a great city, which had then assembled around itself a vast empire. Eventually they had come across the Garsedge Sea, and into Magelaw. They had found a society governed by the Mages, and in order to secure control for themselves, they had wiped them out, or so they thought. In point of fact, the Mages had simply gone underground, prepared to wait out the Quaaman occupation before re-emerging. But in the meantime, the opposition to the invaders, particularly in the north of Magelaw, had proved so fierce that it had ultimately proved to be a province too far, and the occupation had limited itself to the south, and the population more tractable, certainly more inclined to adopt the Quaamans' Mithrasian religion, based around belief in Mithras, The Child of Promise, born at midwinter (Mages could not help but notice that this new god was celebrated at precisely the same time as one of their own major observances, making it that much easier for folk to make the switch).

In more recent times, vassal states had begun to rebel against Quaama on all sides, and she had withdrawn from

Magelaw altogether, her forces too overstretched to be able to maintain their hold on this island province. In one of the last battles fought to drive them out, Thangobrind had sustained a terrible sword wound to his leg, which would never completely heal. As a consequence, pain which for others would be unendurable was his constant companion, but he would never let it get the better of him, and always maintained a sunny disposition, especially towards his customers.

"Ah, Master Troon, if I'm not mistaken." The voice was deep and gravelly, but at the same time friendly and engaging. "I wondered if I might expect a visit from you."

These few simple words put Ben's mind in a spin. To begin with, while everyone in the Academy knew Greywacke Thangobrind, Ben believed himself to have been virtually invisible to all but his closest companions, at least until the commencement of his studies, having done little, or so he thought, to attract the attention of such people as the venerated jeweller.

"How... how do you know my name?" he gasped.

Thangobrind peered at him over the rim of his spectacles, his eyes asparkle. "The mystery child, found in a coracle, adopted by Hasupada and Halldis? Of course I know you. I've seen you around the place since you were old enough to walk. Watched your progress with great interest, I have."

Ben wrestled with his astonishment. "I… didn't know I was worthy of such attention."

"Which is all to your credit, Ben," Thangobrind smiled.

"And how is it that you thought I might be visiting you?"

Thangobrind's smile grew broader. "Well, if you hadn't come to my attention before, you certainly would have when you began courting a certain young lady."

"Ah," said Ben.

"Romantic liaisons within the Academy are always a matter of interest. And Solstice is coming, so it's no surprise that you would be looking for a gift. Now, please take your time, and if you see anything that takes your fancy, I will be happy to bring it out for you to take a closer look."

He handed Ben a lantern to aid with his inspection of the wares in the showcases, the shop being less than adequately lit, and went back to the cloak pin that he was working on.

Ben looked carefully at every piece, trying to imagine what it would look like with Bliss wearing it. There were rings and box brooches, pairs of turtleshell-shaped brooches to pin up a pinafore dress, necklaces of semiprecious stones, amber and coloured glass, some of which might be strung between the turtleshells, bracelets, arm-rings, finger rings, all manner of beautiful things. He looked long and hard at a beautiful knotwork bracelet, in which a pair of fanciful serpentine creatures which might or might not have been dragons, one of silver and the other of gold, were gracefully interwoven, each biting on the tail of the other. He was just about to ask Thangobrind if he might examine it more closely when something else caught his eye.

There was not a great deal in the showcases that was purely gold, but in the corner of one case he spotted a gold pendant. Embossed upon its surface was the image of a pair of embracing lovers.

"Ah, Mr. Thangobrind?"

Thangobrind looked up, smiling. "Greywacke, please, Ben."

"Ah, yes. Greywacke. The gold pendant, may I see it please?"

"Indeed," Thangobrind said, making his way over. "I thought that one might attract your attention." He pulled it out of the showcase into the light of the lantern. "It's engraved on the back."

Ben took the pendant by its chain and laid it in the palm of his hand to get a better view of the figures depicted on it. They were naked, bodies entwined in a passionate embrace. He turned it over and read the words inscribed on the reverse.

I love you more today than yesterday, but much less than tomorrow.

He beamed. "It's perfect."

Thangobrind gave a gratified smile. "I thought you'd like it."

"I'll take it. How much is it?"

"For you sir, three bracteates*. But you need not pay all at once."

Ben opened the pouch on his belt, and pulled out a handful of coins. Immediately visible were two gold half bracteates coins, and these he laid on the counter. He then counted out four testoons* and two bondemarks*, bringing the sum to a total of two bracteates. "I will bring you the rest as soon as I'm able, Greywacke, I swear."

Thangobrind nodded amiably. "I know you will, Ben." He popped the pendant into a small leather drawstring bag and laid it into Ben's hand.

"Thank you," said Ben.

Thangobrind placed his hand on Ben's arm, and fixed him with knowing blue eyes. "May the spirits walk with you and guide you the length of your days, and bring you wisdom and courage in all your doings. Blessed be, Ben Troon, blessed be."

"Thank you," Ben said again, his voice soft with awe. He felt that he had been touched by a world unseen and beyond his comprehension, and ineffable in its power. He slipped the pouch containing the pendant into his own, and walked out of the shop into the sunlight.

*****

There was never any doubt about midwinter. Snow lay in thick drifts everywhere. Hasupada had his young assistants, Owen Ballhatchet and Johannes Moop, out daily spreading salt on the steps, all the way from the waterside to the Academy, and when they were not doing that, they were shovelling madly to clear pathways all around the Academy buildings. The wind had a ferocious bite to it, and brought still more snow, swirling in flurries around cloisters and courtyards, and every now and then, a roof would discharge its chilly burden, to the peril of those walking below.

But all students were agreed on one thing: the ceremony of the Five Dark Days, like all others throughout the year, required that participants be barefoot, to maintain that essential contact with Mother Earth.

Bliss pinned Ben's cloak at his throat, and then pulled his garland of holly and ivy down over his head, feeding his hood up through it at the back and drawing it over his head so that he almost disappeared inside it. He then did the same service for her. They hugged each other briefly, her eyes gleaming with love as she looked up at him from beneath her hood, and then they fell into line behind the other wyffens (who by now, thankfully, had largely become inured to the presence of a pair of lovers in their midst).

It was close to dusk - it seemed a nonsense to speak of sunset when the sun had not been visible for days - as they trekked out to the henge. The great stones reared up, black silhouettes against the orange brilliance of an enormous bonfire in the middle of the circle.

Outside, they stopped and, with deep sighs of reluctance, removed their footwear, all praying silent prayers that the ceremony would be brief, and winced as they stepped through several inches of snow. Once within the confines of the henge, they were relieved to find that most of the snow had been either shovelled clear or at least stamped flat by those who had entered ahead of them, and closer to the fire, the snow had of course melted, leaving instead a well trodden circle of mud.

Mage Waerferth entered the circle from the east, a dramatic figure in his swirling cape, pacing widdershins* around the fire, waving his staff exuberantly in greeting. Students stamped their bare feet, in excitement as much as in an attempt to promote circulation. He returned to his point of entry to the circle and drew a figure out of the crowd. When he was illuminated by the fire, Ben, Bliss and the others could see that he was one of the senior students, dressed in a cloak of holly leaves, complete with red berries.

"The Holly King," Ben said softly. "The King of Winter."

"Yes," Bliss nodded. "I know."

The Holly King made one and a half circuits of the henge, moving deosil*, waving to the onlookers as he went.

When he had taken up his position on the opposite side of the fire, Waerferth drew another figure from the crowd, this one clad in a cloak of oak leaves. He was about to say that this was the Oak King, another senior student, representing spring, when he realised that, of course, Bliss was well familiar with the ceremonies (what did he think they were out in the islands, a bunch of ignoramuses?), and instead merely squeezed her hand tighter. She drew closer to his side in response.

The Oak King, his cloak billowing in the waves of heat coming off the fire, likewise moved deosil around the henge, taking one and a quarter turns before taking up his position.

Finally, without going into the crowd this time, Waerferth raised his hand and beckoned, and the crowd near him parted. A tall, handsome woman with long ebony hair stepped out into the open space, dressed in a low-cut, figure-hugging scarlet dress that showed off her excellent figure to a remarkable degree, leaving precious little to the imagination. At knee level, the skirt flared out, swirling this way and that as she sashayed around the circle, waving to everyone, and smiling broadly. As she passed them, Bliss heard Ben's sharp intake of breath.

"Just you behave," she murmured softly.

When she had taken up her position, Waerferth stepped forward and bowed. In a singsong voice, he began.

"Gather round and gather round.
Come listen to our play.
We make the plays of long time past,
We speak the words the Old Ones say.
So gather round and gather round.
Come, I the Caller say.

First the all father Dagda comes,
Warrior brave who speaks wisdom all.
So heed his words is all we say.
He is the first to enter our play."

Waerferth made a gesture towards the crowd. Again the crowd parted. Grand Mage Styrmir stepped forward, clad in a cloak of leaves, in many different shades of green, sweeping down from his shoulders to the ground, and to shouts of delight he saluted the crowd with his own staff, his eyes sparkling in the firelight.

Waerferth resumed the song, gesturing towards the Holly King.

"Next to come is King Holly, a noble branch of the tree.
He has dispute with his brother King:
The play holds what their fates will be."

From the audience came pantomime boos and catcalls. The Holly King bowed ironically.

Waerferth moved on to the woman in red, making exaggerated gestures, inviting the audience to feast their eyes on her luscious curves.

> "Next to come is the Scarlet One,
> The treasure that does prompt these wars.
> The winner goes to her blessed bed
> When her other husband falls."

> Finally he came to the Oak King, who
> was greeted with wild cheering.

> "Next there comes the Oak King,
> the challenger of the day.
> With sword to sword and battle to battle
> His brother he aims to slay."

This was the cue. From their belts concealed within their cloaks, Oak and Holly drew feather dusters, made of the tail feathers of gullinkambi*, and took up positions for a mock sword fight. Back and forth they went, circling all around the bonfire, thrusting and parrying for all they were worth, the enormous grins they wore an indication the they were having tremendous fun. But finally Holly lost his footing in the mud - whether intentionally or accidentally it was impossible to say - and Oak triumphantly thrust his feather duster home in Holly's chest. An immense cheer went up.

To Ben, it seemed a far cry from oak boughs bearing dripping human sacrifices.

Mage Waerferth stepped forward once more.

> "So gather round and gather round.
> Come listen to our play.
> We make the plays of times long past,
> We speak the words the Old Ones say.
> So gather round and gather round,
> Come, I the Caller say.
>
> This begins the cycle of Spring.
> Our brother light longer dithers tarries and plays.
> For hence for six months he shall win,
> Until the day his brother comes out to play,
> A dark and chilly grin.
>
> The Great Wheel turns."

Grand Mage Styrmir stepped forward, and raised his hands. "Welcome one and all!" he cried. "The feast awaits!"

Gratefully, the students skipped out of the circle and scurried to where they had left their shoes. Ben let Bliss lean against him while she pulled hers on, then he hastily strapped his own. Hand in hand they ran back to the Great Hall, and took their accustomed places at the tables.

The tables themselves were laden with all kinds of festive treats, dried fruits and nuts and exquisite little bonbons in fancy paper, there were flagons of wine, and wandering musicians. Candles flickered, and in the several hearths along the hall, fires were blazing brightly. The whole hall was abuzz with excited conversation.

"Oh!" Bliss gasped, "I do believe I'm able to feel my feet again. I thought I was going to get frostbite if I stayed out there any longer."

She met Ben's eyes. Her own were wide, and reflected the candlelight in a way that he found intoxicating. "Yes, I know," he agreed. "I was the same. I suppose the Mages would say that it's all part of toughening us up for the great wide world."

"I suppose so," said Bliss. "I can't say I feel very tough at the moment."

"Well, it's a long time before we have to worry about that," said Ben, eager to steer the conversation away from discussions of the future. He had stumbled into what was tacitly agreed to be a taboo topic between them.

His hand went to the pocket in his cloak, and the small parcel that nestled there. Around the hall, he could see gifts being exchanged between friends and, very occasionally, lovers. He brought the little package, wrapped in fine paper, with a dainty ribbon to secure it, into the candlelight, and was delighted to see Bliss' eyes light up. She gave him her most radiant smile.

"Thank you," she said, that soft lilting accent of the islands coming to the fore. She took the package, and with her fine fingers delicately pulled at the ribbon, releasing the paper. "Oh," she exclaimed as the box was revealed, "something from Master Thangobrind! It looks expensive."

"Oh, not really," Ben began, dismissively.

Bliss opened the box. "Oh, it's beautiful! Oh, Ben, thank you so much!"

"Look on the back."

She turned the pendant over and read the inscription. Then she threw her arms around him and kissed him passionately.

As he came up for air, she said softly, "It's the most beautiful thing anyone has ever given me." And she slipped the chain over her head, holding the disc of gold up high so it glistened in the firelight.

"While I have your attention," she smiled, somewhat mischievously, "I also have something for you."

From her own cloak she drew out a small rectangular package. "It's nothing as lovely, or as costly, as what you bought me, but I thought you might find it useful."

He took the package from her, smiling with delight. "It doesn't matter what it is," he assured her. "It's from you, so I shall treasure it, always."

He undid the fancy strings and removed the paper. Inside was a box. He opened it, revealing a set of six very small pens, together with a dainty knife for trimming nibs. The feathers were tawny, speckled with black spots.

"Tiny pens!" he gasped with delight. "They're beautiful! But what bird are they from?"

"They are the wing coverts of a glede*," Bliss announced knowledgeably.

"A glede!" Ben exclaimed. "I have never heard of glede feathers being used for a pen!"

"Well, you have now!" Bliss assured him.

Ben's face fell. "Oh, but I don't think I can accept them."

Bliss raised an eyebrow. "Why not?"

"Because I would be too afraid of losing them."

"If you lose them," Bliss said simply, "I will get you some more."

"Oh Bliss," he sighed, running his fingertips lightly over the feathers, "I don't know what to say. Thank you so much."

Their eyes met again and their heads leaned together.

"Now, now, enough of that!" said a voice sharply behind them. They jerked apart as the serving man placed bowls of soup in front of them.

They clasped hands momentarily under the table, then clinked wine goblets and set to, eager to enjoy every moment of the midwinter feast.

And it was truly magnificent, with all manner of roasts and fish dishes and pies and flans and every imaginable kind of savoury. When it seemed as if their stomachs could stretch no more, the desserts followed, a panoply of fruit tarts, syllabubs, baked apples and sweet delights beyond their wildest imaginings, finishing up with plum pudding and the traditional solstice cake, rich and moist, and bursting with all manner of delicious things.

When it was all over, Ben walked Bliss to her door. They walked slowly along the boardwalk, regardless of the cold, stopping every few yards to kiss. When they reached her door, they embraced fervently, Ben clasping Bliss to him with breathtaking fierceness, so she could feel the want in him.

She broke free and they looked at one another through the clouds of their steaming breath. "Not yet," she murmured. "Not yet."

Ben nodded. "I love you, Bliss Tarrant," he said softly.

"And I love you, Ben Troon."

"Goodnight, and sleep well."

"And you."

And she watched as he walked away, torn between desire and fear.

CHAPTER FOUR.

B en, Bliss and the rest of the class sat shivering on benches. It was Adyarren*, the thirteenth month, and the full moon had just risen over the mountains to the east.

"Now," said Mage Zalmoxis from behind them, a quiet, disembodied voice, "focus on the moon, concentrate on it, but at the same time remain in a relaxed state. I realise that this sounds like a contradiction in terms, but that's the secret of calling down the moon. Remain focussed on it until you can see it clearly in your mind's eye."

Ben stared up at the cream coloured orb floating in the blackness above. He could clearly distinguish the Rabbit, facing left, the dark shape of the head and body, with the ears curving upwards and back, following the arc of the sphere. He closed his eyes to see if he could still see it then, but the image was elusive.

"Raise your hand when you feel you are ready to try bringing it down," Mage Zalmoxis said, his voice soporific in the darkness. A few hands went up. "Van Millingen? You would like to have a go?"

There was a low collective groan. Of course Opabinia van Millingen, the teachers' pet *par excellence*, would be among the first, if not *the* first, to volunteer.

"Very well," said Zalmoxis, positioning himself behind her. "Reach out your hand… No, not upwards, straight out in front of you. Reaching upwards like that, you will get tired very quickly… That's it. Now, with your mind, try to summon the moon down into your hand. Don't strain, try to remain relaxed."

Opabinia was not successful in drawing down the moon, nor were any of the others who volunteered. Eventually, Zalmoxis worked his way through the whole class. Each time, he entreated the student to relax, but that was asking a lot, because all of them knew that achieving this particular exercise was the key to performing all other magic.

When his turn came, Ben stared at the moon, whilst at the same time trying to tell himself that it was a matter of the greatest indifference whether he was able to draw it down into his hand or not. Several times, it seemed to him that the moon was indeed drawing down towards him, but in the end it appeared illusory.

By the time they had all had a turn, an hour had passed, and they were all shivering. "I think we might call it a night," Zalmoxis declared. "I would have been astonished if any of you had achieved it first go. Sometimes it takes a good many months. But I think you have all had a first taste of manipulating the forces of nature, which after all is what magic is all about. I suggest we retire to the *Brasseur de Bourbourg*, and I will shout the first round."

This proposal was greeted by murmurs of warm approval, and they were soon ensconced in the tavern, feeling the ice in their veins dissipate in the welcoming glow of a generously heaped fire, helped along by swigs of ale from flowing tankards.

*****

It was only a week or so later that they celebrated Akitu, when Adyarren ticked over into Frigidda*, the first month of the new year. Again there was a great deal of carousing, drinking of toasts and well-wishing for the coming thirteen months. Outside the entrance to the Academy, Hasupada had, as was his custom, deposited a large pile of coal, and after midnight, many students availed themselves of it to 'first foot', ceremonially being the first to cross their chums' thresholds, clutching a lump of coal. Customarily, if the first footer was a tall dark stranger, it was generally considered to be a good omen.

Ben was of course Bliss' first footer.

"Well," she mused, surveying him as he stood in the middle of her parlour, "you are reasonably tall. You're not dark, though, by any means…" She reached up and put her arms around him, and kissed him passionately. "…And you're certainly no stranger!" She poured two glasses of kuass* and they clinked together. "Happy new year."

"Happy new year," Ben replied, smiling. "I wonder what this year will bring."

"Good things, I feel sure," said Bliss warmly. "Good things."

*****

If the students had hoped that the advent of the coldest months of the year meant that they could stay in the warm, perhaps researching spell traditions in the library, for instance, they were going to be disappointed. Having risked chilblains at the midwinter observance, and hypothermia trying to bring down the moon, they now foresaw frostbite as the end result of another exercise…

"Stick-cutting," said Mage Semjaza at the end of a botany class, "doubles as that age-old practice of coppicing. It does the woodlands any amount of good to thin them out, and we get new staffs as a bonus." Mage Semjaza was quite short, with a nest of frizzy brown hair, and a voice that was quite high pitched, and it was not hard to picture him as a wood-elf. "The time of sap-rise is upon us, the perfect time to cut our sticks. So, next week, bright and early. Wrap up warmly, hmmm?"

It was early in Frigidda*, the aptly-named first month of the year, and the heavy frost crunched underfoot as they trekked out in the mist that morning, each equipped with a pruning saw, and all swathed in thick cloaks, scarves, gloves, bonnets and hoods, their breath wafting away in dense plumes as they ascended a step incline.

Mage Semjaza led the way, swinging a bag containing a number of small bowsaws and singing some jaunty folk song in Old Sabellic. They left the manicured grounds of the Academy behind them and ventured into the untamed woodlands beyond. Every so often Semjaza would pause to inspect a branch or a leaf, to read the exact state of the season. They came after a short while to a stream that wound its way through the forest at the bottom of a steep embankment. All along the bank were thick stands of hawthorn.

"Ah," said Semjaza, smiling contentedly. "I think this will do nicely." He wormed his way into the middle of a thicket. "This is the sort of thing we're looking for," he declared, indicating one particular stem of hawthorn. "Long and straight. Perfect for a staff. Raby, pass me the saw." Brancepeth-Raginhard Raby turned to where the saw lay, and stared at it for a moment with an expression of disgust. He clearly considered himself to be above the more "hands-on" aspects of Mageism, an aesthete and an intellectual, not ideal Mage material, Ben considered. Raby picked up the saw with kid-gloved fingers, and followed Semjaza to the point where he could reach the implement across.

"Thank you," Semjaza smiled sweetly, noting with amusement Raby's obvious distaste at getting his hands dirty.

He took the saw and bent down close to ground level, and began sawing his chosen stem as best he could in the confined space. It took only a few brisk strokes to cut it down.

"Somebody catch the end!" he called out as it began to topple. Ben was there and received it into his hands as it fell. "Thank you, Troon," Semjaza panted, slightly winded by his exertion. "Pull it clear of the thicket, please."

Ben did as he was asked, pulling on the stem until it was clear of the others growing there. He had to be careful with the handling of it, as there were sharp spines protruding from the stem along its length, and he did not have kid gloves.

Semjaza disentangled himself from the thicket and approached. From his belt he produced a small hatchet, and working from one end to the other he stripped the spines and small side branches, leaving a denuded staff that was almost as tall as he was.

He held it upright beside him. "Note the height of the stick relative to my height. That is the approximate height ratio that you will be looking to get with your sticks. "Now, pair up, and each pair take a saw. You know the sort of thing to look for, so happy hunting."

Ben and Bliss took a saw and tramped off along the bank of the stream. At one point they came upon a fallen tree forming a bridge across it.

"There are some more hawthorns on the far bank," said Ben. "Let's try there."

"Don't forget that we will have to bring the sticks back across this fallen tree," said Bliss doubtfully.

"I think we can manage," said Ben. "If one of us crosses over, then the other one can pass the sticks across one at a time."

"Well," said Bliss, "if you're sure."

"Sure I'm sure," Ben smiled. He stepped out to the middle of the fallen tree and held out his hand to her. She stepped gingerly onto the trunk and put her hand in his. It felt icy cold to the touch. They carefully crossed over the stream.

On the far side, they saw that the stream followed a U-shaped loop, and that there was a large stand of hawthorns on the further side of the loop. They began to make the short cut across the top of the loop, but pulled up short when they saw that there was a hidden depression in the middle, with a small pond in the bottom.

"Look at that," said Ben, pointing to the water of the pond. It had ripples on the surface where the breeze had blown across it, but the pond was frozen solid. "Gives you an idea of how cold it is," he observed, blowing on his hands to try to generate some shred of warmth.

They skirted around the pond and came to the stand of hawthorn.

"Yes," said Ben with delight as they came close. There were some excellent straight specimens visible within the thicket, perfect staff material. At once Ben began working his way into the middle of the stand, until he could put his hand on the first one that was to be cut out. "Hand me the saw."

Bliss passed him the saw, and he laid the blade against the stem, close to the ground, as he had seen Mage Semjaza do. It was difficult to get a stroke, never mind work up a rhythm, when he was hemmed in on all sides by other stems and tangled undergrowth. Briars snagged his clothing and vines tangled the saw at every movement. He pulled as much of the entanglement clear as he could, and was soon hacking away at the hawthorn stem. It started to fall, but was impeded by all the other growth around it. Ben made his way out into the clear again, and pulled hard on the falling stick to extricate it from among the others. The ground sloped away towards the stream behind him, and it was perilously slippery. At last he had the stick clear, and laid it on the ground.

There were three more to be cut, so they had two each. All went well until the last one, which Ben saw was a beauty, and would make a magnificent staff. Of course, it was right in the middle of the thicket, in the most difficult spot to get to, but he was determined to have it. He fought his way through to it, tiring by now, and hacked away enough of the surrounding brush to be able to lay his saw to it and cut it out. Sawing seemed especially hard this time, and it seemed to take forever to get through the sturdy stem. His breath was steaming furiously with the exertion as he worked the saw blade back and forth, back and forth, until finally it gave, and fell with a crash.

Bliss made some effort to pull it clear, but it was firmly wedged between the other stems, and would not budge. Ben squirmed out into the clear, and taking hold of the upper end of the tree, began to wrestle with it, coaxing it out. It would come a little way and then get stuck again, and Ben would get a new grip slightly lower down the stem and begin again, working it this way and that, and becoming quite frustrated with it.

"It's coming," he said at last. "I think it just needs one last really good pull."

He renewed his grip and put all his weight into freeing the intransigent hawthorn. He leant backwards, huffing and puffing as he struggled to pull it clear. "Nearly there…"

His feet slid from under him in the greasy mud, and he found himself sliding backwards on his bottom, down the slope and into the stream with a splash and a yell.

Bliss hastened to the water's edge as he sat there, momentarily stunned, and reached a hand to him. With her help, he staggered to his feet, soaked from the waist down, and muttering curses he made his way up the bank and retrieved the obstreperous stick. Gathering up the others, they made their way back to the fallen tree. Bliss crossed over, and then he passed the sticks to her one by one. Having crossed over himself, he shouldered the sticks, two on each side, and together they made their way back to where the others were also starting to gather.

At the sight of Ben, dripping and miserable, there was a good deal of hilarity.

Semjaza smiled. "A little brisk, isn't it, for an early morning dip, Mr. Troon? Mind you, that is an excellent staff."

Mage Semjaza began laying into the assembled sticks with his hatchet, vigorously hacking away all that was extraneous. He was quite breathless by the time he was done.

"Right," he panted when he was done. "Pick up your sticks and we'll head back."

Bliss made to pick up her sticks, but Ben wouldn't have it, determined to be chivalrous even if he was wet and shivering.

They arrived back in a small courtyard close to where Mage Semjaza conducted his classes. As they trooped into the quadrangle and laid their burdens on the lawn, Mage Semjaza's assistant, Bohl Mattsdotter, emerged from the building with a trayful of mugs of steaming herb tea. The students accepted them gratefully, and stood clasping them tightly, allowing the warmth to seep back into their chapped and scraped hands.

Mage Semjaza moved among them, distributing to each of them a small sharp knife. "One thing to note that is of great importance, ladies and gentlemen," he announced as he walked around, "is that the bark of the hawthorn is highly toxic. That is why we never take unstripped hawthorn staffs indoors - considered very bad luck, you know - and why we must be very thorough in removing the bark. This is how it's done. Take the knife and begin at one end of the stick and peel off the bark in long downward strokes, the longer the better."

And he began to do just that, paring away long strips of bark.

"The idea is," he went on, "to take off the outer skin, the green layer beneath, and the yellowish layer under that, so that just the pure white wood is seen."

He worked at lightning speed. The others did their best to imitate what they saw, but it was difficult, especially as there were knobby bits where the spines had protruded from the stem. It seemed they were only about a quarter of the way along their sticks when Semjaza announced that he had finished the first of his.

"Of course," he said, being deliberately irritating and smug, "I *have* done this a few times before. And I picked out the smoothest sticks."

With that, he began skinning his second stick, and had finished that by the time the students were half way along their first. He then went around, helping those students who were struggling somewhat, and sometimes doing a few strokes for them, but only ever a few.

By the time they were finished, the neat square of lawn was covered in a snow of stripped hawthorn bark, which Mage Semjaza proceeded to rake into a neat pile that he left on one side for Tradescant's garden staff to deal with. They were well familiar with Semjaza's stick-cutting classes, and knew how to dispose properly of the poisonous waste.

Ben executed the last few strokes on his second stick and stood up straight, flexing his right hand where it was cramping from holding the knife so tightly for so long. Bliss, he saw, was almost finished also. When she was finished, she stood up straight and, catching Ben's eye, smiled at him.

Mage Semjaza was going around with a wooden receptacle in which he had already stored the hacksaws and the hatchet, and he was now collecting the knives, which he deposited in a small rack. "We don't use these knives for any other purpose," he explained. "Now, when you are ready, ladies and gentlemen, please pick up your sticks and follow me. It is of course now safe for you to bring your sticks indoors."

He took them to a lean-to shed in one corner of the quadrangle. Enough light entered through a small window to show buckets lined up along the walls, some of which held sticks that were labelled, while other buckets were empty. Overhead, they could see more sticks stacked among the roof timbers. There was a small desk under the window, with a pot containing small scraps of paper and an inkwell and a pen.

"Please write a label with your name and today's date, and attach it to each of your sticks, and then place them in the empty buckets, which you will note are not entirely empty, but contain a small quantity of neat's foot oil. Your sticks will take about six months to season."

Ben and Bliss waited in line to write their identifying labels, then tied them around their sticks and put them in a bucket. They were now free to go. Ben was still shivering, feeling cold and wet and miserable.

"Come back to my place," said Bliss, "and we'll dry those wet clothes."

It was music to his ears.

They walked into the little parlour. "Come this way," said Bliss, and led him along a short passage and into another room. It was her bedroom. This was her most private place, her inner sanctum, and Ben had the impression that he was stepping onto holy ground. As he looked around, taking in all the feminine touches, inhaling the perfume in the air, Bliss whipped a floral dressing gown off from a hook on the back of the door and pressed it into his hands.

"Get your duds off, mister," she said with a knowing grin, "and put this on." And she slipped out of the room.

He suddenly felt acutely self-conscious, stripping naked in this room, and at the same time, a tingle of excitement ran through him. Then he looked at the robe she had left him to put on, and realised he would look very silly. He was profoundly grateful that none of his chums could see him, still less those of his classmates, like Raby, with whom he shared an active and mutual dislike.

Swathed in primrose yellow, embroidered with large daisies, he walked softly back into the parlour, clutching his wet clothes. Bliss was coaxing a fire into life, and turned to look at him as he entered, struggling, without much success, to keep from laughing.

She set up a drying rack in front of the fireplace. "Give me those," she said, taking soggy bundle from him and arranging shirt, overtunic trousers and socks on the rack.

"Sit down," she said, gesturing to the small dining table in the corner of the room.

When he was seated, she brought him a tankard of ale and set it before him.

"Thank you," he smiled. If it took some discomfort, and looking silly, to be in her company, then it was a price he was more than happy to pay.

"I'll put some soup on," Bliss said. She brought a large cooking pot and hung it on a tripod over the fire, where it would soon come to a boil.

Ben eased back in his chair and took a long refreshing draught of ale. Bliss came with a tankard of her own, putting her hand affectionately on his shoulder as she passed, and settled in at the table opposite him.

Their eyes met, and held each other's gaze for what seemed a very long time. No words were spoken, nor did they need to be.

Ben looked around the room, wanting to drink in every detail of the place Bliss called home, the pictures, the ornaments, the everyday objects, hoping by this means to learn everything he could about the enchanting woman who sat facing him.

Was this, he wondered, a glimpse of the future? Would they one day share a cosy little nest not unlike this one - somewhere, wherever their fate took them - and wallow in domestic - well - bliss? As he watched his clothes steaming, and listened to the bubbling of the soup, anything else seemed unthinkable.

Bliss brought him a bowl of soup and a crusty roll with soft yellow butter, and refilled his tankard. "Are you feeling a bit warmer now?" she asked, placing her hand over his and squeezing.

"Much," he nodded, looking up at her with gratitude and deep affection.

When they had had their fill of soup and ale, they moved from the table to Bliss' comfortable settle beside the fire. Bliss snuggled easily against his chest and was soon asleep. Ben sat for a while, watching the steam rising from his clothes, until his own eyelids grew heavy, and he joined his beloved in the land of nod.

When they awoke, it was nearly dark. They consented to forego the meal provided in the Great Hall, and instead to feast on the delicious, flaky beef and porter pies which were to be had at the *Brasseur de Bourbourg,* as the perfect way to end such an eventful yet cheering day.

*****

Ben had thought Frigidda was cold. The month following, An Frigidda* - meaning simply, "even colder" - taught him a new meaning of the word. Blizzards swept over Dundonald, such that the high towers of the Academy became utterly lost in the clouds and the thick, thick snow that swirled down and swept through every passageway and quadrangle, every exposed corner of the vast edifice, swallowing everything in a vast white silent blanket, and a wind like a whetted knife seemed to slice through clothing, flesh and bone alike, such that every sortie beyond the insulating stone walls became a challenge.

It was a time above all for studying books. Because his remarkable ability to write very small and very neatly - not to mention a certain facility for cartography and illustration - had inevitably come to the attention of the Chief Scribe, Enguerrand Quarton, Ben had been given the task of transcribing one of the various gris-tolkins* in the great library.

The very first morning, Ben and Bliss had settled comfortably at one of the study tables which ran down the centre of the vast book-lined hall. Ben opened a copy of the Erowid, the Mage botanica, essential reading if one wished to remain on good terms with Mage Semjaza, while Bliss began the task of committing to memory the creatures described and superbly depicted in Carr-Gomm's 'Sacred Animals of the Mages'. They had scarcely begun to read when Orgreave Ducange, one of the library's junior scribes, appeared at Ben's shoulder and whispered that Mage Quarton would like to see him in his study.

Ben's first thought was that he had somehow already transgressed some hallowed library rule. "M-Mage Quarton? Wants to see me?" he stammered.

Ducange nodded. He began walking away without further ado. Ben shot a puzzled glance at Bliss and hastened after him.

Ben followed the swiftly pacing scribe into a labyrinth of passageways, all lined from floor to ceiling with bookcases, coming at last to the poky little room with high clerestory windows that served as Mage Quarton's study. It too was filled with books, only some of them appeared to be of considerably greater antiquity than those readily available on the shelves outside. Some of them were enormous, probably requiring two people at least to lift them, Ben guessed, and quite a few were in considerable disrepair, bindings coming away from the pages within, and spines looking as if they had been chewed upon by rodents at some time in the past. The desk which was essentially the only item of furniture in the room was similarly piled high with dusty tomes, such that it was impossible to ascertain whether there was anyone sitting at it or not.

"Mr. Troon to see you, Mage Quarton," Ducange announced, and was gone.

"Ah, Troon," said a voice from behind the bastion of books. "Good of you to come."

The voice had a soporific quality which instantly dispelled in Ben's mind any notion that he might be in trouble.

He decided to take the chance and step forward. He peered over the top of the wall of books. Behind it, a bald-pated elderly man looked up at him with kindly blue-grey eyes over the top of half-moon spectacles.

He extended a bony hand that was speckled with age spots. "Enguerrand Quarton. Delighted."

Ben took the proffered hand and shook it. "B Ben Troon. Likewise."

"Now, Troon, it has come to my attention that you have a particular gift as a scribe."

Again, Ben found himself wondering how it was that people seemed to know so much about him. People of the lofty importance of Mage Quarton.

"I've been told my handwriting is very neat, sir," he managed to get out before his tongue tied itself in knots.

"Exceptionally legible, even when very small, that is what I have heard," Mage Quarton observed quietly. "I wonder if you would be kind enough to give me a small demonstration of your abilities?"

"G-gladly," Ben stammered.

Mage Quarton raised a small bronze bell on his table and shook it. Almost instantly, Ducange reappeared in the doorway.

"Mr. Ducange, could you please escort Troon here to the workbench that has been set up for him?"

"Yes, Mage," said Ducange. To Ben he said, "This way, please."

Ben followed him along a passageway into a large room, well lit by a row of high windows, beyond which high mare's tail clouds could be seen scudding across a crisp blue sky, indicating a brief break in the snowstorms. Ben wished he could be outside throwing snowballs at his friends. Three scribes, two men and a woman, all of middling to advanced years, were perched on stools with a long, high, sloping workbench in front of them. Each of them appeared to be transcribing from enormous dusty volumes with stained and flaking pages. Beyond them, another large book stood open in front of an unoccupied stool. There was fresh parchment, an inkhorn, and small pens in a dainty stand.

"If you could please transcribe the first paragraph or so, and perhaps two or three of the symbols underneath?" said Ducange, gesturing towards the vacant stool.

Ben mounted the stool, and as Ducange sped away with swift, officious paces, he shot a smile at his fellow scribes, and they smiled briefly back at him before resuming their work.

He looked at the writing on the page of the ancient volume set up before him. The ink had faded from black to a light brown, and the writing was crabbed, but not too difficult to make out. It was, he saw, an account of various denizens of the underworld, or, in the common parlance, demons.

He took up one of the pens, examined it for sharpness of the nib, and, taking a small knife from the pen-holder, gave the pen a couple of unnecessary strokes of the blade while he contemplated the text.

He read:

Beware ye also of Agrath, who is the daughter of the demon Ma'hlath*, and like him is in the service of Asmodai*, the*

King of the Demons. She customarily presents herself as a woman of such remarkable beauty that no man can remain immune to her charms, and it is this which she uses with considerable effect to lure her hapless victims into dark servitude in the under-realm.

Drangadróttin, the Lord of Ghosts…*

Ben began to write. When he had completed the required amount of copying, he turned his attention to the symbols. They were mostly circular, but there were triangles, arcs, crescent and full moons, quadrants and arrows. Almost all the symbols were annotated in a language that Ben thought could possibly be Bricriu*, known as the 'poison-tongue', but he couldn't be sure. He felt instinctively that they were connected with some powerful and probably dark branch of Magecraft.

When he was done, Ben set his pen down and turned to see if he might spot Ducange somewhere close by, and jumped, finding him standing silently close by his shoulder. He felt sure he had not been there a moment before.

"Please," said Ducange, his voice seeming ever more unctuous, "bring your work."

Ben took the sheet of parchment he had written on down from the desk and followed the scribe back to Mage Quarton's study.

Mage Quarton took a small cylindrical object from the table and affixed it to his eye socket. Ben saw that it held a lens. The Mage studied Ben's work intently. He muttered softly as he did so.

Abruptly, he looked up and removed the loupe from his eye. "*Very* good!" he beamed. "Very good *indeed*! Mr. Troon, I can happily say, welcome to our team of scribes."

Ben noted with pleasure that he was now *Mister* Troon. He almost floated as he returned to Bliss and his studies.

And so it was that when he was not engaged in his regular studies, Ben would be required to spend some time in the library transcribing ancient grimoires*. He would, of course, have much preferred to spend more of his free time in company with Bliss, but he knew that his was to be a life of service, and that he would have to put thoughts of pleasure aside until the requirements of duty had been satisfied. And, as Bliss reminded him, it was an enormous honour that was being visited upon him, and that he would in all probability learn much that would be useful to him in his later life as a Mage.

Many of the spells were for the usual things, love, luck, wealth, health, protection from evil and so on. Some few, however, were of a darker nature, and some could even kill. Mage Quarton enjoined Ben on his first day of duty, looking into his eyes with an earnestness that spoke of the potential consequences of Magecraft when misused, that it was his, Ben's, business, to transcribe the spells, not to learn them, but sometimes they had a way of working their way into his head anyway, and he couldn't help wondering if that was the tacit expectation of the Mages in setting him to this task.

There was, for instance, one whose very name stirred something deep in his soul: the Call of the Dragon's Breath. Underneath this title was written, parenthetically, "Where smoke becomes solid". In writing it into a fresh volume, the words had wormed their way into his brain, however hard he tried to disregard them.

Cadzal Baldrag
Hendras Fembad
Samiel Schien Hi!

CHAPTER FIVE.

"I think you've changed a bit," Bliss said one evening, as they walked home from the *Brasseur de Bourbourg*. "Since you've been working for Mage Quarton."

An Frigidda had given way to Thraash*, the third month, and the air had, mercifully, a little less of that polar bite about it. It still snowed, but by no means as heavily, and there was a distinct sense that a thaw might indeed be on the way.

"In what way?" Ben asked.

"You've become more serious of late," she said. "You don't seem to spend as much time with Bubonax and the others. You're more distant, I don't hear you laughing as much."

She opened her front door and led him inside. As always, the atmosphere inside was warm and inviting. She put the kettle on the fire to make tea. A plate of toasty brown bannocks was on the table.

Ben gave a deep sigh. It was true. He was young, in his prime, when life should be most carefree, and yet, immersing himself in the books in the library, opening up to him the arcane and mysterious world contained within their pages, it was as if a shadow had fallen across his life. He sat down heavily in his customary armchair.

"It's true," he admitted. "I think perhaps I have become very aware lately of what it is to be a Mage. It's as Mage Waerferth says, we are in the world but not of the world. And we walk a lonely path. It's only other Mages who can grasp what we are about, and once we leave here and go out in the world, meetings with them are likely to be few and far between."

Bliss came and sat on the arm of the chair and put a comforting hand on his shoulder. "Yes," she said, "I know. Perhaps all the more reason to be merry now, while you can. Life is too short not to live it up a little."

He nodded faintly. "Perhaps. I suppose it might be all that stuff that Mage Montelius has been teaching us about the history of the Mages that has made me realise what a very particular and dangerous calling we have been drawn to."

Mage Montelius, every inch the antiquarian, lanky, with long, greying hair flowing down over his shoulders and leather patches on the elbows of his coat, had taught them some of the basic facts about being a Mage. Mages themselves were traditionally the keepers of justice, and kept the seasonal observances. Beyond that, for as long as written records had been kept, they had fulfilled the function of advisor to chieftains, warlords and kings. They wore a red border to their robes. One subset of Mages, whom these leaders of men particularly valued, was the *vates*, who had the gift of prophecy. They wore a purple border. Then there were the healers, identified by green, and the bards, with a blue border to their capes, who were the keepers of history and lore, often preserved in poetry, story and song. Some Mages, Montelius explained, with a hint of disapproval, cut themselves off from society, living as hermits in caves or even hollow oak trees in sacred forests known as nemetons*. But most had resided in seats of learning scattered across the whole of Laurentia. They sought out young children - often ones who had suffered some early childhood sickness or trauma, or had otherwise been "damaged" in some way, as they put it - and brought them to live in Mage academies, sometimes known as Myrfyrions*, and to learn to walk they Magyck path, for the course of study was long, and children were most easily taught. Nevertheless, anyone who came to their door was welcomed, for any small amount of instruction in the ways of the Mage was better than none, and would always pay dividends when the student returned to the world beyond.

All that had changed when the Quaamans had risen to power, bringing with them their Mithrasian creed. As they spread across Laurentia, subduing one tribe after another, they had seen that the Mages were the focus of power and influence, and had, through a series of brutal massacres, sought to eradicate them and their pervasive influence. What they had achieved, of course, was to drive the Mages and their followers further and further into the outer fringes, until Dundonald, essentially on the edge of the known world, was all that remained of that network of colleges. Priests of Mithras took over the spiritual role formerly held by the Mages, as well as that of advisors to kings.

Otherwise, bards continued to live in the courts of nobles, or to travel, sharing their wisdom through poems and tales, and some of them were also *vates*.

Bliss set a cup of tea and a buttered bannock on the table beside him, and he munched and drank thoughtfully, listening to the crackle of the fire.

*****

The early spring brought the first major trial of their careers at Dundonald, the Trial of the Three Fires. They had been thoroughly briefed on what it entailed, but no amount of talking could prepare them for what they were about to experience.

They gathered in the Great Hall on an evening at the dark of the moon. Barbula Beard, a senior acolyte, tall and blonde, with a cheery disposition, came to collect them, carrying a blazing brand.

"All ready?" she smiled encouragingly. A few of the students nodded mutely, though none felt remotely ready. "Good oh! Off we go, then."

She led them through a maze of passages that became progressively less familiar to the wyffens, and then out into the bitter chill of the night air, through a sequence of yards and walled gardens, and then out across open ground, still blanketed in snow, reflecting her torch redly as she passed. They entered the surrounding woods, and followed a narrow path.

After a short time, they saw the flickering light of other torches ahead. Descending into a bowl-shaped hollow, they could make out a long, low building illuminated by torches standing at intervals all around it. Its shallow arched roof was still buried under a layer of snow. The students could discern smoke issuing from a low chimney in the centre of the roof, but the building was completely without windows.

A path had been cut through the snow down steps which led to a low door at one end of the building. Barbula seized the iron ring in the centre of the door with her free hand, and put her shoulder to the door to push it open.

Inside, the only light came from three fires in about the centre of a long hall. The air seemed thick with smoke.

"Mage Vísendakona?" Barbula called. "The initiates are here."

Initiates, Ben thought, as he waited for his eyes to adjust. It was not a word to bring comfort. Bliss edged closer to him, as if reading his thoughts, and squeezed his hand.

"Thank you, Miss Beard," said a woman's voice. "You may go now." The owner of the voice emerged from the shadows, to become a silhouette in front of the flames. The firelight showed her to be a slight, slender woman of advanced years, with pewter-coloured hair pulled back severely into a bun. She was wearing a dark robe, its actual colour impossible to determine.

"Welcome," she said with a warm smile. "There are benches in front of you. Please be seated."

The students edged forward until they came up against the benches, and then shuffled along them, seating themselves on cushions which they were pleased to find there.

"My name is Mage Visendakona. Most of you will not have met me before, since I spend rather a lot of time in here. It is my job to see you through the Three Fires. You will all have been thoroughly prepared on what is to happen here, I think. You see the three fires behind me. Tarrant, explain to us, if you please, what the three fires represent."

"The fire to the left represents the time before birth," Bliss declared in a loud voice, trying not to show the nerves that she felt. "The central fire represents death. And the fire to the right stands for the time after death."

"Well done," said Visendakona, nodding appreciatively. "As you are all aware, each of you is required to run through the fire three times, once tonight, once in a week, and once again about a week after that. You will of course remain here during the intervening period. There are couches along the walls, and food and drink will be brought to you, so you will hopefully not want for anything."

"Mage Visendakona?" The voice was recognisably that of Exomphalus Trillibub.

"Trillibub. Yes?"

"Forgive me, Mage, but I still don't understand how it is that we are not burnt by the fire."

It was not an unreasonable question. The heat could be felt even at the distance the students were sitting from the flames. Nevertheless, a few of those present could not keep themselves from sighing theatrically, particularly as the darkness preserved their anonymity. Or so they thought.

"Mappestone, Raby, Hegedus, you will refrain from making those ridiculous noises," Visendakona snapped. "We will be enjoying each other's close proximity for a good two weeks. Such childishness will not be conducive to good relations during that time." Clearly, there was nothing amiss with Mage Visendakona's hearing. "Now, to answer Trillibub's question, as you pass through the flames, the heat burns off all body hair, turning it into a layer of soot, which in turn protects the skin. All of this happens in the blink of an eye, but, as you know by now, the passage of time can be very relative."

The students took the time to drink in this information. If any of them had thought to titter or make some puerile comment at the mention of body hair, the thought that that instant of passing through the inferno might be slowed down to the extent that one actually became aware of the processes taking place upon one's skin gave definite pause for thought.

"Well," said Visendakona, "if there are no further questions, an evening meal has been prepared for you. I shall pass the food along the rows of benches. Hopefully by now your eyes will be adjusting quite well to the firelight."

It was true. The students found they were beginning to see quite well, well enough to see bowls of lentil soup, baskets of crusty rolls, baked pomdeters* with grated cheese, and cups of cider, as they were passed along the rows. There was a susurrus of soft murmuring which slowly subsided into silence as the students got down to the business of eating and drinking. Mage Visendakona withdrew into the shadows.

When the comestibles had been polished off, the muted conversations began anew. Mostly, the young men and women were talking to calm their fears ahead of the ordeal: they were expected to run naked through a blazing fire, in the hope of coming out the other side unscathed. They had heard the explanation of how it worked several times, but there was still a lot of doubt in their minds as to whether it actually would. Yes, they knew all the older students at the Academy had done it, and they were still here, and surely the Academy would not kill or maim all its new students, but still…

Presently, Mage Visendakona spoke again.

"Well, let's get on. No point in further delaying this moment of truth, eh?" She sounded as if she were trying to be as encouraging as possible. "Ladies and gentlemen, time to put away shyness and disrobe, if you please."

Without further ado, the students divided up according to gender, each group seeking a dark corner in which to undress. Bliss gave Ben a last warm kiss and slipped away to join the other young women, who had gathered into a huddle, a few giggling nervously.

"Are we all ready?" Visendakona called out as the rustling of discarded clothing died away.

"Yes, Mage," came the collective reply.

"Very well," she said. "I shall go to the far end of the hall and call you one by one, in alphabetical order.

When I call, you must run as fast as you can through the flames, and I will be there to meet you on the other side."

She made it all sound so simple.

The young initiates watched with bated breath as Mage Visendakona walked calmly along the middle of the hall, a black shape outlined against the wall of fire in front of her. They gasped as, with no more concern than if she were brushing aside a curtain, she walked through the flames and disappeared from view.

A minute or two later, her voice could be heard from the far end of the hall.

"Right. I am in position. The first through will be Mr. Angenwit."

Bubonax, Ben's best friend, stood up and walked forward. "In position, Mage," he announced loudly.

"When you're ready."

Who could ever be ready for this, Ben thought.

He watched as Bubonax tensed his body, hesitated a moment, and then started into his run. Ben stared. He was really going to do it.

But no. He pulled up short, giving a loud gasp of exasperation, and at once felt himself driven back by the intense heat.

"Sorry," he called out to the invisible Mage. "Have to take it again."

"Very well," Mage Visendakona called back. It was to be expected that there would be a good few false starts.

Bubonax loped back to the starting point and braced himself anew. He sucked in a deep breath and ran, screaming a blood-curdling battle cry as he went, and leapt through the flames. He was lost from sight.

There was silence, no screaming at least. "Mr. Angenwit?" the Mage called out.

"Yes!" came the triumphant reply. "I'm still here! I'm fine!"

The rest of the class burst into spontaneous applause.

"Very good," said Mage Visendakona. "Next is Mister Boarstall."

And so it went on. Those who were able to get through on the first try were in the minority. Many found that adopting Bubonax's battle cry worked well for them. Ben was a little shocked to see Raby leap through on the first attempt. He, Ben, felt honour bound to do likewise.

"Miss Tarrant!"

Ben gave a start. Had they got so far already? He watched as Bliss emerged from the shadows and took up her position. He was desperately aware that he had never seen her naked before, and now here she was on show to everyone. Most of the class had already gone through the fire, but they would all be there on the other side, looking at her. It was not what he would have chosen for that special first moment.

She was a shapely black shape, outlined in red. She had, Ben saw, a perfect hourglass figure. He longed to hold her, to explore every inch of that body.

"In position!" Bliss called out. Her soft islands accent did not seem to carry very well over the roar of the inferno.

"Very well," the reply came back. "Make your run when you are ready."

Ben's heart was in his mouth as he saw her body stiffen in readiness. Everyone else had made it through, surely she would be fine. But he scarcely dared to watch.

She began to run. He noticed that she had that way of swinging her forearms from the elbow that some women had when they ran. Then she let out a roar like nothing he had ever heard from her lips before. It was as if she had been momentarily possessed by some demon, some being that was definitely not Bliss Tarrant.

But whatever it was, it carried her through the fire. She was gone.

There was an extended moment of silence. "Are you all right, Miss Tarrant?" Ben heard Mage Visendakona ask.

"Yes." The word came out as a gasp. Of relief, Ben imagined.

"Mr. Trillibub, please."

Exomphalus Trillibub rose to his feet with uncertainty. This would not be easy for him, Ben saw. Exomphalus was not a runner at the best of times.

"Run, Exo," Ben called to him softly. "Run as if the hounds of Ereshkigal* were about to bite you on the bum."

Exomphalus turned and gave him a little wave of acknowledgement. Then Ben saw that ample derrière turn again towards him, as the tubby fellow braced himself, linking his hands and cracking his knuckles as if he ran through such blazes every day before breakfast.

And then he began running. It was an ungainly motion, not elegant by any means, and not promising any great turn of speed. Exomphalus let out what he clearly intended to be a war cry, but it was a cry that would not scare a walcott*. It was not enough. He pulled up short of the furnace, the war cry turning to a moan of despair.

"Sorry," he called out, as he began stamping back to the starting point. "Have to go again."

"Very well," said Mage Visendakona in a tone that suggested that she expected nothing else.

"Louder!" Ben hissed as he took up his position again.

"What?" Exomphalus hissed back.

"Louder," Ben repeated. "Really, *really* loud."

"All right," said the tubby fellow, with something of a shrug.

He ran again, his bare feet slapping loudly on the ancient stones where so many others had slapped before. His cry was louder this time. The walcotts might have ruffled their feathers with disquiet. But it was still not enough, and he pulled up short again.

"And again!" he called out in a tone that bespoke absolute despair.

"Do your best, Mr. Trillibub," the voice of the Mage carried from the far end of the hall.

Exomphalus slouched back to the starting point.

"Louder still," Ben urged as he took his mark for the third attempt. "Loud as you can. Remember: the hounds of Ereshkigal are biting your bum!"

In the gloom, Ben barely saw the nod of acknowledgement that Exomphalus gave him, but he watched as he turned and stiffened sinews that were slack with disuse.

"Ready!" Exomphalus called out, and this time he sounded as if he meant it.

As he began to run, Ben stood up and began to roar himself, and as if carried along by it, Trillibub added his own. Faster than ever he ran, past the point of no return, and spreading his flabby arms like wings, he flew through the fire.

In the quiet that followed, all that could be heard was a strained wheezing.

"Mr. Trillibub?" Mage Visendakona called out. "Are you still with us, Mr. Trillibub?"

For long seconds, there was no reply, then, "Yes. Thank you."

"Good," said the Mage, sounding mightily relieved. "Mr Troon, if you would get set up for your run, please."

Ben stood up and walked unsteadily towards the starting point. He glanced back into the firelit faces of Uta Vecriga, Ingvar Vidfume and Sidra D'Yahya, the last three after him.

His heart pounded as he walked to the mark. In his head he repeated over and over, the hounds of Ereshkigal, the hounds of Ereshkigal…

He ran, willing every ounce of strength down into his thighs and calves, head down, screaming his war cry, refusing to look at the fire, until the last moment, when enveloped in a cloud of pure heat, and his field of vision was filled with the blinding orange glare of the inferno. He leapt…

…And landed, blinded, stumbling, gasping, his lungs and throat raw. He came to a standstill, the intense heat still roasting his back and legs, and sucked in air gratefully.

"Alive!" he gasped, barely audible.

Mage Visendakona had heard him, though. "Excellent!" she declared. "Miss Vecriga, to your mark, please."

Ben shuffled away into the dark, and as he did so, hands enveloped him in a woollen robe, and he recognised Bliss's tender touch.

"Thank you," he wheezed, still struggling for breath.

Bliss gave a little chuckle. He felt her fingers caressing his bare scalp, and realised he was now as bald as an egg. Tentatively, he raised his hand and lightly touched her head. She was as hairless as he was.

He withdrew his fingers and looked at them in the firelight. They were sooty black. It had worked.

The thought returned to him, as it had many times during the preparatory briefings, that if she was bald on her head, which looked like a large grey egg, then she was, well, bare… down there… He tried to picture it in his mind. It was just too arousing, too unsettling.

Bliss gave his arm a squeeze. Could she read his thoughts, he wondered. Women generally didn't find it too hard to guess what a man might be thinking.

At that moment, there was a loud yell, and Uta Vecriga burst through the flames to a round of applause. She was a perky, popular, red-haired girl. Ben glanced in her direction. She was, of course, just a black shape, standing with her hands against her knees, catching her breath, but Ben, realising that he was looking at her naked, hastily looked away.

"Well done, Vecriga," Mage Visendakona called. Her voice was growing hoarse. "Mr. Vidfume to your mark, please."

"Come," said Bliss, taking Ben by the hand, "The couches are this way."

She led him to where the sleeping couches were laid out. Each had a low table beside it with a jug of water and a beaker. Bliss had already selected two couches side by side. Together they sat down on one of them, and Bliss put her arms around him and kissed him.

"Well done," she murmured in his ear.

"You too," he murmured back.

Ingmar Vidfume's battle cry echoed off the arched ceiling, and in moments he was there among them, being congratulated by his close associates.

Sidra D'Yahya, the last to go, unfortunately took three attempts, and it became apparent that Mage Visendakona's patience was by this time at a low ebb, but at last everyone had passed through the flames, and it had proved to be less of an ordeal than many of them had imagined.

They slowly made themselves at home on the couches. The sound of beakers being filled with water could be heard, and then that water being sluiced down parched throats. A few murmured good nights followed, and soon peace reigned. Ben and Bliss lay side by side and hand in hand in the dark, until sleep overtook them.

There followed a week of eating, drinking and talking, a lot of talking. Over time, everyone told their story, Ben explained as much as he was able of his mysterious arrival in the coracle, and of his adoption by Halldis and Hasupada, and how the Academy was really the only home he had ever known. Even Bliss recounted her suicide attempt, and spoke at length about life on the Tollgate Islands, an isolated community, but enjoying many rare pleasures that mainlanders knew nothing about. In time, all the students knew all about one another in considerable detail, and bonded together as a unified group.

Towards the end of the week, Mage Visendakona began preparing them for the second run through the flames. By this time, a thin layer of body hair had grown back, just enough to give them the necessary protection on passing through the flames.

By the second round of the run through the fire, those who were unable to make the leap on the first go had been reduced to a mere handful. They all knew what to expect, and even if their hearts were pounding, they all had survived unscathed the first time, and there was no reason why they might not do so again.

Another week of talking followed. Every topic was discussed, history, science, love, death, the afterlife, war, the existence of a god or gods, and all opinions were aired and respected. By the end, all knew one another intimately, whatever animosities there had been were put aside, and a band of true brothers and sisters evolved. Which was strange, since they would afterwards take their individual paths in life, and might never meet again, but the bond they had created would sustain their souls until they were quit of this life. And, perhaps, beyond.

Towards the end of the second week, Mage Visendakona began to prepare them for the third and final run through the flames. By now, they were well comfortable with the prospect, and some almost blasé. In the event, not one of them failed to make the leap on the first attempt.

When it was over, they did not sleep, but sat talking for a day and a night (although such terms had ceased to have any meaning for them), discussing matters both esoteric and banal, often with equal fervour. It was as if their very being together served as some sort of intoxicant that made sleep irrelevant.

At last it was all over. Many of the students expressed profound regret that it should be so. When it was time to go, Barbula Beard reappeared. Mage Visendakona had the students form a line, each with a hand upon the shoulder of the one in front. She and Barbula worked their way along the line, tying blindfolds around each head. When that was done, she went to the front of the line and took Bubonax's hand and placed it upon her own shoulder.

"Are we ready?" she called out.

"Yes, Mage," came the collective reply.

"Good. Off we go. Barbula, the door please."

Barbula had taken up position by the door, and opened it. All the students shivered as a blast of cold air swept in and across their bodies. They had been living in a furnace for the last two weeks, and the chill of a night in early spring was a shock to the system.

The Mage moved off, and they all braced themselves for exposure to the elements.

They moved slowly, to avoid stumbling, and the walk seemed to take forever. At last, they felt the change from leaf mould and mud under their feet to gravel pathway, and then, some time after that, to flagstones and cobbles alternately.

"Careful now," the Mage called back. "There are steps here. Go very slowly."

They shuffled up what seemed to be an interminable flight of stone steps, and then the abrupt change in temperature told them they were indoors once more. The heard the complaint of hinges as a large door was swung closed.

"All right," the Mage announced, "you may now remove your blindfolds."

The students did so, many with expressions of relief. They looked around. A small number of wall sconces revealed that they were in the entrance hall of the Academy, the staircase leading to the Great Hall disappearing into the gloom to one side, the great outer doors outlined in faint light to the other.

"Now," said Mage Visendakona, standing by the entrance gate, "it is just past the full of the moon. You may find it a little bright." With that she drew open the great door, and moonlight flooded in. There were gasps, it was so bright. "As you make your way to your quarters, I suggest you keep your heads lowered and avoid looking directly at the moon. Your eyes will be particularly sensitive for a day or so. I suggest that you stay indoors with the curtains drawn for at least tomorrow. Well, class, congratulations! You all did very well. I wish you luck with the remainder of your studies."

"Thank you, Mage," they all called out, and burst into applause.

Shyly, Mage Visendakona gave a bow and slipped out into the moonlight.

CHAPTER SIX.

Normal life resumed. While they had been undergoing the Trial of the Three Fires, Thraash had ended, and the month of Thawl* had begun. Snow had melted, giving way to mud, but everywhere there were signs of new growth, bright green shoots appearing in sharp contrast to the darker green of the previous year's growth, and the weather was distinctly warmer.

Bliss took Ben as her partner to the ceremony of Laa Boaldyn*, a celebration of the coming of spring. They both wore garlands of unopened flowers. Each of them found it deeply strange to contemplate the other with just the barest stubble of hair. Bliss had a pair of gardening shears tucked into her girdle.

The celebrants gathered in the henge, where sticky mud made walking treacherous, and clung to the hems of bright spring dresses.

Mage Kilwinning of the order of Quadishtu, clad in a robe of leaves, officiated, with Grand Mage Styrmir assisting, similarly dressed.

Grand Mage Styrmir assembled the students in the outer part of the henge while Mage Kilwinning remained apart in the ritual area in the centre, apparently communing with the Goddess. Large bunches of wild flowers had been gathered in the early morning from the fields and woodlands all about, and Styrmir set the women to weaving them into more garlands, while the men waited patiently to one side. When they were done, the women walked over to join the men, many waving their shears as a celebration.

There was singing and dancing, and a large goblet of ceremonial brew was passed from hand to hand. Later, Ben noticed that some of the couples were slipping away into the woods for some horizontal merriment, and he felt the urge to take Bliss away for some of their own.

Bliss saw what he was looking at. She seized his hand, and for a moment his hopes soared, but she took him instead to the stepping ground.

"Dance with me!" she urged brightly, and he could not refuse her.

As they drew close in the dancing, she said softly to him: "Not yet, but soon, I promise."

The weather was growing warmer, and the urging in his loins was growing ever more intense. He saw her again, the black shape outlined against the fire, the perfect silhouette. He did not know how long he could hold back. Still, she had promised…

*****

There were shops lining the main street that climbed up from the waterfront to the entrance to the Academy, and there were more in smaller side streets and alleys leading off it. Late in Thawl, when there were few people about, Ben slipped into one of the narrowest alleyways, almost perpetually in shadow, and made for a small, anonymous-looking doorway.

As he was about to enter, he gave a last nervous look about to be sure that he was not observed, and grasped the iron handle.

The proprietor, Tobias Merkin, was a big man with a beer belly, perched on a stool in the corner, which looked much too small for him. He was engrossed in a novel, lit by a small window over his shoulder. He glanced up as Ben entered, said a polite "Good afternoon to you, sir," and went back to his reading. He knew that his customers liked to browse in private, without interference from him. He had his regulars, though, and saw that Ben was not one of them. A "first-timer", in other words. He thought he should add a little extra remark. "If you need any, er, advice, or assistance, sir, just say the word."

Ben mumbled a quick "thank you" and turned his attention to the display cases.

Tobias Merkin was a purveyor of "gentlemen's requisites". And there they were lined up, row upon row of condoms, each displayed on a life-sized phallus of turned wood, just as one might display hats or gloves. Ben gasped inwardly. He had heard stories, of course, but now he was confronted with the visual evidence: the variety was astonishing. Leather was the most popular material, kid leather it looked like, although lambswool was also a popular option. Some were quite plain, others were dyed a host of interesting colours, and others still had been lovingly stitched together in harlequin and other patterns. And then there were the ones with ribs, protruding studs of leather, all manner of peculiar surface patterns. It was bewildering.

Footsteps echoed down the alleyway outside, and Ben was suddenly reminded that he didn't want to be found in here. He had no idea if any of his classmates patronised this establishment. There were certainly a few that he thought might well do.

"I'll take this one, please," he said, pointing to a lambswool prophylactic and trying, unsuccessfully, to sound as if he made this kind of purchase on a regular basis. He wondered if Merkin would pass comment on his choice.

He did not. All he said was, "Very good, sir. That will be one testoon and five sceattas*, if you please."

Ben pulled a handful of coins from his belt pouch and counted out the appropriate sum. While he did so, Merkin wrapped his purchase in plain paper, and he secreted the small parcel in his pouch.

"Good day to you, sir," Merkin said pleasantly, as Ben put his hand on the door handle.

"Good day, sir," Ben replied, struggling to sound Ma'hlath may care about it all.

As he opened the door, he glanced hastily in both directions to ensure he was not observed, then walked briskly back into the sunlight of the main street.

When he had turned the corner and disappeared, Bliss emerged from her hiding place in a doorway further along the alley, a faint smile playing about her lips.

*****

In the dark hour before dawn on the first of Meagh*, the air still had a distinctly chilly bite to it. Bliss pulled her front door closed behind her and wrapped her good wool cloak tighter about herself as he set off along the waterfront. She carried a small earthenware bowl. The air was filled with the sound of lapping water and the hollow clunking of moored coracles as they bumped lazily against each other. Somewhere in the distance, gulls were keening, and here and there came the cries of redshanks.

She made her way up the main street, careful not to trip on the steps in the dark, and came to the entrance hall, where stood a group of similarly cloaked figures, each carrying a receptacle of some kind. They greeted one another with girlish giggles, as if enjoying a private joke. Bliss looked from one face to another in the torchlight. Almost all the girls from her year were there: Sidra D'Yahya, Brilliana Harvey, Clavicula Salomonis, Stella Matutina, Uta Vecriga and Opabinia van Millingen. She was a little surprised to find Barbula Beard there, but reasoned that there was no reason why she should not be, and there were perhaps half a dozen older girls whose names she did not know.

"Is everyone here?" Barbula called out, after they had been milling about for a few minutes. "Speak up if you aren't here!" There were a few polite chuckles. "Very well. Let's go, girls."

She led them off through the Academy, and for a moment Bliss had the notion that she was taking them back to the Hall of the Three Fires, but instead of going into the woods, she turned away into a meadow, where the grass was almost waist high after the drenching spring rains.

"Righty ho," called Barbula. "Collect away, girls. Collect to your heart's content."

The young women moved off, holding their collecting bowls and shaking handfuls of grass. Showers of dew flew everywhere, with much laughter as the women became increasingly drenched. By the time it was light, they had all collected a sufficiency.

They covered their bowls with circles of muslin and tied them with string, then retreated to the inviting warmth of the Great Hall for a cheery breakfast of porridge, apple purée, crusty bread and jam and raspberry leaf tea. Many remarked on the fact that their male comrades would scarcely be stirring yet.

Opabinia van Millingen sat down beside Bliss, her thick spectacles fogging up in the warmth of the crowded hall. "Bliss," she said softly, "I have some wonderful news." And she leaned in close to whisper.

When they were done, they went their separate ways, happy at having shared the experience of Meagh Morning.

Bliss retired to her bedroom and put the bowl down on the washstand. She undid the string and removed the muslin cover. Careful not to spill any, she splashed the icy dew onto her face and worked it into her skin.

Afterwards, she dried her face and looked at herself in a looking glass. Did the dew of Meagh Morning really make her more beautiful? She thought it unlikely, but it was a harmless custom, and she was happy to perpetuate it.

*****

A day or so later, they gathered at sunset to celebrate Beltaine, all dressed in shades of green and wearing garlands of spring flowers. As pre-arranged, Bliss met Ben outside the entrance to the Academy. As he approached and caught sight of her, Ben smiled warmly.

"Hello," he said. "You look particularly radiant today."

So had it really worked then, she wondered. The Meagh dew. She threw her arms around him and gave him a long heartfelt kiss, disregarding the comments made by passing yahoos.

"Mmm," he murmured, coming up for air. "It's good to see you too."

They formed up into a column under the guidance of Mage Waerferth, who paced back and forth, chivvying them into line in his usual grumpy fashion.

"So good to see him full of the joys of spring," Ben muttered, and Bliss gave a laugh. It thrilled him to the core when he could make her laugh.

"Have you heard?" Bliss whispered. "Opabinia is to be the Lady of the Greenwood. She's apparently been closeted for days learning her lines, but she came out for the Meagh Morning dew-gathering, and she told me over breakfast afterwards."

Opabinia van Millingen seemed an unlikely choice for the starring role in the Beltaine ceremony. "How *do* they choose?" he asked.

"I have no idea," said Bliss. "Perhaps they just pull names out of a hat."

Ben nodded. It seemed as good a way as any.

They reached the henge. As they did so, Opabinia emerged from behind a bush, clad in a robe of leaves with a long train, and wearing on her brows a magnificent garland of spring flowers. Her hair was still boyishly short. She carried a long staff of office topped by a globe made of interwoven briar stems. As the students approached, she smiled and waved with her free hand, and took her place at the head of the line. As they passed in single file through the standing stones and took up their positions around the circle, Opabinia walked around the outside of the henge and stood with the sun behind her. It was low, almost touching the distant hills, and it cast long shadows behind the stones. Within the circle, new grass could be seen pushing up through the mud, and the turf felt springy, and in places a little boggy, underfoot.

"Welcome!" said a loud voice behind them, and they turned to see Grand Mage Styrmir standing outside the henge, dressed in robes similar to those that Opabinia wore, but with the addition of a headpiece that sprouted an impressive pair of antlers. "Welcome one and all to our

Beltaine celebration! This is the season of Cernunnos and Ceridwen. We ask for their blessing."

Opabinia raised her arms and recited in a loud clear voice:

"The Cup of Wonder

May I make my fond excuses for the lateness of the hour,
But we accept your invitation, and we
bring you Beltane's flower.
For the Beltane is the great day, sung
along the old straight track.
And those who ancient lines did lay will
heed the song that calls them back.
Pass the word and pass the lady, pass
the plate to all who hunger.
Pass the wit of ancient wisdom, pass
the cup of crimson wonder.
Ask the green man where he comes from,
ask the cup that fills with red.
Ask the old grey standing stones that
show the sun its way to bed.
Question all as to their ways, and learn
the secrets that they hold.
Walk the lines of nature's palm crossed
with silver and with gold.

Pass the cup and pass the lady, pass
the plate to all who hunger.
Pass the wit of ancient wisdom, pass
the cup of crimson wonder.
Join in black winter's sadness, lie in
Lughnassa's welcome corn.
Stir the cup that's ever filling with
the blood of all that's born.
But the Beltane is the great day, sung
along the old straight track.
And those who ancient lines did lay will
heed this song that calls them back..
Pass the word and pass the lady, pass
the plate to all who hunger.
Pass the wit of ancient wisdom, pass
the cup of crimson wonder."

Styrmir walked through the circle of onlookers into the centre. He was joined by Mages Cassegrain and Semjaza, in similar robes of leaves. Together they intoned a cheery song:

"Hal an tow, jolly rumble oh
We were up long before the day oh
To welcome in the summer
To welcome in the Bel oh
The summer is a-comin' in
And winter's gone away oh

Take no scorn to wear the horn
It was a crest when you were born
Your father's father wore it
And your father wore it too."

Grand Mage Styrmir then continued solo:

"Robin Hood and Little John
Have both gone to the fair oh
And we will to the merry green wood
To hunt the buck and hare oh."

Mage Cassegrain took up the next verse:

"What happened to the Bernician
That made so great a boast oh
They shall eat the feathered goose
And we shall eat the roast oh."

It was then the turn of Mage Semjaza:

"The lord and lady bless you
With all their power and might oh
And send their peace upon this land
And bring peace by day and night oh."

Finally, the Mages and Opabinia all cried out in chorus, "Hail to the gods!"

Grand Mage Styrmir stepped forward. "The Great Wheel turns," he declared, "and having turned, moves ever on. Ladies and gentlemen, the Beltaine feast awaits you in the Great Hall. Please enjoy yourselves tonight!"

They filed out of the henge in the reverse order to that in which they had entered, and Opabinia brought up the rear, swinging her staff in a jaunty fashion, and clearly well pleased with her performance.

Ben stood watching the passing parade with Bliss standing in front of him. She leaned back against him with her full weight, completely absorbed in watching what was going on.

"You're leaning on me," he said gently.

She jolted herself upright. "I'm sorry," she whispered. "I hadn't realised."

He put his arms around her. "It's all right," he smiled. "In fact, it's nice that you feel so comfortable with me that you can forget yourself in that way."

They made their way into the Hall. Many were gathered around Opabinia, congratulating her, and she appeared to be basking in her new-found fame. As bowls of nuts and dried fruits and other tasty titbits were passed from hand to hand, Ben leaned close to Bliss.

"I was thinking," he said quietly, "that if the weather is nice on our next free day, we might go for a picnic. I have something I'd like to show you."

Bliss thought back to the sight of Ben furtively slipping out of Tobias Merkin's establishment, and felt she had a pretty good idea what it was that he wanted to show her. "Sounds interesting," she smiled. "I would like that very much."

*****

It was a perfect Meagh day. There was barely a cloud in the sky, and the sun was warm without being oppressive. The water of the inner bay sparkled as Ben rowed his coracle across it, a picnic basket at his feet, with a large plaid rug folded across the top, and his heart sang with anticipation.

As he drew close to the boardwalk, he saw Bliss standing there in a long floral gown, a wide brimmed straw hat shading her face and concealing her skimpy head of hair. A white crocheted shawl lay about her shoulders. As he came alongside her, he saw that she was wearing her most beatific smile, and he felt utterly blessed.

He reached out and took her hand, and helped her into the little craft. As she stepped in, she kissed him on the lips lingeringly.

"Hello," she said.

"Hello," he replied. "You look wonderful."

"Thank you," she smiled. "So do you."

He pushed off from the boardwalk and began rowing. He was unaccustomed to having a passenger, and found it hard work.

"I see you brought the picnic things," Bliss said as she settled on the bench.

"Halldis has given us enough to feed an army," he told her.

"She shouldn't have gone to so much trouble," said Bliss. She had guessed that Ben might not have put a picnic basket together by himself.

"She likes you," Ben assured her. "She seemed to want to do it for you."

"That's nice. I must remember to thank her next time I see her, but please tell her from me I'm most grateful."

"I will," said Ben. "Shall we look and see what we've got?"

Bliss shook her head. "Not yet. I like to savour the anticipation."

"All right."

They lapsed into silence, but their eyes locked, speaking volumes to one another.

Ben rowed past the shallow spit of sand that marked the point between the inner bay and the outer one. From this point, the circulating current, the one that had brought him to Dundonald as a babe, would be too hard to row against. He brought the coracle into the shallows and stepped out. The sea was cold, and he gave a small gasp.

"From here we walk," he explained. He drew the boat up to the water's edge, and gave Bliss his hand to support her as she stepped onto the sand.

Here, the beach ran up to a low bluff of sandhills where tussocky grass grew, but further round the large bay which spread before them, higher limestone cliffs could be seen rising. They took the basket and the rug between them and started walking.

As they drew further and further from human habitation, they became aware of a great number of birds of coast and marshland on the beach and circling in the air, dunlins and sanderlings, ringed plovers, lapwings and godwits.

"This - whatever it is - you were going to show me...?" Bliss began.

"Not far, not far," Ben assured her, looking mischievously secretive. "Not far at all."

Presently they came to a spot where the land behind the beach had begun to gradually rise up, but which was otherwise unremarkable.

"Here we are," said Ben. "Pop the hamper down." Together they lowered the basket onto the sand. "We must tread very softly, and be very quiet," he whispered.

He led her up through the dune grass, and then stopped at the top of the rise, and gestured with his hand for her to come to his side. Filled with curiosity, she came to join him. As she did so, her hand flew to her mouth to stifle a cry of amazement.

Before them was a shallow depression in the dunes, surrounded on all sides by a screen of high grass, such that it gave the impression of a small amphitheatre. On the farther side, facing them, was an enormous white bird, She had trampled flat the grass around her, and this served her as a nest. But it might just as easily have been a throne, so regal was her appearance.

"A mollymawk*!" Bliss gasped. Ben put his finger to his lips.

The great bird eyed them both, unperturbed by their presence, inspecting them with an eye that was as black as jet. As she did so, a slight breeze came up from the sea, gently ruffling the feathers of her breast, a breast of blinding whiteness that spoke of polar regions, so white that it had almost a blue hint, the colour of glaciers. She turned slightly, and then resumed the inspection with the other eye, as if that might provide her with different information from the first one. A different perspective, so to speak.

After considering the newcomers for a spell, the mollymawk rose, with impeccable dignity, and stepped gingerly forward into the middle of her arena. She spread her magnificent wings, gave them a slight shake, and then turned and waddled back to her grassy throne.

She left behind her one of her snowy primary wing feathers.

"The feather of Ma'at," Bliss said softly, reverently.

"Sorry?" said Ben, staring at the feather.

"I've been reading about the Chogans, a desert people, and their beliefs," she explained. "They believe that when you die, a being called Ma'at, in the underworld, weighs your heart against a feather, to determine whether you are good enough to be granted access to the afterlife."

"And if you don't measure up?"

"The heart is devoured by a great beast, called Asag*, and that's the end of it." Bliss gestured towards the feather. "It's a talisman, a feather for your bonnet, to bring good fortune. And the symbol of a traveller, a wanderer."

Ben stepped forward and picked up the feather. "I don't have a bonnet," he said, holding the quill delicately between his fingers.

"That's easily remedied," said Bliss lightly.

"And I'm hardly a traveller," he added. "I've never left the Academy."

"That may well change," said Bliss, and gave him a look that he found faintly disturbing.

"I will only be a traveller if I can have you by my side. Always." And he kissed her warmly.

Bliss did not reply, but led the way back to where the picnic basket stood on the beach. Ben carefully laid the feather in the top, on the blanket. They took their shoes off, and then they each took a handle and resumed walking.

After they had gone a short distance, little waves washing over their Bliss said quietly, "You've brought me back to life."

Ben was stunned, and delighted. "I didn't know I could do that," he said.

Bliss put her arms about him and kissed him, warmly, lingeringly.

They walked along for a while in contented silence until they came to a place where a small stream had carved a deep defile in the cliff face, rushing down in a flurry of white water and then gathering itself in a small clear pool at the bottom before making the last few yards to complete its journey to the sea.

"This seems like a good spot," said Ben, and they set the basket down by the pool. Carefully laying the feather in a sheltered spot, he took the blanket out of the basket and they laid it in the soft sand.

Ben turned his attention to the comestibles. A flask of cider he laid in the edge of the pool to keep cool.

"Let's see…" There was a crusty seed loaf, buttery Warby Red cheese, ham, a jar of pickles, a couple of apples and pears. "Are you hungry?" he called out over his shoulder. There was no reply.

He looked around. Bliss was standing on the sand behind him, naked. Her dress was puddled around her feet, and her arms were at her sides. She was smiling sweetly.

He drew a deep breath and looked her up and down. Her hair, of course, was still so short, and he yearned to see it grown back to its full luxuriant length. The rest of her was perfection. Her breasts were just the right size, neither too large nor too small, with rosebuds for nipples. Her waist formed the classic hourglass shape, her belly curved most seductively. Lower, there was again thin growth, her private parts essentially laid bare, her hips broad, her legs, not long, but elegant. Absolute perfection

"You are utterly beautiful," he sighed, struggling to his feet. "You… you look as if you belong on the arm of some mighty warrior, and yet, and yet, you choose to be with me. That is something I will never understand."

Bliss held out her hands to him. "It is you that I love," she said simply. "That is all you need to understand."

He drew closer to her, and suddenly she was in his arms, his mouth on hers in a fury of passion, his hands roaming over her soft skin, her back and her buttocks, and she clasping him to her as to a lifeline.

She pulled off his shirt unbuckled his belt, fingers frenetically unbuttoning his brayette*, his liberated member bursting forth, furiously erect, to greet the sun. She peeled his breeches down over his hips and he shuffled out of them. Taking her hand, he drew her down onto the blanket, so they were kneeling, facing each other.

"One moment," he gasped, reaching for his belt pouch. He pulled out the lambswool condom and hastily began putting it on.

"Let me help you," said Bliss, tying the laces tightly, her hands brushing intimately against him.

When it was on, she lay back on the blanket. He felt as if he would explode. He made to enter her.

"Wait!" she said, alarmed. "I'm not ready yet!"

Ben had no idea what that meant, but he was far past ready, and plunged into her. She yelped, and then his whole being melted in a moment of pure ecstasy.

Afterwards, she wiped herself with a hankie, and Ben glimpsed a small red stain before she squirrelled it away among her clothes. He rinsed the condom in the pool and laid it on a rock to dry. Putting on the condom had taken longer, he reflected, than the deed itself.

They munched their way through the picnic companionably.

"Do you feel any different… now?" Ben asked cautiously.

"It feels good to have got it done with. The… the first time."

Ben nodded. It was on the tip of his tongue to ask why, if it was such a relief, she had delayed for so long, but he understood instinctively that for Bliss the time and place had to be exactly right, and of her choosing. He had no complaints. He could not have chosen better.

When they had eaten the food and drunk the cider, Ben shambled out onto the sand with the empty flask and set it up. He walked back to the blanket and picked a small stone out of the rock pool and threw it at the flask. He missed. He tried three or four more times, missing each time.

"Let me try," said Bliss.

"Sure," said Ben.

She scooped a handful of pebbles out of the pool and shied the first one at the flask. There was a faint *ping* as the pebble hit it and bounced off. There came a series of repeated *pings* as she threw the rest of the stones in her hand.

Bliss stood up, walked to the flask and bent to pick it up. Ben gasped with delight at the sight of her naked bottom as she did so. Rising, she turned her head and gave him a cheeky grin, then walked further down the beach and repositioned the flask.

She returned to the blanket, Ben again thrilling at the front view of her, sat down, and selected another handful of ammunition from the pool.

Ping... ping... ping...

Every stone found its mark.

"You're a crack shot," said Ben in a voice that mingled surprise with admiration.

"Just the sign of a misspent youth on the beach at home," Bliss replied casually.

And then she was in his arms again, kissing him in a frenzied release of pent up passion, her hands roaming over his body, caressing him, making him feel no longer a boy but a man at last.

And he rose to the occasion. Bliss reapplied the condom, warm after lying in the sun, and fastened it to his rock-hard shaft.

She rolled over and he looked down at her, the pink flower opening between her thighs, just for him. It all seemed like a glorious dream, and prayed never to wake up.

"Here," she said, "Let me show you."

She took his finger and led it between those soft, moist nether lips. "Feel it?"

He felt it. A small smooth knob. She worked his finger over it. "Like this, see?" He did see. "And then, if you like, you might…" And she introduced his finger inside her, inviting exploration of this oven of honeyed delight.

She gave a soft cry as he found a particular spot.

"I'm sorry," he whispered and began to withdraw the finger.

"No, no," she murmured. "It's good. Very good." She looked him in the eye. "*Now* I'm ready."

He determined to go more slowly this time, and entered her this time almost tentatively, thrusting a little at a time, then a little more, until he could go no farther, and his pubic bone was pressed hard up against hers. It was the most delicious sensation imaginable. He became steadily more forceful, until his body took over, requiring no further prompting from his brain. Bliss moaned beneath him, raking his back with her fingers and gasping for air. He saw the veins throbbing on her temple and her neck, felt their sweaty bodies slipping and sliding in exquisite conjunction, and then they both cried out, coming together to a triumphant climax.

He lay upon her, his heart pounding, his breath rasping, until he could gather enough strength to roll away to one side.

"This," he said after a few minutes, "must be why it's called carnal knowledge. Because to be so utterly joined with another person must be as close as one human being can possibly get to knowing another. Truly knowing them."

"Yes," Bliss agreed. "No one can truly know another person, and perhaps it is as well that that is so, but it is, as you say, as close as two people can get."

She lay down in his arms, one thigh extended across his belly, and wriggled comfortably.

They dozed. Slept in fact, for when Ben opened his eyes, the sun had visibly moved down the sky somewhat. He looked into Bliss' face as she slept on his shoulder. Her inky black lashes flickered, and she frowned. Presently she opened her eyes and looked at him with an expression of incomprehension.

"Oh. There you are," she murmured, as if she had been looking for him in her dreams, and was surprised to have found him only upon waking.

She closed her eyes again, and shortly the frown returned. Suddenly she sat bolt upright, her blue eyes wide with fear.

"Get up!" she shouted, scrambling to her feet. She gathered up her dress with one hand and clasped her hat to her skull with the other. "Run!"

Ben hauled himself to his feet. Grabbing his breeches and his shirt in one hand, and dragging the picnic basket by a handle with the other, he raced after her down the sand. She was running towards the sea, away from the cliff, and turned, gesturing anxiously for him to follow.

There came a rumble, and Ben looked back in amazement to see a stretch of the cliff, perhaps twenty-five yards long, break off and come crashing down in huge slabs, precisely where they had been lying.

He stood staring. After a minute or so, he saw the stream, effectively dammed, finding new paths through the rubble and carving its way down the beach in multiple rivulets.

And then, in the same way, after the initial shock and the realisation that he had narrowly escaped death subsided a little, a new truth trickled through his consciousness.

He turned to Bliss, stared into her expressionless face. "You knew!" he gasped. "You knew that was going to happen!"

"I have the Sight," she acknowledged. She picked up her end of the picnic hamper. They began walking back along the beach towards where the coracle was beached. "What is known as *dha shealladh**, in the Fingalian tongue, meaning 'the two seeings', using both physical and subtle sight."

"How… how long…?"

"For as long as I can remember," Bliss said softly. "Passed down to me by Thorbierg, my mother. Every so often, I would get a picture in my head of something that was about to happen. And happen it did. Always."

"Does it just come to you? Or do you seek it out? Knowledge of the future?"

"Sometimes, if I have a particular question. I was so perplexed about coming to the Academy. I felt sure it was the wrong thing for me, that I wouldn't fit in, but the Sight kept telling me to do it."

"And?"

"And the Sight was right. I met you."

As they passed the site of the mollymawk's nest, Ben waved in greeting. Then they moved on, still stunned by what had occurred, and Ben pondering Bliss' revelation.

Ben breathed deeply, drawing in the scents of the sea and the air and of Bliss' body, intoxicated by the sweetness of life. The world seemed like a great golden fruit, and he had taken his first bite, the juice running luxuriously down over his chin. He had the sense that his own self was dissolving into the world, and he gloried in the feeling of being lost in the harmony of all that surrounded him, of not merely being in love but being at one with love.

CHAPTER SEVEN.

"There." Bliss adjusted the new dark green bonnet over Ben's brows and stood back to inspect it. She had pinned the mollymawk feather on the left hand side. "Perfect fit. You look very dashing."

She held up a mirror and Ben looked at himself. He was never comfortable with his own reflection, but nodded approvingly.

"Well," she said, planting a kiss on his lips, "We'd better hurry. Don't want to be late for Mage Semjaza."

*****

"Tell me a story," Bliss entreated.

They had made love with breathless intensity, and were now at peace, lying in each other's arms, but not yet ready for sleep.

Ben searched among the stories that he knew.

"One that I like," he said at last, "is the story of Princess Signý and Sir Eglamour."

"Ah yes," said Bliss. "I like that one too."

"Well, Princess Signý, being a princess, daughter of King Urien map Rheged" Ben went on, " was obliged to make a political marriage, to Prince Mistivoy. But when the guests began to arrive, she noticed Sir Eglamour, and saw the 'love spot' on his brow. She fell in love with him at once. Later, at the wedding feast, with Prince Mistivoy at her side, she asked the King's Mage, Allathurion, to tell her all about the men who were there."

"So Signy and Eglamour could never be together? Never be happy?"

"It seems that way," Ben concurred.

"If we go by what the stories tell us, lovers can never be married."

"Do you think that's how it is in real life?"

"I hope not," Bliss sighed. "I *so* hope not. But I suppose we will have to wait and see."

Ben made no comment. He had fallen asleep.

*****

In the classroom, the chairs had been arranged in a semicircle, with Mage Semjaza's chair in the centre. Beside it was a leather bag with skeins of different coloured wool visible inside it. There were more skeins of wool under each of the chairs, together with reels of red thread.

Mage Semjaza was standing behind his chair. The sticks they had cut in the middle of winter were leaning up against the wall beside him.

"Welcome," he called brightly as the students shuffled in. "Please come forward and claim your sticks."

They were keen to see how their sticks had seasoned, and came forward to pick out the ones bearing their names.

"Stand by your chairs," said Mage Semjaza, "with a stick in your right hand. Unless you are left-handed, in which case, your left hand. Whichever is comfortable." The students complied. "Now raise your stick a little and drop it on the ground." There was a rattling as the sticks hit the ground. "Notice that they bounce? Good. Now, tap the end of your stick lightly on the ground." This they did.

"You feel a hollowness in your stick? A lightness? This is because your sticks are now well seasoned, cured in the neat's foot oil."

"Please be seated," said the Mage. They sat, sticks between their knees. "Now, the next operation is the binding. Please observe."

They watched as he took a reel of red thread from his bag, looped an end around one end of his own stick, knotted it, and then wound the thread in a spiral around the stick till he reached the other end, wound it around the end, then brought it back up the stick in another spiral, forming a criss-cross pattern of thread, until he was back at his starting point, whereupon he knotted the thread and cut it with a dainty knife that he kept tucked into his girdle.

He then pulled a skein of dark blue wool from his bag and began to repeat the operation. "Today we will be using the colours of the Order," he explained, "blue, green, red and purple, which represent…?"

Opabinia van Millingen's hand shot up.

"Opabinia?"

"Mage, they are the colours we see in the shadows in the forest in winter."

"Well done. As I say, we will be using these colours today, but in the future you may want to experiment with other colours. Some very interesting visual effects can result."

He wound the blue wool around the stick against the blue thread on one side, and then on the other. Taking the green, he then repeated the process on either side of the blue, then again with the red and then the purple, until by the time it was done, there were only very small diamonds of stick left visible between the colours.

He held up the bound stick and passed it around for inspection. "This of course brings to mind Arianrod, the goddess who pays out the thread of life. Tradition says that the threads we use here are the leftovers. Perhaps it might serve to remind us that we can never tell when Arianrod will decide to cut our threads."

Ben and Bliss exchanged glances as they wound the sticks through their hands. It was a repetitive process which allowed the mind to wander, and each of them knew that the other was thinking the same thing: recalling the glorious nights of passion they had spent together since that day on the beach, discovering each other's bodies in the most intimate detail. Ben, completely unfamiliar with the female anatomy, found himself fascinated by the way Bliss' breasts changed shape according to whether she was sitting or lying down. Bliss, for her part, was intrigued by the way the penis rose and fell, and that curiosity, the foreskin, and she would run her fingers over the veins running up his member like vines on a great tree, much to Ben's delight.

If Arianrod were to cut his thread now, Ben reflected, he would have no complaints, though at the same time, he prayed to the goddess to give him many, many more years to revel in the warm delights of Bliss' body.

*****

The month of Yune* brought the celebration of the Summer Solstice. Ben was thrilled when he received a note one evening at dinner, indicating that he had been chosen to take the role of First Speaker. He had only a single line to learn, but he devoted himself to putting into it all the dramatic flair he could muster.

On a balmy evening with barely a cloud to be seen, and only the merest wisp of a breeze, the students made their way to the henge, the men in light, open shirts and loose pants, and the women in filmy dresses, all in shades of green, and all wearing garlands of the loveliest summer flowers they could find. They all carried their newly-bound sticks. The grass was soft and springy between their toes, and the rigours of Midwinter seemed but a distant memory.

Outside the henge, Grand Mage Styrmir welcomed them in the guise of the Green Man, in a tunic and pants of imitation green leaves. His tunic left his arms bare, and as he passed, the onlookers could see his tattoos. On his right arm, a circle of thirteen new moons denoted the thirteen months of the year, while the tattoo on his left arm depicted the eight phases of the moon seen through the antlers adorning a stylised stag's head. In one hand he held his Magestaff and in the other his ceremonial goblet. He was smiling broadly, and looked very grand.

Ben gave Bliss' hand a squeeze, and went to take his place in the centre of the circle. He was startled to see that Uta Vecriga was the Fourth Speaker, and he hadn't known: he realised quite how wrapped up in his relationship with Bliss he had become of late, and smiled nervously at Uta. She smiled back, and gave a little wave.

He glanced at Styrmir, who gave him a surreptitious nod in return. Ben raised his arms, holding his stick aloft. He felt acutely conscious of the eyes of the entire Academy upon him.

"Welcome one and all to this, our celebration of the summer solstice!" he proclaimed loudly. "I give greeting to Lugh, the god of the sun, also called John Barleycorn."

The Second Speaker then stepped forward, raising his Magestaff in the same gesture. "I give greeting to Ceridwen," he declared, "the mother goddess of the earth and wife to Cernunnos, to whom all food is dedicated."

The Third Speaker took her turn, a long sage green skirt swirling about her. "I give greeting to Ahviggenau," she intoned, "the goddess of fields and forests, orchards and groves, and sister to the Cailleach, to whom corn dolls, ricks and corn spirals are dedicated."

Uta Vecriga stepped forward and raised her stick. "I give greeting to the Jack of the Green," she announced in a loud, strong voice, "representative of the gods, and keeper and protector of the forests, and invite him to enter the circle. See, he brings the cheering brew that serves to unite the world of men and the natural world in one harmonious whole. Welcome!"

Ben was impressed. It was the longest speech of any of them, and she had delivered it with aplomb. He smiled broadly at her and mouthed the words "Well done". She smiled back, her blue eyes asparkle and relief written all over her features.

Mage Styrmir stepped through the crowd into the centre of the circle. He raised his goblet, and then passed it among the speakers, who each took mouthfuls of the brew until it was gone.

When the goblet was empty, Styrmir raised his staff and declaimed: "The Great Wheel turns, ever on, the Great Wheel turns...."

At this, everyone began to file out of the henge, leaving Styrmir alone at last to break the circle. They all eagerly headed for the Hall for the traditional Midsummer Feast.

*****

It was only a few evenings later that the students gathered once more to attempt the summoning down of the moon. In the intervening months, a few students had already achieved this important objective, including, Ben noted with chagrin, Brancepeth Raby, so the numbers gathered under the great golden orb were somewhat diminished. It gave the gathering a sense of greater intimacy than previously, and most of those present felt that the fewer witnesses to any failure, the better.

"I have a good feeling about tonight," Ben whispered to Bliss as they took their seats.

"Yes," she agreed *sotto voce*. "Me too."

Ben caught her eye. "Have you *seen* something?"

Bliss shook her head. "No. But I have a good feeling all the same."

Mage Zalmoxis called them one by one. "Angenwit."

Bubonax glanced at Ben and they exchanged grins. Bubonax took up his position, shifted until he was comfortable, and looked up at the moon. A few minutes passed, and then he extended his hand in his lap.

Ben looked up, and saw the moon quiver in the sky. It was really happening! The creamy white disc slid slowly down the sky, into Bubonax's hand. Ben saw his fingers close around it, and in the breathless silence that followed, he heard a whispered "Yes!"

"Excellent!" said Mage Zalmoxis. "Congratulations, Angenwit."

A few more tried, most without success, and then it was Bliss' turn. Ben gave her hand an extra encouraging squeeze as she rose, and then she was in position. Ben sat watching her silhouette, willing her to succeed. For a time, nothing seemed to be happening, and then, all of a sudden, the moon had again left its accustomed position in the indigo sky, and was instead enclosed in Bliss' tender grasp.

"Well done, Tarrant," said Zalmoxis. "Mr. Trillibub, please."

As Exomphalus Trillibub rose, Bliss returned and took her place beside Ben. As she turned to face him, he saw in the moonlight the glistening tears of joy on her cheeks. She leaned in to rest her head on his shoulder, and he felt her shaking. He clasped her chilly hands between his own, and felt immense pleasure that she had mastered this hurdle. If she succeeded, he reasoned, then he couldn't *not* succeed.

So engrossed was he in Bliss and her triumph that he was taken by surprise by the ripple of applause from his classmates that marked Exomphalus Trillibub's success.

"Mr. Trillibub, well done," said Mage Zalmoxis brightly. "Mr. Troon, please."

It was Bliss' turn to give Ben's hand an encouraging squeeze. He got to his feet and made his way to the seat at the front. Bliss and Exomphalus had both succeeded. Could he make it three in a row?

He sat down. Composure was what he needed, but his heart seemed to be racing. He recalled everything he had been taught. Look at the moon, but at the same time, *don't* look at the moon. Relax. Pretend not to care whether you do this or not.

He considered the moon, floating there calmly in the evening sky. Far above all mere human concerns. It must be nice, he thought…

Mind on the job, he told himself. He felt as if he knew every last wrinkle of the moon's topography. But did he?

It was now or never. He extended a hand out over his lap, and willed the moon to descend. For a time, nothing happened. He thought again that when he and Bliss had shared so much together, it just wouldn't be right if they could not share this. He felt her eyes upon him, willing him as he was willing the moon.

Was that a movement? No. Wait… yes! It was descending, obedient as a faithful dog, and then there it was, cold and hard in the palm of his hand. He closed his fingers around it, feeling with wonder its solidity, and said a silent prayer to Ceridwen, the moon goddess.

"Congratulations, Troon," he vaguely heard Zalmoxis say. "Mr. Vidfume…"

And then they were in the *Brasseur de Beaubourg*. Ben had no recollection of getting there, but there they were, eyes shining with triumph, offering commiserations for those few who had not yet mastered the technique. But the look in their eyes said it all: they could now call themselves Mages. All kinds of doors were suddenly opened before them.

*****

"Mages!" cried Mage Semjaza, standing in the centre of the courtyard. "And Mages-to-be," he added, with a glance at the handful of students who had not yet achieved the calling down of the moon. He was dressed in a loose belted tunic that left his arms bare, wide-legged pants, and soft leather shoes. He had adopted an aggressive pose, and was holding with both hands a Magestaff that was bound in the middle only, providing a firm grip for his hands while leaving the ends bare. The students' gaze was riveted upon him.

"You all have your Magestaffs now," he continued. "But I'm not sure if you know yet exactly what they are for. Yes, they are the symbol of your calling, they represent who you are as Mages. You will also have been told that they augment your Magecraft, that they are, in a sense, a conduit. But they are not essential for that purpose.

A Mage may perform Magecraft without staff or wand, merely with a gesture of the hand. No, the staff performs a rather more rudimentary purpose than that. It is a weapon. Here at the Academy, we are all friends. But a time will come, and perhaps more quickly than you may anticipate, when you will leave these walls and venture out into the wider world. And a considerable portion of you will be venturing beyond Magelaw, into realms where the followers of Mithras hold sway, and Mages are viewed with suspicion, if not deep hostility. You will need to defend yourselves, indeed, to preserve your very lives!"

Mage Semjaza began rotating the staff from its centre in ever faster figure of eight moves, until it was moving so fast that it could barely be seen, and the air hummed around it. Then he was spinning it over his shoulder, around his back, above his head, to left then right, then left again in a dazzling series of moves that would defy any assailant, even armed with a sword, to approach within range of the swirling stick. Contact with an undefended head would be lethal, and arms, legs, ribs, would be shattered.

The students watched the performance, some open-mouthed with amazement.

Finally it came to an end. Bubonax tentatively raised a hand.

"Mr. Angenwit?"

The students noted that now that they were officially Mages, they were more commonly addressed as "Mister…" or "Miss".

"Mage, surely if we were being attacked, we would use Magecraft to defend ourselves?"

Mage Semjaza smiled broadly. He was barely panting, even after the exertion of his display. "I was hoping someone would ask that. As you have no doubt been told by your teachers on various occasions, performing Magecraft always comes with a physical cost. You will not have grasped it yet, being newly minted Mages, but all Magecraft is draining, much more so than physical fighting. You will discover this in due course. Another point to be considered is that if you are among people who already have their doubts about Mages, using Magecraft in a violent way, even in self-defence, will undoubtedly only confirm their worst fears about us. Much better to use Magecraft only as a last resort. Which brings us to the purpose of today's lesson, namely the use of staffs in combat situations. Mr. Raby, approach."

Brancepeth Raby stepped forward.

"I am going to attack you with my staff. Prepare to defend yourself."

Raby raised his staff horizontally at chest height, as he might hold the oar of his coracle. With a blindingly fast one-two movement, Mage Semjaza rapped his knuckles. Raby let out a howl and dropped his staff.

"Your first and most vulnerable spot, the hands. Be aware that an opponent will target them first and foremost. It is best to alternate the grip, so one hand grasps the staff from above while the other grasps from below. Pick up your stick, please, Mr. Raby."

Raby bent to retrieve his stick from where it lay at his feet. Tucking his own stick under his arm, Mage Semjaza positioned Raby's hands in the manner he had indicated.

The remainder of the lesson was given over to the practice of various defensive blocks taught to them by the Mage. He split them into pairs and had them alternating between attacking and defending, while he moved between them, studying their moves and correcting them.

"If I know you," Ben said to Bliss, after Mage Semjaza had moved out of earshot, "you'd simply pick up a stone and fell an attacker with a shot between the eyes while he was still a hundred ells distant!"

Bliss laughed and nodded.

*****

The early days of Huilay* saw the celebration of Lughnassa, traditionally the time for giving thanks for a good harvest. Everywhere about the Academy there were fresh flowers and garlands and fruit and Lammas loaves.

On a balmy and splendid summer evening, the celebrants flocked to the henge, to be welcomed by Styrmir in his grandest garb, beaming as he ushered them into the circle. In its middle, a large fire was blazing, pouring smoke into an otherwise flawless sky. In front of it stood a small altar bearing a bowl and a flagon of brew.

When the last of the students had passed through the stones, some already tipsy with wine, cider or mead, Styrmir made his way between them into the centre of the circle, in front of the fire. Someone rang a bell, clear and strident, nine times. With a wave of his hand, Styrmir led everyone, and they walked around the circle three times. When they had resumed their places, he raised his staff on high and spoke aloud.

"I am here to honour the god Lugh," he proclaimed. "Bless me, O Shining One, in my working."

Styrmir dipped his fingers into the bowl and brought forth a handful of corn flour, which he scattered on the ground at his feet.

"Great Father," he called loudly, his eyes turned heavenwards, "I am your subject, Father of Light, accept this offering and bless my rite."

He then took up the flagon and poured. A small golden waterfall, glistening in the rays of the setting sun, arced gracefully over the grass.

Styrmir declaimed again, his voice masterful and commanding. Those listening sensed the spirit world pause in their invisible flight to heed his proclamation. "All of you who abide beyond the light of this work's fire, accept this offering and trouble not my working. I have come to do as the ancients did, to keep the rites of Lughnassa, the First Harvest, the Victory of the Growth, the Gathering of the Folk in Peace. Now is the beginning of the Time of Ripening, when the labour of the folk brings the land to bear, the power of the sun gives itself to the power of the earth. I come to make offerings to the powers, to honour the Lady of Sovereignty, Ahviggenau. In this season she is the Earth Woman, the Red Goddess, the Flower Woman whose embrace binds, whose love is fate. I honour especially Lugh, the Shining Young

Hero, the Sacred King. He is the Master of All Skills, the Holy Champion who turns aside drought and storm, protecting the earth. On this day the Golden Rod is wed to the Blossom Goddess, that the earth may come to fruit.

Taking up the goblet again, he this time cast his libation into the flames.

"I make this offering to the keeper of the gates," he announced. "Join your Magecraft with mine and let the fire open as a gate, let the well open as a gate, let the tree carry the spirit to my sacrifice. By this offering and my Magecraft, let the gates be open!"

It was not hard to imagine some great ethereal portal in the heavens swinging its great gates open at his command, to admit all those who stood in the circle into the spirit realm as welcome guests.

From somewhere - was this Magecraft at work, Ben wondered - more goblets of brew appeared and passed among the onlookers.

After the brew had done the rounds, Styrmir began to intone an invocation, his voice seeming still deeper and yet more magisterial.

"Gods and goddesses of elder days
Honour me as I honour you!
Shining ones, accept my sacrifice!

Gods of the dead and spirits three,
Powers of earth and sky and sea,
By fire and well and sacred tree
Offerings I make to thee!"

The brew began to go around the circle again, this time accompanied by crusty slabs of Lammas bread, decorated with seeds in beautiful spiral patterns.. The goblet appeared to be bottomless and the bread inexhaustible. More Magecraft, Ben wondered.

Styrmir called out in stentorian tones to the god Lugh.

"Thou Lugh of the steady hand, I make my grove under your shield, O Lugh, the Falcon of the season, you the Great Archer, you who won arms, a name and a wife, you who died, became an eagle and were restored, be in my midst. Accept this ale in welcome, thou champion, King of All. May we be at peace, and in taking joy in the feast of the Day of Lugh, I offer this bread, that the harvest may flourish by the hand of the ploughman. Thus do I join the Shining Ones' Prince of the Earth. By this may Lugh be the Ward and Guardian of the earth. By this may the earth be the Throne of Joy and Light. May the grain, and our lives, grow green and golden as the active last rays of the summer sun. May the ray of the westering sun be as the arrow of the Champion. Lugh and Epona, hear your child."

The brew and the last fragments of Lammas loaf were passed from hand to hand. Styrmir again threw a shower of brew into the fire.

He spoke again.

> "Let my voice arise on the flame
> Let my voice resound in the well
> O honoured ones, Lugh and Epona,
> Hear me now as I offer up this sacrifice.
> Accept my worship and reverence…
> And give me your blessing."

Again the goblet circulated.

> "I pour the ale of inspiration,
> I draw water from the well of wisdom
> I call upon Lugh and Epona
> To give me as I have given to you.
> O Lugh, O Epona, hallow these waters,
> I open my heart to the flow of your blessing;
> I, your child and worshipper,
> Behold the waters of life!"

Styrmir drank deeply from his cup.

"Shining One, mighty and noble ones, we
thank you for your aid and blessing.

Lugh, I give you my thanks!

Triple kindreds, gods, death and nature spirits:
I thank you for upholding my Magecraft.

Lord of the gates, lord of knowledge,
I give you my thanks.

Now let the gates of the worlds be closed!

The Great Wheel turns, and having turned, moves
ever on! To the feast, ladies and gentlemen, to the
feast!"

As the celebrants began to make their way out of the
circle, Ben glanced again at the fire and did a double
take. Something about it simply didn't look right, and it
took him a moment to figure out what it was. When he
did, he gasped.

He nudged Bliss. "I don't know if that brew was unusually
strong," he said softly, pointing, "but it seems to me that
the flames in that fire are leaping *downwards.*"

Bliss looked where he was pointing. The flames did indeed appear to be starting from high up and snaking downwards towards the ground. "It's Magecraft," she declared archly.

CHAPTER EIGHT.

With the coming of Wrageth*, everything became more intense. The fighting was fiercer, they were studying more powerful Magecraft, all desperate to create a good impression with the Mages who would determine their future.

Ben was intensely grateful to have Bliss by his side. Not only was their lovemaking a wonderful way to relieve the tension after a full day of study, but she was the confidante with whom he could share his hopes and dreams. But the same question surfaced again in his mind over and over: what if they were sent to different places, perhaps far apart?

He asked her the same question, for the umpteenth time: "Do you *see* what's going to happen to us? Don't you have anything with your Sight?"

And for the umpteenth time, she shook her head sadly. "As I've told you, the Sight doesn't come to me on command."

He took her in his arms, clasped her to him. "I love you so much, Bliss," he sighed. "I can't even imagine a life without you by my side."

"It's the same for me," she averred. "But even if we must be separated for a time, we will find a way to be together again. The gods always reunite those who were once lovers."

The thought lurked at the back of her mind that while she believed this to be true, she knew that that reunion did not necessarily have to be in this lifetime. She wished as fervently as Ben that the Sight might grant her some assurance, one way or the other.

With this awareness, the lovers determined to squeeze every drop of joy from their time together, but time they could spend alone together was scant.

*****

And then, almost before they knew it, Sefton was upon them, and with it the responsions*. All day, every day, they sat, pouring out everything they had been taught, pens scratching in the silence of the Great Hall. There were spells to be wrought, and fighting to be done, interviews to be held with the principal Mages.

Suddenly, it was all over. They had nothing more to do but wait while their fates were mulled over and ultimately announced. And that could take weeks. In the interim, they occupied themselves in whatever way they could.

*****

"Ben!"

Ben looked up from the book he was transcribing. Startled to see Bliss standing in the doorway, he almost blotted his copy. She rarely visited him when he was in the library.

"What is it?" he hissed, looking around to see if he was being watched by anyone important. Visitors were not encouraged in the scriptorium.

"The postings! They're out!"

Ben stuck his pen back into its holder. He jumped down from his stool, knocking it over. It echoed noisily as it hit the floor.

Together they hastened - almost ran - to the Great Hall. Bursting in, they saw a large notice board had been erected near the entrance, and students were milling around it, some trying to get to the board to learn their fate, while others, who had already read theirs, huddled with friends to discuss the outcomes.

But when Ben was observed approaching, a hush fell over the crowd. He stopped in his tracks, with Bliss close at his shoulder, conscious that all eyes were upon him.

"What?" he asked softly, glancing from one face to another. Bubonax, Exomphalus, Opabinia, all their faces held an expression of wonder. What in Anoone, he wondered, was going on.

He stepped forward, and the crowd parted. He stepped up to the notice board and looked for his name. There it was: *Troon, B.: To continue his studies at the Magisterium, Lochranza.*

"Morrigan sings!" he gasped.

The Magisterium? The very heart of Magecraft? In Lochranza, the capital of Magelaw? Ben felt a void open up in the pit of his stomach. He felt there had to be some mistake: only the brightest of the bright got to study at the Magisterium.

So shocked by this was he that it took him a moment to realise that Bliss, standing by his side, had taken in the word of his fate and was clasping his hand tightly in hers.

He followed her gaze. Her name was just above his. *Tarrant, B. To pursue teaching and social work in the Tollgate Islands.*

Ben's heart sank still further.

"We must be brave," Bliss murmured. "It will not be forever. One way or another, we will find a way to be together."

Ben looked at her. Her eyes were glistening. His mouth worked, but no words came forth.

Then he looked again into the sea of faces surrounding them. "Lochranza," he said, struggling to grasp the news. "The Magisterium. Is anyone else…?"

They shook their heads. "Only you, mate," said Bubonax. "Congratulations. We're proud of you."

Ben shook his head. "But I'm not Magisterium material. I haven't been a brilliant student."

"Well," said Bubonax, with a jerk of his head towards the notice board, "someone thinks otherwise."

Ben sighed. "I think I need to speak to Grand Mage Styrmir." He looked into Bliss' eyes. "You'll wait for me here?"

Bliss nodded. She watched as he swept away up the grand staircase, his cape billowing behind him. She recalled that first morning, when they had collided, up there, outside the classrooms. It had been almost exactly a year. So much had happened in that time.

Ben continued up the stairs, past the levels where the classrooms were, up to where the Mages had their chambers. It was a part of the Academy to which he seldom came. After all, what student ever wanted to beard a Mage in his den?

There were fewer windows up here, the halls were darker, mustier. Ben had a sense of unseen things lurking here, echoes, perhaps, of dark Magecraft carried on behind these doors.

He came at last to Grand Mage Styrmir's apartment. He paused at the door of the outer office. Carved into its surface was a pattern of hugrunes*. Ben drew himself up, took a deep breath, and rapped.

"Enter," called a woman's voice.

He turned the handle on the door and entered.

Sitting at a desk of dark stained oak that was littered with all manner of documents, books, maps, and objects of unknown purpose was Mage Banfathi, a shalir* and personal assistant to Grand Mage Styrmir. She appeared quite severe, with her iron grey hair drawn back in a chignon, and a black hooded robe, About her neck she wore an assortment of pendants bearing symbols that Ben recognised as belonging to a number of cultures from far distant shores.

She smiled in welcome. "Mr. Troon. Mage Strymir though you might pop up for a chat. Please go straight in."

It occurred to Ben that Mage Banfathi was probably a seer, like Bliss, but then he realised that, given the circumstances, his appearance in Mage Styrmir's rooms probably did not require such gifts to predict.

He tapped on the door.

"Enter!" boomed the voice from within.

Ben stepped into Styrmir's consulting room. On the wall was a large framed wooden almanac, a structure composed of a series of concentric discs each mounted upon the next. The outer part was divided into the days of the year. Next was a circle displaying the phases of the moon, which could be rotated so that they lined up correctly with the calendar. The next circle inward similarly showed the sun, high in the sky in summer and low in the winter. Inside this was a series of progressively smaller hengeforms. At the centre pivoted a pointer, whose needle-like tip pointed at the day's date. All around the outside of the circle, dates of importance were notated. Grand Mage Styrmir, slightly stooped, and with his long grey hair bound as always in a circlet of silver, was looking at it when Ben entered. He had a large snake draped over his shoulders, which moved languidly from time to time.

"Ah, Mr. Troon," Styrmir beamed. He gestured to a comfortable-looking chair in front of the desk. It was ornately carved, and upholstered in well worn chestnut leather. It looked inviting. "Please be seated." Ben did as he was bid. "I regret I haven't had a chance to chat to you personally before now, but I have been following your progress very closely. Your teachers have spoken of you in the highest terms."

"Thank you, Grand Mage," said Ben, flummoxed. Once again, he had the impression that he was the focus of attention amid the high and mighty, and found it more than a little disturbing. "I didn't think I was anything exceptional."

Styrmir smiled broadly. "And your modesty does you credit. Although I must say some of the Mages have said they wished you might be a little more forward in class. None of this hiding your light under a bushel." Ben opened his mouth to say something, but Styrmir raised a hand. "Let me explain something to you. In the vast majority of cases, the Mages who pass through these halls fall into one of two categories. They are pursuants of either the Greater Path or the Lesser Path, and both have an important role to play in the scheme of things. Very, very occasionally, we see a Mage who understands instinctively that there are no paths, only Magecraft. Magecraft, young man, may be limited only by the extent of one's gifts, and in your case, that extent may be very considerable."

"Is this to do with the business of where I came from?" asked Ben, still struggling to comprehend what was being said to him. He had the sensation of floundering.

"I have no doubt that that has something to do with it, yes. What that something is, even I cannot say. It is for that reason that you are to go to the Magisterium in Lochranza."

The Magisterium, often spoken of as 'The Pool of the Wise', was the holy of holies of Magecraft, located far to the south in the capital of Magelaw, the great city of Lochranza. It was the seat of Archmage Caerlugh, known as Porphyrogenitus, or "he who is born to wear the purple". It occurred to Ben that he might even get to see this great man with his own eyes.

Then another thought came to him.

"But…"

Again Styrmir raised the hand. He smiled gently.

"But you are in love with the beautiful Miss Tarrant, whom we are sending in the opposite direction, out to the Tollgate Islands." Ben nodded. "I dare say it must seem as if we are deliberate killjoys," said Styrmir, "but I promise you we are not. We are simply driven by a higher purpose, and must put our young Mages in the places where they are most useful to the wider society. There will be pain. Of course there will. But something I would like for you to understand, Ben, is that everything that happens in your life, the good and the bad, happens for a purpose. The pain is a necessary part of that. It is not an easy lesson. I myself had the greatest trouble coming to terms with it, but there are higher forces at work, and at times they may intervene to adjust matters according to their lights. Love is a wonderful thing, and once you have known it, it is something that you can draw on through the whole of your life, something that can see you through the darkest times."

Ben nodded silently.

"I am not saying that this is necessarily the end of the affair for Miss Tarrant and yourself. Life holds many unknowns, and it may be that you may find some way to be together. But for the present, I fear you must be widely separated."

"Thank you, Grand Mage," said Ben quietly. He felt his heart sinking into his boots. "But... the Magisterium! So great an honour! I don't feel worthy! What in Anoone should I tell them when I get there?"

"Dove's dung!" exclaimed Styrmir. "Mage up, m'boy, Mage up! Tell them that it has always been your aim in life to wear the cloak of office. Tell them that service is the greatest honour imaginable, obedience the greatest good, and that you will strive in all things to further the interests of the Order. They will like that! Now," he went on, scarcely pausing for breath, "to practical matters. In Lochranza, you will be in the care of Ailsa Bleakwill at her venerable bookshop, which stands just across from the principle entrance to the Magisterium. I will write to her and notify her to expect you."

Ailsa Bleakwill, thought Ben, what a name! He could picture her already, an old crone with iron-grey hair drawn back tightly in a bun, a hook nose, perhaps even with a wart on it, probably toothless, and with hair on her chin.

"It's a long and difficult journey," Styrmir went on. "Best if you set out as soon as possible. Certainly you want to be there before the winter sets in. But you will need to be well prepared as well."

"Yes, Grand Mage," said Ben. "Thank you."

He rose from the chair. Styrmir shook him firmly by the hand. He gave a bow, and slipped out of the room.

*****

Ben and Bliss lay in each other's arms after a passionate lovemaking session. When they had coupled for the last time, Ben had felt her muscles contract, holding him inside her for just that little bit longer.

"I love you," he said softly into the darkness. "You know that, don't you? You know that no matter what, I will love you until my dying breath."

"And I you," Her voice came to him out of the gloom.

"Do you see *anything* about us… in the future?"

Bliss shook her head sadly. She had answered this question several times already. However she tried, she was not granted any vision of a future happiness for them. It didn't necessarily mean there would be none, but she felt the omens were not good. "The Sight just doesn't work like that."

He sighed. "I just can't help thinking this is a mistake. That I'll get there, to the Magisterium, and they'll say, "Oh, no, it was another Ben Troon we were thinking of.""

"I'm certain there's no mistake, Ben. Why do you belittle yourself so?"

"Important people go to the Magisterium, and I can in no way think of myself as important. Perhaps I should just go off and make a life for myself somewhere else."

"Ben, listen." Bliss had that tone in her voice that said she would not take no for an answer. "It seems to me that it's always easier to step aside and let someone else do the great deeds in life, to watch the battle from the fringes, as it were. To content yourself with doing the small things. It even seems moral, doesn't it, to say "I'm not worthy of this grace". But I think that if you do that, if you turn away from this opportunity that has been placed before you, you will regret it and sulk about it and be miserable for the rest of your life. And I for one would certainly not want to share that life."

Ben sighed again. "You're right, of course. I suppose I had better start making preparations for the journey."

Bliss kissed him warmly. "So you should." He made a move to get out of bed. Bliss put her hand on his arm. "One other thing, though."

"Yes?"

"While you're doing all these great deeds, try not to be *too* serious about it. Remember, life is too short not to live it up a little."

Ben smiled. "I'll try to remember that."

*****

It was time to go. It was early in Zehnar*, and already there was a slight crispness in the air, a presage of winter. But it was fine sunny morning, and it would be a good day for walking.

They were gathered on the road leading away from the Academy, and there was quite a crowd. All his friends were there, and most of the Mages.

Bubonax shook him firmly by the hand. "I'm going even farther away than you," he grinned. "I'm going to the Taruithorn University, in mainland Laurentia. If your travels ever take you that far, drop in and say hello."

Ben shook his head. "Lochranza is as far as I'll ever get. And I never expected to get that far. But you'll come back one day, won't you?"

Bubonax nodded. "Of course." And the two men hugged.

Halldis and Hasupada were there. They stepped forward, and Halldis brought out a cloak pin. It was the local type, with a many-sided head. He pinned Ben's cloak together. "We're proud of you, lad," he said, his eyes misting. Hasupada was already in tears.

Ben hugged Halldis and kissed Hasupada. "F-farewell," he stuttered. "And thank you for everything."

"Write often, won't you?" said Halldis. "Or your mother will worry."

Ben nodded. "I will."

Grand Mage Styrmir then stepped forward. "Mr. Troon," he said in a commanding voice, "please hold out your right hand."

Ben did so. Styrmir produced a ring of interwoven gold strands, and slid it onto Ben's ring finger. He then presented him with his Magestaff.

"The staff is now fully charged," Styrmir told him. "Provided you don't use it to excess - and I really hope you won't need to use it at all - it will remain charged until you reach Lochranza. And when you get there, remember me to the old place."

Ben nodded. "I will."

Styrmir took a step backwards and ushered Bliss forward. She and Ben looked each other in the eye. Both were close to tears. They had made love the night before, fervently, frenetically.

Now she kissed him passionately, one last time. "Take good care," she whispered. "And remember your promise." He had promised that he would walk away and not look back. "Go now," she urged, "before my heart breaks."

He turned. He set his bonnet with the mollymawk feather firmly on his head. He shouldered his knapsack, which contained a blanket, some provisions that Hasupada had given him, and a few basic necessities. Putting one foot in front of the other, he began to walk. Swinging his Magestaff, he began to develop a rhythm, and steadily began the long march to Lochranza.

CHAPTER NINE.

Ben had never left the Academy before. Everything around him was new. The road south wound through steep hills thick with gorse bushes, a barrier that kept Dundonald hidden from the outside world.

After only a few miles he came upon the first village. The sign declared that it was called Netherburn, and, sure enough, a small stream swept down off the hillside in a cascade, turning sharply to race down beside the road in a deep culvert. Netherburn was evidently a mining village, and the simple slate-roofed miners' cottages lined it on either side. At the centre of the little community was a tavern, and cheery old men with fulsome beards and apple cheeks sat with tankards of the local red ale. They greeted him cheerily as he approached, and gestured for him to join them. Through the open door, he glimpsed a fire, and pretty serving girls bustling to and fro with platters of tasty-looking food. It was tempting: he would only have the one, one for the road…

No. He strengthened his resolve. He had a long way to go, after all, and the more miles he could put behind him the better. He waved back at the men, and walked on.

A few more miles and a few more twists and turns of the road and he came to another village, which was named Bran's Ford. The burn that had been accompanying him now swept across his road, and he had to take his shoes off and hitch up his robes to wade through the ford. The water was icy, and he felt as if he had lost all sensation below the knees, but this first obstacle on his journey was soon passed.

In time, the hills dropped away to either side, and the road continued on over open moorland.

As he walked, Ben saw small groups of ponies. He had heard that it was the custom in Magelaw that travellers might make use of an animal, and when they had got where they were going, they could simply let the beast roam free. As he drew closer, he saw that each animal had a rope halter. The animals appeared quite tame, and made no effort to move away.

He took the rope of a likely looking example, and swung himself up on its back. He tapped it lightly on the rump with his staff and away they went. The pony settled into a gentle trot, and Ben found himself travelling southward at quite an acceptable pace. He began to feel quite pleased with himself.

He became lost in his thoughts, aching at the parting from Bliss, and wondering what the future held.

Late in the afternoon, when he was beginning to feel the distinct pangs of hunger, he came upon a thick stand of hagberry bushes, still burdened with large quantities of ripe fruit. He dismounted and tied the pony to one of the branches, and began to gorge himself.

As he worked from bush to bush, picking the ripest berries, he saw that the bushes were in fact enclosing a space, and when he ventured through a gap between them, he saw before him an enclosed well. On a nail at the entrance were small squares of cloth which one might use in making a wish. He took one from the nail and descended the steps to the basin of water at the heart of the place.

He was overcome by a sense of peace which seemed to diffuse the place. It came to him that such a place might be considered a portal to the spirit world. The sun outside, sinking towards the horizon, cast a golden light over the water. Filled with thoughts about the future, he drew his cloth slowly through the water and made a wish that his journey might end well, and that he might soon be reunited with Bliss (was that one wish or two?). The ripples shimmered across that water and gently subsided.

He remounted the steps, hearing once more the bird calls which had become strangely muted in the well. He untied the pony and continued on his way, sensing that he had paid a brief visit to some other world.

Over the next rise, he saw signs of cultivation, runrigs*, fields divided into long parallel strips running down the slopes of the nearby hills, where he saw bere* and other crops growing, and in the water meadows on the flat land there were wiseats* grazing, cattle that looked to be not so many generations removed from their wild cousins, tough creatures well able to survive harsh winters. Sheep there were too.

Since the villages of Netherburn and Bran's Ford, he had not seen a sign of habitation, and with the sun now well inclined towards the horizon, he was beginning to think of where he might rest his head for the night. He was hoping he might find a farmhouse where he might cadge a cup of milk - perhaps from those very kine that he could see munching the sweet grass - and a little something to eat, and then perhaps a barn to sleep in. But he had no way of knowing whether there was any such thing nearby.

And then he came upon a neat farmer's cottage, its walls of interwoven wattles coated with a daub of mud or clay, and overpainted with a lime wash, bulged outward a little beneath a thatch of reeds.

Close by was a barn, where the bere would be stored, and hay, and which would most likely house the livestock in the winter months. Beyond that was a paddock where more ponies like the one he rode could be seen.

As he drew closer, he could see a woman busying herself in front of the house. He saw that along the edge of the roof there were gutters which collected the rainwater and led it into a large barrel, from which she was filling a saucepan.

She turned at his approach, and smiled, showing no sign of alarm or hostility. She was short, with an ample figure. Her face was round, and she had dark eyes. She reminded Ben of a picture he had once seen of a rearmouse*.

She smiled even more broadly as he dismounted. "Welcome to Simy Folds Farm," she said. "My name is Vitka Amaethon."

"My name is Ben Troon." He slapped the pony on its hind quarters, and it ambled off, unhurried, back in the direction from which it had come. "I am travelling, and I wondered if I might sleep in your barn."

"Nonsense!" said Vitka. "You shall sleep in my house. In a proper bed. You're a Mage, aren't you?" She eyed his staff.

"Yes," said Ben.

"From Dundonald, I presume?"

"Yes," said Ben. "I'm going to Lochranza to continue my studies."

"Lochranza!" Vitka exclaimed. "That's a long way! But come inside and make yourself at home."

She pushed on the battened door and led the way into a small vestibule, where she took off her shoes and Ben did likewise. A turn to the right brought them into what was clearly the main living space of the house. Looking up, he saw how the curved upright timbers, the crucks, met in pairs at the ridge line of the roof, where they were lashed together, with horizontal crossbeams spanning the space between them to support the weight of the roof. And that, he thought to himself with an inward smile, was the matter of the crucks.

The interior of the house was in part quite businesslike, with all the paraphernalia of household chores, such as spinning wheels, brewing vats, a butter churn, moulds for making candles, lacemaking tools and more of the same. The stone wall at one end of the house had the largest of the few windows. In the centre of the room there was a hearthstone, where a small fire was burning. Smoke simply rose and collected beneath the eaves until it found its way through a small hole over the centre of the roof.

But as Ben's eyes travelled around the room, he saw that it was also very comfortably appointed, with large, overstuffed armchairs covered in a faded brocade material. The arms and the ball and claw legs were of a dark lacquered wood, and there were cloths edged with lace draped over the headrests. There was a large bookcase with glass doors, and Ben was curious to see what books it held, as he understood that one could tell a great deal about a person by their reading matter. Vitka's books were an eclectic mix. There were the full ten volumes of 'The Ancient Sagas of Gylfaginning' to begin with, in red leather bindings and with incised gold lettering on the spines. There was 'Waurin's Chronicle', a collection of military exploits, and next to it, 'The Riddles of Aldhelm Tatwine'...

But perhaps the most extraordinary object in the room was the stuffed head of a wapiti*, mounted on one wall, its stupendous antlers reaching almost to the corners and touching the rafters.

"Please, sit down, make yourself comfortable," said Vitka, ushering him towards one of the armchairs.

Ben had not realised how tired he was after his journeying, and it occurred to him that there were a good many more such days to come, with no prospect of such a pleasant welcome at the end of each one.

"Would you like some tea?" Vitka asked.

"Oh!" Ben gasped. "Tea would be wonderful!"

"I have quite a selection to choose from," Vitka told him. "Camomile, sassafras, mint… Let me see… rose hips, fennel, linden, shave grass, sarsaparilla, fenugreek… parsley, of course… oh, and elderberry!"

"Some elderberry would be lovely," said Ben.

Vitka went and busied herself in her small kitchen, from which enticing smells of cooking were wafting, and Ben eased himself deeper among the cushions and let himself drift away.

Presently Vitka returned with a teapot and a cup, and placed them on a small table beside Ben. She then settled into another of the chairs. "I have put on some water to boil so you can have a bath," she announced.

"Thank you," said Ben. "You are much too kind."

"Not at all," she smiled. "I don't get many visitors."

"Do you live here alone?" Ben asked.

"I do now," Vitka replied. "Brodar, my husband was killed a few years ago."

"What happened?" Ben asked.

"He made a journey to visit his relatives on the coast, and got caught up in a raid by barbarians."

"Oh," said Ben. "I'm so sorry." He realised suddenly just how sheltered a life he had led at the Academy. It all seemed so far removed from the realities and the dangers of the outside world. He sipped his tea.

"Come," said Vitka as he drained his teacup, "let me show you something."

She got up and walked to the large window. Ben came and stood beside her. The sun had taken on a warm orange hue, and was suffusing the landscape outside with a warm, aetherial glow as it touched the hillside in the distance.

"You see where the sun is setting?", she asked.

"Yes."

"Well, if you turn slightly to the right…" she placed her hand on his shoulder with a familiarity that made him uncomfortable. "…You can see a cleft in the hills, and that is precisely where the sun sets at midwinter. I believe the ancestor of my husband who built this house positioned it deliberately so we could see that sunset."

"Ah," said Ben. "Very interesting."

She was standing very close to him, looking up at him. He could not look at her without looking down the front of her dress. He could smell the earthy scent of her hair and her body. It was arousing, and being aroused was the last thing he wanted.

Vitka seemed to sense him stiffening, and moved away slightly.

Ben stepped back, and returned to his seat. Vitka remained, silhouetted against the window.

"Your bath water will soon be ready," she smiled.

When it was, Vitka showed him to the scullery, where it was waiting. "Behind the door is a robe. It will be good if your travel clothes can air overnight."

Ben thanked her and closed the door softly behind her. He gratefully stripped off his clothes and stepped into the hip bath. The water was hot, and he luxuriated in its steamy embrace. But it was when he got to thinking about the situation in which he found himself that the sceatta really dropped. An attractive young widow, doubtless missing male attentions, and here he was, wandering along, and, he supposed, passable to look at. He, even *he*, could see where this was leading. He glanced towards the door. Was she, perhaps, peering at him through the cracks? He banished the thought, though he still listened for creaking floorboards outside. Briefly, he contemplated leaving and finding somewhere else to bed down for the night, but it would be dark soon, and there didn't seem to be any other habitation nearby. A night under a bush had little appeal when there was a warm bed here. He dismissed that notion as well. But he would have to tread carefully.

He dried himself and pulled on the robe, presumably one of her late husband's: it seemed he had been a big chap.

The table was laid, with generous platefuls of lamb stew and rye rolls, and a flagon of wine. Ben took his place, and Vitka sat opposite him.

"Hmmm, this looks good," he said, and it did. "You surely didn't make all this for yourself?"

"Well, no," said Vitka. "That is, I make a stew like this, and then I eat the same thing for several days. You were just lucky to have arrived when I made a fresh batch. If you had come in a few days' time, there would have been slim pickings."

Ben ate heartily. Looking around for a topic of conversation, Ben's eyes lighted on the drinking goblet before him. He picked it up.

"These are unusual."

They were staved cups, made of alternating strips of light and dark wood, joined in some skilfull manner to form a tight bond. On top of the strips was a length of green withy* to hold it together.

"It's called a *quaich*, made to hold wine or kuass. The dark and light woods are plane and alder, and they have been feathered to form a tight joint, and to prevent the different woods from expanding and contracting at different rates. The withy shrinks as it seasons to complete the seal."

"I'm guessing this is your husband's work."

Vitka nodded, pride in her eyes. "Brodar was especially good with his hands. He sold them in the local markets."

She raised her own quaich. "Sláinte."

Ben tapped his against hers. "Sláinte."

They talked as they ate, Ben giving an account of his life at Dundonald, though without mentioning Bliss, and talked about what he hoped he might achieve at the Magisterium in Lochranza. He took care not to drink too much of the strong wine.

The evening passed, and the fire burned low in the hearth. When it seemed reasonable to do so, Ben gave a theatrical yawn and stretched. "Well," he said, "it will be a long day tomorrow, so I think I'll go to bed."

Vitka showed him to his sleeping quarters. "Good night," she said, smiling sweetly. "Sleep well." She closed the door behind her. As she did so, Ben saw that there was no means of locking it.

Ben peeled off Brodar's robe, and was about to climb between the bedclothes when he saw his own clothes laid out on the chest at the end of the bed. His bonnet was on the top.

He picked it up and held it to him. Bliss had given it to him, and to touch it was to touch her, to somehow commune with her.

Far away, Bliss clutched the pendant to her breast with one hand, while with the other she began to pleasure herself as Ben had so often pleasured her. It was a poor substitute for his lovemaking, but it would have to do. She had no free hand to wipe away the tears, so she simply let them fall. She lay back on the bed they had shared, and cried herself to sleep.

Ben pressed the bonnet against his chest, and thought of Bliss.

Eventually, with a deep sigh, he put the bonnet aside. He got into bed, blew out his candle, and went to sleep.

He dreamed of Bliss, how she would curl up behind him, her body spooned against his, and he would feel the warmth of her. She would gently kiss his shoulders, while her hand roamed over his chest, probing downwards little by little, running her fingers through his belly hair, until at last she brushed against his straining manhood, and stroking brought him to the heights of desire…

Ben suddenly became aware that he was not dreaming, that he was wide awake. The hand that was caressing him most intimately was not Bliss' hand, and the kisses on his shoulders were not Bliss' kisses. In his head, he heard a voice telling him that this was desperately wrong, that he should not allow this to continue, and yet, and yet… The hands that were exploring his most private places were most expert in the way they went about their business, teasing, arousing him, but not too much, not yet, and the small protesting voice became ever smaller as his passion grew.

He turned over, and began his own exploration of the body beside him in the darkness, desperate now with wanting, running his hands over her soft places until he found the warm wetness between her thighs, and she moaned softly.

He eased her legs apart and positioned himself above her, poised to enter her body. He could feel her back arching as she rose to meet him. Now, now, he could wait no longer…

The sound of whinnying cut through the silence, the sound of ponies in a state of alarm.

"*No!*" roared Vitka, pushing Ben aside as she leapt off the bed. "No, no, no! Not tonight!"

Ben crashed to the ground. Vitka was already out the door. He fumbled and found the flint and lit the candle beside the bed. Hastily donning Brodar's robe and shuffling into his boots, he followed Vitka outside.

A full moon illuminated an extraordinary scene.

The ponies were racing around the paddock in a wild state, with small creatures visible, perched upon their backs. When one came close, Ben could see the ecstatic look on its mischievous face. It had its hands in the pony's mane, twisting it to spur the animal on ever faster.

"Pixies!" gasped Vitka as Ben came up beside her. "To the shed, quickly!"

She ran to a nearby shed, naked in the moonlight, her dark hair flying about her shoulders and, when she turned, that black triangle so stark against the pallor of her skin. Ben followed her into the shed, struggling to keep his candle from going out.

"These are what we need!" Vitka exclaimed. She gathered into her arms some small, curious looking objects. When Ben brought the candle closer, he saw that they were something like corn dollies, but with four legs: imitation ponies, pixie sized, woven from ragwort and rye-grass.

She set them down in the middle of the paddock.

"We need to retire a little," she said, and together they withdrew to the fence.

Presently the whinnying of the ponies ceased, to be replaced by disgruntled snorting. Ben discerned the movement of small creatures, and soft cooings of curiosity and possibly delight.

"That's a good sign," Vitka murmured.

And then the tiny figures were astride the woven steeds. Back upon the breeze came high-pitched squeals of what sounded to Ben like "Horse and hattock". Ben thought his eyes must be deceiving him as he saw the tiny mounts take to the air. The pixies were off, and making for the far side of the paddock, where they disappeared into the shadows.

"Horse and hattock?" he said, turning to Vitka as the last of the cries faded away.

Vitka shrugged. "I have no idea. But it means something to them. Some spell that makes grass horses fly. Come.

Let's go inside. I have something to do before going back to bed."

"Ah," said Ben. "About that…"

"My *own* bed," said Vitka gently. "But there is something I would like to talk to you about first."

Puzzled, Ben followed her back into the farmhouse.

From her candle, Vitka lit a lantern with quartz panels that gave off a warm golden glow, and placed it in the middle of the table. Gesturing to Ben to be seated, she filled two tankards of ale from a barrel in the corner of the room, and put them down on the table. She busied herself cutting bread and hunks of cheese.

"Oh, none for me, thank you," said Ben.

"This isn't for us," Vitka told him. "It's for our friends out there." She gestured towards the paddock they had just left.

"The… the pixies?" Ben exclaimed, aghast. "But they terrorised your ponies! Why would you want to feed them?"

"They did terrorise the ponies," Vitka conceded, "and there is every probability that they will do so again. Even so, it is better to appease them than not."

"Why so?"

Because if they get inside the house, and they are more than capable of doing so, they will do far worse, throwing pots and pans around, breaking things, and making a terrible mess."

She took the platter of bread and cheese outside and placed it on the ground, and then returned, shutting the back door firmly as she did so.

She came and sat opposite him. In the light, she studied him for a moment or so, and in her eyes Ben saw deep affection mingled with curiosity and what might have been a degree of admiration.

"Well," she said, "tell me about her."

Ben looked at her quizzically. "About who?"

Vitka took a long swig of her ale. "Don't be a complete idiot! The woman you are in love with!"

"How did you…?"

"Because, my boy, I put the strongest love potion I have into your drink." Ben started, and stared with deepest suspicion at the tankard in front of him. "Oh, don't worry," said Vitka, chuckling mischievously, "there's nothing untoward in that one. Upon my honour, I'm done trying to seduce you for tonight. But I'm impressed. Even with my best potion clouding your thoughts, impeding your moral judgement, I could still feel you resisting me. Even as you were about to do the deed, even then, I could still feel part of you holding back. So… who is she?"

And so, between mouthfuls of ale, Ben told Vitka all about Bliss. She nodded sagely, and asked the occasional question, but mostly let him do the talking.

When he was done, and the tankards had been emptied for perhaps the third time, she yawned. "Whether you see her again in this life, or whether you don't, you have a love that will be with you, both of you, for all time. I know. Yes, I seek the pleasure of the body with other men whenever I can, but Brodar is my soulmate, and always will be. You will most probably know other women, physically, before you are done, but it will be Bliss that you carry in your heart. Always. And now, since you have a long day's travelling tomorrow, I suggest you get some sleep."

"One more thing," said Ben.

"Yes?"

"Tell me about your love potion. What's in it?"

"Oh that," said Vitka with a cheeky grin. "Pretty basic really. One gill of wine, a small spoonful each of clear honey, rosemary, aniseed, cloves, orange rind, a pinch of cumin and three leaves of rose geranium. Bring to the boil, simmer, sieve. The usual thing."

"I have no idea what half those things are. What's an orange?"

"It's a fruit that grows far to the south in Laurentia. It's the colour of the setting sun. It's very sweet and juicy, but the rind is bitter. I have them sent to me, but I don't have any at present."

"Aniseed? Cloves? What was the other one? C-cumin?"

"All spices from exotic places. You will certainly come across them in your studies in Lochranza. Any more questions?"

"No. Thank you."

"My pleasure," Vitka smiled sleepily. And with that she shuffled away to her own bed.

"Good night," Ben called after her. "Sweet dreams."

CHAPTER TEN.

When Ben arose early in the morning, he was startled to see how neat and tidy the living area was. Every pot and pan was washed and polished, every plate cleaned and stacked, the tankards hung on their hooks, and everything in perfect order. He could smell freshly baked bread.

"Wow!" he gasped. "You must have spent hours doing this!"

"Not I," said Vitka, stirring a pot of porridge. "The pixies. And they have threshed my corn too! I believe they may have been feeling a little ashamed of their activities last night, and have sought to make amends."

Ben sat to eat breakfast. "If you want to shave," said Vitka, "Brodar's razor is still there."

Ben ran his hand across the stubble on his chin and shook his head. "Winter is coming," he announced portentously.

"We Mages let our beards grow in the winter months." He made it sound as though he had been doing so for years, but in fact he had never yet grown a beard. He decided it was time to do so.

Vitka nodded. She pulled down a tankard and poured ale for Ben. "Where is your knapsack?"

"Here," said Ben.

She cut half the loaf that was on the table, and stuffed it into the knapsack, together with cheese, apples, a small pot of pickles, and a filled flagon of ale.

"This should keep you going until tonight," she said. "I'll give you one of the ponies to help you on your way. Not far along from here, you'll join the Great South Road, or what there is left of it these days. It's a bit overgrown, but still easy to find and to follow. When you reach the edge of Coeden Brith, 'The Speckled Forest', turn the pony back. You should make Dunghaven by nightfall."

"The Speckled Forest! Dunghaven! Such names!" Ben exclaimed, wolfing down his porridge and slurping at his ale..

"The meanings will become apparent, I dare say," said Vitka impishly as she led him outside. Ben shouldered his knapsack and followed her. A pony was waiting patiently for him.

"Fare thee well, young Mage," said Vitka, and, embracing him, kissed him passionately.

"Thank you for all your hospitality," he said. "I hope all my hosts are as generous!"

"We can never tell what awaits us on the road of life," Vitka replied. "Now, that is the way you need to go." And she pointed out the path he should take.

He swung himself up onto the pony's back and took the halter in his hand. Vitka gave the pony a slap on the rump and away it went.

Ben looked back and waved. Vitka waved in reply, then turned and went into the house.

The early morning sun was warm on his face. The path led over a short rise. At the top, it presented a view of open land, dotted with stands of yellow gorse, strongly scented in the morning air, and clumps of heather, purple and white, here and there. There was a fringe of trees in the distance to either side, with tall mountains rising beyond that, their heads lost in the clouds. Ahead of him, a sandy cart track wound its way between low banks that were thick with bracken, now starting to turn brown with autumn.

With a kick to the ribs, Ben motioned the pony forward.

After no more than half an hour, the cart track met a broader way, which was paved with regular slabs of stone, but these were now steadily disappearing amid soft tussocky grass that had grown up between them, and was thrusting them aside.

"The Great South Road, I presume," Ben muttered, and turned to the right, so that the sun was now over his shoulder. The pony advanced, picking its way dextrously over the uneven surface of the road.

Ben continued on through the morning hours, singing to himself from time to time to break the silence, while the landscape around him remained largely unchanged. His mind was preoccupied with thoughts of Bliss, and with trying to make sense of the events of the previous night. Yes, Vitka had given him a potion, but he still felt that he should not have given in to his urges as easily as he did. He felt ashamed of himself, and grateful to the pixies for their *coitus interruptus*.

When the sun was high overhead, he stopped and made some inroads into his stock of provisions, and then pressed on.

It was fairly late in the afternoon, with the sun inclining towards the west, when he first saw the forest, a great dark mass spreading across his horizon, and as he drew closer, he saw that the road plunged straight into its midst.

When he reached its periphery, he stopped, dismounted, turned the pony's head back in the direction from which he had come, and gave it a slap on the hind quarters to send it on its way.

He watched with some sadness as it ambled away, and drank some more ale to brighten his mood. Then he set off into the deep shade of the forest.

He had not gone far when he saw that many of the trees had small patches of a reddish-brown fungus liberally scattered across their trunks.

"So," he murmured, "the Speckled Forest indeed."

As he walked, he sought to attune himself to the mood of the trees. The birds whistled and chattered amicably enough, and he certainly did not sense any hostility, as he had read was the case in some forests. But the forest did not feel entirely welcoming either. He had the thought that the trees were reserving judgement until they had better determined what his purpose was as he walked between them.

He listened to the calls that the birds made. Particularly distinctive was the florikan, with its sharp, plaintive cry, and once or twice he saw them, winging their way through the high canopy, the last coppery rays of the sun catching the brilliant blue of their plumage as they flew.

And then suddenly a large crow flew at him from between the low branches of a beech tree, making him cry out. It passed so close that he felt that draught from its wings.

He stopped in his tracks, staring in the direction the bird had flown in long after it had disappeared. It was commonly considered to be a warning of danger when they did that. Ben resolved to be on his guard,

As the sun set, a deeper gloom seemed to seep through the trees like an incoming tide. Here and there, he glimpsed shy neats*, grazing among the undergrowth.

A little after that, he began to see the dark shapes of barbastrelles* as they began the nightly hunt for insects, and he heard the distant cries of flamneus owls as they too set out on the prowl.

He was beginning to think that if he did not reach this Dunghaven soon, he would have to bed down between the roots of a large tree.

He could not say which it was that he became aware of first, the sound of voices in song, and the repetitive thwack of axe on timber, or the smell of woodsmoke, and with it the unmistakeable odour of roasting meat.

But his road then took a slight turn, and there it was before him, a village in the forest. And in case there could be any doubt about its identity, a shabby banner strung across the roadway between two tall ash trees announced, in faded letters, just visible in the last glimmer of light: Dunghaven.

He entered the village. Thatched roofed wattle-and-daub huts lined the main street - the Great South Road - on either side. In one, where the walls only rose to waist height, he saw a blacksmith working the rosy red blade of an axe, while more similar implements could be seen stacked to one side, awaiting his attention. In another, through an open door a man could be glimpsed feeding what appeared to be loaves into a large beehive-shaped oven.

Most of the buildings, however, appeared to be private dwellings of a very modest kind. Each, Ben noted, had a very neat stack of cordwood stacked in a kind of lean-to shelter near the front door. At several, dogs on chains barked threateningly at him as he walked past.

There was no mistaking the building which constituted the centre of the village. It was considerably larger than any other, and had an upper storey. It was the source of the singing, the woodsmoke, which curled from a covered aperture in the centre of the roof, and the cooking smells. It was joined to lower buildings to form three sides of an open courtyard paved with cobblestones. Along one side, furthest from the road, was a stable block, while the third side was occupied by sleeping quarters. A large wagon stood in one corner, with a canvas cover stretched across half-hoops of iron to provide protection from the elements, and another covered whatever cargo it carried. The shaft at the front was long enough, Ben saw, to accommodate a team of six horses, and these were to be seen nodding their heads from stalls in the stable block, along with four or five others. A young stable hand could be seen tending to one of them, cleaning carefully between the three toes of its hoof.

As Ben stood taking it all in, a young girl burst out of a door with her arms full of vegetation, and a lantern clutched in a few free fingers. She could not see past the load she was carrying and almost knocked him over.

"Oops, sorry!" she gasped. "I'm late feeding the horses. It's already dark."

"Here," said Ben, taking the lantern from her. "Let me help you."

"Why, thank you," she gasped, unaccustomed to such chivalry from patrons.

As they came to the first stall, Ben held up the lantern. It was then that he saw what it was that constituted the fodder.

"This isn't hay," he said, "it's…"

"Beans. I know. From the kitchen," the serving girl explained. "This wagon came in too late for putting the horses out to grass. And we've run out of berevechicorn*."

"Bereve…?"

"A mixture of drage* and vetches*."

"Drage?"

The girl rolled her eyes melodramatically. "Drage! A mix of barley and oats! Goodness me! Don't you know *anything*?"

"Nothing that's of any practical use," Ben conceded sadly.

"Ah well, you're young yet. I suppose there's still time." She could barely be a year or two older than he. "Anyway, that being the case, beans it is."

"I wouldn't care to be driving this team tomorrow, then," said Ben, and the girl gave a merry laugh.

"Hedde? Is that you?" came a woman's voice from within the tavern. "I don't pay you to make merry! Get on with your work!"

"Sorry," Ben whispered. "I promise I won't make you laugh again."

"That's all right," said Hedde, pushing handfuls of greenstuff into the manger and moving on swiftly to the next stall. "That's Mrs. Adelaide Neate, the landlady. When she says she doesn't pay me to make merry, the truth is, she doesn't pay me at all. I just get my keep. Still, at least I have a roof over my head, and I don't go hungry!"

Hedde went on with her work with the brisk efficiency that came with daily repetition.

"Have you come far?" she asked.

Ben hesitated. He had been warned that there were many who viewed Mages with suspicion. But Hedde seemed friendly enough. "I'm a Mage," he told her. "From the Academy at Dundonald."

Hedde was just about to answer when the door to the tavern swung open and a cloaked figure stalked out and strode away into the darkness.

"We see your people here from time to time," Hedde told Ben. "Mostly they keep to themselves."

"Uh huh," said Ben, nodding.

He raised the lantern at the next stall. Hedde was very pretty, he saw, with fair hair in plaits and blue eyes, and rosy cheeks that were smeared with soot from the kitchen fires.

"Where are you going?" she asked.

Again he hesitated momentarily.

"You don't have to say if you don't want to," said Hedde, sensing his qualms. "It was just for something to talk about."

"Lochranza," said Ben. "To continue my studies."

"Lochranza!" Hedde gasped. "That's so far away!"

Ben glanced round nervously to see if they could be overheard, but there was no one near enough to hear over the din coming from within the tavern.

When she had finished feeding the horses, Hedde went to a well in one corner of the yard and drew up the bucket on a rusty chain. She then set about filling the trough in each stall, which required several return trips to the well. Ben provided the illumination all the while.

Finally, Hedde's work was done. Together they walked towards the entrance to the tavern. Just before she went inside, Hedde planted a warm, affectionate kiss on Ben's cheek. "Thank you for your help," she said, and gave him a curtsey.

"You're welcome," said Ben with a smile.

"And good luck with your journey!"

And then she was gone, back about her nightly work.

As he was about to follow her inside, Ben glanced up at the lantern-lit inn-sign swinging above the door. The peeling paintwork depicted a fish with its lips pursed, and a musical note next to it. Underneath was the name: *The Whistling Fish.*

Taking a firm grasp of his staff, in readiness for trouble, Ben pushed open the door and stepped inside. He was not prepared for what he saw.

In the centre of the room was a large bonfire, source of tremendous heat and also the principle source of light. Tables and chairs were arranged around it on all sides, as close as one might comfortably sit, and then further benches and tables were arrayed along the walls. The lamplit bar occupied one corner. Most of the tables were occupied by groups of men, many of them with young women perched upon their knees, many of whom were displaying ample expanses of bosom. Ben glimpsed Hedde weaving her way between the tables, and quite a few of the men were making a grab for her hind quarters as she passed, but she seemed well capable of either avoiding their attentions with a deft swerve of her body, or else of fending them off with a sharp slap, at which none seemed to take offence, but rather considered it to be all part of the amusement.

Elsewhere, a solidly-built, buxom, middle aged apple-cheeked women with fair hair in a braid that curled around her head like a coronet, wearing a dark blue dress that amply displayed her finer features, was passing from table to table, exchanging a few words at each. This, Ben assumed, was Mrs. Neate.

The whole room was lit by the wavering ruddy glow of the fire, although it did not reach into the corners, and Ben had the impression of figures seated in the shadows, which made him uneasy. The air was filled with smoke, and carried the mingled smells of spilled beer and roasted meat.

As Ben entered, he saw that the table nearest him was occupied by a group of men playing kapaka*. Like most of the men in the room, their beards were plaited, as was the custom throughout the area. Some men had two plaits, some had four. Ben became acutely conscious that his own hair and beard were woefully inadequate. Most of the men had women perched on their knees, the hands not occupied by cards making frequent forays into the women's unlaced bodices.

One of the men was loudly telling a joke. "And so poor Sir Torrent of Portyngale was ever known as Midsummer."

"Why so, my lord?" asks the woman on his knee.

"Why," said the man, "because he was always the shortest knight!"

All at the table burst into laughter, and the man telling the tale let go a sonorous fart.

"Good sir," said the woman, "your carwitchet I can tolerate, though barely, but I'll thank you to take your Bumbulum outside!"

"Indeed!" replied the man, wiping tears of laughter from his eyes. "Well, Mistress Brazette, I'll thank *you* to bring another Pottle of white Romney!"

"Eftsoons*, my lord." She hopped down from his knee and hurried off to bring the man his wine.

Ben made his way between the tables, further into the light, and as he did so, the hubbub in the room dropped to a low murmur. He looked around and saw that all eyes were upon him. But then, all the chatter resumed, and everyone pointedly looked away. His presence had been noted.

Ben continued on up to the bar. His progress was slow. Where there were not people seated at tables, they were standing at taller tables arranged around the building's supporting pillars. Most tables had evidence of food, but drinking seemed to be the greater preoccupation. There were large foaming mugs of ale and goblets and flagons of wine occupying most of every available surface.

The man serving the drinks was a large, heavily built man with a thick crop of dark wavy hair that looked as if it had not been combed in months. Shaving was clearly not high on his to do list either, as he had several days' growth of stubble adorning his jowls. He had watery blue eyes veined with red, and deep circles beneath them, suggesting that he was more than partial to a tipple himself. Ben hoped most sincerely that he was not Mr. Neate, because in appearance he was anything but.

"Good evening, sir," he said, making what was clearly an effort at amiability. "My name's Wisby Börs. What would be your pleasure?"

Ben's eye lighted on a large pot of steaming mulled wine at the taverner's elbow. "A mug of your mulled wine, please, and I would like a room for the night."

"Very good, sir" said Börs. "That will be four penning for the wine, and five aspers for the room."

Coins rattled onto the counter, and a voice at Ben's elbow announced, "That's for the wine. We'll hold off on the room for the moment."

Ben turned to face the man beside him. He was middle aged, his greying brown locks surmounted by a circlet of gold that rounded his brows. His hair was tied into a pair of plaits, finished off with small silver rings. His eyes, a bluish grey, bespoke experience and wisdom. He had no beard, but long drooping moustaches that were also plaited, the plaits ending in diminished versions of the ones adorning his hair. Beneath the moustaches there was an affable smile. Ben sensed no threat.

"We will?" he said, puzzled.

"Wisselus Smallenburg, merchant,at your service," the man said, extending a callused hand.

Ben switched his staff to his left hand and extended his own right hand, which was swallowed in the grip of the other until Ben feared he might lose circulation. "Ben Troon," he winced, "at yours."

"I have a proposition for you, if you'll hear me out," Wisselus said, gesturing towards a small table in a dark corner. Ben took his mulled wine and followed him.

He stood his staff in a corner, within easy reach, and sat down opposite the newcomer. There was a lighted lamp in the middle of the table, that threw weird shadows up across Wisselus' face, and also showed that nettercaps* had been busy weaving their webs in the corner of the alcove behind him.

Wisselus took a sip from the goblet that was before him. "You are a Mage, aren't you?"

"Is it so obvious?" said Ben.

Wisselus gave a laugh. "Why do you think there was a hush when you walked in? Everyone in this room saw you for what you are the moment you stepped through the door. And I have to tell you, there are a fair few who don't like Mages, for one reason or another."

"But you do?"

Wisselus gave a wry smile. "I am, shall we say, agnostic on the matter. But I have seldom found reason *not* to like your people. Now, where are you bound for, young sir?"

Ben sipped his wine. The warmth of it, and the spicy flavour, felt good as it went down. "Lochranza."

"Lochranza," Wisselus repeated, his eyes lighting up with satisfaction. "Perfect."

"How so?"

"I am, as I say, a merchant." Wisselus glanced around to ensure he was not overheard. "On my wagon out there is a very valuable cargo of amber."

"Amber!" Ben exclaimed. Wisselus' expression turned to one of alarm, and he looked around again, gesturing to Ben to keep his voice down. "But I thought all the amber went by sea," said Ben in a hushed tone.

"It used to," Wisselus agreed. "Because there were many Quaaman patrol ships keeping an eye out for pirates. Now there are far fewer of them, and they seldom venture this far north, so taking cargoes by sea has become much riskier."

"I see," said Ben. "And this proposition of yours?"

"I am in need of a guard," said Wisselus. "My previous employee just left. You may have seen him as you came in." Ben recalled the furtive figure he had seen slipping away into the night as he entered the tavern, and nodded. "He decided the dangers of the journey were greater than he wished to contemplate. I fear he may have found himself an alternative source of income by telling others about my cargo."

"I see," said Ben again.

"That stick of yours," said Wisselus, nodding towards the Magestaff in the corner. "You know how to use it?"

"I have been trained," Ben told him, "but I have never fired a shot in anger, so to speak."

Wisselus nodded, digesting this information. "Ah well, you may get the chance sooner than you might have expected. So, what do you say? It's a long walk to Lochranza. A very long walk indeed."

Ben was about to answer when a voice beside him said, "Hello again."

He turned to find Hedde looking down at him.

He smiled. "Hello again."

"Would you care for something to eat, kind sir?" she said, giving him a curtsey.

"What do you have?" he asked, although he could smell roasting meat, the aroma filling the air.

"We have soup and the roast of the day, which is ox," she replied.

"Well," said Ben, suddenly feeling famished, "yes to both, then."

"That will be one asper, if you please, sir," she said with a giggle. Ben pulled some coins from his purse. It was hard to see which was which in the dim lamplight. Hedde picked one from his palm, and he felt a tingle at her touch. She went away to fetch his dinner.

He found himself looking into Wisselus' eyes. The older man was regarding his thoughtfully. "Yes," said Ben. "I accept your offer."

"Good. The gods have clearly brought us together for a reason," Wisselus said. After a pause, he added, "I wasn't really planning to stop here. It's a real den of iniquity, Dunghaven. But I broke a yoke, and had to stop to get another one made. It will be ready first thing in the morning, they tell me, and then we'll be off."

He took another draught from his goblet.

"What's that you're drinking?" asked Ben.

"Melomel," said Wisselus.

"What's that? I haven't heard of it."

"It's hydromel* that has had fruits such as summer berries added to it. This one, with cowberries, is my particular favourite. Now melomel is not to be confused with metheglin, which is made with herbs. Sometimes I have one made with bog myrtle if I need to stay awake. It's quite bitter. Metheglin with hops, on the other hand, is good for putting you to sleep. The making of hydromel is always a fine art, very much dependent upon the nature of the yeast that goes into it. Our friend Börs there," Wisselus went on, gesturing towards the bar as he warmed to his subject, "has a particularly fine wild yeast that he has cultivated. He cossets it like a mother with a newborn baby, and the result is a very fine hydromel.

One of the plusses of stopping here, definitely. And it's a slow process, too. Depending on the yeast, a brew can take four or five months. But worth the wait. Now, when you add fruit to make melomel, things get rather more complicated, because while the sharpness of the fruit has been well known to get the fermentation going when it gets 'stuck', as sometimes happens, the fruit changes the flavour of the brew, and it should always complement the flavour of the honey, rather than overpowering it. Something like a good marriage, a partnership of equals." He gave an amused cough. "Not that I'd know too much about *that*! But Master Börs again has the touch. Best melomel on the Great South Road."

CHAPTER ELEVEN.

Suddenly a round of applause echoed round the room. A well rounded man with wheaten hair tied into a pony tail, visible beneath a jaunty yellow cap, sporting an assortment of pendants on chains and leather thongs on his dark green tunic, stepped between the tables, acknowledging the cheers with a wave of his hand as he made his way towards the centre of the room. Under his arm he carried a musical instrument which was shaped like a peacock, and in his hand he carried the bow with which it was to be played.

"That's Ailean Dall, the bard," said Wisselus, clapping enthusiastically.

"What instrument is that?" asked Ben.

"That's a taus*," Wisselus explained. "You don't see a great many of them."

Ailean Dall took his seat on a stool near the fire, quickly tuned his instrument, and began playing an old folk song about a maiden's stolen virtue, called 'A Bunch of Thyme'.

While he was playing, Hedde returned with Ben's food, soup, a platter of roast meats, and some fine crusty bread to soak up the juices.

"Could we please each have another cup of your excellent cowberry melomel?" asked Ben, and gave her the money. She gave him another of her coquettish smiles and hurried away again. Ben began making inroads into the generous bowl of soup before him.

When the drinks came, Wisselus gently put a hand on Ben's arm. "Just the one cup," he warned. "To be savoured slowly. Melomel may not seem very strong, but it has a sneaky way of creeping up on you. And you won't be any use to me in the morning if you're nursing a hangover. As, I dare say, many of those here tonight will be."

After playing merry tunes for an hour or more, Ailean Dall made a tour of the room with his yellow cap, and soon it was filled with coins from his appreciative audience.

Wisselus pulled up a leather bag that he had on the floor beside him, and delving into its depths, he drew out a rolled piece of felt cloth bound with a leather thong, and a small carved box.

"Care for a game of halatafl?" he asked, undoing the thong.

"I don't know it," said Ben.

"Ah well," said Wisselus with a smile, "then it's high time you learned. It is, as I say, a long way to Lochranza, and there are many empty hours to fill on the road."

Ben smiled back. "Very well, then."

The square of black felt that Wisselus unrolled between them had yellow lines marked on it. In the centre of the board was a square, with lines radiating outwards from its corners to the corners of four other squares which occupied the four corners of the board.

Wisselus opened the box and took out the small round counters it contained. Half of them were painted red, the other half white. "Twenty-two pieces each," he explained.

On each side of the board, he arranged five counters in a row between the corner boxes, then two rows of seven, and the final three counters to the right of the centre box.

"Now," said Wisselus, "this is how the game is played. "One player moves one of his pieces into the centre square. The other player then has one of his pieces jump over the one in the middle, and takes it from the board. The game then progresses in similar fashion until one player has four or fewer pieces left on the board, at which point he is declared the loser. Pieces move forwards or sideways, but not backwards. They can travel diagonally, but only along the marked lines. A piece can jump another piece if there is an empty space on the other side of it, and when jumping, moving backwards is permitted. Got it?"

"I think so," said Ben, nodding.

"You can jump over any piece, yours or your opponent's, but of course if you jump over your opponent's piece, you take it from the board, that being the object of the exercise. It is possible to make multiple jumps, in any direction, in a single turn. You can enter the corner squares, but you have to leave again immediately by jumping over another piece. You cannot remain in a corner square. Right, let's play."

Wisselus moved his white counter into the centre square, and Ben immediately took it with one of his pieces, and the game was on. The two men became so engrossed that they barely looked up when Hedde brought mugs of ale for them.

They played three games. Ben lost all of them, but with each game, he became sharper, and was eventually able to put up considerable resistance.

As they played, Ben told the other man of his encounter with Vitka. When he had completed his account, he saw that the amber trader was looking at him long and hard, with an expression of deepest concern.

"What is it?" asked Ben, when he could endure the silence no longer.

"It is conceivable, young man, that you have had a very lucky escape," Wisselus said at last.

"How so?" asked Ben, his sense of alarm growing.

"I could be wrong," said Wisselus hesitantly, "but your Vitka may have been a succubus."

"What's that?"

"A succubus is a demon woman, who comes to men as they sleep and steals their seed."

"Gods!" Ben exclaimed. "Whatever for?"

"She passes it to an incubus, the male of her kind," Wisselus explained, "who then uses it to impregnate unsuspecting women, so that they will give birth to half human, half demon mischlings. Moreover," he went on, "it drains the man's life-force. There are those who have even died as a consequence."

Ben stared at him. "A lucky escape indeed, then," he said.

"Indeed," Wisselus agreed. "Shall we continue with the game?"

"Yes," said Ben. "Let's."

Finally Wisselus declared that it was time for bed. "We need to have our wits about us tomorrow," he declared ominously.

"Dove's dung!" exclaimed Ben. "I never got around to ordering a room."

"Not necessary," said Wisselus. "Come with me."

Ben followed Wisselus out into the dark. It took a few minutes for his eyes to become accustomed, but the moon was barely past the full, so it was not hard to see the dark bulk of the wagon. Wisselus went to the driver's box.

"Time to get up, lad," he said, and a shape emerged that resolved itself into the figure of a stable boy. Ben saw the moonlight flash on a coin as Wisselus dropped it into the boy's hand. "I'm much obliged to ye. Now, off ye go to somewhere warm."

And the boy slipped away into the dark.

"I'll take the driver's box," said Wisselus. "You can make yourself at home in the back. I hope you don't snore."

"I haven't had any complaints," said Ben. "What about you?"

"Ha!" exclaimed Wisselus. "My employees don't *dare* to complain!" And he gave a mischievous grin.

Ben climbed into the back of the wagon, unrolled his blanket and made himself as comfortable as he could atop the precious cargo of amber. In moments he was asleep, and unable to testify as to whether Wisselus snored or not.

*****

Ben was awoken by the cries of birds, and for a brief moment he wondered where in Anoone he was. Then he looked up at the canvas stretched over iron hoops above his head, and it all came back to him.

The head and shoulders of Wisselus appeared at the rear of the wagon. "Ah, awake at last, are you, sleepy head? Come and get some breakfast."

Clutching his staff, Ben clambered down from the wagon and looked around. It was barely light, and everything more than a few ells distant was swathed in a heavy mist, turning trees and buildings and people into grey silhouettes. The sun had not yet risen, and when it did Ben guessed it would scarcely be visible. Wisselus' 'at last' seemed a trifle unfair.

He shuffled after the merchant into the tavern, and they took their seats in the same corner where they had sat the previous night. Wisselus seemed to like it as it permitted him to cast an eye over the whole room while at the same time his back was covered.

One young man was scooping up the ashes from the bonfire in the centre of the room, while other lads and lasses were clearing away the evening's detritus.

Hedde appeared, looking as bright as a button, and Ben wondered how she did it. She brought them porridge, hard boiled eggs and bacon, bread and jam and mugs of ale. Wisselus paid her and she slipped away again, but not without giving Ben a cheeky wink. He found himself wishing he might stay a while and get to know her better, but a voice inside his head that he recognised as belonging to Bliss warned him away from such mischievous thoughts.

"Did you sleep well?" Wisselus asked.

Ben felt some aches and pains in various parts of his body. "I believe I have had more comfortable beds," he admitted.

"I don't know how you could tell," Wisselus replied, "since you went out like a light."

"I can tell now," said Ben, yawning and stretching.

Breakfast was swiftly dealt with, and then the two men set off down the main street of Dunghaven. It was Ben's first proper look at the little village. It was, he saw, a community of timber-cutters: most of the menfolk were heading off in different directions into the forest, carrying large axes and saws, and some pulling handcarts to which the felled trees would be lashed for bringing back. It was still barely light, and Ben was tempted to ask Wisselus how it was that they could find their way, but then he realised that these men must know every inch of the forest for miles around, and could probably find their way home in complete darkness.

They were greeted by the carpenter at the doorway of his workshop. He was a tall, rangy fellow with straw-coloured hair and a moustache to match, with assorted tools protruding from pockets in a well-worn leather apron. He introduced himself to Ben as Pod Gryfami, and ushered them inside.

Inside, the lamps did little to alleviate the gloom, but one at least illuminated the surface of a workbench. He picked up the finished yoke and put it into Wisselus' hands. He turned it over, inspecting it in the lamplight. Ben saw that its rounded profile had been cut from a block about four inches square, and a little over an ell in length. In the middle, a graceful curve about five inches in length had been carved out, where the yoke would sit over the animal's neck.

"What sort of timber is it?" asked Ben, by way of making conversation.

"Brush box," said Pod. "It's a good timber to use because it gives a nice smooth finish. We cut the piece out of a log across the grain." He pointed to where the grain of the wood could be seen, deeper in colour than the honey tone of the surrounding outer wood.

"We must be on our way," said Wisselus. "Ten aspers I believe we said?"

Pod nodded. "Ten aspers it is."

Wisselus counted the coins from his pouch into the carpenter's outstretched hand. They shook on the transaction. Then Wisselus picked up the yoke, and they walked swiftly back to the tavern.

The stable boy who had been sleeping in the wagon the night before appeared, leading Wisselus' horses one by one. As he brought them out, Wisselus harnessed them to the wagon. He led the reins back along the shaft, passing them through iron rings which were affixed to the shaft by means of a lower fixing loop which was enclosed beneath a skirt of four oak-leaf shapes. Above the two loops which held the reins there was an iron acorn as further decoration.

"They're called terret rings," said Wisselus, noting how Ben observed his actions.

"I'm no expert on such things," Ben admitted, "but six horses seems a lot."

"There are places where the Great South Road is not so great," Wisselus told him. "As you will see. Now, climb aboard and we'll be on our way."

Ben scrambled aboard, making sure he had his knapsack and his staff close by him. Wisselus flicked the reins and the horses moved forward, hauling the wagon out of the yard and onto the road, southbound.

Ben glanced up at the banner strung across the road at the southern end of the village, and then glanced back. A slight dip in the ground soon hid it from view.

Once they were out of the village and clear of any foot traffic, Wisselus increased their pace somewhat.

Ben sensed the other man's tension. "You are expecting that someone will ambush us."

"I would put a lot of money on it," said Wisselus. "And I'm pretty sure I know where they will try it."

"Where's that?"

"You'll see soon enough, Ben Troon. Soon enough."

They had not gone far when one of the horses let loose a sonorous fart. And then another did the same. And a third. Before long there was a flatulent chorus.

"Ye gods and little fishes!" gasped Wisselus. "*What* have these animals been eating?"

"Beans," volunteered Ben. "From the kitchen at the *Whistling Fish*."

"I see," said Wisselus, giving him a suspicious glance. "And you know this because…?"

"I was there when Hedde fed them. She said she didn't have time to let them forage properly."

"Hedde," said Wisselus. "She wouldn't happen to be the filly that served us last night?"

"The very same," Ben acknowledged.

"No wonder she was giving you the goo-goo eyes, if you just stood there and let her feed the horses *beans*!"

"Well," Ben replied with a mischievous smirk, "I didn't know then that I'd be riding behind them."

"So it's all right if some other poor sod has to suffer their gaseous eruptions? Thanks very much! Is that what they teach you at Mage school?"

Ben didn't answer. It was all he could do to keep from exploding into laughter every time another horse let go a fart.

They pressed on at a goodly clip, lapsing into silence. As the sun rose, the mist quickly burned off, and it looked like being a fine autumn day. The branches of the trees formed a tunnel over their heads, the deciduous ones turning to brown and gold and red, the conifers remaining solidly green.

A little before midday, Ben observed that the trees were thinning out. He could see more daylight ahead. Presently, the wagon emerged from the forest, and Wisselus reined in the horses.

Ben gave a gasp. They were at the top of a high escarpment, looking out over a landscape of woodland and rolling moors that swept away as far as the eye could see.

"How is it that we are up so high?" he asked.

"You have in fact been climbing slowly but steadily more or less since you left Dundonald," Wisselus told him. "Or soon after. This is Ravening Edge."

"How do we get down there?" asked Ben, pointing at the land below.

"The road drops down the face of the scarp," Wisselus explained. "But first we have another obstacle to deal with."

With a snap of the reins, he set the wagon in motion, following the road as it turned to the left, running along the ridge.

After a few minutes, Ben heard the sound of rushing water, and they came upon a deep cleft carved through the escarpment.

"This is Givold's Fosse," said Wisselus. "At the bottom is the Brodribb River, making its way down to the lowlands."

Ben saw that the road ahead led across a bridge spanning the gorge. It was an impressive structure, built of oaken beams, perhaps five ells in width and several hundred feet long, supported by a network of trestles built out from the rocky sides of the gorge.

"We have two very good reasons to be careful here," said Wisselus, slowing the team to a walk as they approached. "One is that this bridge was built by the Quaamans when they came here many years ago, and it has not been kept in good repair since their departure. Some of the timbers may well be rotten."

"And the second?"

"The second," Wisselus answered with a sigh, "is that if we are going to be ambushed anywhere, it will be here. Keep your stick ready."

Ben tightened his grip on his staff. The wagon rumbled onto the bridge. The timber decking boards began to creak ominously under the weight of the wagon. Both men tensed as Wisselus eased the team forward.

Ben glanced down. He could see the rushing waters of the river far below them, and his pulse raced. He sensed he was in greater danger than he had ever known in his life.

Suddenly there was a loud cracking, and a board beneath the wheels split in two and plunged into the abyss. Both men gasped in shock.

"You were right," Ben whispered. "This bridge is in a bad way."

The groaning of the timbers continued incessantly as they progressed. The horses snorted, also sensing their precarious situation.

A quarter of the distance was passed. Then they were right in the middle of the gorge, with nothing but empty space all around, the bridge seeming like a slender reed on which to rest their hopes.

As the far side drew closer, little by little, Ben felt his hopes slowly begin to rise.

Wisselus, too, seemed to draw a breath. "Perhaps I was wrong," he murmured.

Almost as if he had heard, a man stepped from behind a rock on the far side of the gorge. He was thickset, with dark curly hair, dressed in homespun tunic and leggings. He was holding a sword, and had a dagger in his belt.

"Oops," said Wisselus softly. "Spoke too soon." He addressed himself to the man. "And you are?"

"My name's Bassewitz," he announced, "and I am proposing to take your wagon and its cargo, if you'd be so kind."

Wisselus could not restrain a chuckle. "You and whose army?"

"Not quite an army," said Bassewitz, "but I do have a companion." He gestured past them.

Wisselus and Ben turned their heads and looked back along the bridge. Standing on it, perhaps two hundred ells behind them, was a formidable female figure, clad in a long, ragged black cloak, with raven dark hair flying wildly in the wind. She was grinning, and Ben realised he was looking into the face of pure evil.

"This is Kwepkas," said Basselitz with mock affability. "She's a witch, and her Magecraft is ten times that of your young Mage there."

Kwepkas brought up her hand with lightning speed, and a bolt of blue-white light slammed into the tailgate of the wagon. Wisselus and Ben stared, as wisps of smoke rose into view.

"So please don't try any hocus pocus on us," Bassewitz went on, "because it will go badly for you."

Wisselus remained staring fixedly at Bassewitz. Out of the corner of his mouth, he murmured, "I can run down our friend in front, if you can get a shot off at the witch. Ready?"

There was no reply. He glanced around, but the seat beside him was empty. "Damn you, boy!" he hissed. "Thought you'd be more use in a crisis!"

He could see that Bassewitz too was wondering where Ben had gone. It was now or never. With a "Yah!" he snapped the reins and the horses bolted forwards, amid the sound of splintering timbers. He felt Kwepkas' bolts slamming into the back of the wagon, and even heard the hum as they swept past his head.

Bassewitz threw himself aside as the wagon rumbled off the bridge, but he recovered with speed that Wisselus had not anticipated, and in moments he was up alongside the merchant, swinging his sword.

Seeking to dodge the swirling blade, Wisselus ducked and at the same time released his grip on the reins. The wagon hit a pothole and lurched, and he was thrown backwards through the air, landing heavily on the ground. Bassewitz leapt down beside him. He had dropped his sword, and was fumbling for his dagger.

Wisselus leapt forward and brought his fist sharply into Bassewitz' stomach, then, as he doubled up, Wisselus jerked his knee into his groin. He went down, and Wisselus leapt on him, seeking to disarm him, but again the other man recovered with alarming speed, and the two men were soon wrestling furiously in the dirt.

*****

If Wisselus did not know where Ben was, Ben himself was none the wiser. He was on his hands and knees, with his staff thrust through his belt across his back, and he could see the timber deck of the bridge below him. But something was decidedly odd, for he and it were in deep shadow, not the bright autumn sun of a moment ago. While he sought to get his bearings, he became aware of the sound of rushing water booming loudly in his ears. But again there was something amiss, for he could swear that the sound was coming from *above* him. He craned his neck upward, and sure enough, there was the river, pounding through its gorge, *over his head*. But it appeared to have slowed down, flowing now like molten honey, and the sound it made was deeper, far deeper than before. It was all very puzzling.

And then it all came back to him. In the moment that Kwepkas' bolt of energy struck the wagon, Ben had suddenly felt very distant from everything that was going on, and a rhyme had come into his head, completely unbidden.

> *Nettercap, nettercap, grant me your power,*
> *For my need was never greater*
> *Than it is at this hour.*

He was willing to admit it was not great poetry. The worst of Dundonald's bards could do better. But as an expression of will - and that, he had been told repeatedly, was the essence of a spell - it would serve its purpose. Indeed, it *had* served its purpose, for here he was, on the underside of the bridge, like the nettercaps that clung to the ceiling in the *Whistling Fish*. And he knew what he had to do.

He scampered along the bridge, touching it with his hands and feeling a slight attraction at each movement. And time had slowed down. Was this how nettercaps viewed the world?

He tried to judge how far behind the wagon Kwepkas had been standing, and went a little further. Then he clambered over the bridge guard rail and drew a sigh of relief. Kwepkas was standing with her back to him.

Standing on the deck, he swiftly pulled his staff from his belt and set down the wooden tip. He was about to strike the top with his ring when he paused. He couldn't shoot someone in the back.

Whether it was the soft sound of the staff striking the deck or merely some sixth sense, but Kwepkas spun, and in the same moment launched a bolt from her hand. At the same time, without even having formulated a notion to do so, Ben slammed his ring down on the top of the staff.

Even as Kwepkas' bolt sizzled past his shoulder, Ben's shot struck her full in the forehead. She did not scream audibly, but Ben heard it inside his head, a final anguished cry from one wielder of Magecraft to another.

And then she was gone. Not merely dead, but vanished, reduced to smoke and ashes swept away on the breeze, leaving only a black cloak on the deck.

Ben was about to look at it more closely when his attention was drawn by sounds of struggle, and looking up he saw the two men fighting on the ground at the end of the bridge. Even as he watched, Bassewitz was raising a dagger, its polished blade glinting in the sunlight, poised to end Wisselus' life.

Ben thrust out his hand and launched another bolt of energy. Bassewitz screamed as it struck him on the shoulder, dropped the dagger and fell forward across Wisselus' supine body. As Ben ran up, Bassewitz' body was still twitching, and then it lay still.

As Ben approached, he saw that a large hole had been burnt into Bassewitz' tunic. The flesh beneath where the bolt had struck was blackened, surrounded by a ring of crazed, angry looking red lines.

Ben's jaw dropped. "Is he…?"

"Yes!" growled Wisselus. "Now pull him off me, for the love of Ceridwen!"

Hesitantly, Ben dropped his staff and slid his hands under Bassewitz' armpits. He began straining to pull him off the merchant. Bassewitz was a big man, and as a dead weight, quite literally, he was not easy to move. But slowly Ben dragged him to one side, and Wisselus staggered to his feet.

"All right," said Wisselus, "Let's get rid of him. You have the arms already, you might as well stay there."

He took the dead man's legs, and led the way back along the bridge, almost to where Kwepkas' cloak still lay.

"All right," said Wisselus. "Heave him up over the rail."

Together they hauled the body up onto the guard rail, and then it only took a slight shove to send it careering down through the air, arms and legs flailing wildly, suggesting for a moment that there was still life within it. It hit the grey, foaming water with a distant splash. Air trapped beneath the man's tunic caused it to balloon out, and then it drifted into the fast midstream current and was swept away out of sight.

Ben turned his attention to the sinister black shape that was Kwepkas' cloak. Shuddering slightly, he picked it up between his fingers and tossed it over the rail. Caught by the breeze, it spread out like the wings of a terrifying bird and slowly floated downwards, drifting out over the river until it settled on its surface, and swiftly becoming waterlogged, was sucked under. It was still visible as a shadow below the surface as it was carried around the next bend and was gone.

"Good work," said Wisselus, brushing his hands together. "Now, let's put this place behind us, shall we?"

CHAPTER TWELVE.

At the end of the bridge, Ben stooped to retrieve his staff, and then they walked on. A few hundred ells further on, the wagon had stopped by the side of the road, and the team was munching on fresh green grass. Wisselus and Ben climbed aboard, and Wisselus snapped the reins to get them moving again.

"Good job they stopped when they did," he observed, "or we'd be in some even deeper strife."

He gestured ahead, and Ben saw that the road was beginning to descend a long, steady incline across the face of the escarpment. Had the runaway horses continued on down the slope, the consequences were likely to have been disastrous.

They began the descent, Wisselus with his hand on the brake lever, easing the horses down the hill as he had done many times before.

"I see you still have your bonnet," Wisselus observed.

"I…?" Ben's hand went to his head, and snatched off his bonnet, still with the mollymawk feather in the side. He had been upside down under the bridge, and yet it had remained firmly affixed to his head. "I do indeed," he said with a broad grin. "Now that truly *is* Magecraft."

He stared at his headgear in disbelief, before replacing it firmly upon his head.

Not many minutes had passed before the farting started again. Both men exploded into laughter. It was as much as anything the sense of relief that they had escaped with their lives, and could now comfortably return to the world of the mundane, if not the absurd.

At the bottom of the slope, the road took a broad turn to the right, and they were once more heading in a southerly direction.

It followed a course across open moorland, and as they progressed, the two men lapsed into silence. Ben could not imagine what Wisselus might be thinking about, but he was vividly reliving the events he had just experienced. He reflected numbly that he had just killed two people, and no matter how much they may have merited it, he was unable to feel good about it. He prayed to all the gods he could think of, especially Morrigan, the Queen of Battle, that he might be spared ever having to be in that position again.

And then there was the puzzling matter of his Magecraft. The words of the nettercap chant had come to him from he knew not where, and had granted him the ability to take on the characteristics of the nettercap, and at the same time to somehow slow down time. Then he had thrown bolts of energy when they were needed, to save himself and Wisselus, without volition. As he pondered it all, he was suddenly reminded of Styrmir's words during their interview, about how there were for him no paths, just Magecraft. Was this what the Grand Mage had meant? That for him, Magecraft was somehow innate, instinctive? It was all so perplexing.

One thing was certain, though: he was tired. Performing Magecraft seemed to have drained all the energy from him. His muscles ached, and he struggled to get comfortable on the hard wooden bench. He dozed fitfully, but the feeling of listlessness remained with him all through the rest of the day.

*****

"I have a question," Ben said a little later.

"Spit it out, then," said Wisselus.

"Why is amber considered to be so precious and important?"

Wisselus slapped his forehead theatrically. In all that carry on, I completely forgot! You haven't actually laid eyes on our cargo, have you?"

"No indeed," said Ben.

"That must be rectified at once," said Wisselus, and drew the wagon to a halt by the side of the road. "Come," he said.

Glancing up and down the road to be sure they were unobserved, he uncovered the boxes that filled the wagon bed and opened one. He pulled out one of the pieces of the translucent, golden amber that were within.

"Amber is highly prized by the natural philosophers, many of whom are to be found in Lochranza, drawn to the Magisterium as bees are to nectar," he told Ben. "Amber is very special because it exhales a form of effluvium, a vapour, so to speak. Now, there are a number of other substances that do the same thing, including stones such as carnelian, agate, jasper, chalcedony, some metals, pearls, sea oak…"

"What in Anoone is sea oak?" asked Ben.

"As the name suggests," said Wisselus, "it comes from the sea. It is hard, brittle in fact, but resembles oak leaves and other plant matter. Now, these materials all give off an effluvium if you rub them, but because they are so much denser, and contain a great deal of earthy matter - even the sea oak - the vapour which they exhale is thick and heavy. They may draw iron to them, but only slightly if at all. Not so amber. Observe."

From within his tunic, Wisselus drew out a pendant on a chain. Ben saw that it represented the war-axe of Agrona, the slaughter-goddess, a popular item of personal adornment in Magelaw.

"The Axe of Agrona is made of iron," said Wisselus. With his finger-tip, he rubbed the amber.

"Notice," he said as he did so, "that I rub vigorously, but my touch is at the same time very light. This is the best way to achieve the desired effect. In this way, I draw out the amber's most subtle effluvia, which are trapped in the moisture locked within the resin. Amber is of an oily nature, which aids in the release of the effluvia, and winds from the north or the east, which are common in these parts, and clear skies, are also beneficial in achieving the desired effect. Humid winds, winds from the south, are mostly counterproductive, as is cloudy weather. Now, watch the Axe of Agrona."

He raised the piece of amber, and as he did so, the pendant rose too, drawn irresistibly towards the amber.

"Not Magecraft as such," said Wisselus, "but simply an effect of nature."

"But isn't that all Magecraft is?" retorted Ben. "Simply applying the forces of nature to serve the will of the Mage?"

"Ah well," said Wisselus, replacing the amber in its box and covering it over once more. "Perhaps that's so. But that's a discussion for wiser heads than mine. We'd best be on our way."

*****

When night was coming on, Wisselus drew the wagon off the road. He set stakes in the soft tussocky grass so the team could graze, and he and Ben built a fire. They ate some of the provisions they had brought with them from Dunghaven and passed a flagon of wine back and forth between them, chatting idly about their lives, their hopes and dreams.

They lay back and contemplated the stars. Wisselus pointed out the constellations that he knew, the Ro-éich, or Great Horse, rearing on its hind legs and pawing at the inky firmament, the bulky shape of the Serimner, the Boar, and the long, sinuous stream of stars that everyone knew as Ormurinn, the Serpent.

When they had exhausted their knowledge of the heavenly bodies, and their fire had burned low, they took to their bedding rolls underneath the wagon, the grass making for a softer bed than the boxes of amber Ben had slept on the night before.

The following morning dawned grey, with the landscape shrouded in mist. A rain was falling that was so light that they barely felt it.

"Soft weather they call it in these parts," Wisselus told Ben between mouthfuls of bread and cheese and slurps of wine.

Ben helped him get the horses into harness, and they were soon on their way again.

The landscape, or what they could see of it through the mist, was not much different to that of the day before. Occasionally they had to ford a fast-flowing stream, otherwise the journey was uneventful. After noon, they passed through a range of low hills.

In the far side, they came to a broad, shallow river, braiding around long banks of gravel. A bridge carried the road across that was of the simple post-and-lintel type of construction, posts set at intervals into the river bed carrying beams onto which the decking was laid.

"This is the Ussuri River," Wisselus announced. "We are now officially leaving Magelaw and passing into Luthany."

"I thought Magelaw was much larger," said Ben.

"It was, once," Wisselus agreed. "But when the Quaamans came, they gave the southern part the name of Luthany. The northern part was too hard to conquer, so they just left it, and it remained Magelaw."

The wagon rattled over the bridge.

"Why didn't they change the name back to Magelaw after the Quaamans left?"

"A lot of people in the south, as you will see, became very attached to Quaaman ways, and so the name Luthany stuck."

They continued on. The "soft" weather seemed to be turning distinctly harder.

Presently, Wisselus gave a grunt, and pointed ahead. Ben could see that what remained of the old Quaaman road surface had disappeared completely. In its place they could see a quagmire of mud.

"I wouldn't be surprised," said Wisselus, "if some farmer has helped himself to some of the road stones to repair a wall or a pig sty or some such. Well, Ben m'boy, this is where you earn your keep."

"I thought I already did that," Ben retorted with the ghost of a smile.

Wisselus grinned. "Well, let's put it this way. If you'd rather ride to Lochranza than walk, we're going to have to get the wagon through that lot."

As they approached the mud patch, which extended along the road for perhaps a hundred ells, Ben descended from the wagon into the driving rain.

"Just keep shoving from the back," Wisselus instructed him.

"Am I really going to make that much of a difference?" Ben asked.

"You'd be surprised," Wisselus assured him. "Every little helps."

Ben put his weight against the tailgate of the wagon, while Wisselus urged the team onwards through the glutinous mud. It was so sticky that Ben feared he might lose his boots. The horses struggled to find their footing, and Ben heard them snorting in protest, but slowly they edged forward. Wisselus called out encouragingly to both them and him.

They had almost reached the point where the stone road surface resumed when Ben suddenly heard a noise that he had not expected, the sound of pounding hoofbeats.

A rider appeared behind them, his mount travelling at full gallop. He was swathed in an oiled cloak and hood, and had bulging saddle bags on either side. He seemed oblivious to the rain and to them, and swept past, his horse's hooves throwing up a spray of mud that splattered across Ben from head to foot. And then he was gone.

When the wagon was back upon solid ground, Ben clambered aboard.

"Who was that?" he asked.

"Just the mail courier," said Wisselus. "It's how people stay in touch. He might even have been bringing some letters from your Academy."

"I believe Mages have other ways of communicating," Ben observed.

"Maybe so," said Wisselus, "but there's still something nice about a good old-fashioned letter." And he urged the horses into motion once more.

Ben mused about what the mail courier might be carrying. Vitka's oranges, perhaps. He knew that before long such a rider would be carrying passionate letters between Bliss and himself. Her lovely face came to him again, and he yearned to hold her.

Twice more that afternoon they encountered mud patches, and when they stopped to camp for the night, Ben's muscles were aching. There was certainly no possibility of looking at the stars that night, for a blanket of cloud covered the entire sky, and Ben was soon sound asleep.

The following day, the weather eased, and the landscape took on a gentler aspect. The barren moorlands gave way to more verdant rolling hills.

"These hills are called the Long Mynd," Wisselus declared.

As they trotted on, they heard curlews calling and sheep bleating, and they passed through frequent stands of birch and beech, often with babbling streams scoring deep gullies through them, passing through culverts under the road.

As the emerged from one such copse, they saw the remains of an ancient building silhouetted against the sky atop a low hill.

"What's that?" asked Ben.

"An old Mithraist temple," said Wisselus. "Fallen into disuse. This is probably the farthest north that the Quaamans brought their religion. It's probably only a matter of time before the stone is pillaged as building material."

Ben nodded.

Here and there, gaunt square peel-towers could occasionally be seen, marking out this or that warlord's territory. One of the most impressive was mirrored perfectly in a lake.

"Haddeby Noor," said Wisselus. "The tower marks the border of the realm once dominated by the mighty Tarr Lunn, a celebrated warrior who made life in these parts very difficult for the Quaamans."

"Indeed?" said Ben. His knowledge of history was shaky in places, and it was a thrill to imagine the great battles that must have been played out in the land over which they were travelling.

As the day wore on and the sun grew lower in the sky, they once again began to look for a place to stop for the night. They crested a low rise, and there before them lay a large complex of stone buildings with a paved driveway leading up from the road.

"Ah," said Wisselus, "that'll do nicely."

"What is it?" asked Ben.

"An abandoned Quaaman villa," Wisselus replied. "A very big one. I think this may have been the residence of the regional governor."

"You're sure it's abandoned?"

"Oh yes. The Quaamans have long since left this part of the world. And look, it's not in a good state of repair. You can see where the wind has pulled tiles off the roof, and they haven't been replaced."

"What about local people? Wouldn't they have moved in after the Quaamans left?"

"You might think so," Wisselus agreed, "but in fact they give these places a wide berth."

"Why so?"

"The people here have a different approach to living from the Quaamans. The Quaamans like to impose themselves on the country, building these big stone houses where they can cut themselves off from nature and wallow in their creature comforts, regardless of what the weather is doing outside. Local people like to build with wood, local materials, with skills that have been passed down for generations. They don't impose themselves on the landscape, they live within it, blending in with the hills and the valleys, the forests and the rivers."

"Like Dunghaven."

"Exactly. The Luthanians like to live in small villages and hamlets, and don't have a lot of use for the big towns that the Quaamans built, although their chiefs often take them over as their headquarters. They make use of the buildings, but the towns work in a different way to how they did during the occupation."

Wisselus had turned the wagon off the road onto the driveway, and he let the horses pull up to the porticoed entrance to the villa. He and Ben jumped down and unhitched the horses, and led them to what had once been finely manicured lawn, but was now waist high with wild grasses.

Wisselus waved his hand towards a circular building that was an adjunct to the main villa, surrounded by an elegant colonnade.

"That would be the bathhouse," he explained, walking towards one of the windows let into the outer wall. "It has two entrances, so that local people can use it as well as members of the household."

Through the window, the empty baths could be seen, with the patchy remains of fanciful mosaic patterns decorating the floors.

"Keen on baths, are they?" asked Ben, peering in.

"The Quaamans bathe every day."

"*Every day?*" exclaimed Ben, aghast,

"And the locals got into the habit as well. So the bathhouse here would have got plenty of use. But no more."

Ben shook his head in bewilderment at such alien behaviour.

Wisselus made his way up the front steps and into the entrance hall, Ben following a few paces behind, his eyes on stalks as he tried to take in everything around him. It was all on such an enormous scale.

"So how many people lived here?" he asked.

"Just one family. And their retainers," answered Wisselus.

Ben was staggered. For so few people to occupy such a vast edifice seemed like a huge waste of space. "No one needs a house this big," he said.

Wisselus laughed, the sound echoing off the high vaulted ceiling above them. "You have much to learn, m'boy. It's not about need. It's about status, about telling the world how rich and powerful you are, and not to mess with you."

"I see," said Ben. He was beginning to.

They crossed another room and came to the courtyard that was in the middle of the complex. In the middle was an ornate fountain, long since dry, and ranked around the perimeter were oversized statues, most of them still standing, although nearly all were disfigured with birdlime, and a few even had nests where there was a convenient niche.

They pressed on to explore the rest of the house. There were larger rooms which Wisselus said were for entertaining, and smaller rooms which had undoubtedly once been bedchambers. But large or small, every room had its mosaic floor, many depicting mythical creatures. Others showed scantily clad young women running and tossing balls to one another.

To the rear of the building was a hall easily as long as the Great Hall at Dundonald. The mosaic floor was largely intact, and showed what at first glance seemed to be hunting scenes, but a closer inspection showed that the animals - strange, exotic beasts that Ben could not recognise - were not being slain but rather trapped with nets and herded onto ships.

"What is happening here?" he asked.

Wisselus scowled. "The Quaamans hold tremendous spectacles where warriors pit themselves against these creatures to demonstrate their prowess. Thousands of the animals are killed every year. There are places where the predation of the Quaamans has been such that these magnificent beasts are no longer to be found."

"Morrigan sings!" Ben gasped. "That's awful!" He pointed to one extraordinary-looking animal. "What's that?" he asked. "It looks like it has a serpent in the middle of its face!"

"That, my friend, is a gompotherium*. Needless to say, the places where they live are far away and strange."

"A gompotherium," Ben repeated, savouring the word like some strange new dish. He had barely suspected that the world could be so immense as to contain such wonders, and stood for long minutes staring at the monstrous creature at his feet.

A few of the rooms still contained items of furniture, and Wisselus soon had a good fire burning in one of the smaller chambers. He still had a couple of rabbits that he had trapped the day before, and he quickly spitted them and had them cooking. He and Ben spread their bedding on the floor close to the fire, and settled in for the night.

When they had eaten, and the fire was burning low, they passed a flask of wine back and forth between them and spoke idly of this and that.

"Have you ever heard of Ösel Island?" Wisselus asked.

"No," said Ben. "Where is it?"

"If it exists at all," said Wisselus, "it is far out in the great ocean to the west. It is known as the Island of the Immortals, and Luthanians believe it is where we go when we die."

"If that's the case," said Ben, "it would be getting quite crowded by now."

Wisselus smiled broadly. "Imagine, if you will," he went on, disregarding Ben's comment, "that you are standing on top of a hill. You see a barque approach, and she lowers a boat that comes to the shore. You can see that the boat is full of the old and the sick, those upon whom the shadow of death lies long. You and your friends approach to welcome the newcomers. As the boat beaches, the boatman jumps out, and one by one he carries these people ashore. As he sets them down upon the sand, a remarkable thing happens. The years fall away from them, and suddenly the flower of their youth returns to them, they become virile men and lissom women again. As this transformation takes place, they look about them in amazement, and the people of the island embrace them and kiss them and give them to eat the fruit of immortality."

"It sounds wonderful," said Ben, stifling a yawn. He looked across at Wisselus, his face aglow in the dying light of the fire.

"I live in hope that it proves to be true," said Wisselus, and with that they settled for the night.

*****

The next morning it was sunny but there was a brisk chill in the air, a distinct sense that winter was not far away. They had another look around the great villa before taking to the road again. Presently they came to a village.

"This is Wyke Champflower," said Wisselus. "We can stock up with provisions here, and have some lunch at the inn."

He tied up the wagon at a hitching rail outside the general store, and they went inside. Ben stared around at the cornucopia of goods that it held, while Wisselus went from one barrel to another, helping himself to quantities of flour, oats, dried beans, mushrooms, dried fruits and the like, fresh vegetables and smaller quantities of herbs, a small cask of wine, oil for lamps and for leather, needles and thread, and much more besides.

When he had completed his purchases, and they had loaded them onto the wagon, they went to the inn and had a pasty and a mug of mead each. The landlord made small talk, and they sipped and munched contentedly

When they had finished, Wisselus said, "There is something I would like to show you."

He took Ben along a small lane behind the inn, which began to climb a hill towards a building that was visible on its summit. As the road ascended the hill, it passed under a low bank which was held back by a rank of large flat stones, perhaps two ells in height, some of them damaged, others leaning drunkenly.

"What you see on the hilltop is of course the Mithraist Temple built by the Quaamans. These stones that you see lining the route - how many are there, would you say?"

Ben ran his eye over them and made a quick assessment. "Perhaps a hundred?"

Wisselus nodded. "Not far off. Do you see what they are?"

Ben looked again. "Why, they have been taken from henges!"

"Exactly," said Wisselus. "Pillaged by the invaders for their own purposes. The next place that we come to, Bovetown, has something similar. All the stone circles in this part of the world have been dismantled."

"Clearly the Quaamans have no respect for the spiritual paths of others."

"You've got that right," Wisselus agreed.

They returned to the wagon and resumed their journey. In Bovetown, which they reached a couple of hours later, Wisselus pointed to another wall made from recycled standing stones, but they did not stop.

"If we make good time, we should be in Carrick Bend by nightfall," Wisselus told Ben.

"What's there?"

"The Slagenbekken River."

And indeed, the late afternoon sunlight was filtering through the trees lining the road when they came to a wall. The road passed through a large round arch in a double gatehouse that loomed threateningly above them.

"Good timing," said Wisselus as they passed beneath. "Much later and they would have closed the gates."

Are they afraid someone will attack?" asked Ben.

"There's no specific threat, but the frontier mentality still holds. They prefer not to take chances."

They emerged into the light once more.

"Who do they think is going to attack them?"

"Why, you people of course!" said Wisselus. "Savages from the north!"

They entered the market square in the centre of the busy little town. There were fine half-timbered merchants' houses all around it. Ben saw one house that was undergoing some major repairs. He could see that it seemed to be resting on the timber remnants of some earlier structure, and where the ground had been dug away in front of it, he saw alternating layers of gravel and stone, and what appeared to be drainage pipes made from hollowed logs.

There was a large, fortified building in one corner of the square.

"That's the Roland Tower," said Wisselus. "A place of final refuge if the walls are taken."

Beyond the square, they soon came to the port area, bustling with activity.

"This is Gammelgarn," said Wisselus. "In the old tongue, it means "old port"."

The quay, a broad boardwalk along the river's edge, with cranes set at intervals along it, was lined with large sheds, granaries, Ben soon saw, from which men were rolling out barrels of grain. He could smell the dust that always accompanied the storage of cereals. At one point on the water's edge, there was erected a large stone slab incised with three spiral patterns. This, he knew, meant, "Do not tie your boat up here."

Tied up at the wharf was a large flat vessel, onto which barrels of grain were being loaded. Wisselus brought the wagon to a halt close to a ramp providing access to the vessel. A man of medium height, with thick grey hair and a curly grey beard was overseeing the operation.

"Issa!" Wisselus called out as he jumped down from the wagon.

The man turned, and beamed. "Wisselus, you old rogue!"

Ben climbed down and approached. "This is my assistant, Ben Troon, a Mage. Ben, this is Issa Fofone, the captain of this disreputable hulk. He will take us to Lochranza."

"Willing to chance your arm, are you, on this 'disreputable hulk'?" said Fofone, grinning. "Welcome aboard. We sail first thing in the morning. Egino!" he called. One of the men loading grain came over. "Help get the wagon aboard."

The man called Egino and Wisselus positioned themselves either side of the lead horses and led them up the gently sloping ramp onto the barge. It was manoeuvred into position and secured with ropes, the horses unhitched and given nosebags of feed and a trough of water.

"Time for us to head for the trough too," said Wisselus, when he was satisfied that all was well.

"Will the, er, cargo be safe?" Ben asked.

"Issa's men will keep an eye on things. He knows I carry a lot of valuable merchandise."

They made their way to a waterfront tavern to eat, drink a little hydromel and perhaps hear some merry music.

CHAPTER THIRTEEN.

For three days they sailed down the river. The progress was slow, sometimes barely more than a walking pace, particularly where the helmsman had to negotiate a path between mudbanks or large trees that had fallen into the water. Ben had the impression that the weather was becoming milder as they headed south.

For much of the time, the river wound its way through woodlands, and the air seemed alive with choirs of insects, for they were certainly all around, effusions of spindly legs and gauzy wings, hanging in the midday air with effortless grace, sometimes motionless, and at other times caught up in rapturous dances, following some steps that only they knew, but able to turn aside if a breeze threw down a drop of water from the leaves above.

Ben was taking it all in from his favourite vantage point on the roof of the wheelhouse.

"It's all very beautiful, isn't it?" said a voice beside him.

Ben turned, and looked at a short, dapper man of middle years, dressed in an elegant velvet cloak and hood.

"Yes," Ben agreed. "The insects sing so enthusiastically."

"My thoughts exactly," his companion concurred.

"Although," Ben went on, "it would be nice if we could travel just a little faster. Winter is coming on."

"Indeed," said the man. "I fear this may be one of the last grain runs into Lochranza before the weather closes in."

"Grain?"

"Bercilak De Hautdesert at your service, Luthanian Ministry of Food inspector. It is my job to make sure that the reserves of grain are adequate, to see Lochranza and Luthania generally through times of drought, and to ensure that the grain is of suitable quality."

"How efficient," said Ben.

"We have learned our lessons from hard times. We keep a network of granaries well stocked at all times. But it will soon be impossible to ship grain into Lochranza for the winter, so we need to move stocks in before that happens."

They stood a while longer in silence, watching the swift, intricate gavotte of the dragonflies and the beetles.

The forest on either side of the river began to thin out. The barge rounded a bend, and on the riverbank on the right they saw a landing stage, and a long low building that bore the sign 'Customs House'. The barge approached, and on the wheelhouse a bell was rung.

A man in shabby work clothes emerged from the building and took the rope that was thrown to him.

"If you'll excuse me," said Bercilak, "I have business to attend to."

"Of course," said Ben, and watched as he nimbly skittered down the companionway onto the deck below.

As he did so, a contingent of well-armed men suddenly emerged from behind the customs shed and boarded the barge. Startled, Ben watched as they entered the wheelhouse beneath him and emerged with Issa Fofone, his wrists secured by manacles. Wisselus, who had been talking to his old friend, came out of the wheelhouse close behind him.

"Gentlemen, my apologies," Bercilak called out, "but I regret to inform you that the voyage will be terminating here. My name is Bercilak de Hautdesert of the Ministry of Food, and I am arresting your captain, Issa Fofone, on corruption charges relating to the transportation of tainted grain."

Ben saw Wisselus' jaw drop.

"You will necessarily have to continue your journey to Lochranza by road. The Great South Road is just a short distance in that direction." Bercilak pointed in the direction of the customs house.

Ben raced swiftly down the steps. The guards led Issa around the shed to where a horse-drawn wagon with barred windows was waiting. He was hustled inside, and the guards followed him. Bercilak climbed up beside the driver, who snapped a whip and the wagon sped away.

"Damned idiot," growled Wisselus as they returned to the barge. "Well, there's nothing for it but to get back on the road."

*****

For four more days they travelled. The wild country was well behind them now, and the road passed through farmland, villages and small towns. No longer was it necessary to camp by the roadside. They could stop each night at an inn that had a yard with high gates, and often a dog or two, to deter would-be thieves. They could sleep in warm, comfortable beds.

But nothing could prepare Ben for his first sight of the city.

In late afternoon - the sun was setting noticeably earlier now - the wagon laboured up a long steady slope. All around them were other vehicles and walkers, almost all heading in the same direction as them, up the hill, as if drawn by some unseen force beyond.

They reached the top, and Ben gasped. Wisselus drew the wagon to the side of the road and reined in the horses to allow Ben to drink in the view before them.

In the valley directly below them, the sun was glinting on water. Ben could see the Slagenbekken River, whose course they had been shadowing, and that it was flowing into another river.

"That's the River Lond over there," Wisselus explained, pointing to the second waterway.

Before them, there was a walled city. The Lond flowed through a broad, shallow arch beneath the wall, where gates had been inserted to allow river traffic to flow through, but which would be closed at night. Ben could see a number of craft that seemed to be making haste to get into the city before that happened.

He let his eye roam. The city seemed to fill the whole valley before him, its walls continuing as far as he could see, punctuated at intervals by watch towers. He could see at least two other roads leading into the city. In front of the walls, there was a ragged collection of huts, shanties and small cottages, the overspill from the metropolis within. Beyond the walls, he could see a mass of tiled roofs, with a high tower thrusting up between them here and there. In the distance, in what he judged to be the centre of the city, he could see a large, solid-looking edifice of dark stone.

"What's that?" he asked, pointing.

"That, my young Mage, is the Magisterium. Your new home. Welcome to Lochranza."

Wisselus urged the horses on. Soon the great gate loomed above them.

"This is the Mezentian Gate," said Wisselus, "Where the Great South Road reaches its destination."

They passed beneath, through a long dark tunnel, and emerged into the hubbub of the great city.

Ben looked about him. He had never seen so many people before, many of them dressed strangely, all of them appearing intent on getting where they had to go with the minimum of fuss. There seemed to be no inclination to stand idly chatting, as one might do in a village. There was a greater earnestness in their movements. He found it all exciting and a little unsettling.

Wisselus turned the wagon off the street into a yard that had a high wall around it.

"Wisselus! You're here!"

A bald, tubby man in a stained apron emerged from a doorway and came running towards them.

"Shortflatt!" Wisselus laughed, jumping down from the wagon. He threw his arms around the other man. "Yes, I'm here, thanks in large part to my friend here, Mr. Ben Troon."

Ben clambered down from the wagon, and the man called Shortflatt seized his hand and pumped it vigorously.

Shortflatt cast a quick beady eye over the wagon, and noted at once the scorch marks. "Trouble?"

"A witch named Kwepkas, but Ben here slew her. He's a Mage."

Ben quaked inwardly at the memory. He had sought to put it from his mind, but he knew it would always be there, lurking amid his memories.

"One moment," said Shortflatt, raising a stubby forefinger, and waddled away across the yard, yelling as he did so, "Cenwulf! Gifemund! Get off your lazy arses and come and unhitch the horses!"

"This is where we part company, Master Troon," said Wisselus, reaching down Ben's knapsack and his staff. He gave Ben a hug.

"How do I get to where I'm going?" Ben asked.

"Turn left out of this yard," said Wisselus, "and just keep going until you reach the water. Then you can see the Magisterium, and you say this bookshop is near the main entrance? Easy."

Two young boys, whom Ben took to be Cenwulf and Gifemund, emerged from the building, gave Wisselus a shy wave, and set about releasing the horses from the harness.

Shortflatt returned with a small leather pouch on a thong. Ben could hear the clink of coins, and began to say that payment was not necessary, but Shortflatt would have none of it. "Wages well earned," he declared. He put the thong around Ben's neck and tucked the pouch away inside his cloak where it was hidden from view. "You're in the city now," he said softly. "Take care."

"And remember," Wisselus added, "there are a lot of people here who don't like Mages."

A final handshake, a wave, and Ben was off, swallowed up in the great throng that was Lochranza.

He walked quickly, marking his paces with his staff, off about his business like a man who had lived in Lochranza all his life and knew exactly where he was going.

The sun was just setting, and it was that magical moment in the day when all is suffused with a golden aura that says all is well with the world. Shopkeepers were busy shuttering their shops for the night, and market barrows were being wheeled away to wherever it was that they passed the night hours. As he walked on through the deepening twilight, lamplighters appeared as if from holes in the ground, going from lamp to lamp, providing what minimal nocturnal illumination there was. And people hurried to get indoors quickly. Ben observed that many were well-dressed, and that the wearing of wigs was customary in these parts.

Just then, bells began ringing out, some close by, others further off, including one, far off, that sounded louder than all the rest. Some were just slightly out of time with the others. Ben counted the chimes. Six o'clock.

He was, he realised, in a place where time was measured rigorously, mechanically... It was further proof, if it were needed, that he had entered a different world.

Ben walked on, aware that he was steadily descending. It grew darker, and except around the taverns, where the nightly carousing was already distinctly audible, there were few people to be seen.

It was fully dark by the time he reached the water's edge. He could see lights reflecting in it, far off. This was not a river, he realised, but a lake, in the middle of the city, the "loch" in Lochranza.

Looking to his right, he perceived an enormous black bulk, standing in the water perhaps a hundred ells from the embankment. It was really only visible on account of the lamplit windows punctuating its tremendous walls, going up some five storeys. Ben was struck dumb. It dwarfed the buildings of the Academy: he could scarcely conceive that such an immense structure was possible, and yet there it was: the Magisterium, the heart of Magedom, in the midst of a city that was ambivalent at best where Mages were concerned.

He began walking alongside it, sensing the power it exuded and feeling very small and insignificant.

After what seemed an eternity of walking parallel to its walls, glimpsing figures moving within the illuminated rooms on the ground floor, heightening his curiosity about what went on within, he came to what was clearly the main entrance.

There was a bridge leading across the water from where Ben was standing. In sharp contrast to the solidity of the edifice, the bridge appeared spindly, fragile almost. Recalling what Wisselus had said about the unpopularity of Mages, Ben had the impression that the people might, if they chose, sever this tenuous link with the mainland and send the island on which the Magisterium rested floating away out of their lives.

At this point, the building stood further back from the water's edge, so that there was an open space, a courtyard, to be crossed before reaching the entrance doors. Anyone approaching the doors would be clearly observed and, he supposed, dealt with as necessary. As Ben stood looking across the bridge, he saw a movement at one of the windows beside the gate, and realised he was being watched.

He moved away, and as he did so, he heard the striking of a tremendous bell in the darkness above him. It made him jump. Moments later, he heard other bells chime in, at a distance, but their sound was lost in the sonorous roar coming from above him. He looked up and tried to make out the clock tower, but could only define it by the absence of stars at that point in the sky.

The huge echoing bell struck seven.

He walked on, and suddenly became aware of the sounds of music and merriment. On the far side of the street running along the water's edge, he saw the lighted windows of a tavern. He walked across to it and read the name on the shingle above the entrance: *The Five Bells and Blade Bone*.

Two men brushed past him and entered. As they crossed the threshold, one turned to him, holding the door open. Ben saw within a bright fire in the fireplace, and men and women clutching tankards of ale, laughing and singing.

"Coming in?" asked the man holding the door.

It was an enticing prospect, but Ben had other business. He had to make the acquaintance of this Ailsa Bleakwill, and thought he should not delay too long in the dark in this unknown metropolis.

"No," said Ben, shaking his head. "Thank you."

The men entered the tavern and Ben walked on. There was a row of shops, a small restaurant, a bakery, an ironmonger…

And then there it was. The bookshop. A lamp lit beside the door cast its light upwards over faded, peeling yellow paint, which bore the words 'Bleakwill's Bookshop'. The shop was in darkness, but there was light visible in a window on an upper floor.

Beside the door was a brass bell mounted on a bracket. Underneath was a plaque which bore the single word 'Welcome'.

"Well," said Ben to himself, "here goes." He set down his pack on the pavement and leaned his staff against the wall.

He took the bell-cord in his hand and rang the bell.

Almost at once, the lighted window opened and a silhouetted head and shoulders appeared, which Ben took to be female from the sweep of long hair falling down over the shoulders.

"Leo? Is that you?" called a woman's voice. Ben was surprised that it sounded so youthful, not at all the croaking of a crone that he had anticipated.

"My name is Ben Troon," he called up. "Gr... Styrmir sent me. From Dundonald."

"The Mage!" the woman shouted excitedly. Ben glanced around nervously to see if anyone could hear. "You've arrived! Wait there! I'll come down!"

The window closed. Ben heard the rattle of hurried footsteps on stairs. There was the clatter of locks being undone, and then the door flew open and a female figure threw herself into his arms, locking him in a warm embrace. Ben inhaled a heady, almost intoxicating perfume.

She released him at last and stood back. She was certainly no crone. Youthful, of medium height, her raven-black hair was parted simply in the middle, falling over her shoulders and framing an oval face that featured a pair of glistening dark brown eyes that flitted over him, taking in his appearance with evident satisfaction, a pert nose that was decidedly wart-free, and a pair of full, sensuous lips that were curved upwards in a welcoming smile, and in their turn creased a pair of dimples in her cheeks.

She was wearing a close-fitting dress of dark blue samite with swirls of silver thread woven through it, over the top of a white linen under-dress. The samite was secured at the shoulders with a pair of oval silver brooches, between which were strung three rows of beads of glass, cornelian, rock crystal and silver, and around her slim waist she wore a fine silver chain-link belt from which an assortment of keys hung on their own small silver chains.

For an instant, Ben felt his heart flutter.

"Are you… Ailsa Bleakwill?" he asked hesitantly.

"Yes, of course," she replied. "Who did you think I was?"

"It's just… you weren't quite what I was expecting."

A black eyebrow arched itself. "And what *were* you expecting?"

Ben fumbled for his pack. "Oh, it doesn't matter!"

"Indeed!" said Ailsa gaily. "Come in, come in!"

She led him inside and up a narrow flight of stairs. Ben tried not to notice the pert wiggle of her bottom as she did so. Every step on the dimly lit staircase was piled with books, and more piles of books seemed to occupy every spare corner that he could see. Picking his way cautiously up the steps, he followed her to the first floor, and into a living room that appeared to double as a study, library, dining room, and who knew what else besides. In the centre of the room was a table surrounded by chairs, and around the walls were large, comfy-looking armchairs in front of crammed bookshelves that reached from floor to ceiling. In one corner was a door leading to what appeared to be a kitchen, and there were two windows set into the wall facing him, surrounded on all sides by bookcases. Still more piles of books were on the floor and one or two of the armchairs. One small space at floor level was not filled with books. Instead it was occupied by a marbled cat that eyed him for a moment as he entered, then went back to sleep.

Following the direction of his gaze, Ailsa said, "That's Cairbre."

"Delighted," said Ben.

Ailsa took his pack and threw it on a vacant armchair, then put his staff in a corner. She took his cloak and bonnet and placed them with the pack, then pulled out a dining chair. "Please, make yourself at home. After all, this is to be your home for the foreseeable future." Ben sat. "I'll get you some tea, while I put on something for you to eat. You must be hungry, thirsty and tired."

She went into the kitchen. Ben suddenly realised that he was all of these things.

While he waited, Ben looked around. He saw that Ailsa had cleared a space on the cluttered table, and was working at something by the light of an oil lamp. Curiosity got the better of him and he got up and walked around the table to see what it was that she was doing.

There was a sheet of parchment pinned to a baseboard, and next to it an inkwell and a pen with a very fine nib. On the parchment was a drawing. A seabird, with exquisitely graceful outstretched wings hung over a rocky coastline, while a wild sea tossed in the background. In tiny writing on one of the lichen-covered rocks in the foreground was the artist's name: Ailsa.

Ben stood staring at it for a long time. He could almost feel the wind blowing through his hair. It was superbly executed.

In time he drew himself away, and began to wander around the room. There was not much on the shelves apart from books, but here and there he found some intriguing little treasures. Small stones, worn smooth as if in a river, were painted with runes, brightly coloured, with quirky little decorative details around them. He saw Ailsa's hand in these too.

He was holding one in his hand, examining it with curiosity and delight, when Ailsa returned with a tray bearing a teapot and two mugs. With one hand she pushed aside a mound of yellowing papers and books to make a space. Some of them fell to the floor. Putting the runestone back on its shelf, Ben hastened to pick them up.

"Thank you," said Ailsa. "I'm afraid the place gets terribly messy."

"Your work is beautiful," said Ben, finding a new place for the errant papers.

"My…? Oh, the stones!"

"And this," Ben said, gesturing towards the drawing.

"Oh, thank you," Ailsa smiled. "I find it very fulfilling. It takes me away from the troubles of the world. Now, tea."

She poured tea into a mug and handed it to Ben, who had seated himself at the table once more. He lifted it to drink, and was at once enveloped in a delightful fragrance.

"What kind of tea is this?" he asked.

"It's called Monk Pear," Ailsa replied. "It comes from a place far in the south of Laurentia, further even than Quaama."

Laurentia: the great continental land mass that lay across a narrow sea from Luthany and Magelaw. It seemed impossibly far away, but now here he was drinking this tea that had grown there. It was all so exotic.

"Well," said Ailsa, seating herself across from him, "dinner won't be long, but we might as well start while we're waiting. Tell me all about yourself, Ben Troon. Where you were born, your family, how you came to the Academy. What's it like there? I've never been."

And so Ben began to tell his story, about his mysterious origins, his being found in the coracle, his life with Halldis and Hasupada, his impressions of the Academy, and so on. He was just about to come to his meeting with Bliss when Ailsa stopped him.

"I think dinner should be ready by now," she said. "Could you make some space on the table? Just pop everything onto one of the armchairs. Or on the floor. I'll sort it out later."

Ben did as he was bid.

Ailsa returned from the kitchen with two plates of some sort of vegetable mixture, and two tankards of ale. They sat down to eat.

Ben took a mouthful. "This is really good," he said. "What is it?"

"It's called chole*. It's made from chickpeas with onions, tomatoes and spices, particularly Grains of Paradise."

"I'm familiar with onions," said Ben with a laugh. "The rest is new to me."

"Well, the Quaamans did introduce us to a lot of new things. Tomatoes wouldn't grow where you are, they need more sun."

"Ah ha," said Ben, and continued eating heartily.

When his plate was empty, he pushed it away with a grateful sigh and took another swig of tea.

"More?" Ailsa asked.

"Herne, no," said Ben. "I'm full."

"Not too full for dessert, I hope."

"Dessert? Goodness!" Ben gasped.

Ailsa went back into the kitchen and returned with a large bowl, a pair of smaller ones, a couple of small pots and some spoons.

"Saffron rice pudding with whipped cream and dewberry jam," Ailsa said, spooning the golden pudding from the larger bowl into the smaller ones, and then adding jam and cream from the pots. "I trust it's to your liking?"

"I have never tasted such delights," Ben declared, spooning it into himself with gusto, "but yes, it is most certainly to my liking!"

In almost no time, he had polished off firsts, seconds and thirds.

"I have a sitting room upstairs," Ailsa said, when he was done, "where we can be more comfortable. If you'd care to join me?"

"Certainly," said Ben, following her up more book-laden steps to the floor above.

Ailsa gestured to the door at one end of the passage. "That's your room along there," she told him. "We'll make your bed up in a little while. And that," she went on, pointing to the other end of the passage, "is my room. And this, between them, is the sitting room."

They entered a small, cosy room, largely filled with capacious armchairs and lit by a blazing fire in the fireplace. Here there were fewer books and more pictures, mostly landscapes, which Ben now recognised as being Ailsa's own work.

From a small cupboard in one corner, Ailsa produced a bottle and two elegant glasses. "Metheglin*?"

"Oh yes, that's like hydromel, isn't it?"

"Yes." Ailsa poured two generous measures and passed one to Ben. They clinked glasses. "To your safe arrival," she smiled. "Sláinte*!"

"Sláinte!" Ben replied. He sipped the drink. It was delicious and warming, and went down very well. For a brief moment he recalled the last woman who had plied him with strong drink, but an inner voice told him he had to stop thinking that every unattached woman was out to have her way with him. "Mmmm. It's very good," he beamed.

"Sit yourself down," Ailsa urged, "and tell me all about your journey."

Ben began to tell his tale. He hesitated when he got to the part about Vitka, but then he decided that concealing what had happened between them served no purpose, and so he told Ailsa about the potion.

"I'm not about to do that to you, by the way," Ailsa interjected as he spoke.

"That's a relief," he answered. He made it sound like a joke, but it wasn't.

He started to pick up the threads of his tale again, but was interrupted by the loud booming of the bell across the street.

"It's that bell again," Ben said loudly over the din.

"Great Tom, striking eight o'clock," Ailsa explained.

"Horns of Herne!" Ben exclaimed. "Does it do that all night?"

"Only till midnight," Ailsa reassured him. "Then we get some peace until seven in the morning."

Ben went to the window and looked out, but beyond the lighted windows he could see nothing of the Magisterium, just across the road.

He returned to his chair, and when the clock had finished striking, he resumed his account of his travels.

He was just getting to his account of meeting Wisselus when the bell began striking again. "Now what?"

"Ten minutes past eight," said Ailsa. "The bell strikes a hundred and five times to recall the hundred and five original Mages who made up the Magisterium, centuries ago. It is said that the first Archmage, or Lord of Stones, as he was then known, a man named Kapnobatai, chose the island there in the lake as the place for the Samildánach, or conclave of the Mages, but to build the Magisterium he embezzled the money from his master, King Cuneglassus, and paid for that with his head."

"I see," said Ben. "Not an auspicious start for the Magisterium."

"Indeed not," Ailsa agreed, "but we have put all that behind us and moved on."

"I notice you say 'we'," said Ben. "So you are a Mage yourself?"

"Sort of an associate Mage," Ailsa told him. "I don't have the full powers of a Mage. But the Bleakwills have always been the purveyors of books to the Magisterium."

"Embezzlement, eh?" Ben mused. "I thought Mages were supposed to be above all that venal stuff."

"They're supposed to be, yes," Bliss conceded. "But we do have our fallen angels, so to speak."

When Great Tom had finished his hundred and five chimes, Ben continued his story, telling Ailsa all about the battle on the bridge, and then the events that had marked the remainder of the journey. Ailsa listened intently, refilling Ben's glass and her own from time to time.

Before he knew it, the bell was striking ten. Ben could not suppress a yawn.

"Come on," said Ailsa. "We'd best make up your bed. We've got a big day tomorrow."

"We do?"

"Well, *you* do. You'll have to gain entry to the Magisterium, and then go through the process of induction."

"Gain entry?"

"You'll see. You'll need to bring your staff, and be prepared to use it."

"As a...?"

"As a weapon. I'm not supposed to tell you anything."

Ailsa went into the room she had identified as Ben's, and pulled bedding from a chest at the foot of the bed. He looked around. It was comfortably furnished, with its own privy in an alcove, and a mansard window. Easing the curtain aside, Ben saw only the lighted windows of the Magisterium.

While she was sorting out the bedding, Ben gave the mattress a gentle prod. The softness betokened feathers rather than rough plant matter, and the mattress was covered in a wool twill material.

Ailsa put down a linen underlayer, then a striped twill overblanket, followed by a top layer in a piled weave fabric. The pillows were of feather down, in cases of linen diamond twill.

"There," she said, hands on hips, when she had made the bed to her satisfaction. "You should sleep well in that."

"I certainly will," Ben agreed.

"Good night, then."

She gave him an affectionate peck on the cheek, and slipped out, closing the door behind her.

Ben got undressed and climbed into the bed. It was the most comfortable he had ever known, and he wriggled happily, content to have reached journey's end.

His last thought as he drifted into sleep was that he would have so much to tell Bliss when he wrote to her.

CHAPTER FOURTEEN.

The morning light, when it filtered through his curtains, was grey and uninviting. He was awoken by Great Tom striking seven.

*****

In a corner of the room was a washstand. He poured some water from the ewer into the basin and washed his face. The water was icy, but he was quite used to that.

Standing up straight he gave a start. There was a mirror on the wall, and he had seen himself for the first time with a beard. It was coming along quite nicely, he thought, giving it an affectionate stroke.

"It's almost Nosgalan*, Winter's Eve," Ailsa told him over breakfast when he commented on the weather. "That's why I was worried you wouldn't get here before the storms began.

"Winter's Eve?" asked Ben.

"What you would call Samhain," Ailsa explained. "It will be your first ceremony at the Magisterium."

"Why don't *you* call it Samhain?"

"Smacks too much of Magecraft for many people's taste here. We have to be a bit careful. And in any case, Luthany has a slightly different calendar. Some of the names of the months are different."

"Such as?"

"Well, the month which begins straight after Nosgalan is called Anagantios*, which means the month of inability to leave the house. You, of course, will pay no heed to that, as you will be leaving the house many, many times, between pursuing your studies and earning your keep doing bookshop business."

"I see," said Ben, scraping the last of the porridge from his bowl.

"Have you finished your tea?"

"I have," said Ben. He was beginning to get rather a taste for Monk Pear.

"Well then," said Ailsa, pulling a battered leather cloak from a hook on the door and wrapping it around herself, "time's a-wasting. Here!" She tossed Ben his staff. "Let the business of the day begin. And may the old gods favour us with good fortune." She fastened the cloak with a pin that matched those on her dress, and hastened down the stairs.

Ben had barely time to pop his bonnet on his head before following her.

They went downstairs and out into the street. Ailsa hung a sign on the front door which said simply, '*Back in the Foreseeable Future*', locked it and slipped the key into a pocket in her cloak. Stepping out briskly, she led Ben towards the entrance to the Magisterium.

It was Ben's first opportunity to study the imposing edifice in the light of day. Its size, he saw at once, dwarfed even the Academy at Dundonald, the largest building he had known hitherto. It was essentially a rectangle, occupying the full length and breadth of the small island in the lake, and it was several storeys high. Over the gateway arose the clock tower containing the bell, Great Tom. It was surmounted by an ornate, onion-shaped dome, flanked at its corners by smaller turrets adorned with miniature onion domes, which suggested that it was a later addition tacked on to the original fortress-like edifice. The clock said it was a quarter to eight.

As they crossed over the narrow bridge, Ailsa dropped back, allowing Ben to advance ahead of her. He stepped onto the flagstones in front of the entrance, and two imposing figures clad in short black tunics, black pants and high black boots emerged carrying quarterstaffs, which they crossed, barring his way.

"Name and purpose!" demanded one.

"My name is Ben Troon," Ben replied, trying not to let his voice quiver, "and I have come to the Magisterium to further my studies as a Mage."

"Then you must come through me!" declared one of the two guards, stepping forward a pace while the other withdrew into the shadow of the building. He took hold of his staff at its centre and twirled it, windmill-fashion, so that the air hummed, and it spun so fast that it was barely visible. Then he rotated it over one shoulder, around his back, then over the other shoulder, in a bewildering display.

"Defend yourself!" he commanded, and suddenly ran at Ben.

Ben barely had time to react, bringing his staff up just in time to parry a blow from the other that jarred his arms, and then suddenly he was swinging his staff this way and that to fend off blow after blow. All the while he could see deadly earnest in the steely blue gaze of the other man. This was no exercise. The man clearly meant to do him serious harm, if not kill him.

Ben told himself that he had not come all this way, fought a witch, and pushed Wisselus' wagon out of umpteen muddy quagmires, just to fall at the first hurdle, within the shadow of the Magisterium itself. But, he recognised, it called for more than simply parrying the other man's blows. He would have to lay a few of his own, and began to look for openings.

Gathering his resolve, he began to fight back, trying desperately to recall all that he had been taught by Mage Semjaza. His hands were placed an ell apart, gripping the staff from either side, and he danced lightly across the stones, diving this way and that, trying to make his moves as unpredictable as possible. Co-ordination of eye, hand and foot were the key. He furiously raised his weapon to fend off blows from above, from the sides, from below. With lightning speed, he swung the staff, striking with alternate ends, and managed to get in a few blows on his opponent's arms, but it never seemed to be enough.

Then he managed to get in a heavy blow that connected with the other man's ribs, momentarily winding him, and in an elegant follow-through, Ben swung the staff through a broad arc so that the opposite end came around instantly and smashed against the side of the guard's head, laying him out on the stones.

Ben took a step back as the other guard came and crouched over his comrade. From a pouch on his belt he took out a small mirror and held it to the other man's mouth.

"Is he…?" Ben struggled to bring the words out. He saw again Bassewitz stretched out on the ground.

"He lives," said the guard. "He will recover in due course."

Ben stiffened. Was he now expected to fight the second guard?

"Well fought, Ben Troon," said the other man, looking up at him, and a broad grin cracked open across his weathered face. "Welcome to the Magisterium. You may enter at will."

Ben and Ailsa passed through a dark tunnel, where the only real illumination was the window of the porter's lodge.

Ailsa pointed to the honeycomb of boxes affixed to the wall alongside the window. "See these pigeon holes?" she said. "Always look in the one marked with a 'T', for there may be letters in there for you."

Ben nodded. They emerged into the light, such as it was on that dull morning. As they did so, Great Tom above them struck eight o'clock.

They were in a spacious quadrangle, with a raised walkway around the perimeter, within cloisters that faced the walls of the building on the first two storeys. The walkway was interrupted only where they were standing to accommodate a carriageway which ran around the edge of the quadrangle within the cloisters. At the four corners were fortified towers from which it would be possible to fire on intruders.

In the middle of the quadrangle was a circular pool, in the centre of which was an enormous bronze statue of a dragon, perhaps five ells in height, sitting on its haunches like a dog. One foreclaw was resting on its knee while the other held up a pearlescent sphere, from the top of which a fountain bubbled, dropping a continuous circle of raindrops into the pool below.

Ben put his hand on Ailsa's arm. "That man, that guard…" he began, jerking his head backwards towards the tunnel, as if there could be any doubt as to the man he was alluding to. "I nearly killed him."

"Yes," said Ailsa calmly. "You fought well. I'm proud of you."

"On the other hand, I thought he was going to kill me."

"He certainly meant to. Or at the very least to seriously injure you."

"Why?" Ben asked, perplexed. "What is the purpose?"

Ailsa turned to him, took him firmly by the arm, and looked into his eyes with those intense, liquid-brown orbs of hers. "Ben," she said, "You have to understand. We have become an oppressed minority. When you were taught stick-fighting at the Academy, it wasn't just for the exercise. You have to be able to defend yourself, or else you are no use to us."

"I see," said Ben. He was beginning to.

"Look around you," Ailsa went on. "This place was designed as much as a fortress as a centre of learning."

Ben saw that it was true.

They walked over to the pool. Ben saw that there were ornamental fish swimming in it.

"It is known as the Pool of the Wise," Ailsa told him. "Draigh Maae, the dragon, holds the pearl of wisdom, to which we must all aspire."

"Wisdom," Ben echoed, a little mournfully. "I doubt if I will ever achieve that."

"It comes at the end of a lifetime," Ailsa observed, "if it comes at all. But certainly a first step is knowing how little you know, and how very much there is still to be known. A good dose of humility helps, too."

"Let's be on our way," said Ailsa. "We have a lot to do, and I'd like to get back to the shop as soon as possible."

They entered a passageway and came out in another quadrangle only slightly less grand than the first. A shallow circular ditch contained within it a circle of stone slabs, into which were set gold letters and symbols, indicating all the points of the compass, the places of rising and setting of the sun at the solstices and the equinoxes, and a variety of arcane symbols, some of which Ben recognised, others he did not.

"There are four of these open spaces," Ailsa told him. "You will no doubt be familiar with every corner of this place before you are done."

She led him into a staircase and up to a higher floor. They stepped out into an arcaded gallery, from which Ben could look down at the henge below.

"It feels strangely warm in here," he remarked, "compared to outside."

"The hypocaust fires have obviously been lit," said Ailsa as they began to walk along the gallery. "Another sure sign that winter is coming on."

"Hypocausts?"

"A legacy of the Quaamans," Ailsa replied. "They certainly did leave us a few useful things. Roads, a legal system, central heating… Fires are lit in the basement, and the warm air is carried through a network of tunnels underneath the floors, and up through the walls, to steadily warm the building. It is very clever."

Ben gestured out of the windows they were passing. "What is the function of all these buildings? They can't all be for teaching, surely."

"Some are lecture rooms, certainly, but there are rooms dedicated to particular ceremonies, there are the dormitories where your less fortunate fellow students sleep, there are kitchens, armouries, and all sorts of other rooms. As well, of course, as the offices of the senior Mages."

And with that she halted and rapped on a door. Ben saw that the name-plate on the door read: *Mage Noaidi: Intendant of Shavelings.*

"What's a shaveling?" Ben asked, but Ailsa had already opened the door and passed inside.

A thin man with lank grey hair flowing down over his shoulders and half-moon spectacles perched on a beaky nose was writing at a desk under a window, and looked up to see who his visitors were.

"Ailsa!" he beamed. "Delighted to see you!" He rose, came round the desk, and gave her an affectionate hug. He then looked past her at Ben. "And this must be Mage Troon, whom we have been expecting to join us." He hesitated. "I presume, since he's here, that he…"

"He knocked Gondlir unconscious."

"Good show!" Mage Noaidi enthused. "That's what we like to hear!" And he shook Ben vigorously by the hand, the strength of his grip taking Ben by surprise. "Welcome, Mage Troon. Welcome to the Magisterium. Now, let's get all the business out of the way, and you can commence your studies."

He turned to a shelf on which there were a number of rolled sheets of parchment, each tied with a red ribbon and with a small label attached, upon which a name was written. He sorted through them until he found the right one, and handed it to Ben with a flourish.

"This is your certificate of matriculation," Mage Noaidi told him. "You aren't anything in this world until you have a piece of parchment that says you are what you claim to be. Now, you are living under Ailsa's roof, so your accommodation is all taken care of. I dare say she will feed you well, but there are several refectories in various parts of the Magisterium, should you wish to take advantage of them, and anyone here will direct you to them, especially as a shaveling."

"What's a shaveling?" asked Ben.

Mage Noaidi glanced at Ailsa. "Oh, you haven't told him?" he said with a faint smile. "Well, that's the next order of business. Come along."

And he swept out of the office and along the gallery at a sprightly pace, leaving Ben and Ailsa to follow in his wake as best they could.

A short distance away, Mage Noaidi entered another room. "I have a customer for you, Wiggod."

Ben entered behind the Mage, with Ailsa at his heels. The room, he saw, was well lit, but largely bare, with no floor covering, and chairs lined up along the walls. A larger, more comfortable-looking chair occupied the centre of the room, with a small table placed alongside it. On the table was a box containing scissors, razors and shaving brushes. Alongside was a bowl of what Ben took to be shaving soap, and from the side of the table hung a leather strop. It was, evidently, a barber's shop.

Wiggod, a man of middling height, with a slight paunch and a neatly trimmed grey beard, was sweeping hair clippings into a neat pile in one corner of the room. He looked up as the newcomers entered, and put his broom to one side.

"Mage Noaidi," he smiled, "what can I do for you?"

"We have a new shaveling," Mage Noaidi told him, gesturing towards Ben.

"Aha. Would this be the gentleman from the far north?"

"It would indeed," said the Mage. "Please take care of him in your regular fashion."

Ben found it a little unsettling that so many people seemed to know of him, and to have been awaiting his arrival.

"That I will do," Wiggod assured the Mage. Turning to Ben, he indicated the chair in the centre of the room. "Please, take a seat, Mr... ah..."

"Troon," said Ben. "Ben Troon."

Behind him, Mage Noaidi swept from the room, while Ailsa sat on one of the chairs against the wall, positioning herself where Ben could easily see her, to offer him encouragement.

Ben sat himself down in the big chair. Wiggod produced a cloth which he wrapped around Ben's shoulders. He whisked off Ben's bonnet and tossed it to Ailsa. Smoothing the mollymawk feather, she settled it in her lap.

Brandishing a businesslike pair of scissors, Wiggod began snipping off Ben's hair. Ben sighed. It seemed he had only just got back a decent head of hair after the Ceremony of the Three Fires, and now here he was having to lose it all again.

Suddenly he remembered his beard. His hand went reflexively to his newly hirsute jaw. "What about this?" he said, suddenly alarmed.

"The beard can stay," Wiggod reassured him. "Though it might look a bit strange. With nothing up above it."

"I can live with that. How long do I have to keep my head shaved?" Ben asked, as Wiggod slopped shaving soap onto his bared scalp.

"Oh, we only do this the once," Wiggod replied. "It marks you out as a newcomer, a… what is your word?"

"A wyffen," said Ben.

"A wyffen. Precisely. Then everyone here knows your status, even if they haven't seen you before, and they know that you are unfamiliar with the Magisterium, and will help you out. Over time, your hair grows back, and by that time everyone knows who you are anyway. And then you cut your hair every seven years. Cut, mind you, not shave."

As he spoke, Wiggod drew a razor from the box beside him and gave it a few quick strokes on the leather strop. Then he began working over Ben's pate, taking off every last vestige of stubble. He worked quickly and efficiently, and in very little time he was finished. He wiped the last of the soap away and held up a mirror for Ben to inspect himself.

Ben didn't generally spend a lot of time looking in the mirror, but he had a certain idea of what he looked like, and the person looking back at him from the mirror seemed like a complete stranger. His appearance was a bit odd, he conceded, a bit like a bearded egg. Was that the intentional result, he wondered, to make him seem to be a different person?

He examined his naked scalp, so bare and pink and vulnerable, the contours of the skull beneath so plainly mapped out.

"It's going to be a cold winter," he observed.

Wiggod glanced across at the bonnet in Ailsa's lap. "I dare say you will be permitted to wear headgear out of doors," he commented. Ailsa smiled and nodded.

"That's good," said Ben, rising from the chair.

"Welcome, Mr. Troon." Said Wiggod, extending a hand. Ben shook it.

"Thank you."

Ailsa gave Ben his bonnet, which he held in his hand. As they left, Wiggod was already reaching for his broom to add Ben's locks to his growing pile.

"Where now?" asked Ben as they set off along the gallery.

"Back to Mage Noaidi's office," said Ailsa. "He will give you your study timetable, the times of your lectures and tutorials, and a reading list, although I already know what's on that, and can fix you up back at the shop."

As they walked, Great Tom struck nine. Ben had passed his first hour in the Magisterium.

*****

 Duly equipped with the timetable and reading list, Ailsa and Ben returned to the shop. Ailsa whizzed around, pulling books off from various shelves while Cairbre watched with bemusement.

At the shopkeeper's post in the middle of the shop, Ailsa settled Ben in with his pile of books, and briefly initiated him into the essentials of running the shop.

"Every book has the price pencilled on the flyleaf," she explained. "When you make a sale, you simply write the title in the record book, here." She indicated a large ledger on the desk, bound in black leather, with a red ribbon to mark the page, and an inkwell and pens. "Lock the door if you want to make some lunch, or if you need to visit the privy. I have a little Magecraft business to attend to. I'll be back this afternoon." She gave him a peck on the cheek. "So glad you're here," she said as she walked towards the door. "It's been really difficult without an assistant."

And then she was gone. Ben wondered about her Magecraft business, but realised it would be pointless, and probably rude, to pry into her affairs.

He opened the ledger and examined the entries, all written in what he came to recognise was Ailsa's florid, elegant handwriting. The handwriting of an artist, he thought. The books were on all manner of subjects, from the 'Lacnunga*', or 'Manuscript of Healing', to the 'Rule of Chrodegang', or 'Book of Correct Behaviour'. He inspected the pens, and almost without thinking, pulled the little penknife from its receptacle alongside the inkwell, and trimmed the nibs down to the finest point he could manage.

He was still focussed on this task when the doorbell rang, and a sprightly, elfin-looking man of advanced years swept into the shop and, advancing to the desk, inspected him with sharp blue eyes.

"Ah," he said with a note of satisfaction, "the new shaveling."

Reflexively, Ben's hand went to his denuded cranium. "Ben Troon at your service," he declared. "How may I help you?"

"Mage Vitolfus at yours. I believe you will be attending my classes from next week." He extended a thin hand covered in liver spots, and Ben shook it.

He shuffled through the papers on the desk in front of him until he found the timetable. He sought out the Mage's name. "Ah yes," he said, "Mage Vitolfus, 'Advanced Healing Magecraft'."

Mage Vitolfus looked through the stack of books on the desk, pulled out one hefty tome and repositioned it on the top of the pile. Ben saw that it was 'The Leechbook* of Bald'.

"Best you start your reading with this one," Vitolfus told him, patting the tome affectionately. "The healer's most important work of reference. Now, as for how you can help me, I am seeking the Lacnunga of Sváfnir the Sleep-bringer, but since you are new, and I know where Ailsa keeps the leechbooks, it is probably more a case of me helping myself."

"Very well," said Ben. The logic was irrefutable.

Vitolfus made his way to a particular corner of the shop, as if he had trodden that path many times, and cast his eye over the shelves. Ben followed him with his eye, eager to learn as quickly as possible where different kinds of books might be found. Vitolfus muttered as he perused the volumes so, and occasionally uttered a more audible remark along the lines of "Oh, she has *that* one! Ah well, next time!"

Finally, he made a grunt of what Ben took to be satisfaction as he found the volume he was looking for. He brought it to the desk.

Ben looked on the flyleaf. "That will be five mancus*," he said.

"Worth every fyrk*," Vitolfus agreed. From a purse on his belt, he drew out five gold coins. Ben was not sure how Luthanian money related to that of Magelaw, but it looked like a remarkable amount of money. As Ben popped the coins into the cash box, Vitolfus glanced at the open ledger. "Am I your first customer?" he asked.

"You are indeed," Ben replied.

"Oh good!" exclaimed Vitolfus, clearly delighted. "Until next week, then," he said cheerily, tucking the book under his arm. "Don't be late!"

As he left the shop, the bell chiming, Ben picked up his newly trimmed pen, dipped it in the inkwell, and made his first entry in the ledger.

When all was quiet, he locked the shop and made himself some bread and cheese and a pot of tea, and opened the 'Leechbook of Bald'.

In the course of the afternoon, he sold complete booklists to two students, an angular youth of medium height with lank brown hair that flopped into his eyes, who introduced himself as Henric Forbus, and a short, friendly fellow with fair hair and an amiable smile, who said his name was Onund Treefeet, and a book of the Ephemerides* to a sallow-skinned, unsmiling man who identified himself as Mage Simeon.

When Ailsa returned in the late afternoon, she was well pleased with how he had fared. She looked at the ledger.

"Goodness!" she gasped. "What wonderfully neat, petite handwriting you have!"

"It has been remarked upon from time to time," Ben conceded modestly. "But yours is prettier."

Ailsa smiled sweetly. "Bless you. Now, I was thinking that we would go and have a celebratory dinner at the *Five Bells and Blade Bone*. In a wee while, after we've closed up."

"That sounds good," said Ben.

*****

The *Five Bells and Blade Bone* was packed to the doors when Ben and Ailsa made their entrance. Ben quickly scanned the room. There were bewigged men who looked to be too hot in their perruques, and a goodly few dark green cloaks were in evidence, Mages for certain, and a number of younger men and women whom he took to be students, one or two he felt sure he had spotted about the Magisterium, and a few who were sporting mere stubble on their heads, thus shavelings barely more advanced in their studies than himself. He suddenly felt much more at ease.

"I see we are amongst friends," he remarked, as Ailsa began shouldering her way through the crush in the general direction of the bar. He had to struggle to make himself heard above the raucous din of a hundred alcohol-fuelled conversations going on around him.

"Well, yes," Ailsa agreed. "So close to the Magisterium, there will be many of our kind. There is certainly safety in numbers here. In other parts of the city, it would be unwise to enter taverns at all, but I will tell you about them before I send you out on errands."

They reached the bar, which was a magnificent sight, perhaps twenty ells in length, of dark, glossy timber, with four large vats of ale and metheglin ranked behind, each furnished with a tap of gleaming brass. To either side were shelves lined with a bewildering assortment of bottles containing liquors of almost all the colours of the rainbow, many of which Ben felt he had no hope of even identifying. In one corner was a stand with hooks, on which hung individual tankards, each of which had above it a small handwritten label naming the owner. Hanging above the bar in ascending order of size were the five brass bells, and next to them the enormous shoulder blade bone of an ox. Ben made a mental note to ask, at some appropriate time, about their significance. But for the moment, that would have to wait, as their presence had been noted by the landlady, Mrs. Fiddymort.

To say she was large would have been a polite understatement. She looked to Ben like a lorcha* under full sail that he had once seen in a book. Her bright, round, rosy-cheeked, blue-eyed and scarlet-lipped face was surrounded by a cascade of blonde kiss-curls, and a bouffant abundance of more of the same had been piled up in picturesque disorder on the crown of her head. But all male eyes in the room were irresistibly drawn to the huge expanse of bared bosom that preceded the rest of her, her lace trimmed décolletage of dark blue satin cut so low as to leave precious little to the imagination. And she was making a bee-line for the two of them.

"Ailsa!" she exclaimed when within hailing distance. "How lovely to see you again!"

Ailsa smiled. "But it's only been a few days!"

"No matter, no matter!" Mrs. Fiddymort enthused. "I always miss you when you aren't here!"

"Ben, this is Mrs. Fiddymort, landlady of the *Five Bells and Blade Bone*. 'Mrs. Fiddymort, this is Ben Troon…"

"Well, aren't you the woman of mystery?" Mrs. Fiddymort gushed. "It seems to me you have a different man in tow every time you come in here! And so young, this one! You, cradle-snatcher, you!"

Ben glanced at Ailsa, and she glanced back at him, forcing a nervous smile. It could have been a trick of the light, Ben thought, but he would swear that she was blushing.

"That's another little thing I must chat to you about," she said quietly. Turning to the landlady, she said, "Mrs. Fiddymort, I was about to say, this is Ben Troon, and he's a new student across the road. He's also my new assistant in the shop. He's *not*, well…"

Mrs. Fiddymort's chubby, ring-encrusted fingers went to her lips. "Oh, Ailsa! Have I spoken out of turn?"

Ailsa smiled. "No, no, not really."

Relief swept across the tavern mistress's features. "Oh good! Now, what can I get you?"

"We're celebrating Ben's first day as a shaveling," Ailsa explained. "We would like a bottle of the usual, and whatever is best on your menu." She glanced around. "*If we can find a free table!*"

"Don't you trouble about that," said Mrs. Fiddymort with a theatrical wink. She approached a small corner table where two men were drinking quietly, and leant over to speak to them, giving them ample time to ogle her womanly charms as she did so. Ben was unable to hear what she said, but the two men, seemingly mesmerised, eagerly rose and found themselves another corner in which to drink and talk.

Ben and Ailsa took the men's places at the table, and had barely settled in before Mrs. Fiddymort was back with a bottle of metheglin and two glasses.

"Might I suggest the venison hotpot?" she said. "It's especially good tonight."

"That sounds excellent," said Ailsa. "For two."

"I'll bring you something to nibble on while you're waiting," the landlady added. She hurried away.

"She seems to like you very much," Ben observed when she had gone.

"I'm something of a regular here," Ailsa acknowledged, "as you might have gathered. And I encourage most of the students to eat here."

"I see," said Ben.

"Most of the people you see here practice the Craft in one way or another," Ailsa went on.

Mrs. Fiddymort returned with the first course. "Deep fried cheese balls," she announced, placing the plate in the middle of the table, then swished away. Ben could not help a glance at her ample derrière as she did so.

He turned his attention to the dish on the table. The cheese balls resembled nothing so much as oversized rabbit turds. He speared one with his fork and it flew through the air, landing on the floor and skittering under a neighbouring table. Ben cursed softly, grateful that the occupants of the table had failed to notice.

Ailsa pressed her fingers down on another ball. "Now try," she said.

Ben speared the ball, successfully this time, while Ailsa licked the grease from her fingertips and turned her attention to the bottle of metheglin. They looked into each other's eyes and laughed together.

"Perhaps I should use the Craft on these cheese balls," Ben muttered.

Ailsa's expression grew serious once more. "Don't even think about it," she said earnestly. "The Craft is not a toy. Avoid using it in public at all costs."

"I wasn't serious," Ben told her, chastened.

"I know, but sometimes it can be very tempting."

"Now, what was this little thing you wanted to chat about?"

Ailsa's cheeks coloured again. "Ah, well, the thing is..." she began. "I do have a few men friends, and they often stay the night. I expect that sometimes you will hear... things."

Ben nodded. "Ah. All right. I'm guessing one of these men friends is called Leo?"

Ailsa's jaw dropped. "How did you...? Oh, that's right. When you arrived I called out to you, thinking you were him. Leodigaris Grymaldo. Yes, he's one of them."

Had that only been twenty-four hours previously? So much seemed to have happened in the interim. Ben steered to conversation onto other topics, safer ones. It was no surprise that an attractive, vivacious woman like Ailsa would have her beaux, but somehow he didn't want to know about them.

Presently the starter plates were removed, and then the bowls of hotpot arrived, with warm crusty bread to soak up the sauce. Ben began to feel the warm glow of the metheglin coursing through him. He took the first mouthful of the hotpot, and found it delicious.

"Slainte!" he cried, lifting his glass. "This must surely be the food and drink of the gods!"

Ailsa smiled sweetly. "I'm glad you approve."

When they were done, and the plates had been removed, Ailsa said, "Would you care for a game of Nine Men's Morris?"

"I don't know it," said Ben, "but if you'll teach me how to play, I'll have a go."

"That's the spirit," said Ailsa. She got up from the table and went and fetched a board from a corner of the room where games were stored. When she set it down, Ben saw that the playing surface was circular, with a field marked on it, consisting of three concentric squares, with places for up to four players. In front of each player, set into the board, was a velvet-lined receptacle which contained the playing pieces, nine for each player, which resembled soldiers, each set wearing different colours. Ailsa showed him how to set up his pieces on the board.

"The object of the exercise," Ailsa explained, "is to reduce your opponent to two men, or to prevent him from making any legal moves. You make your move by sliding your piece along to any square which is vacant. When you have a line of three pieces, you can take an opponent's piece, but if theirs is one of a line, you can only take it if there is no alternative."

As they began to play, Ben saw that it was a kind of a mix of chess and noughts and crosses.

They played four games, and Ailsa won them all, but by the end Ben was beginning to get a feel for the play of it, and they went home happy.

CHAPTER FIFTEEN.

It was early morning, very early. It was just barely light, and the streets were swathed in a fog that had come up the River Lond from the sea. Everything was silent. Ben was on a mission: another bookseller, a man of Quaaman stock named Vespasiano Da Bisticci, who had a shop in another quarter of the city, had acquired a rare copy of the 'Sefer Yetzira'*, or 'Book of Creation', and Ailsa had a buyer among the Mages, so Ben was being sent to collect the book. A rare book like that would be an inviting target for a thief, so it was felt that the best time to carry it across the city was in the early morning when - it was hoped - most self-respecting thieves would be tucked up in bed. Ben carried his staff, but was warned not to use it unless absolutely necessary. He also had a map of Lochranza, absolutely essential while he was still learning how to find his way about.

He followed the directions on the map with great care, heading down Fishamble Street, then right into a narrow side street which brought him to the top of the appropriately named Breakneck Stairs. At the bottom of the steps, another narrow street opened into Conduit Court, a small square graced by an ancient yew tree growing in the middle, lifting the cobblestones with its roots. In one corner of the square was an old Mage meeting house called Caerdderwen*, 'The House of the Oak', surrounded by a high wall, and stately but withdrawn. From there it was but a short walk to Hagmatana, the Place of Assembly, a big open plaza. Where once had been held religious gatherings, there was now a fruit and vegetable market, and Ben found himself thrust from deserted streets where all that was to be heard was the echo of his own footsteps to a frenetic hive of industry, a teeming, shouting, swearing, scuttling community, which seemed to be self-contained within the confines of the square, an ants' nest where all the ants wore leather aprons and pushed trolleys and wheelbarrows, communicating loudly in a language that seemed to be all their own, while early shoppers wandered between them, interlopers almost, comparing goods and prices from one stall to the next, shuffling through a detritus of crushed, mashed vegetables.

The produce on sale included all the usual garden fruits, such as apples, pears, cherries and nuts, and a host of vegetables. There were huge quatities of leeks, which were popular as vegetables, and also as a flavouring for a range of dishes. Then there were onions, beans, cabbages, turnips and parsnips, radishes and carrots, the last appearing in the customary orange, as well as yellow, purple and white. There were beets, though Ben saw that people bought the leaves and often discarded the roots. There was the fruit of the vine also, used to make verjuice for cooking and - particularly in the autumn - for pickling.

In one corner of the square, a tavern purely for the purveyors of greenery dispensed ale at an hour when the sun was barely above the rooftops. It was all very strange.

Crossing the square, Ben entered Winetavern Street, and quickly found the bookshop. His business done, he was soon heading home, eager to sit down to a hearty breakfast.

Sometimes Ben's errands took him through the butchers' quarter, where blood ran in the streets and congealed stickily underfoot. He wove his way through Tripe Street, Slaughterhouse Street, Spider Street - a reference to the four-pronged hooks used to hang meat in the open air - Knacker's Yard Street, Fish Stone Street - where the butchers also sold fish - and the Vale of Tears, where there was a market selling poultry, game, lamb and goat, as well as eggs, butter and milk. On these occasions, Ben always tried to do his business early in the morning, before the heat of the sun made the stench and the flies intolerable.

At other times, he was out and about in the middle of the day. His missions took him through Hagmatana and other open spaces when they were crowded with people, and Ailsa warned him to be on his guard against cutpurses. Some of the most brazen amongst them, she told him, often resorted to theatrics to distract their victims, and duly warned, he was able to watch their performance from a safe distance.

One such villain, Augustus De Morgan, had a large and popular eating establishment, but not content with the income from this legitimate source, he also employed a small army of fingersmiths*. The way they went about their business, among the unsuspecting citizens of Lochranza, was this. They had amongst their number a particularly handsome lad called Mogens Hvat, who went about through the crowds, kissing women at random, fondling breasts and bottoms with the utmost boldness. When their menfolk responded in the predictable fashion, seeking to lay hold of him, he always managed to slip away, and it was upon innocent persons that they laid their hands. These in turn would lash out at their assailants, often knocking off wigs, and it was, as the saying goes, on for young and old.

The disturbance thus created provided the perfect opportunity for De Morgan's light-fingered felons to go among the crowd, cutting pursestrings to left and right with great abandon, their crimes going unnoticed in the chaos until it was far too late. Watches were lifted from pockets, and sometimes whole coats were spirited away.

De Morgan could never resist the urge to watch the spectacle, and would mount a wagon parked outside his establishment, dressed in the white coat and pants, and the tall chef's hat, which his voluptuous wife Elioxe had persuaded him were necessary to give his establishment the air of superiority which would draw the better off clientele (his kitchen assistant, Oddketil, and the serving girls, similarly wore starched white uniforms, and the tables were graced with elegant white linen tablecloths and napkins, which he had found amply repaid the cost of daily laundering by allowing him to inflate his prices quite considerably). De Morgan was a diminutive figure, portly as all good chefs are, and he could be seen bouncing on his stubby legs with excitement, and often waving a meat cleaver or a rolling pin or other culinary implement as he watched with ill-contained glee the pandemonium in the square,

Sometimes Ben's errands took him through the main brothel quarter, known as the Court of Miracles, and while he was never tempted to purchase the delights which he saw on offer - he had little money and less time for such pleasures - he would sometimes stop to simply chat with the 'ladies of negotiable affection', especially the young ones, just starting out in the business, known as punketees*, with whom he felt a certain affinity, and got to know the names of a few of them, and heard some of their stories.

For example, Sköka was a common subject of gossip. She was in her late twenties, and was not a regular, but would appear on the Court whenever the need for money drove her there. She was, to some men at least, a provocative beauty, and even occasionally favoured Ben with one of her radiant smiles as he passed. She lived on nearby Alksnãja Street, and the other women noted the somewhat furtive manner in which she came and went. She had about her something that bespoke better times, when she had known greater security, and her aloofness and her sense of her own superiority generated a degree of resentment among the other women. Ben grasped that she was truly a "fallen woman", and felt sorry for her.

*****

Occasionally, Ailsa would shut the shop and accompany him on long walks. She made a point of showing Ben some of the most destitute parts of the city. Small manufactories and workshops, taverns and bakeries, were jumbled together, sharing a partition wall, no space between them. It was evident that over time, any green fields had been built upon, and genuine countryside pushed ever farther from the core of the metropolis, as farming folk were lured into the city by the evanescent promise of greater wealth to be found there. She took him through rambling networks of lanes and over ditches, passing rows of houses fronted by dismal patches of garden, squalid in aspect, fenced off from the public road by old doors, some evidently taken from coaches, and barrel staves and ragged lengths of oiled cloth, with dead bushes, iron pots, many with their bottoms rusted out, and sundry other scraps pushed into the dirt to fill any gaps in the barrier. Ben found it all quite depressing, but Ailsa insisted that it was an important part of his education that he see how so many denizens of Lochranza eked out their existence.

*****

While Ailsa's business was the selling of books, not their production, she occasionally became involved in the latter. To which end she sent Ben into the quarter known as Hormiga, 'The Ant's Nest', along the bank of the Lond, where a parchment-maker named Hamun Le Stare had his workshop among all the others involved in various aspects of the leather trade.

Ben had no doubt about whether he was in the right place. The first impression of the Hormiga was the stench, like nothing he had ever experienced before. It almost knocked him off his feet. In navigating the jumble of alleyways and narrow streets of the quarter, in search of Mr. Le Stare's place of work, Ben found himself looking at every facet of the trade. There were the fellmongers, those who dealt in the raw hides, still bloody from where they had been stripped from the animals, and who claimed the prize for the most putrid stinks of all. At the other extreme, there were the curriers, who dealt in fine coloured hides, such as might be used to bind exquisite books which scholars would treasure till their dying day. Judging from the name-boards over the entrance to each establishment, Ben concluded that they were almost all run by single families, from the smallest, perhaps with just one man, to the largest, 'Botair of Akubek and Sons', which occupied almost a trev* of land, and claimed, with apparent justification, to be the largest leather-working establishment in all of Anoone.

When he finally tracked down Hamun Le Stare in his workshop, the leather man greeted him effusively, and while he bundled up the required sheets of parchment into a convenient parcel, he chatted amiably about the business he and his neighbours were engaged upon.

"There's a lot of different materials needed to turn a raw hide into a sheet of the softest leather," he said. "There's sumach, a spice from far off Tassili N'Ajjer, we use a lot of that. Alum, lime, old fashioned salt. And eggs."

"Eggs?" said Ben.

Eggs," Le Stare confirmed. "Hundreds, nay, thousands of eggs, brought in from the outlying farms all around the city. Very important."

"Goodness," said Ben. "I would never have imagined…"

"Nor you nor most other folks," said Le Stare, "but there you have it."

*****

On another occasion, Ben's errands took him to a street called the Street of the Necromancers.

"Master Gooseflesh the printer has a new edition of the 'Mathematica Alchandri'' Ailsa had told him.

"Master Gooseflesh!" Ben had exclaimed. "What a name!"

"It's Master Gooseflesh's name," Ailsa told him, "and it would be politic not to let him see that you find anything intrinsically risible about it."

She said this with a straight face, but the slight upward twitch at the corners of her mouth betrayed that Ailsa too found Master Gooseflesh's name intrinsically risible.

It was dusk, and shadows were advancing quickly. The street was narrow and arcaded, with dark, mysterious shops on the ground floor, and tall, narrow merchants' houses above, with stepped gables and cranes above the loft windows for hoisting goods into the attics for storage. The façades appeared innocent enough, but, with a name like that, Ben could not help wondering what sinister secrets dwelt behind them.

Master Gooseflesh was a large, shadowy presence in an ink-smeared apron, his shop filled with stacks of freshly-printed volumes, filled with the smells of ink and hot metal, and from behind a curtain came the sounds of industry being carried on. Ben kept a straight face throughout his interview with the printer.

His business completed, he found his way quickly back to well-lit boulevards, where he saw women, dressed in their finest clothes, carrying bunches of carnations, a sign, he had quickly learned, that they were on their way to a romantic assignation. As it happened, when he returned to the bookshop, he met Ailsa, just leaving, dressed in her finery, and wearing her formal hennin*. She was carrying just such a bouquet.

"Ah," he grinned as they passed, "I know where you're going. Have a nice evening."

"Thank you," she smiled. It was on the tip of her tongue to say "You too," but she recalled just in time that he would most likely be spending it immersed in his studies, so she desisted.

It was late, well after Great Tom had struck for the last time, and the candle he read by was almost used up, when he heard the front door open and footsteps on the stairs, awkward, unsteady footsteps, as of people whose heads were befuddled by wine or metheglin or both. The footsteps were accompanied by muffled laughter.

He heard two sets of footsteps in the passage outside his door, Ailsa's familiar light steps, and another set, heavier, that made the floorboards creak, and whispered conversation as they receded towards Ailsa's room.

Not long after, he heard the unmistakeable sounds of lovemaking, and tried to remain focused on his study, but the noises were impossible to ignore. He simply had to wait until they ceased, which wasn't long.

In the morning, he delayed his appearance at the breakfast table until he was sure that Ailsa's nocturnal guest had gone, and this became his practice on subsequent occasions.

*****

Only a few days after that, it was Nosgalan, the Winter's Eve Festival. New Year's Eve, Ailsa explained, was generally one of the quietest times of the year, as it was considered a time of flux and transition…

"'The time when the veil between the worlds is thin'," Ben intoned, recalling the Samhain ritual from the Academy..

"Exactly," said Ailsa. "Boundaries between this world and the spirit world become fluid, and mischievous gods and spirits walk abroad in Anoone, and common folk, especially followers of Mithra, think it wisest to stay indoors."

She took Ben to the formal opening ceremony at the henge within the Magisterium explaining that it would be his first chance to see, albeit from a distance, Caerlugh. the Archmage Porphyrogenitus, the Mage of Mages.

"Porphyro…?" said Ben.

"Porphyrogenitus," laughed Ailsa. "It means, 'He Who Was Born to Wear the Purple'."

"Ah."

It was thrilling. So few Mages got to actually see the Grand Master of the Order. Ben shook as much travel dust as possible from his cloak - washing them was not permitted - and wondered what this extraordinary personage might look like.

In the event, he proved to be tall and well built, but more than that it was hard to say, because he wore a stag's head, complete with an impressive rack of seven-point antlers, that obscured his features. He wore a cloak of leaves, artificial ones of course, in multiple shades of green and brown, which swept the ground and swirled around him as he walked, and he carried a large staff, carved and richly decorated with ornate bands of silver, and topped with a large crystal that glowed a soft purple.

The ceremony seemed to usher in the days of fierce cold.

One morning, Ailsa appeared wrapped in her warmest cloak, her neck swathed in a plaid whittle*, a bonnet pulled down over her ears, lambswool-lined mittens on her hands and matching boots on her feet. She was carrying a capacious basket.

"Wrap up warmly," she told Ben as he gobbled his breakfast. "We'll go to the Nosgalan Market."

They left the shop and walked along the embankment, right past the end of the Magisterium, past the end of the street that Ben had walked down on the evening of his arrival - he wondered in passing how Wisselus was doing - and on.

They reached a park that ran for some way along the waterfront. Crowds of people were converging upon it.

"This is the King's Garden," Ailsa explained. "Centuries ago, when Lochranza was really beginning to grow, a king who was friendly towards the Mages, King Galafre, decreed that it should be laid out here to give Mages, who love nature, a place to experience it in the heart of the city."

"That sounds like an excellent idea."

The open space within the park had been taken over by lanes of identical wooden booths selling all manner of goods, and Ben and Ailsa joined the ambling throng passing along them, inspecting the myriad wares on offer.

They came to a stall where a small crowd had gathered and some disputation was being carried on. They drew closer.

"Ah," said Ailsa after a pause. "The stallholder is being fined by the inspectors," she explained.

"Why?"

"He's selling butter on the same stall as fish, which is forbidden by the public health regulations."

They moved on, and as they did so, a further snatch of the argument came to their ears.

"And, further," one of the inspectors was saying, "for adulteration with marigolds, ten mancus."

"Oh," said Ailsa. "That too! Oh, he really is in trouble."

"Why would you adulterate butter with marigolds?" asked Ben, when they had put a little distance between themselves and the stall.

"Just to give it a more appealing colour," said Ailsa. "Ah, here is someone selling butter, but no fish!"

On this next stall there were large earthenware pots, which, on closer inspection, were seen to contain pats of butter wrapped in sorrel leaves and immersed in salt water. Ailsa bought one and put it in her basket.

Even though it was the middle of winter, every shop that they passed seemed filled to overflowing with all manner of delectable treats. Even the humble onions looked fat as monks, their bronze bellies swelling as they jostled one another, seeming to compete for the attention of the pretty young women who came to buy for their Solstice feasts, hovering enticingly under bunches of mistletoe as if just waiting to be kissed. Great mountains of apples and pears overflowed from their shelves, and luxuriant bunches of grapes, brought into the city from some more clement southern climate had passers by agog amid the winter turpitude. Nuts, too, filberts, hazels, chestnuts and walnuts, recalled autumn days spent shuffling pleasantly through drifts of fallen leaves. It was all calculated to bring joy and excitement into the darkest days of the year.

Ben stared at the comestibles with delight: golden-crusted pies, puddings, cakes, dainties of every description, hams, delectable sausages large and small, delectable smallgoods, pickles and preserves of kinds he could not even name, it was just never-ending. And then there were clothes, coats, scarves, boots and shoes. He saw an excellent pair of kid gloves and tried them on: they were a perfect fit, and a very reasonable five thrymsa*. He snapped them up, eagerly passing the coins across to the dark-haired girl running the stall, and pulled them on.

In spite of wearing almost every item of clothing he possessed, Ben was nevertheless beginning to feel the cold. It was just then that he heard a woman's voice singing from a booth nearby.

> "Take spices of Procyon, and of Algol too -
> Nutmeg, cinnamon, allspice and clove
> And honey or sugar to sweeten the brew,
> And sweet orange slices, fruit of the grove.
> Put in a saucepan and add red wine -
> A wine good enough, but not of the best,
> And simmer awhile with fruit and the rest
> Until all is mingled and tastes divine."

Hastening over, Ben saw that she was selling mulled wine, a big steaming pot of it sitting on a stove at the back of her stall.

"Oranges!" he exclaimed. "I've heard of them!"

The woman looked at him quizzically, then glanced at Ailsa, who had appeared at his shoulder. "Not from round here, then, is he?" she asked.

"A country cousin," Ailsa explained with an apologetic tone of voice, and a cheeky smile.

"Well then," said the woman, smiling. "One cup of glow-wine with extra orange it is."

"Two," said Ailsa, handing across a mitten full of fyrks.

They walked away from the booth and clinked wooden beakers. "Happy Nosgalan," said Ailsa.

"Happy Nosgalan," Ben replied.

He drank. The aroma of the red wine and the exotic spices and the sweet orange pieces was intoxicating, and he delighted in the wonderful warming sensation as it coursed its way down through his chilled body. It was well worth feeling cold, he thought, if this was the cure.

At another stall, they found an assortment of leather goods, including items such as fetels*, but most particularly an array of footwear. There were swiftlers*, hemmings*, and pampooties*, among others. . Ailsa inspected some rivlins* of rich russet-coloured leather, lined with lambswool, with bronze buckles to secure the side straps.

"They have good thick soles," she declared. "And they are well made. Try them on."

Ben threw up his hands. "They look much too expensive for me. I can't afford them."

Ailsa turned to the shoemaker. "How much are they?"

The shoemaker, an affable, rotund fellow, gave her a wink. "To you, lady, three mancus."

Ailsa snorted. "You're right. They are too expensive. I wouldn't give more than one. Come on, Ben." She turned and started to walk away.

"Two," said the shoemaker.

Ailsa stopped and turned on the ball of her foot.

"But..." Ben began.

"One mancu, five thrymsas."

"Done," said the shoemaker.

"But I still don't..." Ben protested.

"I'll give them to you as a Solstice present. And for working hard. Try them on."

Leaning against the booth, Ben undid one of his own shoes and pulled it off. He began pulling on the rivlin, but it seemed a tight fit. Then, as he was still struggling with it, it suddenly seemed to expand to exactly the right size. Startled, he glanced at Ailsa. It was her turn to give a wink.

"They're a perfect fit," he announced.

"I thought they would be," said Ailsa with a slight smile. She handed over the coins. Ben put on the other rivlin, and they walked away. "They should serve you well while you're traipsing all over the city in the rain and snow," she told him.

"Thank you," he said.

*****

Anagantios gave way to Dumannios*, The Darkest Month, as it was known on the Luthany calendar.

One afternoon, while Ailsa was out and Ben was minding the shop, a tall man with a long grey beard and long grey hair tied in a ponytail entered the shop. He had a slight stoop, and an avuncular smile. He wore a decidedly dishevelled green cloak, and carried a staff that was bound with wool in myriad shades of blue and green, in such a way that the pattern appeared truly three-dimensional. On the top of the staff was a bronze tercel*. He lowered it until the bird's beak sank into the flesh of Ben's shoulder.

Ben looked up at him. He was staring at Ben over a pair of half-moon spectacles, and as Ben looked into those steely blue eyes, he momentarily had the impression of looking into a tremendous abyss. He felt a slight chill, and suppressed an urge to shudder.

"Can… can I help you sir?" Ben stammered.

"Indeed I hope so, young man," the customer replied in mellifluent tones. "I am looking for a copy of the Book of the Grey Goose."

"I… I'm not familiar with it."

"Not yet, I dare say," said the grey-haired man. "But you probably will come across it in due course. You're the new Mage from the north, are you not?"

"Ben Troon is my name, sir."

His customer was already perusing the shelves. "It's an old book of laws. Most interesting reading."

"Laws!" said Ben brightly, clutching at straws in his efforts to please this mysterious visitor. For a moment he had the absurd notion that he had seen him somewhere before, but than considered that if he had, he would have been unlikely to forget it, and dismissed the idea at once.

"In that case, it's probably in this bookcase here," and began running his eyes over the spines.

As he was doing so, the door opened and Ailsa entered. Her mouth gaped as she took in the tall figure in her shop.

"Maier…" she began.

The man's finger went straight to his lips, giving a little jerk of the head in the direction of Ben, whose back was still turned. Ailsa's mouth snapped shut, and she composed herself.

"What is it you're looking for, Ben?" she asked.

"Ah! Ailsa!" Ben gasped, swinging round at the sound of her voice. "The Book of the Grey Goose."

Ailsa hurried over, running her finger along the spines until she found one that was appropriately grey in colour. "Here it is. The lettering is a little faded. That's why it was hard to spot." She drew the weighty tome off the shelf and looked on the flyleaf for the price. "It's three mancus. It's quite rare."

"Not an outrageous price by any means," said the man. He delved into a pouch on his belt and produced three shiny coins, which he popped into Ben's hand. At the touch of his fingers, Ben felt a peculiar little frisson.

"Thank you so much," said the man, taking the book from Ailsa and slipping it under his arm. He took up his staff and made for the door.

Ben raced to open it for him. "Thank you sir," he said. "Please come again."

"Thank you," said the man. "I certainly shall. Good afternoon."

And with that he strode briskly away in the direction of the Magisterium.

Ben turned to ask Ailsa who he was, but she had already gone upstairs. He made a mental note to ask her later, but somehow it slipped his mind.

*****

Sometimes Ben would study until late in the evening in the Magisterium library. He would emerge to find his surroundings blanketed in a thick fog. The sea, he had discovered, was not that far away down the River Lond (he made a mental note that when the weather was warmer, he would make a journey there, to see if it looked any different here to how it looked at Dundonald), and it was not uncommon for sea-fogs to envelope the city. When this happened, he would walk across the great quadrangle, past the Pool of the Wise, and see the lamps lit around the perimeter of the square glowing dimly, diffusely, and he delighted in the aura of mystery which then pervaded everything.

So wrapped up in his studies and his work for the bookshop did he become that he scarcely noticed the approach of the Solstice festivities, although on one of his forays into the city markets he found a beautiful scarf of taffeta-sarsuet*, dyed a beautiful coppery brown and bearing a pattern depicting the Irminsul*, or Tree of Life. The price, three thrymsas, ate a not insignificant hole in his carefully hoarded savings, but Ailsa had been so kind to him that he felt he had to get her something really nice. Especially when he thought of the rivlins.

*****

Then came one morning when he awoke and knew at once that there was something different in the world. There was a different quality to the light that filtered through his curtains. He threw them aside and gasped with delight. The city was enveloped in a blanket of snow, and even the lake had frozen over, for he could see figures out walking upon the great plain that it now formed, stretching away beyond the Magisterium's grim walls.

He could hardly wait to get out and about. The air had a crisp bite to it that was invigorating, and all was transformed to a dramatic chiaroscuro, the shapes of trees and buildings starkly contrasting with the brilliant whiteness all around. Even the most insalubrious of streets were somehow purified, the usual piles of rubbish hidden from view by nature's great veil. He loved the sound and the feel of the snow as it crunched beneath his every step. Children throwing snowballs invited him to join them, and for a few minutes he did so, delighting in the innocent pleasure of the game.

But it made walking precarious, especially on hills and steps, and he witnessed quite a few falls. Horses, too, struggled to find their footing as they pulled carts through the streets. Still, it was exciting.

When he returned to the shop, Ailsa grinned to see him with rosy cheeks and little icicles in his moustache and beard.

"You look like Old Man Frost himself!" she declared.

CHAPTER SIXTEEN.

Solstice Day came, and Ailsa formally presented Ben with his rivlins. He in turn gave her the scarf, and she was genuinely surprised and delighted, not expecting anything from him. The shop was closed, as all shops were, so they spent the day sitting in the parlour, reading and chatting idly, sipping on metheglin. In the afternoon, Ailsa busied herself in the kitchen, declining all Ben's offers of assistance.

"It's your first Lochranza Solstice," she told him, "so I want it to be a bit of a surprise."

As the afternoon wore on, a tantalising odour of roasting meat drifted up the stairs to where Ben was sitting. He started to feel hungry.

But the Solstice ceremony came first. As it grew dark, they wrapped themselves in their warmest clothes and their cloaks, Ben in his bonnet and Ailsa in her hennin, and joined the throng that was streaming towards the Magisterium and the great henge within. It was packed. Every practitioner of the Craft in the city was there, shoulder to shoulder. It was hard to see anything, but Ben was able to glimpse the Archmage again, wearing his ceremonial purple robes and the stag's head mask.

The ceremony was essentially the same as the ones Ben had attended at Dundonald. As always, the participants were barefoot, and Ben feared he might get frostbite before it was done, There were audible sighs of relief when it was done and everyone could put their shoes on again.

Ben and Ailsa returned to the shop. Ailsa sat him down at the dining table, specially cleared of the usual clutter for the occasion, and dressed with a fine linen tablecloth, stiff with starch, and a candelabra made of glistening orichalc*, holding three fine, festive red candles.

"Ta-daa!" said Ailsa, emerging from the kitchen bearing a large platter on which sat steaming a golden brown roasted bird, surrounded by the accompanying vegetables. "The traditional Solstice roast heronshaw*," she announced, and setting it down in the middle of the table, she took a large knife and began to carve.

The meal was delicious. Ben could not recall even Halldis cooking better.

"That was brilliant," he declared, munching on a fig. "You've clearly missed your vocation."

Rising from the table, Ailsa gave a curtsey. "Sweet of you to say so. Now, I hope you're not too full for a little walking, for the evening's entertainment awaits."

Ben arched an eyebrow. "Entertainment?"

"Indeed," said Ailsa, passing him his cloak and bonnet as he stood up. "A special treat for your diligent work and study."

He wrapped the cloak around himself, and Ailsa helped him pin it closed. He settled the bonnet on his head, and she passed him his staff. "We might need this to light us home," she explained.

They left the shop and swept away through pathways dug through the snow, coming soon to a part of the city that Ben as yet knew only slightly. They walked along Long Wyre Street to the spot where it met Short Wyre Street, a spot well known as Beetlebung Corner, where a grand flight of steps led up to the Arnamagnean Library. From Short Wyre Street, Ailsa led the way into a broad, well lit avenue. Ben recognised the imposing colonnaded edifice that was the Temple of Tefarin, a name meaning 'The Sun in the Tree of Life', but beyond that he was in unfamiliar territory.

Ailsa diverted from the main avenue into a maze of smaller side streets.

"We could perhaps do with some light here," she said.

"Light!" said Ben, and the tip of his staff at once began to glow a soft lilac colour.

"Almost there," said Ailsa.

*****

They turned a corner and came upon a crowd of people gathered around the front of a small building. A signboard outside announced it as *Bodinière Theatre: Home of Lochranza's Puppet Master, Wagang Kulit.*

Ben turned to Ailsa with a quizzical expression. "Puppets?"

Ailsa nodded. "The best you will ever see."

They shuffled inside the theatre, grateful for the warmth. Wagang Kulit himself was standing there, tall and jovial, with an avuncular smile, and shook the hand of every patron as they entered. Behind him on the wall, in a display case, was a tiny suit of armour, lovingly crafted down to the last detail.

Within the auditorium, the seating was rudimentary: hard wooden benches. Those in the know had brought their own cushions. At the front, just under the stage, stood a man with a hurdy gurdy, who would provide the musical accompaniment to the drama

*****

When everyone was seated, the lights went down and the action began. The plot was an old story taken from the Annals of Tigernack, a tale of an abducted princess, Princess Keltine, and a hero, Bödvar Bjarki, who goes to her rescue. Along the way, Bödvar fights the giant, Tom Hickathrift, and slays Iormungand, the serpent which circles the world at the bottom of the sea. In the grand climax, he does battle with the villainous Biflindi, the 'Shield-shaker', not merely slaying him, but hacking him to pieces. Bödvar then of course claims the lovely Princess Keltine as his prize, and they live happily ever after.

Ben sat transfixed. He was so caught up in the drama that he barely noticed how uncomfortable the bench was. He was fascinated by the inticate movements that the puppets were capable of, all of them operated from above by Wagang Kulit. Bödvar and the other characters were capable of drawing swords, doffing caps, grasping maidens by their willowy waists, and a host of other intricate manoeuvres. One of the moments that amazed him the most was in a scene of comic relief, when a puppet dog ran onto the stage, lifted its leg and peed real water.

Ben turned to Ailsa in amazement as the audience roared with laughter. "How does it *do* that?" he exclaimed.

Ailsa threw up her hands. "Beats me!" she said.

Apart from a few such moments of ribaldry, however, Ben was surprised to find that the performance lacked the expected knockabout farce, with the stock comic characters, and instead adopted a tone of inculcating moral precepts.

When it was over, they took a few moments to talk to the puppet-master. Ben remarked on the unusually weighty subject matter.

"And why not?" asked Wagang Kulit. "We go to considerable lengths to make our characters as realistic as possible. Why should they not grapple with serious matters of crime and punishment, just because they are made of wood rather than flesh and blood? I have seen many shows which had no greater aim than to make the audience laugh, and cannot say that I found them satisfying. I would much rather present some lessons in the right and wrong way to behave, which I believe is as legitimate for our little theatre as for any of the grandest stages in the city. I seek to improve my customers just as they do."

Ben seemed unconvinced. "Perhaps you're right," he said. "I certainly meant to cast no aspersions on your ability or your creative talent. I merely missed the figures I have known in the past."

Ben and Ailsa made their way out into the street again. It was snowing lightly, and their breath billowed in thick clouds in front of them.

They had come out at the same time as a number of other places of entertainment were closing, and the crowds filled the streets. It was hard to make any progress.

"I'm getting cold," said Ailsa. "I feel as if I'll turn into an icicle before we reach home." She gestured down a narrow side alley. "We can take a short cut down here. Give us some light on your staff."

Ben looked dubiously down the alley. "Are you sure?"

"Yes, yes," said Ailsa, growing impatient. "We'll be quick. I know where it comes out."

"Light," said Ben, and the tip of his staff glowed, this time a ruddy crimson, and brighter than before. He couldn't even recall thinking about crimson: the staff seemed to have made up its own mind what colour light it wanted.

They began down the alley at a brisk trot. It seemed very dark and forbidding.

"Ooh," said Ailsa, "I'm glad I'm not coming down here alone."

"Yeah," Ben concurred, "so am I."

Ailsa gave a peal of laughter that echoed off the walls.

As the sound died away, Ben suddenly became aware of another, softer sound, the shuffling of feet in slippers of thin, worn leather on the stone paving slabs. He realised that they were not alone.

At the edge of the pool of light created by his staff, Ben saw a small, furtive figure, a boy of no more than ten, pale and unkempt, in a ragged robe.

"Money," the boy said in a faint, hoarse voice, and extended his left hand as he took a step towards Ailsa.

But Ben neither heard the word nor considered the left hand, because the light of the staff was glinting like a bloodstain from the dagger that the boy was grasping in his right.

"*No!*" he yelled, and before he had even had time to formulate the thought, a brief blue-white bolt shot from his staff and struck the boy full in the chest. He gave a brief, strangled cry and fell in a heap.

"Bring the light closer!" Ailsa commanded as she crouched over the inert body. Ben obliged.

She looked up at Ben, her rich brown eyes seeming to grow larger as she did so. "He's dead," she declared quietly.

She stood up and took Ben's arm. "I think it's time we made ourselves scarce," she told him, urging him away along the alley.

Ben hastened alongside her, their shoulders brushing the walls. He barely seemed to have command of his own feet. His head reeled: he had killed *again*, and this time a child! And now, his muscles seemed to have gone to water. He could barely put one foot in front of the other, even though he knew the urgency of them making their escape. It was the same feeling he had had after the battle on the bridge, a feeling that all his strength had simply drained away, leaving him empty and lethargic.

They swept out of the alley and merged with the river of Solstice Night merrymakers. They traversed two or three crowded avenues, and then, when they reached a corner, Ailsa stopped Ben and drew him to her. Before he knew what was happening, her mouth was on his, her tongue pressed hard against his, her hips likewise against his. It was his instinct to sweep his cloak around her, enveloping her in its folds, as he responded in kind to her passionate embrace.

And then something happened that seemed even more remarkable. It was as if a tide of new energy were sweeping through him in the midst of it, imbuing him with renewed vigour and vitality, and he knew that it was Ailsa's doing.

At last she broke off to suck in lungfuls of air, but her eyes did not leave his.

"I *think*," she said at last, "that he only intended to use the knife to cut my purse from my belt. I don't think he meant to harm me. But you were my knight, my Bödvar Bjarki, protecting me, and I am very grateful. But…" She paused, and her voice changed from starry-eyed heroine to schoolmarm in an instant. "…This is a valuable lesson in how dangerous Magecraft can be if the practitioner is in a state of high emotion. At such times, the need for absolute control is essential."

Ben could only nod mutely.

"Come on," she said, adopting a tone of enforced brightness. "Let's go home."

He had no recollection of how they came to be at the bookshop once more. His mind was in a whirl. But there they were, in the parlour, safe and warm.

"Would you like a nightcap?" Ailsa asked.

Ben's thoughts were jolted back to the here and now. The kiss - had she intended it as an invitation to further intimacy? He scuttled back into his shell.

"No, thank you," he said with a wistful smile. "I think I'd like to just get some sleep, if that's possible."

Ailsa smiled back. Not the right moment, then. It was of no consequence. She was happy to bide her time.

He turned to go.

"Ben?" He turned back. "Happy Solstice."

His smile was more ironic this time. "Happy Solstice, Ailsa."

*****

Ben was delighted to discover that Solstice Night was but the first of a sprinkling of festivals which served to punctuate and brighten the dull winter months. It was shortly followed by Modranect*, the Night of the Mothers. Although Ailsa was not a mother - "Well, not yet anyway," she added with a sly grin - she insisted on going out and celebrating nevertheless, and Ben discovered that many non-mothers similarly seized the opportunity to make merry at midwinter.

She took Ben to a cosy restaurant called Musa's, where, so popular belief had it, the same cauldron of stew had been on the fire, constantly being added to and taken from, for nigh on a century. Ben rubbed his hands with delight as a bowl of this extraordinary concoction was placed in front of him and a platter of seed-encrusted rolls with golden butter and a foaming tankard of ale to accompany it, and Ailsa told him that he was "eating history".

Dumannios was replaced by Ogronios*, the Month of Ice, the first month of the new year, when Luthanians customarily made vows to break bad habits and live better, few of which were ever honoured.

*****

After Ogronios came Riuros*, quite simply the Month of Cold, and with it came another grand festival, Oimelc, celebrating the fact that ewes began to give milk at this time.

By Samonios*, the Month of Sowing, the days were growing appreciably longer, and the wind had lost that knife-like chill that made any time out of doors a trial of endurance. The last grubby piles of slush had been swept from the streets by the spring rains, although the downside of that was that the usual rubbish was now in plain sight once more. There were even some sunny days when it was almost pleasant to be outdoors, harbingers of more pleasant days to come.

The real warm weather came with Giamonos*, the Month of New Shoots, so much so that Ben decided it was time to shave off his beard, and bought himself a razor and a brush and soap, and a little leather case to put them in. Soon the beard was gone. He looked at himself in the mirror, contemplating the difference in his appearance. At least his hair was growing back, so he was no longer truly a shaveling. He felt he was going up in the world. Slowly but surely.

"Ben, I want you to… oh!" Ailsa gasped when he appeared at breakfast. "You've shaved!"

"Spring is here!" he announced, reaching for a loaf and a knife to cut himself a slice. "You want me to what?"

"I want you to go to Mr. Da Bisticci's and bring me a copy of the 'Dragmaticon'. He's expecting you."

"I'm on it," he said.

"Oh and Ben…"

"Yes?"

"The Great Spring Fair is on in the Hagmatana. Try not to dawdle there *too* long, hmmm?"

*****

With the 'Dragmaticon' wrapped in plain brown paper tucked under his arm, Ben wandered through the aisles of stalls and amusements filling the great square of the Hagmatana. So many tasty treats, so many beautiful crafted items, pins and buckles and gewgaws of every kind, silks and taffetas and exotic cloths, intricate wooden toys and puppets, perfumes and maquillage, lamps and bowls and pots kitchenwares, many painted with delicate interweaving patterns, a cornucopia of delights for the eyes, and indeed all the senses. It was hard not to linger.

On the periphery of the square were a host of sideshows and entertainments of all sorts.

Ben was walking past a shy, where people sought to knock bottles off a stand with small wooden balls. He stopped abruptly.

There was a woman about to take her turn in trying to knock over the bottles. She was of medium height, and slender, wearing a white linen dress over which she wore an overdress of lace, which, as she moved and it swirled about her, cast intricate shadows on her body. She was not beautiful in the traditional sense, but there was an elfin quality about her that made Ben want to stop and look at her. She had long fair hair and a finely sculpted face, pleasingly oval, in which the most striking features were her almond shaped blue eyes. To Ben's mind, she looked as if she had just stepped through a portal from Mag Meld*, the Land of the Fay.

Just as she was about to throw the first ball, she shifted her head slightly, and held Ben's eyes with her own. She smiled, although whether it was intended for him or was the consequence of some inner notion of her own, he could not tell.

She threw the balls. Every one hit a bottle and knocked it into the sand box below. She was a crack shot, Ben thought. Just like… just like…

Bliss! Morrigan sings! He buried his face in his hands. How could he have forgotten her? He had not written her a line! What must she think of him? He must go home at once and put a letter into a courier's saddlebag this very afternoon!

He turned to go. Then something prompted him to look again at the mysterious woman, but she was nowhere to be seen.

He set off across the square at a loping half-run, dodging between people, his mind already engaged upon composing a letter to his beloved, entreating her forgiveness for his failure to communicate.

But even as he did so, another thought came into his head, unbidden. The mysterious woman's enigmatic smile reminded him somehow of another, very much like it, that he had seen once before, and in spite of himself he began sifting through his memories to find it. It was the image of Bliss, sitting across from him on the floor in the hallway at the Academy that brought it back. It was the smile on the face of Mage Adoy when he had seen them there, a satisfied smile that bespoke some secret plan that was unfolding precisely as it was supposed to.

Nonsense, Ben told himself. He banished the thought from his mind and turned his whole attention to the letter he was going to write, and he was still engaged upon that task as he burst through the door of the bookshop, deposited the book on the counter beside Ailsa, and hastened upstairs to his room.

"Good morning?" she inquired of his departing back. There was no reply.

> *Dearest Bliss,*
>
> *What must you think of me? Please accept my most humble apologies for failing to write to you before this. It certainly hasn't been the case that I have not been thinking of you, far from it. But between my intensive study at the Magisterium, where I am learning the ways of Deeper Magecraft, and my duties at the bookshop (where Ailsa is very friendly, and not at all the hag I had envisaged!), it has been quite*

exhausting. But now it is spring, and this young man's fancy turns to thoughts of the one he loves.

Pack your bags, come to Lochranza any way that you can (so long as it is a safe way, of course!). There is so much that someone with your talents could do here, and there are so many wonderful things to show you in the Big City!

I long to hold you again. I can't wait to start a proper life together. I love you and I miss you so much.

Write soonest!
All my love,
Your Ben.

He read it over. It seemed very brief. But he wanted above all to re-establish contact, to hear from Bliss as soon as possible. He could write her a longer letter, share all his news the next time.

He scattered fine sand to blot the ink, folded it, sealed it, addressed it. He threw on his cloak and raced to the courier's office. In the yard there were horses saddled, the mail bags ready to go. It was perfect timing. He hastily paid the postage, and saw the courier's clerk slip his letter into one of the bags.

He paused long enough to see the courier emerge into the yard, mount his steed, and head off at a gallop in the direction of the Mezentian Gate. His letter was on its way.

He returned to the shop, his heart singing. Ailsa looked at him: she could not remember seeing him in such an ebullient mood.

"You seem very happy," she observed.

"It's love," he told her. "I've written to the one I love, told her to hurry and come to the city."

"Ah ha. That explains it," said Ailsa, and went about her business.

*****

The suspense of waiting for the reply almost drove him insane. He could barely keep his mind on what he was supposed to be doing. He was studying the 'Book Antimaquis', and found himself reading the same page over and over again. Concentration was impossible. Everywhere he looked, he saw Bliss' lovely face smiling back at him.

One week passed, and then two, and then three. What was taking so long?

"This came for you," said Ailsa one morning as he returned from an errand. She was holding up a letter. Ben saw at once Bliss' elegant handwriting, and when he drew close he could smell her perfume on it, made from powdered onycha shells. "Your lady friend, I presume?"

"Ah! Yes! Yes!" shouted Ben in an ecstasy of delight and relief. He took the letter from her, scarcely able to control the urge to snatch it, and scampered to his room like a child on Solstice Morning, eager to see what gifts Betana* has brought.

Throwing himself on his bed, he broke the seal and began to read, his eyes devouring the words.

> *Dearest Ben,*
>
> *Thank you so much for your letter. I am so glad, and relieved, that you got to Lochranza safely* (he wondered if he should tell her about the battle on the bridge, or whether it was better just to keep her in ignorance about that) *and that you are enjoying your life in the big city.*
>
> *I'm sorry that it has taken me a while to answer your letter, but I am now living back in the Tollgate Islands, and sometimes if the sea is rough, the courier's boat cannot land.*

Dear Ben, you say you want me to come and live with you in Lochranza. It sounds like a wonderful idea, but alas I cannot. I am betrothed to another man. We will very shortly have our official handfasting.

I waited so long to hear from you, and when no word came, I thought that you didn't love me any more. I see that I was wrong, and for that I am sorry. I would like to keep you as my friend, and hear all your news.

Fare well, dear Ben.
Your Bliss.

Ben stared in disbelief at the paper in his hand. No, it couldn't be. He reread it.

I thought that you didn't love me any more. It was like a spear through his heart. But he had not sent her a single word, so how could he blame her for thinking that? How could he have been so *stupid* that he had failed to realise that as soon as she got out there in the wider world, there would be other men who would fall for her charms just as he had? He could imagine this nameless other man whispering in her ear, perhaps even suggesting to her that he, Ben, had not written because he had himself found someone else. But could she not have at least let him know what was blowing in the wind? You can hardly accuse her on that score, said a voice in his head, when you failed so miserably to even send her one line about your own doings.

His world had come crashing down. He threw himself back on the bed and wept.

In time, however, he composed himself. He sat at his little writing desk, put the 'Book Antimaquis' and all his other texts in a pile on the floor, and prepared to write a reply to Bliss.

> *My Dearest Bliss,*
>
> *Thank you for your letter. It was such a joy to hear from you again after all this time, and well worth the wait.*
>
> *I can't pretend I wasn't shocked to hear that you have found someone else, when I had such dreams for our life together, but I can fully understand why you might think that I had stopped loving you, and I have only myself to blame for letting you slip away from me. I will probably spend the rest of my life kicking myself for that.*

You say that you want us to remain friends. This places me in a horrible dilemma. Of course I don't want to lose sight of you altogether, and I so much want to know about your life. But at the same time, to hear your news would mean hearing about your new man, and it would be more than my heart could stand, I think, to be constantly reminded of you in the arms of another. So perhaps it is best simply to let go.

All my love,
Ben.

Again he sealed his letter and addressed it. Bliss had sent him an address in the Tollgate Islands, so it would not have to be redirected this time.

In sharp contrast to the previous time, he trudged miserably to the courier's office. He didn't care if his letter went that day or not for a week. He did not stay to see the courier leave.

He descended into a pit of despair.

"Is everything all right?" Ailsa enquired.

"It's just a personal thing," he told her. "A bit of bad news, that's all"

"Ah. Well, if you want to talk about it, I'm a very good listener," she told him.

He smiled weakly. "Thanks. But not right now."

*****

And then one day when he walked into the shop, Ailsa held up a packet for him. It had the same elegant handwriting, the same onycha shell perfume. Bliss had written to him again.

"Thanks," he said, taking it from her. He went upstairs to his room.

Although it was spring, the air still had a chill to it, and Ailsa had lit a fire in his hearth. The room was warm and inviting.

He paced up and down, barely two paces in either direction, hefting the package in his hands, examining its thickness. If it was a letter, and it clearly was, it was a very long one. What might she have to say that required such length? He hoped and prayed it did not involve intimate details about her new love - *that* he did not want to read! Whatever it was, it must have taken a long time to write. She must have poured her heart into it. He turned the packet over, pondering.

As he did so, a magma of anger and frustration welled up inside him. No, whatever it was she had to say, he didn't want to read it. He was hurting, hurting too much for that. He threw the unopened packet on the fire.

He went to the window and stared out at the Magisterium, trying to keep his confused emotions from running riot. She was Bliss, she was the centre of his universe, her every word was precious to him…

"No!"

He turned, reaching out towards the fireplace, but saw at once that it was too late. The packet was reduced to ashes. He would never ever know what she had tried so hard to say to him. It was over.

*****

The days shuffled by with little to differentiate them. Ben felt as if he had died, but his body just hadn't got the message yet. He continued his studies, but without commitment. He wandered around in a daze. The weather was getting steadily warmer, but he felt no joy of it. Invitations from his fellow shavelings to join in lunchtime games of kubbe* on the Magisterium lawns, depending on the depth of his despair at that particular moment, were either met with a polite refusal or else were simply ignored, swiftly earning him a reputation as aloof if not downright rude. Young women, attracted by his good looks, sought him out as a dancing partner at the revels, and he did dance tolerably well, or else they would sit beside him in the great dining hall, where he ate only when it was unavoidable, and they talked to him about their mutual friends, about life in the Magisterium, about where he came from in the far north, or about Magecraft in general. But he never took the acquaintance any further. He tended to be absent-minded about invitations to parties, theatrical presentations, and many lesser social gatherings. And he came to be looked upon as cynical and a recluse. But he didn't care. He didn't care about anything any more. His life had ended before it had properly begun.

The days merged until they became weeks. One, then two, and then three.

And then one day he walked into the shop and Ailsa had a letter for him. It was from Bliss. He took it from her, forced a smile, and ran to his room.

He broke the seal. It had her perfume as always, but as he began to read, he could almost smell the anxiety over the top of that.

Dearest Ben,

I don't know what has happened. I wrote you a letter, a really long letter, to try to explain about everything, and I waited for your reply, but it hasn't come, so I don't know if my letter went astray or what. I realise now that you still love me, and I have made a terrible mistake. All I can do is ask for your forgiveness.

Please write soon.

Bliss.

Ben sat down at his table and pulled out a fresh sheet of paper. As he pondered what to say, he spent an inordinate amount of time trimming his pen. At last he was ready. He dipped his pen in his inkwell, drew a deep breath, and began to write.

My Dearest Bliss,

Thank you for your letter. It is my turn to ask forgiveness. Your letter did arrive here, but I am ashamed to say that I was angry with you and threw it on the fire without even opening it. I realise that it must have cost you a great deal of pain to write it, and I will never know what it was you had to say. For that, and for everything else, I shall spend the rest of my life kicking myself.

You ask me to forgive you. As I see it, there is really nothing to forgive. You acted in the most sensible way imaginable in the circumstances. But if forgiveness is what you need, then yes, of course you are forgiven. Forgiven but never forgotten. May I dare to hope that you will say the same of me? It breaks my heart to think of the tears you must have cried when it seemed you had lost me.

I hope the man you have found is a good man, and that he will make you happy. Your happiness is my number one wish. Of course, I wish it were me bringing you happiness, but it is not to be.

For myself, I have no way of knowing what the future holds in store. But I will say this. If I should chance to meet another woman (at the moment I can't imagine it happening), she will never be able to claim my whole heart, because a corner of it will always remain a shrine to you.

Go well, darling Bliss, and may your life be all that you wish of it. I don't imagine you will hear from me again, but I will love you until my dying breath.

Your Ben.

He scattered sand across the page, to blot both ink and tears. Mechanically, he sealed it and addressed it, then with a leaden heart he trudged to the courier's office and handed it over.

It was done. Now he wished only to die.

CHAPTER SEVENTEEN.

And so he went on from day to day, a black cloud of despondency hanging over him perpetually. Life had lost all meaning. He pursued his regular activities as if by rote, listless, glum. He tried to tell himself that perhaps he had been wrong about Bliss, that she had not been the right woman for him after all, but that nagging voice in his head told him straight away that that was merely self-delusion of the worst kind. Of course she had been right for him, far more right than he deserved. He just hadn't been right for her. Well, now she had found a good man - and Ben sincerely hoped he *was* a good man - she would have the happiness she truly merited.

Ailsa noted all this, and it wasn't hard to guess the cause. But she refrained from prying. She felt sure that it would come out, all in good time.

"Would you like to go to the circus?" Ailsa asked.

It was a warm summer evening and they were standing on the embankment just past the end of the Magisterium, watching the spectacle out on the lake. It was the Ball-Within-A-Ball, the highpoint of Lochranza's social calendar. All the city's wealthiest people gathered together in a giant sphere of timber and glass, lit by hundreds of coloured lanterns, which floated down the River Lond and across the lake, before rejoining the river on the seaward side of the lake. The sounds of merry music and raucous laughter carried across the water to where Ailsa and Ben were standing.

She had let him stew for quite a while. Giamonos had come and gone, giving way to Simivisionos*, and Ben showed no signs of emerging from his gloom, and so it seemed to her that it was time to take some affirmative action.

Ben considered the invitation. The last time they had gone out together, it had not gone well, but he would not let that be a jinx. He had to accept that his life was stretching out ahead of him, with or without Bliss, and that it seemed pointless to be eternally miserable.

"Yes," he said at last. "I would like that very much."

"Good," said Ailsa, relieved. "Tomorrow night, then?"

*****

"Wow!"

Ben stared. Ailsa had entered the parlour. She was wearing a dress that he had not seen before, of crimson velvet, that clung delightfully to every curve of her body. It had a high collar and full length sleeves, so there was not an inch of bare flesh below her chin or above her wrists, but her shape was nevertheless there to admire in every detail.

"You like it?" she asked flirtatiously.

"I do indeed."

"Well then, let's go."

She took his arm as they promenaded along the water's edge to the King's Garden, and Ben became aware of the admiring looks of other men as they passed. They are jealous of me, he thought, with growing pride.

A large tent had been erected in the park, and the crowd moved eagerly towards the entrance.

Inside there were the mingling smells of sawdust, manure, and the tasty treats that the vendors were hawking. Around the edge of the ring were little stands offering sausages in bread, pies, jellied eels, and little bowls of fruit, as well as wine, metheglin and ale. Ailsa bought two of the sausages, two pies, and two mugs of ale.

They made their way to their seats, just a few rows back from the ring, Ailsa taking the steps with some difficulty in her tight dress. Ben gave her his arm to lean on.

Ben felt good, happily getting into the spirit of the evening. The acts presented by the ringmaster, Ithuriel Pesrut - a man whose name meant 'Red Cloak', and was suitably enveloped in a cloud of swirling scarlet cloth - were the usual circus fare of tumblers, jugglers, trapeze artists, performing animals and, of course, clowns, all of whom were dressed in fantastical costumes, and all of whom put on a tremendous show. The audience cheered, gasped, laughed and applauded with gusto. Among Ben's favourites was Engastrimyth the ventriloquist, who had the crowd in fits of laughter with his engaging repartee with his dummy, Loddfafnir, a name meaning "Everyman".

About three quarters of the way through, the ringmaster introduced the twins Uziel and Abiel Bethel and their performing tarpans*, wild relatives of the domesticated horse, which they had tamed to the extent of being able to get them to leap over obstacles as they ran in circles around the ring.

And then something completely unexpected happened. A man who had clearly had more metheglin than was good for him suddenly lurched from the crowd, mounted the barrier around the ring, and, in a feat remarkable for someone stone cold sober, not to mention one pickled to the eyeballs, he threw himself at the tarpan as it flashed past, and managed to get on its back. Grasping its bridle like grim death, he hung on, as the animal, clearly unused to having a rider, pitched and cavorted, doing all it could to unseat him. Every time the tarpan bucked, the man's legs flew up in the air, but by some miracle, he managed to come back down across the beast's back. Round and round the ring they went together, while the Bethel twins did all they could to catch them. Sometimes the man wound up hanging off one flank of the horse or the other, his feet often grazing the sawdust in the arena, but always somehow retaining that vice-like grip on the bridle, and managing to haul himself back up onto the animal's back.

All the while, the audience was on its feet, cheering and stamping, many laughing till the tears rolled down their cheeks.

Ben felt Ailsa's hand tighten in his own, and he realised that, like himself, she was far from amused. Fearful, rather, that the man was in mortal peril if he was thrown from the tarpan. He could easily break his neck, or else be trampled under the hooves.

Ben became aware that Ailsa was murmuring something under her breath, a far away look in her eyes. As she did so, the horse slowed its pace and ceased the tossing, until the twins were able to secure its bridle and get the drunken interloper off its back. He was firmly escorted out of the circus tent.

As they walked home, Ailsa was still holding his hand. He sensed something, some of his life force being drawn from him, the reverse of how he had felt when she had held him after the death of the child on Solstice Night, but in a less extreme way. She was drawing strength from him, and it thrilled him to be able to help her in that way.

But even after the sensation had ceased, and she appeared to have revived, she continued to hold his hand.

"You probably saved that man's life," he observed.

"Yes," she answered softly. "I probably did."

And then her arms were about him, and she was kissing him with a ferocious hunger.

*****

They were sitting in the parlour with glasses of metheglin, in armchairs on opposite sides of the fire. Ailsa had taken off her shoes and was wiggling her toes contentedly.

"That was quite a show," said Ben, smiling now. With the danger past, he could see the funny side of it all.

"Yes it was," Ailsa agreed. After a long pause, she said, "Do you want to sleep with me tonight?"

Ben was struck dumb. It was so unexpected. But then, he asked himself, was it such a bombshell? Had it not always been there in the back of his mind as at least a possibility since the moment he arrived at the bookshop. She was, after all, a *most* desirable woman.

She raised an eyebrow. "Well?"

Ben cleared his throat. "One half of me does. Very much so."

"And the other half?"

"Is scared to death."

Ailsa laughed. "Scared? No one's told me I was scary before."

"Ah well, that's just it," said Ben. "The others. See, you've never made any secret of the other men in your life. In fact I hear them from time to time. And me, I'm *almost* a virgin. By comparison. And I don't think I could stand it to be the worst you ever had, which I think is a distinct possibility."

Ailsa gave a knowing smile and shook her head. "Not possible, I assure you."

"But there's more," Ben went on. "I'm afraid that if I sleep with you I'll fall in love with you, and then you'll get bored with me and end it, and I will get hurt, and I'm not ready to go through all that again."

He had blurted it all out in a rush.

Ailsa gave him her sweetest, most beatific smile. "Love is always a gamble," she said. "There's never any guarantee it will last. Sometimes you have to just jump in with both feet." Ben nodded slightly, but said nothing. "You know," she went on, "they do say that it's a rare person that goes to their grave without regrets. And what's more, they also say that people end up regretting more the things they didn't do than the things they did do. The fact is that acknowledging the things we have done that we shouldn't have, or the things that we didn't do that we wish we had is well and good for keeping us on the right road in life. We learn from our mistakes, and are careful not to make the same ones in the future. But if we let the regrets take hold, and simply degenerate into excessive breast-beating, then simply clinging to the memory and wallowing in self-hatred and self-blame serves no purpose. It only leads to continued suffering which you bring upon yourself. I know it is hard to let go, but if you can manage it, your scars will heal over all the quicker."

"Yes," said Ben, brightening a little. "I suppose that's true. Though I don't imagine they will go away."

"No," Ailsa agreed. "Some scars stay with you for life. But that's what makes us who we are. Would you like to tell me about her?"

"Who?"

She gave him a look of mock contempt. "*Who*? Why, the woman who broke your heart, of course."

"Well, the truth is, I think I broke hers first," Ben conceded. Ailsa made no reply. "It's a long story," he said. "Are you sure you want to hear it?"

Ailsa gave a little shrug and settled back deeper in her armchair. "I'm not going anywhere."

Ben took another mouthful of metheglin and began his story.

When he was finished, Ailsa said quietly, "My question remains. Do you want to sleep with me tonight?"

"Do you really want me?" Ben asked. Before Ailsa could answer, he slipped from his chair onto his knees on the floor and shuffled over to her. "No, no, let me rephrase that. Do you really want *me*?"

Ailsa looked down at him and gave him that smile again. "Why wouldn't I?"

"It's just that I've always thought of myself as being wholly unattractive to the opposite sex."

Ailsa stood up. She took his hands in hers and drew him upright, until she was looking up at him. Those liquid brown eyes with their heavy black lashes had never looked more enticing. "Well, you're not," she assured him. "Now, come to bed."

Still clasping his hand, she led him out of the parlour and along the passage to her room.

Ben had never been in her bedroom before. He considered it her inner sanctum, her holy of holies. It was the same size as his own, but the bed was much larger, occupying most of the space in the room. It occurred to him that it must have been assembled there in the room, for there was no way it could have got through the door. It was covered by a large bedspread that was a patchwork in shades of deep green, wine and plum, with embroidered motifs and a border of gold thread. The curtains were of the same opulent material.

On the walls, there was scarcely an inch without pictures. Some of them were recognisably Ailsa's own, but many were in other styles, by other hands: landscapes, portraits, still lives, every possible subject. A number of them were highly erotic.

"What you see there is the theory," she told him. "It's time for a practical demonstration." And she gestured to him to come to her.

His trembling fingers found the top button of her dress, directly under her chin, and he undid it, working downwards until he had undone it enough for her to disengage herself from the sleeves and step out of it. It fell in a billowing crimson heap at her feet, and she stepped away from it.

He looked at the undergarment in which her torso was encased. "What is *that*?" he gasped.

"Ah, you have no experience of women's corsetry, do you? That, sir, is a Symington Side-lacer. If one has no lady's maid to secure one's laces, then lacing at the side is a boon, to say the least."

In spite of his eagerness to do away with this last barrier to his heart's desire - in truth it was another organ that demanded satisfaction - he studied the garment with curiosity. Her breasts and the whole of her upper body were enclosed within a bodice of stiff white material that had bands of reinforcement stitched across the front in a criss-cross pattern.

Enough, his lust declared, His hands went to the lacing, tied at her hip, and hastily pulled it undone, opening up the corset and flinging it aside.

Finally there was her shift, which he hoisted over her head and tossed it to join the rest of her clothing on the floor.

He stood before her as a pilgrim before a shrine, his eyes drinking in the glories of her naked body. Where Bliss had had the perfect hourglass figure, Ailsa inclined a little more towards the pear shape, with smaller breasts and broader hips. But her breasts were no less delightful, with large dark nipples and seductive curves. His eyes ran down over the equally delightful contours of her belly and her hips to that dark foliage between her thighs.

And then her hands were all over him, pulling at his tunic, hoisting it over his head. Underneath he wore a thin undertunic, and with patience wearing thin she simply ripped it open. Her mouth fastened upon his nipple, while at the same time her hands worked expertly at his pants until she had them loose.

She pulled them down and at the same time dropped to her knees in front of him, and before Ben could grasp what was happening, she had taken his tumescent member into her mouth. It was almost - *almost* more pleasure than he could bear, and he gave a groan of delight.

He feared he might come too soon, but Ailsa, sensing his degree of arousal with a refinement of judgement that came from considerable experience, released him, then falling back on the bed, drew him down on top of her.

"Take me," she gasped. "Take me now!"

And Ben was only too happy to oblige, thrusting into her, trying desperately to hold back the seminal deluge he felt coming, but it would not be denied. And they both cried out together.

When it was over, and he had recovered his breath, but was still inside her, he said, "Thank you. Thank you so much."

"My pleasure," Ailsa replied with deep sincerity. "My pleasure indeed."

In moments he was asleep. Ailsa lay awake a while longer, her head resting pleasurably on his shoulder. "Not the worst," she murmured. "Not the worst by any means."

*****

When Ben awoke, the sun was streaming through the window. He looked into Ailsa's eyes, heavy-lidded with sleep.

"Good morning," he said softly.

"Good morning," she murmured back.

Suddenly conscious of the time, he sat up. "We're late!" he exclaimed. "What about the shop?"

Ailsa put her hands on his shoulders and drew him gently back down onto the lace-trimmed pillows. She straddled him and began massaging his privates. "The shop," she said quietly, "can wait. We have more important matters to attend to."

Already stiffening, Ben lay back, his arms outstretched. "I cannot tell you how pleased I am to hear you say that."

Ailsa taught him every amatory skill she knew, and Ben was an eager pupil. He swiftly learned how to use her tenderly and yet thoroughly, and in a short time he had acquired the ability to extend his lovemaking, bringing her almost... *almost!...* to a climax, and then hold her there, trembling with expectation, gasping for breath, the veins on her temples throbbing visibly, whimpering and desperate for him to finish the job, and then he would, and she would find herself dropping into a chasm that seemed to have opened up where there was none before, and then finally, her body drenched in sweat, she would open barely focussed eyes to behold him still there above her, and still deep inside her.

Ben stopped sleeping in his own bed, and the late night visitors ceased coming.

*****

One lunch time in Thermidor*, the hottest month of the year, Ailsa came into the shop from the street. She was smiling broadly, and looked radiant.

"Ben! Good news!" she declared loudly. "At last I know why you have been sent to us!"

"You do?" said Ben, puzzled.

"Yes!" she beamed. "Go upstairs, tidy yourself, put on best bib and tucker. We have an appointment with the Archmage. Well, that is, *you* do."

Ben's face fell. What heinous crime had he committed? "With the… Archmage?"

"Yes! He has something he wants to talk to you about. And you're to bring a sample of your writing. One of your workbooks, something like that. Off you go!"

CHAPTER EIGHTEEN.

With his hair neatly combed, and in his formal cloak, staff in one hand, the other clasping his workbook, he strode along through the great quadrangle, past the Pool of the Wise, struggling to keep pace with Ailsa. Although her demeanour was chipper, Ben could only feel dread.

Great Tom struck two. They entered the building, and were soon in a part that Ben had never visited before. After climbing what seemed an infinity of stairs, and passing along a long, sumptuously decorated passage, they came to a door which might have been taken from the main entrance to some vast, imposing fortress.

There was a bell, with a rope attached. Ailsa reached out to pull it, but as she did so, the mighty door swung open.

They entered the outer office. Surrounded by cases of swords, racks of sticks, all manner of Magecraft paraphernalia, portraits, maps, tapestries, all thick with dust and cobwebs, sat an elderly woman at a desk. With her neutral-coloured clothing, half-moon spectacles, and grey hair caught up in a snood, she was the picture of respectability.

"Hello Ailsa," she said, looking up. "Haven't seen you in a while."

"Hello Therda," Ailsa replied. "No, I haven't had much cause to speak with Maierlinden much lately."

So Ailsa was on regular speaking terms with the Archmage! Ben was astonished. Her place in the Magecraft hierarchy was much higher than he had realised.

"And this must be Mister Troon," said the woman called Therda. "He's to go straight in. He's expected."

As she spoke, a door beside her desk swung open, and she waved her hand to indicate that Ben might enter.

Ailsa turned to go. "Good luck," she said with a cheery smile.

His heart pounding, Ben stepped through the door. It closed with a soft click behind him.

The room was empty. In the centre was an enormous desk that looked as if it could house a small family. The surface of the desk was cluttered with books, papers, a Sacrobosco sphere*, a couple of crystal balls, what appeared to be children's wooden puzzles, and a variety of objects Ben could not immediately name. Gingerly moving a few items, Ben cleared a space and laid his workbook down on a corner of the desk.

Behind it was a large chair of intricately carved polished wood and leather, with wolf heads on the armrests, which drew to Ben's mind that of Grand Mage Styrmir, although this one was even grander, almost a throne. On the nearer side of the desk was a much humbler chair.

One corner of the room was closed off behind an ornate screen. Ben wondered if he might take a peek behind it, but hesitated to pry. He turned his attention elsewhere.

Much of the wall space was occupied by bookshelves, and Ben cast his eye over the names on the spines. There was the 'Panchatantra'*, the 'Corpus Hermeticum', 'The Deceits of the Alchemists', books by Heinrich Hexenhammer, the 'Mathematica Alchandri', Marie Keyser's 'Astrological Almanac', the 'Picatrix' of course, 'The Sworn Book', the 'Popol Vuh'...

What wall space was not occupied by bookcases was given over to hengeforms and other complex mathematical shapes, an almanac with a pointer to mark the positions of the sun and the moon, and some mysterious pictures. One in particular, directly behind the enormous chair, drew Ben's attention, and he made his way around the desk to examine it more closely.

"Shall I tell you what it represents?" said a voice, only inches behind Ben's back. He jumped visibly.

He spun around and found himself looking into a familiar face. "You!" he gasped. "You came to the shop! 'The Book of the Grey Goose'!"

"A most worthy volume," said the newcomer. "So glad I could get my hands on a copy."

Ben's hand was on his heart, in a desperate attempt to keep it from exploding out of his chest. "You're... you're the Archmage Porphyrogenitus?"

"You may call me Caerlugh," the owner of that name told him.

"But... Ailsa called you something else."

"I have many names," Caerlugh said simply. Ben was struggling to draw his gaze away from the abyssal depths of the other man's piercing blue eyes. "Nomophylax*, or 'Keeper of the Laws'? No? What about Maierlinden*?"

"Yes, that was it!"

"'Guardian of the Trees'. Now, about this picture. What it depicts is Hu, the Spirit of Life, conjoined with the male form, Hesus, who appears in the guise of an oak tree. Also to be seen here are Bel, the sun-disc, and the sacred bull, Tauros Trigaranus, which is to say, 'Of the Three Cranes'. He is the thunder-god, with the triple stripe. Around him are three trees, and upon his back are the three cranes of wisdom. Together, all these elements represent an idea, the spirit of Hu develops into and inspires the force of nature, especially trees, hence the oak. Hesus, the man, the adult, is seen to emerge from the oak. Sometimes he is shown as a kind of wolf-man. The tree spirit stands for growth and revelation, both of which, I might say, we have observed in you. Also in animals, such as the bull. And Hu, as the seed-spirit, is always behind everything."

"I see," said Ben nervously, not sure how one should address the head of the order. "Or at least, I think I do."

Caerlugh seated himself in the big chair and motioned Ben into the smaller one opposite. He drew out a small pipe, and filled is with a substance from a round box in front of him that had on the lid the face of the Green Man, grinning from amid a halo of foliage. He struck a flint to a small taper and lit the pipe. For a moment, he sucked contentedly, considering the young Mage before him, as if sizing him up.

"You've brought a sample of your writing, I believe?" he said at last.

Ben darted out of the chair, snapped up the workbook and delivered it into Caerlugh's hands. The Archmage opened it and squinted.

"Pass me the maggot-frying glass," he said.

"The… what?"

"There. On the desk. In front of you."

Ben picked up a magnifying glass with a bone handle and a brass frame to the glass. "This?"

"Yes, of course that," snapped Caerlugh impatiently. "What other maggot-frying glass do you see?"

He took the glass from Ben's trembling hands and perused the workbook.

"Hmmm. Excellent handwriting. Even magnified, there is scarcely a slip to be seen."

"Thank you sir. I was honoured to be given work in the scriptorium at the Academy."

"Yes, I know," said Caerlugh, somewhat abstractedly. "Grand Mage Styrmir has given me a full account of your activities." He closed the book and put it back on the desk. "Writing is about more than just words, you know. It's a cosmological act, a recording of the great events of the world."

"A cosmo…?"

"Exactly. Now. You fell in love with a fellow student, I believe?" Ben blushed and nodded. "And then you lost her to another man?" Ben nodded again. "Of course, officially, we don't approve of affairs of the heart. They complicate matters quite remarkably. But it happens, and generally we turn a blind eye. Personally, I take the view that one should give one's love of one's own free will. If one reaches the point where one cannot cease to love, it becomes a tyrannical yoke that one must throw off. Otherwise, as the sage Telliamed says - you know him? The philosopher of the Prasinophyceans? - lovers become like two hypnotists doing battle in a locked room. Yes, yes, I know, terribly unromantic of me. Still, as Mages, we have a job to do, and we can't have you mooning about as you have been doing, neglecting both your duties and your studies."

"No, sir."

"Well, to business, then," said Caerlugh, as if suddenly recalling the purpose of the meeting. He leant forward, engaging Ben with those abyssal blue eyes. "I would like you to consider the possibility that everything that has happened to you in your life, the good and the bad, has all been to one end, namely to bring you to this place, to that very chair you are perched upon, at this precise moment in time."

"Very well," Ben replied hesitantly. "I accept that possibility. Sir."

"Good. Because I have a job for you, if you are willing to take it on."

Ben was not about to deny the Archmage Porphyrogenitus anything. If he had a job for him, it could only be an honour. "Of course, sir. Whatever is in my power."

"Excellent. Tell me, what do you know about sheep?"

Ben was not sure if he had heard correctly. "Sheep, sir?"

"Sheep. What does a sheep's life consist of?"

Was this a trick question, Ben wondered. His mind raced. "Well, I suppose it consists of standing around in a field for a few months and then being eaten."

Ben saw the corners of Caerlugh's mouth twitch upward, and had the impression that the Archmage was repressing a laugh.

"Good answer," said Caerlugh. "We might leave the last part to one side for the moment. Let me put it another way: what does the sheep know of the shepherd?"

"Well," said Ben, "apart from at shearing time, I suppose not a lot." He was still desperately trying to figure out where this was all leading.

"Indeed," Caerlugh concurred. "Which is a funny thing, wouldn't you say, given that the shepherd guards the sheep, and keeps wolves and other predators away."

"I suppose so," Ben conceded.

"Well, I would like you to consider that all of us here on Anoone are sheep, all of us, and we are about to receive a visit from the shepherd."

Ben struggled inwardly to consider this notion. "Who is that, sir?"

Caerlugh waved his hand towards the ceiling to indicate the realm beyond Anoone. "A Siderial Nuncio, a messenger from the stars, come to see how we're getting on."

"I see."

"I'm not sure you do," Caerlugh remarked. "But no matter. We need a written report that we can present to this extranoonian visitor, and I would like you to write it, if you are willing. It will mean, quite simply, that you will travel all around the world, recording everything that you see. It is quite likely that you will travel further than any one individual on Anoone has ever travelled before. And make no mistake, it will be dangerous. Very."

"If you think I'm up to it, I'd be honoured to do it for the order."

"Good," said Caerlugh, appearing relieved. "I do think you're up to it. In fact, I think you are perhaps uniquely suited for the task, hence my earlier comment. Now, what do you know already of the geography of Anoone?"

Ben swallowed hard. "Not much," he conceded. "The extent of the Quaaman Empire, as it was, to some degree, but nothing really beyond that."

"Well, that's more than some folk," said Caerlugh. "That's about to change though. The scholars of Delgnat the Beautiful, which I trust will be on your itinerary, believe that what is generally thought of as the "habitable" world occupies about a quarter of the surface of Anoone. How much of the rest is land and how much is sea is one of the things you will doubtless determine on your travels. There is a school of thought that the land masses must necessarily form a half of the whole in order for the whole thing to balance, and I'm sure you've been taught about the importance of balance in nature?" Ben nodded. "Good. Shamsiel of the Phylosophantes argues for the existence of a great southern continent which has been named Sahul. You may perhaps determine whether he was correct."

It all seemed too much for Ben to take in. What was it he had agreed to?

Caerlugh stood up. "Right. There are many things that need to be done before you are ready to depart, but first things first. You will not be travelling alone. Motria, if you would step forward, please."

A woman emerged from behind the screen, and Ben's heart leapt in his chest, for she appeared to him to be remarkably similar in appearance to Bliss. She was about the same height. She had the same oval-shaped face, likewise framed by long hair, although this woman's was honey-coloured rather than Bliss' light brown, and wavy rather than straight. Her eyes were a limpid blue, and she was smiling. Around her brows she wore a ring of animal fur, as if a fur hat had lost its crown, and a heavy brocade coat - or it might have been a dress, Ben couldn't be sure - in a rich, earthy brown, that swept down to the floor. Ben's first impression was that she looked as if she came from somewhere cold.

"May I introduce Motria Leborcham, from Hyperboria?" said Caerlugh.

"Hello, Ben," said the owner of the name, extending a hand. Ben took it and shook hands distractedly.

"Hyperboria?" said Ben, perplexed. The name rang a distant bell, but that was all.

"It means 'Beyond the North Wind'," Caerlugh explained. So, a cold place indeed.

Ben felt his heart sinking into his boots at a tremendous rate. Moments before he had felt thrilled at being given this extraordinary task to fulfil, and now he was being told he had to do it in the company of a woman, and an undeniably lovely woman at that. He could already foresee all sorts of complications that he could really live without.

"Oh, no, no," he moaned. "I don't want to be rude," he said, glancing nervously in Motria's direction, "but I'd really rather do this alone."

"Unfortunately," said Caerlugh, "you don't have that option. For one thing, there is the Book. You won't be able to carry that and all your travelling requisites. For another thing, there will be places where you will not want to draw attention to yourself, and a man and a woman travelling together can often be less noticeable than a man travelling alone."

"I see," said Ben, crestfallen. He shot another glance at Motria. His treacherous heart was already beating out a faster rhythm.

Caerlugh turned to Motria. "Would you excuse us a moment?"

Motria smiled engagingly. "Of course," she said, and feigned a rapt interest in the books on Caerlugh's shelves.

Caerlugh took Ben to one side. "You remember the story, don't you, of how the first people came to Magelaw?"

"Yes, of course," said Ben. "It's one of the first things they teach you at the Academy."

"So you remember who it is that they met when they came there?"

"Certainly," said Ben. "They met the three goddesses, Erin, Banba and Fódla."

"And they are…?"

"Well, the three manifestations of the triple goddess."

"Good," said Caerlugh, with a smile that Ben found most unsettling. "Now, I would like you to consider that the three women you have been and are most closely connected with, to whit, Bliss, Ailsa and now Motria, are similarly three manifestations of the triple goddess."

"All right," said Ben, somewhat reluctantly. "But I see a problem with the analogy."

"And that is…?"

"Well, the three goddesses married the three founding kings of Magelaw, Cuill, Checht and Gréine, the Hazel King, the Plough King and the Sun King."

"I would like you to consider that you in yourself represent a manifestation of all three kings."

Ben was silent for a long moment while he digested this. "Very well," he said at last.

"So you will accept Motria as your travelling companion?"

"It rather looks as if I have no choice."

Caerlugh beamed, and slapped him on the shoulder. "That's the spirit! Now, the next item on the agenda…"

He went to a cupboard in one corner of the room and opened it. Motria stood close by, watching with interest as he did so. From a shelf he took down a box measuring perhaps half an ell by a third, and about six inches deep. On the top there were four square panels framed by a plain moulding. Within this was a second moulding of narrow step fret, suggestive of lightning, or bolts of magic energy. On the sides was an additional strip of step fret which terminated with a twist. A knotwork design of a ring-knot made from two concentric circles threaded by four return loops was incised into it, and Ben felt that there was some deep inner meaning contained within the design. There were other little knobbly bits contained within the design which seemed to serve no particular purpose.

Caerlugh placed the box in Ben's hands. It was heavy. "The wood is cheetwood," he informed him. "When the box is closed it is waterproof and buoyant, fireproof and is protected against all but the strongest Magecraft. Open it," he said.

Ben was intensely conscious of the other two observing him. He ran his fingers over it. After a moment or so, he found two small hinged legs which could be pulled out of the casing, and could be secured to turn the box into a sort of lectern. He pushed them back into their housing, and marvelled at the way they became almost invisible when one did so. With some further probing, he found that one of the decorative accretions could be depressed.

"Well done," said Caerlugh.

Ben slid open the box. Inside was a large book, bound in leather of varying shades of green. Incised into the leather were mysterious sigils that Ben was unable to recognise.

"Open it."

With trembling fingers, Ben lifted the front cover to reveal the first page. The parchment was black, and bore in ornate gold letters the simple words: 'The Book'.

"The black parchment was immersed in a solution containing iron and copper, and only lead white, gold and silver ink may be used upon it. Contrary to popular misconception, the black signifies luxury, *not* mourning."

Ben turned to the next page. It was blank, creamy white, and silky to the touch.

"Three hundred pages of uterine vellum, that is to say, from the skin of unborn or still born calves," Caerlugh told him. "With your small writing, that should be ample for your report."

Ben stroked the page thoughtfully with his fingertips. It would take him a lifetime to fill three hundred pages!

Caerlugh returned to the cupboard and from the bottom pulled out what appeared to be a well-made leather knapsack. On either side there were pockets. He unbuckled the flap on one of these and pulled out a small case. He opened it to reveal rows of small quills with very fine points, together with a small pen-knife.

"These are the wing feathers of the knot," he said. The pens are admirably suited for someone who writes as finely as you."

Ben studied them. "They are the finest pens I think I have ever seen," he declared. "Thank you."

From the other pocket Caerlugh drew a leather-bound flask. "Ink," he explained, "made from boiled evergreen bearberry with young osiers and black tincture in a medium of gum and water. It will refill as and when necessary."

He replaced the pens and the ink in their respective pockets and secured them. He took the box and fitted it into the knapsack, which was evidently tailor-made to receive it. "Turn around," he said. Ben turned around.

Caerlugh lifted the knapsack. "Put your arms through the shoulder straps." Ben did so. "How does it feel?"

"Comfortable," Ben replied. "But you certainly know you have some weight on your back."

"Precisely," Caerlugh concurred. "You see why you need a travelling companion, to carry all your necessaries. Or vice versa."

"Yes," said Ben, though still without enthusiasm. "Yes, I see."

"Now," said Caerlugh, "the next thing you will need is a map."

"A map?" said Ben in surprise. "I thought I was going into uncharted territory."

"Well, you are," Caerlugh agreed. "But you will have to cross a fair bit of charted territory first. We want to help you as much as possible. Let's go and see Senex, the mapmaker."

*****

They found the mapmaker's workshop two flights of stairs and half a dozen corridors away. The room and the man himself were largely as Ben might have expected them to be. The walls were covered with framed, yellowing maps, shrouded in atorcoppe* webs,

While every shelf and much of the floor space was occupied by large rolls of parchment. Ben's eyes were immediately drawn to those maps which showed lands bordering on unknown territory, and he was filled with a desire to fill in the blank spaces.

"My maps are all completely accurate, of course," said a reedy voice behind him. "Unlike those of Joris Carolus, whom they call 'a congenital inventor of islands'." The figure which emerged from behind a veritable mountain of charts on the large drawing table at the centre of the room was similarly reed-like, tall and slender, a wild frizz of white hair surrounding a dome-shaped bald pate. He had watery blue-green eyes with wrinkly bags beneath them. A straight, thin ridge of a nose formed the centrepiece of the visage, and beneath it a pair of thin, clenched lips and a weak chin that had sprouted a few grey whiskers.

"My name is Senex," he said. "How may I be of assistance?"

"His name is Ben Troon," said Caerlugh, emerging from a shadowy corner of the room, with Motria close behind, "and he's going on a long journey. Longer, perhaps, than anyone has undertaken before. He needs one of your special traveller's maps."

"Archmage," said Senex. "Forgive me. I didn't see you there. One of the special maps, you say? Goodness, haven't had a request for one of those in quite a few years! Quite a few! Well, I'm sure I have one here somewhere."

Ben was consumed with curiosity as to what it was that was "special" about these maps. He glanced at Caerlugh, but his expression was blank, then he turned to Motria, but she merely shrugged as if to say that she was as much in the dark as he.

Senex took a little time, rooting through bundles of parchment, muttering to himself as he did so, and sneezing as he threw up clouds of dust that had lain undisturbed for a considerable period of time. At last he emerged from one of the furthest corners of the room, clutching a roll of yellow parchment.

"Found it!" he announced. "Come and see!"

They gathered around the map table, and he unrolled the parchment, weighting the corners.

"Observe, Mister Troon," said Senex, waving a proud hand over his creation.

Ben looked at the parchment. The whole known world was laid out before him. Instantly recognisable was the island shared by Luthany and Magelaw, lying in the Garsedge Sea, a little off the coast of the great continent of Laurentia. Mountains appeared to rise up in long chains, capped by snow on their peaks, rivers sparkled, lakes and great seas glistened, and then it all slowly faded away at the edges, where the mapmakers had not yet ventured.

"Now, should you wish to acquire a closer view of a particular part," Senex went on, "all you have to do is think about it. I would suggest you focus on here, Lochranza."

Ben did as he was bid, focussing his thoughts on the city, and as he did so, it was as if he were plunging down out of the clouds, falling at a great rate. He could see the city walls, the houses, the River Lond snaking through, then broadening out into the great lake, the island of the Magisterium close to the southern shore, and then the river resuming its course towards the sea. In his mind, he ordered a halt to his descent, and found himself hovering as a seagull might over the rooftops of the Magisterium. He could even pick out the bookshop across the embankment.

"And of course it works the other way too," said Senex. He removed the weights and rolled up the parchment, and it seemed to shrink to a much smaller size than previously. Easy to fit into a pocket.

He handed it to Ben. "Take care of it," he said. "There aren't too many like it."

Ben took it, shook his hand, and they took their leave.

CHAPTER NINETEEN.

"Right," said Caerlugh, leading the way along the passage at a brisk pace. "That's that. The next thing you will need is a sword. There will be times when Magecraft will not be appropriate, and perhaps not even possible. We will pay a visit to our swordmaker, Lothar Ilmarinen."

As they walked, Ben conjured up a picture of the swordmaker in his mind. He had got it pretty right with Senex, a studious old man, tall and lean. The swordmaker would be a giant of a man, with glistening raven-black curls, bare-chested and with forearms like ham-hocks, pouring rivers of sweat as he pounded glowing metal with a hammer that Ben would scarcely be able to lift.

Again Ben found himself walking through parts of the Magisterium that were new to him. They came at last to the quadrangle furthest from the main entrance. As soon as they emerged from the connecting passageway, they heard the sound of iron slamming down on steel, again and again.

One part of the square was enclosed and roofed over, with dark smoke pouring from a central chimney. As they drew closer, they could see that the interior of the enclosed space was lit with a ruddy glow. Ben thought it looked like the workshop of K'daai Maqsin*, the underworld smith in the ancient tales.

As they drew yet closer, Ben felt a jolt of surprise. The smith was hammering a sword on the anvil, a large block of stone, making sparks fly in every direction. He was not the colossus Ben had pictured in his head. Indeed, he was not above average height. Lothar the Swordmaker did not have huge musclebound arms. He had wavy red hair that was turning to grey, blue eyes that sparkled over the top of a pair of spectacles - spectacles on a smith! - and a grey goatee. He was clad all in black leather, a long workmanlike apron with assorted tools stuffed into the pocket, black leather pants and heavy black boots that looked as if they could withstand an anvil being dropped on them.

"Master Lothar," said Caerlugh as they approached, "your services are required."

"Archmage. When has it ever been otherwise?" said Lothar gruffly, desisting from his hammering. "What can I do for you?"

"This gentleman is Ben Troon," said Caerlugh, nudging Ben forward. "He is going to go on a long journey on our behalf, and needs a sword."

Lothar looked him up and down. "Do you use a sword much?" he asked.

"N-no," Ben replied. "Not much."

"So something to defend yourself with? Nothing too fancy?"

"Y-yes," said Ben. "I suppose so."

"I would suggest a scramaseax. A straight, single-edged blade, more for hacking than thrusting, a good all-purpose weapon. Pattern-welded."

Lothar glanced towards Caerlugh, who nodded in agreement.

"Leave it with me," Lothar said. "Come again in about five weeks." It was clear they were being dismissed.

"A man of few words," Ben observed as they were walking away.

"Indeed," Caerlugh agreed. "But there is no finer swordsmith in Luthany. Two weeks will give us time enough to get you well familiarised with the sword before it is time for you to depart. I certainly want you to be across the sea before winter sets in. Now, there is one more thing we have to do today, but it is perhaps the most important."

*****

"Now, Motria," said Caerlugh as they were walking away, "I have not forgotten you. I believe that in your home country you are quite the hunter?"

Motria, who had said little during the foregoing, shook her head. "I don't know about 'quite the hunter'," she replied modestly. "It was necessary to hunt game to eat, certainly. We didn't hunt for pleasure, as some do, and we always used every part of the animal."

"That's good to hear," said Caerlugh. "I would expect nothing less. What I was meaning, though, was that you know how to use a bow."

"Oh!" Motria exclaimed. "Well, yes, of course. But I don't have one with me."

"That," said Caerlugh, "is about to be remedied."

In the opposite corner of the same quadrangle where Lothar had his forge, there was another workshop, similarly sheltered from the elements with a thatched roof and light walls made of wattle hurdles. In one corner there was a small area that was screened from view.

In front of it a man sat straddling something which loosely resembled a child's rocking horse. An upright bar passing through the main body pivoted, and was held in position by the feet of the man. It thus held in position a bow from which the man was shaving thin slivers of wood with a two handed plane. When he had taken a small amount from the body of the bow, he released it by dropping his feet, and held it up so he could look along it and examine the precise contours. It was when he was thus looking along it that he beheld his three visitors.

"Archmage!" he cried. Setting down the bow, he threw his leg over the bow-jig and leapt to his feet.

He was, Ben saw, a stunted, sickly-looking individual who appeared to be unable to stand straight. He looked pale and lacking in vitality.

"This is Multhesius Schmedding, our bowmaster," said Caerlugh.

"At your service," said Schmedding. "How may I help you, Archmage?"

"My friends here are going on a long trip. This lady, Motria Leborcham, will be largely responsible for catching their dinner, and she needs a bow."

"Just a straight yew bow? Shouldn't be a problem. In fact, I have a limb from the Great Yew of Ankerwyke."

"That would be perfect," said Caerlugh, "I was thinking… sharpened cowhorns on the tips would make it a good weapon for close range fighting."

"Oh, it's that sort of trip," said Schmedding. "I can arrange that."

"How long would it take?"

"Oh, not long," Schmedding assured him. "Three or four hours to cut the yew stave, another five or six to finish it. I could have it done in a day. Or a day and a half."

"Excellent," said Caerlugh. "Though there is no particular hurry."

While they were speaking, Ben, curious, reached for the unfinished bow-stave beside Schmedding. The bowmaker snatched it away.

"Yew," he said. "Best not to touch it in its raw state. Speaking of which, if you'll excuse me?"

He dropped the stave and ran to the closed off part of his workplace.

"The runs," said Caerlugh *sotto voce*. "Bowmakers suffer terribly from it, handling yew all the time."

"Is that why he looks so unwell?" asked Motria.

"Exactly," said Caerlugh. "We might just discreetly withdraw. There is one more important bit of business to do, and then we can call it a day."

*****

Ben and Motria followed Caerlugh's swirling robe as he led the way back inside the Magisterium. The passageways had a bewildering sameness to them, and Ben quickly felt that he was becoming lost.

Then Caerlugh opened an enormous door and passed through. Ben, following behind him, gave a gasp, as did Motria bringing up the rear. If he had felt bewildered before, now Ben was utterly speechless.

They were standing at one end of an enormous hall. Ben thought he had explored most of the Magisterium over the past few months, and could not conceive of how such a huge space could have escaped his attention, unless - and he thought he could kick himself for not considering the possibility earlier - there was some powerful Magecraft governing the accessibility of this place.

He looked around, flabbergasted. Along the walls were intricately carved wooden screens, perhaps ten ells high, with exotic creatures forming the finials, and, looking further up, he saw the magnificent fan-vaulted ceiling. Off to one side, halfway along, an ornate throne in some dark timber stood raised upon a stepped pediment: the seat of the Archmage. In front of it, a circle of six immensely tall columns, reminiscent of a grove, supported a dome, high above, interrupting the roof vaulting and casting illumination down upon the floor below.

As they drew closer, they saw that set into the floor were two concentric circles of tiles, the outer circle white, the inner one violet.

"This is the Place of the Spirit," said Caerlugh, indicating the circles. "The heart of the Magisterium, and indeed the Order itself. The holy of holies, if you wish. Here, the elements of earth, air, fire and water are harmonised, reconciled, transmuted and transformed."

From the centre of the circle, an elegant stone staircase ascended to meet a strange structure which occupied almost the whole width of the hall somewhat further along its length. In the middle of the floor stood a short column of white marble which supported a plinth of the same material. This in turn supported two more small columns, above which was a further, slightly longer, plinth bearing three more columns, then four above that, and then five, and so on. At a certain point, the process went into reverse, each plinth becoming shorter than the one below it, and supporting one less column, so that the entire structure had a diamond shape. At the top, where the staircase met it, the final column held a small platform upon which stood a circular mirror, more than man-height in diameter.

To either side of the mirror were a pair of long slender windows, and through them Ben saw the ruddy light of a setting sun.

At the same time, he became aware that an elderly servant was hastening along the side of the hall, lighting lamps that were affixed to the wooden screens. It occurred to Ben that Caerlugh, or himself for that matter, could light the lamps with a wave of the hand, or even with just a thought, but then he recalled the admonitions that he had heard that Magecraft was not a toy, and definitely not to be used for frivolous purposes.

"Get undressed, please, Ben," said Caerlugh quietly.

The request took Ben aback. "Completely?"

Caerlugh nodded. "Completely."

He took his own shoes off and with a little hop crossed over into the circle.

Acutely conscious of Motria looking on, Ben disrobed. With the same little hop, he joined Caerlugh in the circle.

"Kneel," said Caerlugh. Ben did as he was bid. "Ben Troon, why have you become a Mage?" Caerlugh asked.

Ben's mind reeled. He gave the only answer he could think of. "Because I have never wanted anything else in this life."

Caerlugh seemed content with this. "Whom do you serve?"

"Why, yourself. And the Order."

Caerlugh said nothing, but nodded. He placed his hands on Ben's head.

Ben cried aloud. It was as if a dam had burst, and a vast torrent of thought was flooding through his mind, the memories of countless lifetimes, many of them of staggering antiquity, ideas, notions, experiences, far, far too much to absorb, visions of extraordinary places and strange events swept through his consciousness, engulfing him.

Caerlugh lifted his hands from Ben's head. Ben found he was struggling for breath. But suddenly there was this wealth of ancient wisdom there inside him. More than he could fathom in a single lifetime. It was beyond comprehension, and at the same time, intoxicating.

"Take some deep breaths," said Caerlugh soothingly. Ben did so.

"What just happened?" he asked.

"We call it the ritual of transmission of the gnosis," Caerlugh explained. "To grossly oversimplify it, a special status has been conferred upon you, by Ruad Rofhessa, founder of the Order and a lord of great knowledge. Very few have been so honoured, Mr. Troon. Now, Motria, if you could toss him his clothes?"

Motria obliged, and Ben hastily dressed. When he was ready, Caerlugh ushered him up the staircase. At the top they stepped onto the small platform. Ben made a point of not looking down, as there was no guard rail or balustrade of any kind.

Instead he looked at the mirror. He saw himself reflected, standing next to the Archmage. It made him feel small and insignificant, and not at all up to the task which he had taken on.

"Behold," said Caerlugh, and gave a wave of his hand.

At once the reflections vanished. The image that replaced it was of an ocean. It was as if Ben had been transformed into a seabird, flying low over the crests of the waves. He could almost feel the spray on his face. Then a coastline appeared, steep cliffs of brown rock, he could see the strata bending this way and that. Before he knew it, he was over land, farmland. He could see wagons bringing in the harvest, streams snaking between pastures with growing crops, and villages with thin streams of smoke rising from chimneys: at one point he actually flew through the smoke. Then a large city appeared in the distance, and he found himself looking down at grids of streets, large squares, palaces and other official buildings, before he swept on, moving over the land at breathtaking speed, crossing lakes and forests and then rising up into a range of snow-capped mountains…

And then it was gone, and the reflections of Caerlugh and himself returned.

"You get the picture," said Caerlugh. "With this, we are able to track your progress. However, and this is a major stipulation by the Siderial Nuncio, no matter what happens to you, *we can not interfere.*"

"I understand," Ben said quietly.

"Yes?" said Caerlugh. "Come what may, you and Motria are on your own."

"Yes," Ben assured him, "I understand."

"Very well," said Caerlugh.

They descended the staircase once more.

"Well," Caerlugh sighed when they reached the ground, "it's been a long day. You should go home and get some rest. We will commence your training tomorrow."

He clapped Ben amicably on the shoulder.

"Thank you, Archmage," Ben said. "Thank you for having confidence in me. I hope it isn't misplaced."

"If I didn't think you could do it," Caerlugh smiled, "I wouldn't have offered it to you, believe me."

Ben nodded. He turned to Motria. "Good-bye, Motria," he said, with a nervous wave of his hand.

"Good-bye, Ben," she replied with a smile. "We'll meet again soon."

With that, Ben walked away. He took the handle on the great door and pulled it open. In a few minutes, he was out in the great quadrangle, which was bathed in golden evening light. As he passed the Pool of the Wise, Great Tom struck seven o'clock. He had no notion that he had been away so long. Time seemed to have become distorted while he was inside the Magisterium.

Ailsa was cooking in the kitchen when he walked into the living room. Delicious smells were wafting through the air.

"You're back," said Ailsa when she saw him. "How did it go?"

Ben felt suddenly exhausted. He fell into her arms.

"There's a lot to tell," he sighed, his face in her hair.

*****

"Well," said Caerlugh when Ben saw him again a few days later, "you're getting a sword. It's time you were taught how to use one. You need to go and see our resident swordmaster, Anthime Spinnewyn.

Anthime Spinnewyn. To Ben's imagination, the name suggested a spider, and he was gratified to find that for once he was right. The master of swords was a gangling, long-limbed fellow with beady eyes. His movements were jerky and appeared deceptively uncoordinated, but he was lightning fast, and Ben soon came to realise that he would not like to be a fly in *his* web.

"Let's see what you can do," Anthime said, when they first met in a secluded courtyard. Ben duly showed him.

"Hmm," said Anthime, after he had effortlessly disarmed Ben for the fourth time. "It seems we have our work cut out. But no matter. I enjoy a challenge. Now, we begin with the standard blocking moves…"

Anthime worked Ben until his arm ached and he could barely lift his sword, let alone fight with it. Day after day, the sword master honed Ben's skill with all manner of thrusts, parries, ripostes and counterripostes, until he was fluent.

"Well," he said, as Ben stood panting at the end of a particularly arduous bout, "I think I have taught you all you need to know. Almost."

"Almost?" gasped Ben.

"Almost," Anthime repeated. "Take a rest, have something to drink, get your breath back. And then I will teach you the 'Boar's Thrust'. Who knows, it may save your life one day..."

*****

Ben's training grew more intense from then on. Besides more instruction in the deeper ways of Magecraft, he was given instructors in combat with quarterstaff, sword, axe and pole weapons, as well as daily archery practice, which he did alongside Motria, who had her new yew bow from Master Schmedding. Ben no longer worked in the bookshop, Ailsa happily taking over full time.

Caerlugh taught Ben many aspects of unarmed combat. He showed him how to bring a man to the ground, seizing the wrist with the fingers of one hand so as to twist the arm upward, whilst at the same time applying pressure with the other hand to the upper arm - just above the elbow, on the bicep, or closer to the shoulder, depending on the size of the opponent in question - and all sorts of other crafty manoeuvres. He taught him how to fall without hurting himself - "Learning how to fall is perhaps the most critical skill of all," the Archmage told him - and many other such skills. He also taught Ben how to apply pressure on the neck in such a way as to cut off the blood supply to the brain and thus render an opponent unconscious… or dead.

He was, without question, the most remarkable person Ben had ever met, or, he felt sure, ever would, and yet he was able to make himself utterly unremarkable. As he watched Ben exercising, he would be dressed in robes so faded that it was virtually impossible to say with any certainty what colour they had originally been. In a crowd, he would blend in utterly, no one would give him a second glance.

He was also able to make himself genuinely invisible - that had been established from day one - and he used this in Ben's training. He might come at Ben from one direction, and then throw his voice, calling to him from another direction entirely. In this way, Ben learned to disregard distractions, and remain focussed upon the antagonist directly in front of him. But it took many painful blows and hard falls before he learned this lesson to Caerlugh's satisfaction.

Caerlugh also used his invisibility to teach Ben to home in on cues that were other than visual, such as heavy breathing, or a person's body odour. In time, Ben became proficient at combating even an invisible enemy, but even when he had used the arm grip to bring the master to the ground, and then applied hand pressure to his neck, he could not help but suspect that Caerlugh had allowed him to do it.

"Perhaps I did," Caerlugh conceded, "but unless you have the grave misfortune to run up against an opponent whose abilities are of the same calibre as mine, you should be able to outmanoeuvre and overpower any enemy that you come up against."

It was exhausting but exhilarating.

Cantlos*, the Month of Song, came round, and with it the Midsummer Ceremony. Ben found it strange watching Caerlugh conduct the ceremony wearing the stag's head, knowing now what he looked like. Within the circle were twelve pots each containing a small ash sapling, and Ailsa pointed out to him that the fire buring in the centre of the henge was also of ash wood.

*****

Knowing that their time was coming to an end, Ben's and Ailsa's lovemaking grew in intensity.

"I can't imagine not having to wrestle any more with your Symington Sidewinder," he declared one night, as he undid the laces of the aforementioned undergarment.

Ailsa gave a peal of laughter. "That's Side-*Lacer*, idiot!"

She took delight in sharing with him amatory techniques that were beyong his wildest imagining, ways of stimulating all the senses, sometimes one at a time, sometimes all together, and ways of delaying the climax to extend the pleasure far beyond what was considered usual, and of course, with all that he learned, Ailsa herself was the immediate beneficiary. Sometimes Ben wondered what the neighbours must think of the ecstatic vocalising that accompanied their amours, but at heart he didn't particularly care.

Gasping for breath on sweat-soaked sheets after a spectacularly athletic bout of such fornication, he said to her, "That is the most amazing magic I have ever known."

"Why, thank you, young man," she panted back. "You're not so bad yourself."

*****

One afternoon word came from Caerlugh that Ben's scramaseax was ready for collection. He met the

Archmage and Motria in the great quadrangle and went swiftly to Swordsmith Lothar's lair.

He was sitting at a sandstone wheel when they arrived, putting a final razor-sharp edge to the sword. His visitors stood and watched him at work for a few minutes, oblivious to all around him, until his bellows boy noticed them and politely cleared his throat.

"Oh, you're here!" said Lothar, jumping from his stool. "Hold out your hands," he told Ben.

Ben put out his hands, and Lothar laid a cloth over them, and then delicately laid the sword across his palms.

"Best not to touch the blade with bare hands if you can help it," Lothar said. "The acid in sweat pits the steel very easily."

Ben inspected the sword. The cutting edge was slightly shorter than the back, the leading edge angled back to meet it: definitely a sword for hacking rather than thrusting. But what drew Ben's attention first of all was the runes inlaid in silver, F-U-Th-A-R-K, the first six runes of the Elder Futhark, the runic alphabet, twice along each side of the blade.

He glanced questioningly at Caerlugh.

"Silver, of course," the latter replied to the unspoken question, "is potent against dark forces."

"Dark forces?" echoed Ben. "Do you expect…?"

"There is no telling what you may encounter," Caerlugh answered quickly. "It is as well to be prepared for all eventualities."

"And why twice, on each side?"

"That makes twenty-four runes in total," Caerlugh explained. "And the number twenty-four in itself has a beneficial influence."

Ben turned his attention again to the blade. There was inticate patterning all along it. It resembled the skin of a living creature.

"This patterning on the blade…?"

"Appropriately enough," said Lothar, "it's called pattern welding. It is achieved by layering strips of steel, hammering them together, folding them over and repeating the process, over and over again, perhaps a thousand times. It's what takes up most of the time in making a sword."

Ben thought back over the past weeks. While he had been in ecstasy in Ailsa's bed, Lothar had been hammering and sweating to forge his weapon. He felt more than a little guilty.

"This particular style is called wurmtinting, because it is supposed to resemble the hide of a dragon. I've never seen a dragon myself, and I don't know anyone who has, so I can't say whether it does or whether it doesn't."

Ben looked then at the hilt. It had a slight curve to it, and sat most comfortably in his hand. It was covered in some sort of black material that was slightly rough to the touch, and it was ornamented with gold wire in a criss-cross pattern.

"This hilt isn't wood," he observed. "What is it?"

"It's the tooth of a walrus," Lothar told him.

"What's that?"

"It's a large sea-creature that lives in the cold north," Lothar explained.

"Hyperborea?" Ben asked, glancing at Motria.

"Among other places, yes," Lothar agreed. Ben made a mental note to ensure that Hyperborea would be on their itinerary.

"The black material," Lothar went on, "is called shagreen. It's the skin of a kind of fish called a ray. As you see, it provides an excellent grip in all circumstances, even when slick with sweat and blood."

Ben was suddenly jolted back to reality. What he was holding in his hand was not some fancy ornament, it was a weapon, and its purpose was to kill. He gave a slight inward shudder.

Not slight enough, for Caerlugh noticed it. "You'll have to give it a name," he said, deftly redirecting Ben's attention.

"Yes," said Ben, brightening visibly. "I've thought about that. All the swords in stories have names, and I came across one that I like."

"Yes?" said Caerlugh and Motria in unison.

"Fragarach. The Answerer."

"It's a good name," said Caerlugh. "Fragarach it is."

"Thank you, Lothar," said Ben. He made to give him back the cloth.

"Keep that," said Lothar. "It's a polishing cloth. It's been soaked in melted tallow with ground glass mixed through it. You'll need it, especially after it's been used."

"I'll take it," said Motria, and stuffed it into a pouch that she had slung across her shoulder.

"Oh," said Lothar. "Almost forgot. There's this."

From behind the grinding wheel he picked up a leather scabbard incised with knotwork patterns. He took the sword and slid it in.

"Now, you're familiar with sword etiquette, I presume?" he asked. Ben looked blank. "If you are going to fight, you draw the sword out of the scabbard. If you are removing it for any other reason, you draw the scabbard away from the sword. It's a subtle difference, but there are times when having your actions misinterpreted could cost you your life, so be careful."

Lothar's blue eyes, behind his spectacles, were intense. Ben took the point.

"Go well, Mage Troon," said Lothar, formally placing the sheathed weapon into his hands. "And come back safely."

It was yet another reminder that the time for departure on this hazardous undertaking was drawing ever nearer.

"Thank you," Ben said. "With Fragarach at my side, I'm sure I shall."

The following month was Bassemánnu*, the Holy Month. It was barely a few days old when Caerlugh appeared at one of Ben's and Motria's archery sessions. He beckoned to them.

"Come with me," he urged. "There's someone I want you to meet."

Ben passed his bow and quiver of arrows to their instructor, while Motria slipped her own bow, almost as tall as she was, into its case, and shouldered it.

"Where are we going?" Ben asked, as they walked out through the main gate.

"To the wharves," said Caerlugh.

CHAPTER TWENTY.

Beyond the lake, the River Lond, wider now, resumed its course to the sea. Along its banks were the wharves where all manner of cargoes were loaded and unloaded. It was a part of the city he had never visited before, and he had heard it said that it was a dangerous area, and that one should, at the very least, keep a close eye on one's purse.

Weaving their way between barrows and horse-drawn drays, packed with barrels and sacks and boxes of every size, and men hastening hither and thither with large loads on their backs or their shoulders, they came at last to a dry dock, where a ship of moderate size appeared to be undergoing repairs. At the prow was mounted a silver-painted star, which Ben took to be of wood. He read the name painted on the bow: *Realt Fanad*.

"It means *The Star of Fanad* in Lepontic," Caerlugh told him. "Ah, there's Captain van Brodick."

The Archmage gestured towards a large figure distinguished by an imposing beaver-skin hat, from beneath which wild red hair protruded in all directions. He wore a dark blue tailcoat and pants of an indeterminate colour that were remarkably baggy. Ben saw that the men around him were attired in similarly voluminous drawers.

"Captain van Brodick," Caerlugh hailed him as he approached, "these are your two passengers, Mage Troon and Miss Leborcham."

"Pleased to meet you," the captain said amicably. From close up, Ben saw that he had a ruddy complexion, a consequence, perhaps, of long exposure to sun and wind. A meaty paw enclosed first Ben's hand and then Motria's. "Come aboard."

They descended the gangplank onto the deck, and then van Brodick led them into the bowels of the vessel.

"Do you know much about ships?" he asked. The question was directed at Ben, for he was clearly of the opinion that a woman could not possibly know anything about ships.

"Not a thing," said Ben, who decided at once that honesty was the best policy.

"Ah," said van Brodick, looking slightly deflated. But then he brightened, realising that he had a new pupil before him whom he could dazzle with his erudition on matters maritime. "Well. You're standing in the hold of what is known as a wherry. Sits fairly low in the water, carries cargoes of timber across the Garsedge Sea into Laurentia, specifically the country of Pilappelanth, on the coast. Which is what we will be doing as soon as we have finished repairs. Now, under your feet here is the keel, which is the timber which runs the length of the ship, a single piece of wood, mind you. Ours is about seventeen and a half ells long, and varies from fourteen and a half to sixteen and a half inches in thickness. Stems then join to the keel with short transitional pieces. The hull is what we call clinker built, which is to say that the boards overlap instead of being edge to edge. The planks are called strakes, and there are sixteen of them from the keel to the gunwale. They are secured with rivets and caulked, that is, waterproofed, with animal fur dipped in tar and pushed into all the gaps. Now, above the keel is the keelson, which supports the mast, which you will notice is at present distinguished by its absence. The keelson is a heavy longitudinal timber. Well, it is in this case. Other ships have them going crosswise. It has notches cut into it to accommodate the floor timbers, which are connected by other timbers called knees. These are timbers that have grown naturally with two branches approximately at right angles. As you see, there is another natural branch projecting vertically directly in front of the hole where the mast will go when it is ready, which will hopefully be in the next few days. Now, there is one other little thing…"

"Yes?" said Caerlugh, slightly flummoxed by van Brodick's lecture.

"We will be sailing at night."

"Why's that?" asked Ben.

"Glad you asked," said van Brodick, looking discomfited and not at all glad. "The thing is, I have, well, a few debts, shall we say, and would like to slip away under the cover of darkness, before my creditors twig that the *Fanad* is even seaworthy again. So you might not get a lot of notice that we're sailing."

"I see," said Ben.

Van Brodick finished his conducted tour and took his guests back to the main cabin, where a flask of metheglin was passed around.

When they were done, Caerlugh, Ben and Motria returned to the Magisterium.

Word came that the *Fanad* would be sailing at eleven that night. It would be Ben and Ailsa's last day together.

They made love with the morning light streaming through Ailsa's window, then went for a long walk around the lake shore. It was a beautiful day, and they held hands all the way, stopping every few ells to kiss one more time.

When they returned to the shop, Ailsa said, "Caerlugh wants you to perform the Fath-Fith before you go. I have a special farewell dinner for you. It will be ready when you come back."

Ben nodded. He took his staff and walked across the street and through the great gate of the Magisterium one last time. He crossed the quadrangle, past the Pool of the Wise, and headed on to the henge.

Caerlugh was there in full ceremonial robes. He was alone. There was a fire burning in the centre of the circle. Ben felt odd, conducting a ceremony without crowds of people milling around. He took of his shoes and hopped into the circle.

"Ben Troon, seeker after knowledge!" Caerlugh said in a commanding voice. "Walk three times sunwise around the fire." Ben did as he was told. "Now go home and recite that Fath-Fith."

Ben exited the circle. "Is this goodbye?" he asked.

"Herne, no," said Caerlugh, "I will be there tonight to see you off. I have a couple of little last-minute presents for you."

Intrigued, and hoping these presents were not going to be too difficult to carry on his journey, Ben returned to the bookshop.

He took up position in the doorway, looking out across the lake, pressing the palms of his hands against the flaking paint of the frame, and began reciting the incantation.

*****

> "Fath-fith
> Will I make on thee,
> By Mary of the augury,
> By Bride of the corslet,
> From sheep, from rain,
> From goat, from buck,
> From fox, from wolf,
> From sow, from boar,
> From dog, from cat,
> From hipped-bear,
> From wilderness-dog,
> From watchful scan,

From cow, from horse,
From bull, from heifer,
From daughter, from son,
From the birds of the air,
From the creeping things of the earth,
From fishes of the sea,
From the imps of the storm."

All the creatures in the incantation were those which a simple subsistence farmer might expect to see when looking out from the door of his or her cottage (though the more exotic among them might perhaps only appear after a noggin or two of kuass).

When the incantation was done, Ben went inside and ascended the stairs, where he was met by the delicious aroma of roasting heronshaw.

When the meal was over, Ailsa took Ben by the hand. "One more for the road!" she shouted exultantly as she scampered up the stairs.

In the bedroom, Ben was torn between the urge to sink himself once more into that oven of hot, mysterious delights, and the desire to make this final foray between her creamy thighs last as long as possible. They employed every technique they had worked out together to delay the climax until every last sweaty ounce of passion had been squeezed from their coupling, and finally, with shared animal ululations, they came together.

In the aftermath they dozed, side by side, the bedding a rumpled mass on the floor.

"Sceatta for your thoughts?" asked Ailsa idly.

"Oh," said Ben, "just the usual."

"Namely?"

"Oh, you know. I just expected that you would have tired of me long before this. You have such a brilliant, bubbly personality, and I thought you would soon be bored with someone like me."

Ailsa hoisted herself on an elbow and looked him in the eye. "Ben Troon, you are not the dull old stick you make yourself out to be. Why do you always undersell yourself?"

"It's the way I've always been, I suppose," Ben replied with a sigh. "At the Academy, I never wanted to seem brighter than my friends for fear that they might think I was, well, up myself."

"And did they ever show the least sign that that was what they thought?"

"No…"

"No. I didn't think so. In fact I suspect they were rather proud to have you in their midst."

"I don't know about that…"

"And as for me, well, far from being bored with you, I have reserved for you a unique privilege."

"Oh?" said Ben. "What's that?"

"You, Ben Troon, the dull old stick who didn't think he could compare with my other lovers, have fathered the next Bleakwill."

And she passed a hand meaningfully over the curve of her belly.

"What?" gasped Ben. "You mean…?" Ailsa nodded. "But… I'm going away. I won't have any part in…"

"The men never do," Ailsa assured him. "Mine certainly didn't. It's part of the Bleakwill tradition."

"I won't even know if it's a boy or a girl."

"Oh, it will be a girl," Ailsa remarked matter-of-factly. "It always is. But…"

"Yes?"

"I *will* let you pick a name."

"Hmmm…" Ben pondered. It was all so sudden and unexpected. "I have always liked the name Andraste*."

"The invisible one," Ailsa smiled, "The goddess of victory. Very well, Andraste Bleakwill it shall be. Now, time is getting on, and there is one more little thing I want to do before we leave. So get your clothes on, Master Mage."

*****

Ailsa cleared the dinner plates off the table and made a space. From one of the shelves she pulled down a small box. "Come and sit beside me," she said, pulling up a chair and settling herself. She placed the box on the table in front of her and opened it. Inside was what appeared to be a deck of cards.

"Cards?" said Ben, bemused.

"The Tarot of the Mages," Ailsa replied, fanning out the deck. "Now, you are required to draw one card, and one card only. That will tell us all we need to know. So choose carefully."

Ben's fingers hovered over the deck as it lay on the table. He picked one. It depicted a cloaked figure holding a staff not dissimilar to the one in the corner of the room. Behind the figure there was a globe, which appeared to be spawning an infinity of smaller globes, trailing away into the distance.

"Ah, the Traveller," said Ailsa, with a contented expression. "I had a feeling it might be. Now, behold the infinity of worlds. On the spiritual plane, this card represents the primary motion, the infinite possibility of movement and transformation of the spiritual dimension. It is not subject to any specific law, but constantly creates new possible "laws" to abide by. At the level of the soul it represents full emotional and instinctual freedom, not in the sense of indifference or insensitivity, but rather the transcending of pleasure and pain into something much more abstract - pure sensation. On the physical level it represents freedom from forced interaction, the exception that does not deny the rule, but manages to escape it."

He understood. After Caerlugh's transmission of the gnosis, there were many things he understood that he would have had no hope of understanding before.

"Now, on a more pragmatic note," said Ailsa, getting up from the table and returning the cards to their place on the shelf, "I have a parting gift for you."

From another shelf she drew down a small leather purse. Ben opened the drawstring and peered inside. He saw the glint of gold and silver within.

"Your purse will never run dry," Ailsa told him. "And what is more, it will always contain the correct currency for the country you are in."

"Wow," said Ben. "Thank you."

Ailsa threw herself at him and locked him in one last steamy kiss, her hips grinding against his as she did so.

At last she had to come up for air. "By Herne, I will miss you, Ben Troon," she gasped.

At that moment Great Tom began striking ten.

"It's getting late," she declared. "Time to be going."

Ben looped his money purse onto his sword belt, and buckled it on, Fragarach in its scabbard slapping against his hip. Ailsa helped him into his cloak and settled his bonnet with its jaunty mollymawk feather onto his head, then lifted the small pack he had packed with a couple of changes of clothes and a few other necessaries, and he put his arms through the straps. He took his staff in his hand. Cairbre, sensing a special moment, rubbed himself against Ben's legs, and Ben stooped to scratch him behind the ears.

Ailsa swung her own cloak about her. "We're off!" she announced, trying hard to sound upbeat, but not really succeeding.

They clattered down the stairs one last time, and went out into the warm evening air. Ailsa locked the door, and they set off at a brisk pace towards the wharf district.

*****

The *Realt Fanad* was moored by the river's edge. She had acquired a mast, from which hung a large square red-brown sail, bellying out in a stiff breeze. In the flickering torchlight, Ben saw that the sail was peppered here and there with little rents which had been neatly stitched together. She was quite low in the water, laden with a deck cargo of beech logs. Captain van Brodick and a crew of four men were busying themselves with the final preparations before sailing.

Caerlugh and Motria emerged from the shadows. He was holding a staff in one hand and the straps of the Book's knapsack in the other. Motria was carrying on her back another knapsack containing the essentials for a long journey. On her shoulder were her bow-case and a quiver of arrows.

"Good evening," said Caerlugh. "Ben, we don't have a lot of time, so if you could transfer your possessions into Motria's knapsack?"

Ben took the pack from his back, undid the straps and pulled out his clothes, stuffing them into Motria's pack. He hoped there would be enough room, and somehow there was.

"Good," said Caerlugh when he was finished. Ailsa shouldered the empty pack. "Now, I have already equipped Motria with a quiver of arrows that will never empty, and I believe Ailsa has given you a purse that does the same trick?"

"Yes," said Ben, as Caerlugh lifted the pack containing the Book, and Ben took the weight on his shoulders. He shifted slightly until it was comfortably balanced.

"Now, as I said," Caerlugh continued, "I have a couple of small gifts for you."

He lifted the flap on a pouch he carried on his belt, and drew out a large ring of gold on a fine chain. He held it out for Ben to inspect.

Ben turned to the nearest flickering wall sconce and examined it. The ring was inscribed with a circle of runic insigils.

"Bindrunes," Caerlugh explained. "Two or more runes in combination. Together they form a very powerful amulet."

"There are some here that I don't recognise," said Ben.

"I dare say," said Caerlugh. "Some of them are very ancient, and contain power to defend against dark forces." Ben looked into his eyes, hoping for an elaboration, but none was forthcoming. Instead, Caerlugh hung the chain around Ben's neck, tucking the amulet well away inside his clothes, and said, "Draw Fragarach, please."

Ben withdrew the scramaseax from its scabbard in the manner he had been taught, pulling the scabbard away from the sword rather than the other way around.

Caerlugh took the sword and turned so that his body shielded the sword from the sight of the crewmen rolling barrels across the wharf behind him. He laid his hand flat upon the blade, and at once small blue and orange flames leapt from it, weaving themselves into spiral patterns in the air above it. The two men and two women smelled a strange bittersweet perfume.

"Notice the helical pattern formed by the flames?" said Caerlugh in what was almost a whisper. "That is the pattern that underlies all of nature." Again, Ben waited in vain for an elaboration. Instead, Caerlugh said, "All is well. Sheathe your sword." Ben replaced Fragarach in its scabbard. "Now, the last gift I have for you."

He held up his staff. It had a fork at the top that was a perfect U-shape. "I would like you to have this staff instead of your own." Ben hesitated. He and that stick of hawthorn had been through a lot together.

"Inspect it," Caerlugh urged him.

Ben took the proffered staff in his hands, placing it across his fingers to find the balance point.

"The wood is… ash?"

"Correct," said Caerlugh. "As is the World Tree…"

The World Tree. Legend had it that this enormous ash tree existed in some distant land, with its roots thrusting down into the demon-haunted Underworld, its trunk rising through the world of men, and its branches extending up into the realm of the gods.

"…And as are some of our own sacred trees, Tortu, Dathi and Uisneach. Now, consider the runes which are carved upon it. Mage Gaut, our runemaster, has done some fine work here."

Ben turned the staff over in his hands. A series of runes wound in a spiral around it. "The whole Elder Futhark is here," he observed. Each rune was credited with a different power. Together in combination like this, they represented a tremendous magical force.

Ben continued his inspection. The intricately carved knotwork which formed the handgrip reiterated the theme of the helix. Further down the shaft were more runes. "What are these?" he asked.

"Ramrunes," said Caerlugh. "More runes of power."

Ben's eye was drawn back once more to the U-shaped fork at the top. The tips of the arms of the U were encased in bronze, and from each tip a bronze wire spiralled downwards, both joining to a bronze ferrule just below the fork. The foot of the staff, Ben noticed, was similarly encased in bronze.

"Bronze is almost as good as silver in warding off the agents of darkness," Caerlugh said.

There it was again, the talk of dark forces. Ben said nothing, hoping that he might be allowed to simply slip through Anoone largely unnoticed, complete his mission and return home in one piece.

He ran his fingertips over the U shaped fork. "This looks unnatural," he commented.

"Trained is the word you're looking for," said Caerlugh. "The ash sapling was trained to form this fork."

"It looks as if there should be something there, mounted in the fork."

"Well observed," said Caerlugh. "What that something is will be revealed to you in the course of your journey."

"Ah," said Ben. "So you *do* know where we're going?"

At that moment, Great Tom began sounding eleven o'clock. That the bell should begin sounding at that precise moment was just too convenient to be a coincidence. Ben glanced suspiciously at Caerlugh, but he was wearing his best butter-wouldn't-melt expression.

"Sorry to interrupt," said Captain van Brodick, "but we need to be on our way."

"Of course," said Caerlugh.

Ailsa stapped forward and kissed Ben one last passionate time. Close up, Ben saw that she had tears welling in her eyes. "Be safe," she murmured.

Van Brodick gestured to a tall, lugubrious man standing beside him. "This is Mister Beaglehole, my first mate," he said. "Mister Beaglehole will show you to your quarters."

With a last wave, Ben and Motria followed the mate down the gangplank. The mooring ropes were already being cast off.

Beaglehole showed them into a small cabin with two narrow beds. They put down their belongings and hastened back on deck. The wherry was sliding away from the wharf, her sail filling, and she was already picking up speed.

Ben and Motria stood at the rail until the figures of Ailsa and Caerlugh had been swallowed by the night.

"Well," said Ben, "it's just us now."

End of Part One.

MAGELAW CALENDAR.

Mons o'der Yarr, be Loonas Yarr a Rotan der Serlis.

(Months of the year, according to the lunar calendar and the rotation of the sun).

Frigidda (January)

An Frigidda (February)

Thraash (March)

Thawl (April)

Meagh (May)

Yune (June)

Huilay (July)

Wrageth (August)

Sefton (September)

Zehnar (October)

Radnyr (November)

Midyar (December)

Adyarren (Thirteenth Month).

AWORDESLIEST.

(**Glossary of unfamiliar words, or terms specific to Anoone**).

A

Adyarren: The thirteenth month (Magelaw calendar).

Age of Unpolished Stone, the: The distant past.

Agrath: Daughter of the demon Ma'hlath (q.v.).

Aji: Chilli

Akitu: New Year's festival in Magelaw.

Alcamy: Seabird.

Alichino: Demon.

Alvis: The all-wise god.

Anagantios: The month of inability to leave the house (Luthany calendar).

Andraste: The goddess of victory, the invisible one.

An Frigidda: The second month (Magelaw calendar).

Arachlor: A toxic being.

Arathkone: Racoon-like creature.

Asag: Monster in the belief system of the Chogans, a desert civilisation.

Asmodai: The King of the Demons.

Asp: Willow.

Astropelekia: 'Axes fallen from the sky'.

Atenoux: The divide between the light and dark halves of the month.

Atorcoppe: Spider.

Atropos: The goddess of fate.

Attagen: Game bird.

B

Bagattine: Smallest unit of currency (Quaama).

Balestrin: Small folding crossbow.

Banba: Goddess.

Barbastrelle: Bat

Barding: Horse armour.

Barmkin: Small courtyard.

Bartizan: Projecting turret in a tower or wall..

Basilisk (here): Large cannon.

Bassemánnu: The holy month (Luthany calendar).

Batjorn: Petrel

Baudkin: Rich brocaded material.

Baunajig: Rare bird.

Bavins: Kindling.

Behistun: The abode of the gods.

Bengodi: Paradise.

Bere: Barley

Berevechicorn: Animal fodder made from barley, oats and vetches (see below).

Betana: A good witch who brings gifts at the winter solstice.

Bewpers: Bunting.

Bilander: Two-masted merchant vessel.

Bis: Rye bread.

Boanerges: The mythical Son of Thunder.

Bombazine: Twilled fabric, in which the warp is silk or cotton and the weft is worsted.

Bondemark: Magelaw currency. Two bondemarks equal one testoon (q.v.).

Bracteate: Magelaw currency. May be a coin or a stamped gold talisman.

Brannaimh: Board game.

Brayette: Codpiece.

Breacan: A tartan-type pattern in cloth.

Bricriu: The 'poison-tongue'.

Bridge of the Gatherer: The passage into death.

Buckler: Lightweight shield.

Bumbulum: Fart.

Byrnie: Suit of mail armour.

C

Cachalot: Sperm whale.

Caerdderwen: The House of the Oak

Cailleach Bhéarra: Goddess of wilderness and forests.

Calcabrina: Demon.

Caliver: Firearm.

Caltrop: A device consisting of four metal spikes, such that however it is thrown on the ground, one spike is always pointing upwards, to maim horses.

Camlet: Material of wool, goat's hair or silk.

Cantlos: The month of song (Luthany calendar).

Caper: Privateer vessel.

Carucate: Measure of ploughland, generally for taxation purposes.

Carwitchet: Pun.

Carynx: War-trumpet.

Catafalque: Temporary structure resembling a tomb, or raised funerary bier.

Cataplasm: Poultice.

Chirimia: Shrill trumpet.

Chole: Chickpeas with onions, tomatoes and spices.

Clencher: Old, worn out vessel.

Clepsydra: Water clock.

Clotto: Goddess of Fate.

Cocket: Rye bread.

Coehorn: Small bronze mortar.

Coleworts: Cabbage.

Collops: Fried bacon.

Companionway: Staircase on a ship.

Corant: Dance requiring a running or sliding step.

Court-bouillon: Stock with carrots, celery, shallots and herbs.

Crayer: Single-masted trading vessel.

Cresset: Lamp.

Cuddy: Mess room on a ship.

Cuirass: Breastplate.

Curtow: Deck-mounted ship's gun.

D

Deosil: Clockwise.

Devip: Oystercatcher.

Dha shealladh: 'The two seeings', using both physical and subtle sight.

Distater: Coin (Quaaman currency).

Dovekie: Seabird.

Drage: Animal fodder made from a mixture of barley and oats.

Drangadróttin: The Lord of Ghosts.

Drungus: Body of infantry.

Dumannios: The Darkest Month (Luthany calendar).

Dyker: Cormorant.

E

Eftsoons: Immediately.

Ell: 1140mm

Ephemerides: Astrological almanac.

Ereshkigal: Afterlife/underworld.

Etrog: A cirus fruit.

F

Falcater: Single-edged sword.

Falchon: Curved sword.

Farandine: Silk cloth mixed with wool or hair.

Farmatir: The god of burdens.

Fetel: Leather money pouch.

Fidnemed: Forest shrine.

Fidhchneall: A game similar to chess.

Filbert: A variety of hazel nut.

Fingersmith: Pickpocket.

Fios: Oral, esoteric knowledge of the universe.

Flake-hurdle: A portable gate-like hurdle.

Florikan: Forest bird.

Foist: Small vessel propelled by oars and sails.

Frigidda: January (Magelaw calendar).

Fryse: Coarse woollen cloth.

Fulminate: Gunpowder.

Fyrk: Smallest unit of currency (Luthany).

G

Gaflak: Javelin.

Gallinule: Water bird.

Galliot: Small swift galley.

Gawkroger: Clumsy person.

Genitor: Light horseman.

Gessa: Magical prohibition.

Giamonos: The Month of New Shoots (fourth month of the Luthany calendar).

Gilguys: Sailors' gadgets.

Glede: Kite-like bird of prey

Gleek: Three-handed card game.

Godweb: Shot-silk taffeta.

Gofannon: The smith-god.

Gompotherium: Large tusked mammal, similar to a mammoth.

Grains of Paradise: Spice.

Grampus: Orca, or killer whale.

Grigri: Mountain goat.

Grimoire: Book of dark spells.

Gris-tolkin: Book of spells.

Grivny: Small coin (Pilappelanth currency).

Grumfit: Pig.

Gullinkambi: Cockerel.

Gyllou: Vampire-demon.

H

Habirchon: Sleeveless coat of mail.

Hagbutter: Soldier armed with a firearm.

Hawser: Rope on a ship.

Hemming: Rawhide leather shoe.

Henge: A ceremonial circle made of stone or wood.

Hennin: Woman's headdress.

Heregeld: Soldiers' pay.

Heronshaw: Young heron.

Hiraeth: Longing for the homeland.

Hobiler: Light cavalryman.

Horagállis: Thunder-god

House of Office: Latrine.

Hu: Sun-god.

Hugrunes: Runes of mind power.

Huilay: July (Magelaw calendar).

Hulan: Soldier.

Hydromel: Mead.

I

Iaqeb: Crane.

Inanna: Quaaman love-goddess.

Irminsul: The Tree of Life.

Ivy-tod: Thick bush of ivy.

J

Jaserant: Plate armour.

Jugera: A measure of land.

K

Kalila: Jackal-like creature.

Kapaka: Card game.

Kasturi: Type of deer.

K'daai Maqsin: Underworld smith.

Kuass: Spirituous liquor.

Kubbe: An outdoor game, a curious cross between lawn bowls and chess.

L

Laa Boaldyn: A celebration of spring.

Lacnunga: Book of healing.

Lagopus: Blue fox.

Laima: The goddess of birth and fate.

Lamashtu: Female demon.

Lammsmäcka: Grilled, parboiled half lamb skull, complete with eye.

Leechbook: Book of healing.

Leechcraft: Healing art.

Lindorm: Earth dragon.

Liuthrindi: Disruptive patterning on shields, designed to dazzle an enemy.

Lochesis: Goddess of fate.

Lodesman: Navigator.

Lorcha: Type of ship.

Lorica: Mailcoat.

Luchtar: God of carpenters.

M

Ma'at: Underworld spirit in the belief system of the Chogans, a desert civilisation.

Mag Meld: The Land of Delights.

Ma'hlath: Demon

Maierlinden: 'Guardian of the Trees'.

Malabathrum: Cinnamon.

Mancu: Large unit of currency (Luthany).

Mantlet: Concentric outer wall of a fortification.

Meagh: May (Magelaw calendar).

Medimnus: Measure of wheat, barley, peas, etc.

Megin: Inner power.

Metagnomy: Awareness beyond intelligence.

Metheglin: Mead.

Meurette: Fish casserole.

Midyar: December (Magelaw calendar).

Minion: Cast-iron or bronze muzzle-loading gun firing cast-iron shot of 3¼ lbs.

Mithras: The Child of Promise, born at midwinter, founder of the religion of Mithraism, followed by most Quaamans.

Modia: Measure of grain.

Modranect: 'Night of the Mothers' - Luthanian festival.

Mollymawk: Albatross.

Morkosh: Household goddess.

Murderer: Type of cannon, breech-loading and swivel-mounted.

Musquetoon: Stand-mounted handgonne.

Myrfyrion: Academy of Magecraft.

N

Naginah: Stringed instrument.

Neat: Deer.

Neeps: Turnips.

Nemeton: Sacred wood.

Nergal: The underworld.

Netsik: Seal.

Nettercap: Spider.

Nidhog: Dragon.

Nirrup: A beast of burden resembling a donkey.

Noce: Nutmeg

Nomophylax: 'Keeper of the Laws'.

Nodons: God of healing.

Norns: Spirit beings who govern the fate of every person, cutting the thread of their life when their time is up.

Nosgalan: Winter's Eve (Luthany calendar).

Nu: The mythical agent of chaos.

O

Oakum: Rope fibres.

Odachi: Sword.

Ogronios: The month of ice - First month of the year on the Luthany calendar.

Onager: Wild ass.

Orichalc: Copper alloy.

P

Painter: Rope for mooring a boat.

Pampootie: Moccasin-like soft leather shoe.

'Panchatantra': 'Five Books of Wisdom'.

Parrel: A loose collar that rides up and down the mast of a ship, raising and lowering the yard arm.

Partan bree: Crab soup.

Perspicillum: Telescope.

Petard: Small bomb used in sieges.

Pateroe: Very small cannon.

Picatrix: Manual of astral magic.

Pinnace: Large ship's boat.

Pomdeter: Potato.

Porringer: Small bowl with a handle on one side.

Portimpo: Water god.

Potin: Small coin (Quaaman currency).

Pourpoint: Tunic.

Punketee: Apprentice prostitute.

Q

Qeblur: Protector-deity.

Qeladim: 'The Insidious Creepers'.

Quanun: Zither-like instrument with 81 strings.

R

Radnyr: November (Magelaw calendar).

Rēaf: Garments and weapons taken from the dead.

Rearmouse: Bat.

Responsions: Exams.

Riuros: The Month of Cold (second month of the year on the Luthany calendar).

Rivlin: Type of boot.

Rokea: The evil one.

Rossmar: Walrus.

Rowbarge: Small warship, using oars as well as sail, with no upper deck.

Runrig: Division into elongated fields running downslope in parallel bands.

S

Sackbut: Trombone-like musical instrument.

Sacrobosco sphere: Armillary sphere.

Sagares: Double-headed axe.

Saker (or saker falcon): Cast-iron or bronze muzzle-loading gun firing cast-iron shot of 5lb.

Samonios: The Month of Sowing (third month of the year on the Luthany calendar).

Sarcenet: Rich, thin taffeta cloth (see Taffeta-sarsuet).

Sator: The Creator.

Sceatta: Silver penny (Magelaw currency. Ten sceattas make one testoon (q. v.).)

Scorpe: Sand or mud bank.

Scuppernongs: Wild grapes.

'Sefer Yetzira': The Book of Creation.

Sefton: September (Magelaw calendar).

Sequana: River spirit.

Shalir: One possessed of supernatural knowledge.

Shawm: Clarinet-like musical instrument.

Silver popolin: Large denomination Quaaman coin.

Simivisionos: The Month of Brightness (fifth month of the Luthany calendar).

Skadi: The polar god of skiing and hunting.

Skein dhu: Small dagger.

Skyr: Curds.

Slaínte: "Cheers!"

Snekka: Fast warship.

Sook: Crab.

Spaewife: Witch.

Springald: Pivot-mounted heavy crossbow.

Spritmast: Small spar projecting above the bowsprit, often carrying a heraldic device.

Susselman: Mayor or governor.

Swiftler: Soft leather slipper.

Swithers: Jellyfish.

T

Taffeta-sarsuet: Very fine silk.

Tarabagan: Squirrel-like creature.

Targe: Circular shield.

Tarpan: Wild horse.

Taus: Stringed musical instrument.

Tercel: Falcon.

Testoon: Magelaw currency. Five testoons equal one bracteate (q.v.).

Thalium: A heavy metal.

Thawl: April (Magelaw calendar).

Theriac: Anti-poison medication.

Thermidor: The Hottest Month (sixth month of the Luthany calendar).

Thraash: March (Magelaw calendar).

Thrymsa: Mid-denomination coin (Luthany currency).

Tibert: Wild cat.

Tiecelin: Raven.

Toft: An enclosed field around a homestead.

Top armings: Long strips of painted canvas that hide the ship's crew from view.

Topstreamer: Mast-top pennant.

Torngat: God of the frozen north.

Tourte: Bread made from rye flour.

Toxophila: "Lover of the Bow".

Treen: Turned wooden bowls, cups and trenchers (plates).

Treenails: Wooden ship's nails.

Trev: A measure of about five acres.

U

Ull: God of the frozen north.

Uppowac: Tobacco.

Uxellimus: Father of the gods.

V

Vargulets: The language of the cosmos.

Verethragna: God of battle.

Vernage: Sweet white wine.

Vetches: Members of the bean family.

Virodactis: Mother goddess.

W

Wad-dirrak: A close relative of the platypus.

Wadmal: Coarse, undyed woollen cloth.

Wafter: Escort vessel.

Walcott: A dainty, feathery creature

Wapiti: Elk.

Welkin: Sky.

Wendigo: Were-bear

Whimbrel: Wading bird, smaller than a curlew.

Whittle: Fringed shawl.

Widdershins: Counter-clockwise.

Wiseat: Cattle. Many cattle domesticated from wild animals.

Witangemot: Meeting of the ruling council.

Withy: Willow.

Wolawant: Flatterer.

Wortcunning: Medicine.

Wrageth: August (Magelaw calendar).

X

Xibalba: The underworld.

Y

Yama: The Lord of Death.

Yune: June (Magelaw calendar).

Z

Zehnar: October (Magelaw calendar).

Zinziber: Ginger.

Zippiril: Rosemary.

Zurvan: The god of time.